The Lamplighter

by Ellen Gardner

Stephanie,
My favorite
heroine is
Hannah! ♡

Ellen
Gardner

ISBN-13: 978-1492780557

ISBN-10: 1492780553

This book is lovingly dedicated to all of the
Lamplighters of my life – my family and friends;
You hold my hand daily,
You love and support me unconditionally,
I will forever carry you within my heart.

Most Especially,
To my beautiful mother, Marie.
You taught me the meaning of true courage and strength.
You are my Grace Padgett!

The Lamplighter
A Special Dedication

Atop the precipice of human darkness,
In the hollow of the soul's abyss,
The Lamplighter brings forth
A spark of light, a ray of hope;
A stranger's smile, a gentle whisper,
A warm embrace, an unexpected kiss.

The spirit suffers at the mercy of fear,
Courage falters as year passes year,
The Lamplighter breaks through
The shattered spirit, the lost soul;
Healing open wounds, conquering despair,
Forgiving transgressions, wiping away tears.

In the midst of a shattered heart an eternal light glows,
The supreme Lamplighter dwells within each living soul,
Bringing peace to the weary, hope to the desperate,
Truth to the uncertain, faith to the lost;
Yet, it is love that restores us and makes us anew,
In our darkest hour, His greatest gift unfolds.

~Ellen Gardner~

I dedicate this book to every human soul who has
suffered tragedy, anxiety, depression, and phobias. In
the heart of your suffering, there is hope.

ONE

Andy Padgett winced as he drove down the rural Texas highway that led to Nana Padgett's house. The road was under construction and threatened to damage his newly painted 1972 Chevy pickup. The Chevy had been a gift from his Paps just before he died, a day short of Andy's sixteenth birthday. He treated the old truck like it was gold and the thought of ever replacing it never crossed his mind. He intended to keep it forever. His ex-wife, Jean, always referred to it as his mistress, because he spent so much time and money working on it and repairing it. Its fresh new paint job, carnal red, had been an extravagance he had lent himself after his divorce. This extravagance had royally ticked-off Jean because she no longer had control where he spent his money. If he wanted to go into debt, it was his business. Andy smiled smugly as he recalled the look on Jean's face when he first picked up the boys in the newly painted Chevy. He heard loose rocks beat against the bottom of his truck and his smile faded.

"Just great," he murmured to himself. "This is just great ... the beginning of a beautiful day in Blossom, Texas."

Blossom, a small East Texas town with a population of just over eight hundred, had been his Nana Padgett's home since Andy was fifteen. Before that, Nana and Paps had lived in the country just south of Blossom on a twenty-acre farm. As a boy, Andy had spent every summer and every free weekend with his Paps and Nana on their farm, helping with the crops and the animals. Even though Andy went to school near Dallas, where his parents lived, he knew that some day he would be a farmer like his Paps. Andy brushed the tears that began to fill his bloodshot eyes as he recalled the painful, dark period when his dreams started to slip away. It began the day his Paps and Nana sold their farm because of Paps' declining health and moved to Blossom.

Less than a year later, Paps died. The doctors said he died from complications due to a stroke. Andy knew differently. He knew that Paps had died the moment he left his farm and the life he loved so well. Andy thought of Nana. He hadn't taken care of her the way he had promised Paps he would. Truth was, he missed Paps too much and Nana was a constant reminder of what he had lost when Paps died. It was too painful, so he left the duties of taking care of Nana to the rest of his family. When Andy married shortly out of high school, he drifted even further from his promise.

There were his usual excuses. He had his new job at a *Peary's*, a Dallas grocery, that kept him busy. He and Jean had just had their first child, a son, and later, two more sons followed. One year turned into two and then three and before he realized it, nearly fifteen years had gone by. He recently learned that Nana's health was declining and she wasn't getting around as well. A lump filled his throat. Now he wished his family had visited more often.

He rubbed his forehead. He felt as if his life was dealing him a series of bad hands. This last hand, his divorce from Jean, had almost killed him. He always imagined that he would be married to Jean forever. He thought he would be married and working at *Peary's*, where he had recently been made an assistant manager. He laughed aloud. Now, even his job was uncertain. Talk around the store was that a larger chain might buy out the grocery. If that happened, Andy had no idea what direction his career would take.

His head was throbbing now, a consequence of having too little sleep and possibly too much to drink last night. It was an occurrence that had been happening more frequently these days. He knew he had to get control of himself. Each day he vowed this would be the day, but then life would throw him a curveball and he would be back to square one. He reached into his glove box and pulled out a bottle of Tylenol. His hands were shaking and his nerves were on edge.

A few days ago, Jean threw another lightening bolt at him. She said that she was considering taking him back to court. She wanted full custody of their three boys and possibly supervised visits. She ran on about his drinking and women chasing being out of control and him not being a strong role model for them. Hell, what was she thinking? He never drank in front of his boys and the only girlfriend he ever brought around was Liz. Since Jean approved of Liz, he had no idea what she was thinking. Maybe it was because he broke it off with Liz awhile back. He didn't know. He only knew that he loved his boys and he was a good father. If she wanted to take him to court then *bring it on.*

The thought of not seeing them on a regular basis was unthinkable. Nothing meant more to him than his boys. He would give his life for them. The thought of Jean and her recent actions cut him deeply. Whatever she thought of him, he didn't care, but to take his boys away? This divorce wasn't his idea. Ripping his family apart wasn't his idea. She was the one who wanted her freedom. She wanted to grow in her career. His heart raced. He and Jean had been together since they were sixteen. They grew up together. She said they had been drifting apart for years. Andy gripped the wheel tightly. Maybe she had been drifting, but he always loved her — still did. He would take her back tomorrow if it meant having his family together again. Before he could indulge further in self-pity, he saw the turn to Blossom and his mind focused on his driving. In a few minutes, he would be at Nana's house. A gentle comfort filled him as he recalled the Nana of past days, who would fuss over him and made life better just by her presence. Andy felt a sense of peace for the first time in months. Nana would make things better.

Hannah Martindale woke up feeling sixty instead of thirty-four. Just when she had finally fallen asleep last night, the intrusive morning showed its cruel face through her window. It teased at her, pretending to be a promise of a beautiful day, when all along it was a culprit, hovering over her like a dark cloud that never quite went away.

Cautiously, her eyes scanned the stream of light. As if programmed, Hannah pulled herself from her bed and went about her daily routine—brushing her teeth, haphazardly moving a brush through her unruly hair, dressing into an outfit she may or may not have worn yesterday. She tripped over an area rug inside her bathroom, forcing her to look up into her full-length mirror. Hannah panicked when she saw the image reflected. A stranger was staring at her. As quickly as her panic had come, it left. She touched her face gently. The familiar features, though more aged, were recognizable. A funny thing about panic—it can take you to another realm of reality in the blink of an eye. One thing Hannah knew. It always brought her back. Each dark day proved this.

Putting on a pot of fresh coffee, she looked outside her kitchen window and saw two sparrows dancing around her abandoned birdbath where yesterday a late evening shower had filled it. Hannah felt a piercing pain. Had she really picked out that very birdbath and planted roses in the nearby garden? A vision of lush flowers blooming where weeds now overran, filled her mind. She could almost smell their sweetness. She sighed. That was a lifetime ago and she was another Hannah. Once outgoing and vibrant, today, she barely had the inclination to recall what she had once been.

Still, Hannah clung to the fragments of her former life, hopeful that some miracle might release her from her self-imposed bondage. Almost immediately, dread soured her belly. No miracle could change her past. No miracle could bring the life she once had back. Hannah looked at the clock that ticked.

She waited. For what? For Grace to call or come over? Ah, yes, sweet, precious Grace Padgett, her neighbor and confidant. Grace always called her about this time. She would call and break the dreaded silence. Hannah resisted picking up the phone and calling Grace. She might be sleeping and she knew she needed her sleep. She had been so tired lately. Grace hadn't been well.

For well over three years, Hannah had rarely left her house. The occasional times she had been forced from her home, left her in such a state or torment, she was powerless to do anything for days. The ordeals set her back, both physically and emotionally, so she avoided them at all costs. This consequently sent her into a deeper state of confinement and she remained literally housebound except for her night trips to her front porch and her visits to Grace's house. More often than not, Grace would find her way to Hannah's house and the two would spend the greater part of the morning drinking coffee and discussing any news Grace had to tell. Grace's news and stories were the highlights of Hannah's days. When they didn't visit, her days were long and often dark. Grace was one of Hannah's few links to an outside world that had been so cruel to her. Hannah didn't realize it, but she was quickly becoming Grace's lifeline, as well.

They were an odd pair. Grace was almost eighty, where Hannah was thirty-four. Both were widows. Both had lost a child. Both were restricted to their homes, Grace by age and declining health and Hannah by fear and tragedy. Both women clung to the past except for the occasional times when they were forced into the present. The most prevalent concern to Hannah was Grace's health. She saw her friend faltering more each day—her slow walk, her speech, and her failing memory. She feared Grace would have to be hospitalized soon and then what would she do? She prayed God would give her the courage to be the friend Grace deserved and that she wouldn't let her fear abandon Grace in her time of need.

Hannah's thoughts were interrupted when she saw a red truck pull into Grace's driveway. A tall, dark-headed man got out and made his way to Grace's backyard. Hannah remembered that Andy would be coming to help Grace out this weekend. Grace was so excited, because it had been months since she had seen Andy. In reality, it had been years since Grace and Andy had really visited. Hannah watched Andy intently. He was not the person she remembered from years past.

She first met Andy a few months after she had moved next door to Grace. She was nineteen and almost a new mother. Andy was eighteen, a cocky senior in high school, who was near the brink of manhood. He swore too much and gave his father and mother fits with his rash behavior. He had always challenged his parents and done things the hard way—almost failing school, skipping college to go to work, marrying right out of high school, and starting a family shortly after. Although Andy was rash and impulsive, he was also the most endearing of Grace's grandsons. He loved deeply, giving his heart and soul to something or someone he deemed of value. He wasn't afraid of work and had made a good living for his family. Grace always said that he wore his heart on his sleeve and loved unconditionally. Hannah studied him as he knocked on Grace's back door. She wondered when he had gone from a reckless boy to a responsible man. She had to guess it was during the lost years of her life.

Just then, Hannah saw Grace open the door and watched the two embrace. Grace was reluctant to release Andy, but she did as they went inside. Hannah understood then that Grace would not be visiting today. She was okay with this because she knew how much this visit meant to Grace. Usually, Grace's other grandsons, Charlie or Ben, came to help their grandmother on the weekends. Sometimes they would take her to their houses for the weekend. Lately, they just visited because Grace didn't get around as well. Of all her grandsons,

Hannah knew that Grace favored Andy, simply because Andy reminded her so much of her late husband, George Padgett.

Grace's back door slammed and Andy reappeared. He stood in a slump, staring in no apparent direction. Hannah edged toward the window and watched him. He seemed lost and her heart tugged for his recent sorrow. She understood all too well, what it was like to feel alone. While their situations weren't the same, he had lost his family. Andy stood for some time before he made his way to Grace's shed where he found her mower. Minutes later, she heard the hum of the motor and the smell of cut grass filled the late morning air. Hannah closed her blinds and slid quietly once more into the obscure corner of her world.

Andy saw the two boys run suspiciously behind Hannah Martindale's house. He let the mower idle while he followed them around the back. Andy guessed them to be around ten or so, just a few years younger than his oldest son, Mathew. He watched as the boys dug around in Mrs. Martindale's garden, or what used to be a garden. While the heat from the sun had absorbed most of the water from yesterday's rain, the boys managed to find a muddied section in the garden. He let out a chuckle when they started walking in the mud, giggling and smudging each other's clothes. Just as Andy was about to resume his mowing, he saw the larger boy ball some mud in his fist and throw it toward Hannah Martindale's kitchen door. The small boy followed his lead. Andy saw a fleeting shadow emerge at the door. The boys threw a second handful and shouted out cruelly.

"Crazy Hannah Banana! Crazy Hannah Banana!"

Before he realized what he was doing, Andy ran toward the boys and grabbed them by their shirts. Why he walked them toward Mrs. Martindale's door, he wasn't sure. He just knew he couldn't let them get by talking to her this way.

"I like a fun time same as the next guy," he said to them harshly. "But I draw the line at cruelty. You boys are going to apologize to Mrs. Martindale. You hear me?"

"I'm not," the larger one spat and then squirmed out of Andy's hold. Somewhat stunned by the boy's strength, Andy said little when he ran off. Still holding the other boy by his shirt, Andy used his free hand to knock on Mrs. Martindale's door. During their wait, Andy quizzed the boy.

"What's your name, son?"

"I ain't telling."

Andy clutched him tighter.

"Some friend you have. He left you to take all the blame. Are you always going to be a follower? That was mighty cruel what you two said and did."

The boy looked at Andy confused. "Why? Everybody knows that old lady Martindale is crazy. She ain't been right for years."

"That's not the point. You invaded her privacy and did harm to her property. Besides, if truth be known, you more than likely made her feel bad inside."

Andy knocked the second time.

"She won't answer," the boy said in a matter of fact tone. "She don't ever answer her door. Why me and Jimmy have been coming..."

"Oh, I see," Andy interrupted, somewhat amused. "You boys have been here before and probably playing your same mean pranks. Haven't you?"

The boy shrugged, "Maybe."

"Do me a favor," Andy said. "Leave Mrs. Martindale alone. If you promise me this, I will let you go and I won't tell your parents what you did today."

"You don't know me and you don't know my parents," he spat not too sure of himself.

Andy grinned. "It's a small town, son. There aren't too many people to know in a small town. It would only take a few calls."

The boy thought for a moment and then answered, "Okay."

Andy loosened his grip on the boy and within seconds, he could only see the flash of his jeans as he ran out of sight. Andy had to grin. He knocked one more time on Hannah's door, but there was still no answer. Not blaming her one bit for not answering, Andy made his way to the mower and the unfinished lawn. Hannah stood within inches of her door and followed Andy's form through her window until he disappeared. When he came into view again, Hannah watched his strong stride as he pushed the mower across Grace's back lawn. A stirring of emotions overcame her as she recalled the unexpected compassion Andy had shown toward her just moments ago.

"Thank you for standing up for me," she whispered. "It's not often someone defends the honor of *Crazy Hannah Banana*."

Hannah made Grace and Andy an apple pie. It wasn't fresh, because she didn't have fresh apples, but even so, she turned out a delectable pie using her grandmother's recipe. It had once been said that Hannah's desserts were the best in Blossom. Until today, it had been years since she had baked for anyone other than herself. As she pulled the pie from the oven, its sweet juices circled the air and an intimate feeling filled her spirit. Arms wrapped around her waist and lips nestled within her neck. Hannah closed her eyes and saw Sammy's face. Her late husband was smiling at her, enticing her to love him.

"Sammy," she whispered.

Within that same inclining of pleasure and desire, Hannah felt a sharp pain in her heart. Sammy wasn't really with her, but in memory. He was dead, buried over four years ago, and ripped from her life forever.

"My Beloved," she cried. "What brought you here today?"

Then she knew. It was the apple pie. Sammy loved her apple pies. They had been his favorite. Why today of all days had she done such a thing? She thought it would be a kind deed for Grace and her grandson—sweet, gracious Andy.

"Of course," she thought. "The way he handled those boys today, so strong and in command, reminded me of Sammy."

Hannah sat at her kitchen table staring at the pie. She heard Andy's voice.

"If truth be known, you more than likely made her feel bad inside."

Hannah felt her eyes grow moist. "Oh, Andy, if you only knew. I rarely feel anything but lost inside."

Hannah eyed the pie. It was cooked and she wanted Grace and Andy to have it. She wanted to thank Andy not only for the incident with the boys, but after he had finished mowing Grace's lawn, he mowed hers. This was something Ben or Charlie had never done. Before she lost her nerve, she picked up her phone and called Grace.

"Hannah," her elderly neighbor's voice soothed. "I was just about to call you. I thought it would be a good time with Andy in the shower. Oh, Hannah, Andy told me about those horrid boys. I'm so sorry, dear. Oh, and one of them was the youngest Renfroe boy, Benny. Paul and Sue would be mortified. I've a good mind to call them right now."

"Grace, let it go. We both know it isn't the first time and it sure won't be the last. They aren't the reason I'm calling you. I made a pie—for you and Andy. He mowed my grass, you know."

"Oh, how thoughtful, but Andy wanted to mow your lawn. He's always been such a worker. Oh my, how that boy loves to be outdoors, just like his Paps. He's like his Paps, you know, the way he holds his pain inside of him. I'm so worried about him Hannah. It's been well over a year since his divorce and he can't move on. Now, this thing with Jean and the boys..."

"It can't be easy," Hannah consoled. "How are the boys?"

"Who really knows? They don't come around me much."

"Divorce is hard, Grace. It's like, well, a death almost."

"You are so insightful, Hannah. But we must not talk about this any more. Andy is coming now. He gets so upset. So, you made us a pie, did you? I'll send Andy over to get it. Better yet, bring it over and have dinner with us. I know Andy would like a nice visit with you."

Hannah froze in her tracks. "Dinner? Oh, heavens no, Grace! I couldn't do that...you know. I'm not up to it. But I do want to thank Andy."

"I do understand, Hannah, but Andy isn't a stranger."

Hannah wanted to say that he was to her, but she didn't. When they hung up, Hannah mustered the courage to take the pie next door before Grace talked Andy into coming over. She tapped on the back door gently, laid the pie on the step and ran quickly to the security of her home. Grace moved outside and picked up the pie.

"Such a gentle bird," Grace said to herself. She knew what courage it took for Hannah to make this gesture. Anything beyond the norm was such an ordeal for her friend. "Oh, my sweet Hannah, you just don't realize your strength. You are stronger than you think you are." She looked toward Hannah's house for some time before going inside. "Dear Lord, make her strong. I know I won't always be here to watch after her."

Grace convinced Andy to stay for the night. Truth was, he had no better plans and being with Nana had restored him somewhat. Listening to her stories about Paps and his mom and dad took the sting away from his present situation. Long after midnight, Andy lay awake, lying in the very bed he had slept in as a teenager. Nothing in Blossom changed, not even the still May nights. It was as if Blossom and the surrounding country were frozen in time. Andy walked to the open window and lit up a cigarette, an occasional vice he afforded himself at the end of a long day. He knew Nana would have a fit if she found him smoking, but he also knew she was fast asleep.

The air was close and his throat was dry. With a million thoughts swimming in his head, he wasn't really focused on any particular one. He just stared out the window. His eyes drifted down the dark street with the rows of lamplights shining reminiscent of an age long ago. He happened to hear the front door of Hannah Martindale's house open and it caught his attention. He thought of the pie she had made for dinner. She had made it to thank him for mowing the lawn and for reprimanding those boys today. Damn little shits. What did they know about crazy? To some folks, Andy had been known to be a little crazy. Jean and her parents thought so. Even Nana had said that anyone who drank his life away the way Andy had done at the beginning of his divorce was just plum crazy. She told him that no woman was worth it. Andy thought of his boys. He missed being a part of their daily lives. This every other weekend crap was for the birds.

"Jean," he thought. "Now she's crazy."

Just then, Andy heard what he thought was humming and seconds later, he saw Hannah walking down her front sidewalk to her mailbox. The lamplight between Nana's house and hers exposed her figure. Along with the humming, he watched as she moved back to her house. She was fairly skipping as she lightly glided onto her porch where she sat down on a swing.

"What the hell?" he thought. "Fear keeps her bound during the day, but she comes out at night, skipping and humming? Maybe she is crazy."

A vision of the woman Andy had known years ago formed in his imagination. Hannah Martindale had once been beautiful; so beautiful in fact, Andy on numerous occasions had indulged in fleeting fantasies about her. Oh, it was nothing serious, but her tall, slim form, flowing black hair, and large brown eyes, demanded a man to look twice. She was a classic beauty, like Audrey Hepburn, and as untouchable. Her smile was slanted and she had a small dimple on one cheek. She had a soft, gentle voice and when she spoke, her southern draw flowed eloquently from her lips. She was captivating and desirable, but elusive. While a man might have passing thoughts of being near her, he understood she was off limits. Andy had always been appreciative of Hannah's beauty. Even though Hannah was slightly older than he was, she always came off to Andy as much older, because of her carriage. Tonight, his curiosity peaked. He was experiencing these same familiar sensations.

In the past, Andy had been so busy with his family and work, and Hannah with her family, her church, and charities, their paths rarely crossed. Sometimes he would hear tidbits about her through Nana or his parents, but the interest wasn't there. He had his life and she had hers. In his life, he had maybe a dozen conversations with Hannah and these were always superficial. Just once, he had an in-depth visit with her. It was ironically, several weeks before the car accident that took her family from her and destroyed her life.

Her husband, who was a high school principal in Blossom, was considering taking a position near Dallas as a principal. It would mean more money, but it would also mean uprooting his family. Hannah asked him about the schools near Dallas, the shopping centers, and the general atmosphere. She was apprehensive, having raised her children in such a small town. They were rooted and she knew the change would be drastic. What he recalled most about the conversation was just how devoted she was to his Nana, considering her to be much like the mother she never had. This always gave Andy comfort, knowing Hannah was next door, watching over his Nana.

Through his window, he heard her soft humming echoing in the night. He closed his eyes and let the sound ease away his own misfortune. He felt immensely lifted.

"Crazy?" he thought to himself. "No, not crazy, just misunderstood. Oh, Hannah, we are all running and hiding from something. We are all one step from crazy."

Two

Sixteen-year old Paul Renfroe, Jr. knocked twice on Hannah Martindale's front door. Like every Sunday afternoon, he was delivering her weekly groceries to her. He set down the bags on the porch next to the door. Underneath the worn welcome mat, she always left a card. Inside the card, there would be a new grocery list, a check, and a twenty-dollar tip.

Paul Jr. knew she was watching him from inside like a scared cat and this gave him the creeps. This woman wasn't the gentle person he had known as Gabe's mom. This woman was a stranger, a witch of some sort, who now possessed what used to be Hannah Martindale—Gabe's mom. If it weren't for what Gabe had meant to him, Paul Jr. doubted he could face Hannah week after week. Gabe was a few years younger than he was, but they were still best friends. That's why every Sunday, he would go to the local market after church and pick up what was on the list she had left the week before. Then, he would deliver her groceries to her house.

He knocked a third time and then walked to his car. Inside, he opened up the card and didn't bother to read the note she had written. It always said the same thing, *"Thank you and God will bless you...blah, blah, blah."*

He put the check for next week's groceries in his wallet and crumbled up the card before tossing it on the floorboard. He shoved the twenty into his pocket and smiled. He knew when he got home, his parents would give him a matching twenty, unaware that Hannah was generous. He sure wasn't going to tell them. After all, he had more than earned every dollar just getting close to the loon. With Crazy Hannah taken care of, he turned the radio up full blast and picked up his speed. Paul Jr.

had the rest of the afternoon to do what he wanted to do. Inside his glove box were three rolled joints. He took one and lit it up. He was going to fly high.

Few people in Blossom had forgotten Hannah Martindale and the woman she used to be, but still, most had become complacent about her condition. They well remembered the vivacious woman who used to charm their community just by walking down the street. They recalled with sadness the pride she had always had in being a devoted wife and mother. Yet today, if they happened to be driving past her house, most simply shook their heads, remembering her meticulously groomed lawn and the rich floral schemes that once identified her touch. She'd been known as Hannah with the magic touch or Hannah with the green thumb, because she could take simple flowers and trees and arrange them into works of art. Those who had been particularly close to Hannah might even shed a tear or two at the sight of her crumbling surroundings that epitomized the state of her spirit. Yet only a handful saw to her welfare.

One person who did was Paul Renfroe, Sammy Martindale's best friend. Paul cared deeply for Hannah ever since he met her some eighteen years ago, when she started dating Sammy. Paul was already married to Sue, his high school sweetheart. The four grew close and lived within blocks of each other. Hannah was the baby of the foursome. Paul, Sammy, and Sue graduated five years before Hannah. They always teased Sammy that he had robbed the cradle. Still, Hannah was graceful and mature beyond her years and she fit well within the circle. The two families went to the same church, Blossom First Baptist Church, and socialized in the same circles. Their children grew up together and became inseparable. Rarely was one family seen without the other.

Yet, in the years the two families had kept their close relationships, Paul harbored a secret. He was in love with

Hannah. Always careful to keep his feelings for her hidden, he never wanted those he loved to know, especially Sue. He did this because of his deep faith in God and the sanctity of his marriage. Sue was a woman he had known his entire life and he loved her with all his heart. Paul loved Sue differently than he did Hannah. He didn't feel the passion he felt for Hannah, but he respected Sue deeply. Sue took care of him and kept him on the straight path of life. She was God-fearing and dependable. Most importantly, she was the mother of his two children, Paul Jr. and Benny.

Paul felt guilty, as he always did, when he thought of his boys. Paul Jr. and Hannah's Gabe shared the same birthday, but were born in different years. Gabe Martindale would be fourteen had his young life not been cut short by that fatal accident four years ago. Pretty little Julie, the carbon copy of her mother, Hannah, would be almost ten. Sammy, Paul's closest friend in the world, a man he loved like a brother, would be celebrating forty years of life this coming October. Even now, Paul often lost control when he thought of his friend and not being able to sit down and discuss the every day things of life with him. The world had surely been right with Sammy in it and his beautiful family. Paul wasn't sure if anyone who loved Sammy and Gabe and little Julie would ever be the same. He knew he wouldn't be — nor his precious Hannah.

As Paul sat in the living room reading the Sunday paper, he could hear Sue's footsteps moving back and forth upstairs. She was busy getting things ready for the church garage sale, a project she had been working on for months. He knew she would be busy all day. He decided this would be a good time as any to go to the cemetery, if there ever was a good time. He made his way upstairs and found Sue in their bedroom, knee high in old clothes. She gave him a quick smile.

"Mind if I take a ride to the cemetery?" he asked.

Her smile faded. "Today? What about the church shrubs? You promised that you would trim them today. And I could use your help here."

"I'll get the shrubs after I go to the cemetery. Besides, I won't be gone long. It's just..." his words faded.

"I know," she noted softly. "It's that time of year."

Paul slouched on the bed, "Yea, that time of year."

She let out a heavy sigh. "I'm sorry, Paul. I'm being selfish. Of course, I don't mind you going to the cemetery. Funny..." Her eyes got wet.

"What?" Paul asked kindly.

"The cemetery comforts you, but it breaks my heart."

"At least you have your best friend still," he said with a slight cut of anger, meaning she still had Hannah, but Sammy was gone forever.

"I get it," she spat. "You think I should go visit Hannah. Is that it? I've tried. So many times I've tried. She doesn't want to see me. She's made that very clear. Can't you see? She's just as dead to me as Sammy is to you."

Sue sat on the bed and wept into a pile of clothing. Paul sat next to her. His anger left him and his compassion for his wife surfaced. He reached for her and brushed her cheek.

"I can go later. Hey," he smiled warmly. "Paul Jr. is gone for the day. Benny is next door with Adam. We could lock the door and..."

Sue looked at him half-exasperated, yet relieved that they were discussing anything but Sammy and Hannah. She punched him slightly in the arm.

"You mean to tell me with everything I have to do, you want to fool around?"

He cocked his eyebrow, "Yea, sounds good to me."

"You," she spat jokingly. "Who's going to get these clothes priced by next weekend?"

He pulled her close to him and kissed her long and deep. "You will, and I'll help."

She let out a short giggle when he threw a bundle of clothes to the floor leaving room for them.

"You're impossible, you know," she said, all the while encouraging him to continue. She moved her hands over the buttons of his shirt. In all the years they had been married, she had never refused him, nor he her.

"And you are wonderful," he said truthfully. He removed her blouse and within minutes, the afternoon was filled with the sounds of their lovemaking. She wanted to please him as he always pleased her. He was praying a silent appeal of forgiveness for briefly wishing his wife was another woman.

Sundays were difficult for Andy. He used to love them. When he was married, it was a day set in rituals. First, the family would go to Mass and then out to eat or he would cook out on the grill. After that, Andy would spend the day with the boys. If the weather were bad, they would play games inside, video games or board games or watch a game on TV. Most of the time, they were outside, biking, hiking, or playing some sort of ball. In any event, Sundays were his days to be with his boys. Jean would do her thing with her friends or mother. After the divorce, this changed. He got them every other weekend and one of the weekends included Monday, his usual day off. This particular weekend, Jean had some family thing going on Saturday, so he was limited to having them one less day. Thankfully, it was his Monday weekend. Every day it seemed the world as he knew it was diminishing further. It cut him like a knife.

Early this morning, he and Nana packed up Nana's Buick and drove to Dallas. They were going to spend the day with the boys and then later go to Andy's apartment and spend the night. Because he had off Monday, he would take the boys to school and bring Nana home later. Her Buick was newer and roomier than his Chevy truck, more practical for traveling with Nana. She bought the car new a few years ago because at the

18

time, she was still driving and her family insisted she have reliable transportation. These days, Nana rarely drove, but still had a current license.

The easiest part of the day was the ride to Dallas, even when he had to stop to let Nana walk or use the restroom. She was a trooper and they joked around the entire drive. This was a promise for a great day in the making. While the drive went smoother than Andy anticipated, when he drove up into Jean's driveway, his former residence, he saw that look on Jean's face. She was standing by her car puffed up like a smokestack. She barely waited until he parked before she started in on him.

"I have an appointment in fifteen minutes and it will take me at least twenty minutes to get there. I am going to be late because you are so inconsiderate."

Andy looked at his watch. "You said noon and it's noon."

Jean kicked his tire and realized he wasn't driving his truck. This got her imagination running wild.

"Whose car is this? One of your girlfriends? If you think the boys are going with you and one of your trysts, you are crazy."

Nana edged slowly out of the car, but was quick to defend Andy. She hobbled toward Jean.

"Jean, I'm sorry we are late. I'm afraid it's my fault. Andy had to stop more for me than he's used to and time got away from us. I guess he didn't allow time for traveling with an old lady."

Jean let out a heavy sigh when she saw Grace. She loved this woman, always had. The very sight of Grace eased her irritation.

"Grace," she said moving toward the woman and hugging her. "I didn't know Andy was bringing you back with him. I'm sorry I sounded like a lunatic. It's just that, well, this isn't the first time that Andy has been late picking up the boys. In fact, it's becoming a bad habit of his."

Grace kissed Jean's cheek. "He's trying, Dear. Go on to your appointment. I'll make sure every thing is locked when we leave."

Jean nodded. She sent Andy a scornful look.

"The boys are hungry. I didn't want them to ruin their lunch, so I wouldn't let them snack after church."

Andy brushed by Jean without as much as a *good-bye*. He walked up to what used to be his front door and Bobby, his six-year old, ran up to him, hugging him tightly. Then, he let out a loud whistle and called out the names of his other two boys, "Mathew, Jeff, time to roll."

Jean shook her head frustrated and then leaned to kiss Grace. She watched as Andy locked the door. Within minutes, he had the car loaded with kids, bags, and Nana.

"Don't worry," he snipped at Jean before she could remind him. "I'll have them showered and ready for bed at a reasonable hour. I know tomorrow is a school day. You had better go. Wouldn't want you to be any later for your appointment than you already are."

Jean watched as he pulled away. The kids waved but Andy didn't. She felt her blood boil. Why did she let him get to her this way? Andy was Andy. He wasn't going to change. The tug of war game they played was growing old. Andy had to let go. Their marriage was over. He just couldn't accept this. Her insides were churning. She looked one more time down the empty road where Andy had just driven. Even after so many battles, she knew one thing. Andy loved his children. He'd do anything for them. She could not dispute this. That's why this last legal battle had been particularly difficult. Her lawyer wanted her to find Andy unfit in order to gain full custody of the boys. She knew she couldn't do this. She also knew it wouldn't be good for the boys. She would tell him tomorrow when he brought the boys home from school. She would also have to find the right time and the courage to tell him that she was in love with another man.

20

Later that evening, Paul did go to the cemetery and then, he drove by Hannah's house. He was secretly hoping to catch a glimpse of her, but he didn't. He had to wonder if after all these years if she knew that he drove by her house at least once a week and just parked — watching and waiting. He had to guess that she didn't. This was his only contact with her, this and Paul Jr. doing her grocery shopping, and the occasional flowers he and Sue sent her on her birthdays and the anniversary of the accident. He wanted her to know he was still there for her.

Sue had long since given up calling her or coming to her house. Half the time she didn't answer her door and when she did, she begged her to leave. It was too painful, she told her. She didn't want Sue to see her the way she had become. Finally, Sue did stop coming by, but not Paul. Oh, he never knocked on her door, but parked down the road and just watched the house. On rare occasions, he did catch a glimpse of her on the front porch, or with Grace. He knew this indulgence wasn't healthy, but he couldn't help himself. Maybe he wanted her to see him so that she would know she wasn't alone. Maybe he wanted her to know that there was someone in the world who cared for her deeply and would never forget her. He rationalized that loving Hannah this way was safe and that no one was getting hurt. It was better than not loving her at all. It was certainly more than he deserved.

Andy tucked the boys and Nana in bed. Nana took his bed and the boys each had their own beds. He would sleep on the couch tonight. The day had been good. They went to lunch and then the mall. Everyone got new clothes, compliments of Nana. The boys had a blast pushing Nana around in her wheelchair. It was good for them to get to be with her ... and good for him. Andy felt almost normal, like old times. He hadn't laughed so hard in months. He would make sure the boys saw more of

Nana. He stretched his long legs out on the couch. He was tired from the long drive and the day was catching up with him. It was a nice kind of tired and he caught himself laughing out loud thinking of the day. He flipped the channels trying to unwind. Maybe he could catch the news. Then, he heard Bobby crying. He walked into his room.

"Hey, Sport, what is it?"

"I need my blanket."

Andy sighed. Bobby was six and gave up *blanket* several years ago, but since the divorce, he was regressing and asking for it. Jean let him have it when they first split, but was now working hard to keep him from sleeping with it again. Andy thought she was right and supported her on this matter.

"Hey, how about you come sleep with me on the couch. We can watch TV for a while."

It was a tight squeeze, but the two settled down on the couch. Andy let him switch the channels for a while. After a bit, Bobby's eyes were drooping. Andy knew he was almost asleep.

"Daddy," he asked softly. "Are Frank Gordon and Mommy getting married?"

Stunned by the question, Andy stiffened his body and dared to ask him why he would say such a thing. Frank Gordon was Jean's boss at *Texas Computers*. He was ten years older than Jean, balding, and slightly pudgy. Andy shook his head at the idea wondering where Bobby had gotten such a notion.

"Frank Gordon is Mommy's boss, Buddy. That's all. Where did you get such an idea?"

"Well, he comes over a lot and I saw them kissing once."

Andy balled his fists. He felt like someone had kicked him in the gut. Surely, Bobby was mistaken. This couldn't be real. Trying to keep his emotions in tact, he rubbed Bobby's hair gently and kissed him.

"You're mistaken, Buddy. It's late now and you need your sleep. Don't you worry about anything tonight. We can talk about this tomorrow."

"Okay, but Daddy, I think they are getting married. Mathew told me if they did, he was going to live with you."

Andy could barely breathe.

"Shhh, hush now. Time to sleep or you won't be able to learn tomorrow."

Within minutes, Bobby was asleep. Andy was wide-awake. He thought of Frank Gordon. He had always considered him to be a nice guy. This just couldn't be true. Andy worked hard to try to connect the dots, to make sense of this sudden bolt of news his son had thrown out of the clear blue sky. Frank Gordon? He was married, wasn't he? Maybe not. No, man, he lived with his mother. That was it. His mother died a few months after Jean started working at *Texas Computers*. Andy remembered Jean going to her service.

Andy edged off the couch and went out on the deck outside of his apartment. The air was still and humid. He stared out into the darkness. Several events started to pop into his mind like radar. All of the company meetings Jean had gone to and stayed out late into the night. The many nights she worked late. He had always been proud that she was trying to better their lives. Once he came home unexpectedly from work and Frank was at their house. Jean told Andy he was there to fix their computer. He had no reason to question the truth of this. The computer was broken. He was a computer man. Then, a vision of Jean with untidy hair and smudged lipstick came to mind. She had been nervous and was rushing Frank out the door.

"You fool," he told himself. "She didn't want her freedom. She just wanted freedom from you. She's in love with another man and has been for quite some time."

He had been duped by them because Frank Gordon was an unsuspecting combatant and he had no reason to suspect his wife of such conduct. His hands were shaking uncontrollably. His heart was racing. He wanted a drink desperately, but he wanted to be sober when he talked to Jean. All of these months she had judged him, his drinking, his going out to clubs, his constant badgering her, his reckless behavior. He was looking for answers as to why his life had been turned upside down, when all along, the truth was right in front of him. He knew he should wait until his anger was more in tact before calling her, but he couldn't. It was more than time for her to face what she had done to their lives. He reached in his pocket and pulled out his cell phone. He called Jean.

"I get it," Andy said coldly. "All of these months I've been beating myself up trying to figure out what I had done wrong. Now I know. It wasn't what I did. It was what I couldn't do. Frank can give you all the things I never could. I wish I could be happy for you and Frank, but I guess I'm not that big of a man. But I do know one thing. You will regret losing what we had. Some day you will look at Frank and none of the things his golden pocket can give you will matter. You will be left wondering what the hell you threw away."

Andy arranged for Jean to pick up the boys at his apartment after work. They were ready and waiting for her, homework done, supper, and baths, all by six o'clock. Their clothes were clean and their bags packed. When Jean arrived, the bitterness Andy felt was obvious. His demeanor was cold and detached. He said and did all of the right things, but he was void of emotions. Jean didn't offer to explain further her situation. She knew this wasn't the time or place. Shortly after the boys left, Nana and Andy were on their way home to Blossom.

The drive was quiet, except for the humming of the motor and Nana's occasional snoring. She slept most of the ride and when Andy pulled into her driveway, he gently nudged her.

"Wake up, Sleeping Beauty. We're home."

"Already? My goodness, what time is it?"

"Almost nine-thirty. Time to tuck you in bed."

"Stay with me tonight, Andy. I don't want you driving back this late."

He looked into her sleepy eyes. He really needed to get back tonight, but then he thought of his empty apartment. He didn't have the heart to go back there. Not tonight.

"Okay, but only for my girl. I'll be gone early though, probably before you get up."

Satisfied, she smiled. Andy helped her out of the car and up the back steps. Within a half hour, she was in bed and fast asleep. It wouldn't be as easy for Andy to fall asleep. So many thoughts and ideas were racing in his head. He piddled in the kitchen and made a quick sandwich. He went outside to check on his truck and everything was in tact. He laughed aloud at the absurdity of him checking on a truck. Jean would laugh, too. Jean? Who really cared what Jean thought? He heard one of Nana's screens banging against a window and so he went to secure it. That was when the distinct noise of a swing moving back and forth told him he wasn't the only one awake.

He couldn't explain why, but he started walking toward Hannah's house. When he came into view for her, Hannah's heart jumped. Cautiously she stood and moved toward the security of her front door. He watched her silhouette in the moonlight. Her robe was swaying in the wind, as well as her long hair. He knew that he might frighten her, but was compelled to acknowledge her presence. Hannah wanted to retreat, but he was at her porch before she could. He could hear her breathing and suddenly he was as nervous as she was. Both stood immobile staring into each other's eyes.

She was a vision, especially in the moonlight. Where was the mad woman the boys had ridiculed? Where was the shadow that hid behind her door? This woman was making his heart leap to his throat. Maybe *he* was finally losing his mind. He swallowed hard, praying he wouldn't say something that would send her running inside. For some unknown reason, he wanted her here, needed her here. Moonlight dipped over her face and he could see her fear. There was something else he saw, but couldn't identify it. She gripped her robe and moved near a post to steady her nerves. Andy couldn't stop staring. The eyes and hair and mouth he had often fantasized about were the same, perhaps even more erotic. No, tragedy hadn't diminished her beauty. Andy was lost in a mirage of flowing black hair and mystic eyes, making him more vulnerable than the frightened woman who possessed them.

"Hannah," he said uneasy. "May I call you Hannah?"

She didn't speak, but her eyes told him that he could. He let out a deep sigh. Hannah gripped the post she was standing near. Andy saw her chest constrict and then let out a heavy breath.

"Am I frightening you? Do you want me to leave?"

She didn't answer. He laughed nervously.

"You are going to have to help me out here. I don't know what you want. I don't want to leave, Hannah, but if you want me to, I will."

She shook her head so slightly that he thought he might have imagined it. But then, she shook it again. He smiled and walked up the remaining step so that he stood directly beside her. He felt her retreating again, so he moved back and rested against the stair railing just below her. He began to relax somewhat and reached into his pocket for a cigarette.

"Do you mind?"

Again, she shook her head. A steam of smoke filled her nostrils and she remembered the times when Sammy had smoked his cigars. These were fond memories and through the darkness, she smiled. Andy smiled back warmly.

"Hannah," his voice spoke softly. "I want to thank you for seeing after Nana. She loves you, you know, like a daughter. I think maybe as much as she loves her only son. Maybe even more than her grandsons. I think it's because you understand

26

each other. She tells me how you help her with things like bathing and dressing when she can't. She tells me that you often cook for her. I know you won't believe this, but you are the strong one. Nana says you have more courage than an army of soldiers. Anyway, thank you from my family — and me. We — I owe you a debt of gratitude."

Andy shifted his weight so that his other hip held it. Hannah barely moved. He turned to her and she was looking at him intently. They made eye contact again and he took in every detail of her features. They were almost too perfect to be real. He noticed her fidgeting, so he turned away. She watched him from behind. He was a large man, tall and muscular and ruggedly handsome. She could tell that he had taken care of himself, but his recent ordeal was taking its toll on him. The worn lines told his suffering and the dark circles were signs that his drinking might be getting the best of him. What cut Hannah's heart more than anything, was his carriage, a droop that defined a lost spirit. She knew this droop all too well. Like her, Andy Padgett had little hope. As if sensing she was studying him, he turned to her.

"Do I turn you off, Hannah?"

She lent him a puzzled stare. Immediately, he realized she misunderstood his question. She was probably thinking he was fishing for a compliment or something.

"That didn't come out the way I wanted," he said nervously. "I'm glad you can't see I'm blushing. What I meant to ask was, do you find me unfit? My ex-wife does. She thinks I'm unfit for my boys. She thinks I'm setting an immoral example for them, which to me is ironic. I mean in all the years that we were married, I never once cheated, never once considered it. I gave her my paycheck every Friday and never questioned where she spent it. I knew she was a better manager than I was. Maybe I gave her too much, because when she left, she said I was drowning her. I couldn't make sense of it...until yesterday."

Andy flicked his cigarette into the darkness and watched its slight flame smolder into nothingness. He ran a hand through his thick hair. Then, he sat on the top step and continued talking.

"I found out yesterday that she's in love with another man, her boss. Isn't that a cliché? I believe in my gut that their affair started before the divorce. She says that it began after we split. Guess it doesn't really matter. They are a couple. Hell, why didn't she just take a knife to my chest? It would have hurt less."

Andy dropped his head into his hands. The air was thick with pain and broken dreams. He wanted to cry, but he couldn't. He lifted his head and stared into the bleak night.

"I've lost her, Hannah. In many ways, I've lost the boys, too. You can't be a real father when you live in another house. I'm empty. Broken. Nothing matters now."

He wasn't sure why he was spilling his guts to Hannah. Maybe he needed someone to listen to him that would not judge him. Or maybe he knew her pain was so deep, she would have empathy. In the heart of his sorrow, Hannah did the most remarkable thing. She did it without thought or outcome. She sat next to him and ran a gentle hand though the back of his hair. He turned to her startled and that's when he noticed her face. It was covered with tears. He groped through his pockets for a hanky or tissue. Of course, he didn't have one, so he wiped her tears with his hand.

"Hannah," he apologized. "I'm so sorry I made you cry. Please don't cry – not for me. I'm not worth it."

She felt in her robe pocket and pulled out a tissue. She blew her nose and once again found herself looking into his eyes. So badly she wanted to reach out to him, but she just couldn't break through her protective walls. He was a virtual stranger. Still, she was no stranger to pain and he was filled with it. She gently took his hand and held it. The two sat for some time on her porch saying nothing, easing away each other's sorrow. After some time, he stood and held his hand out to her. Reaching for it, they stood one last time facing each other. Then, he walked her to her front door and smiled kindly.

"Thank you for tonight, Hannah. You will never understand how much you helped me." Then he made light of the situation. "Be careful. I hear there's a crazy man lurking next door."

Hannah laughed and then covered her mouth. For the first time since she could remember, her laughter was genuine.

THREE

Hannah sat in the quiet of Grace's kitchen, after cleaning up this morning's breakfast dishes. It was mid-morning and she had just put Grace down for her morning nap. Grace was tired a lot lately and her health, Hannah knew, was becoming a serious issue. In the past several weeks, she had literally seen Grace deteriorate before her eyes. It was time, past time, for her to contact family to seek medical help. The week after Andy had been here, Charlie came. Ben skipped this week and asked Hannah to keep a close watch on her. She knew that Grace had been to her family doctor several months ago, because Charlie had taken her. Grace told Hannah that her doctor said she was healthy as an ox and would live to be a hundred. Hannah had her doubts about that and decided to make an inquiry to Dr. Thorn, Blossom's one and only practicing physician.

His nurse, Trudy Blaine, was speechless when Hannah relayed her concerns about Grace's health. She told Trudy that she understood she couldn't divulge information to her because Hannah wasn't family, but maybe she should call Charlie or Ben. Trudy told Hannah that she, in fact, was on Grace's list as a family member that could be given medical information. Hannah soon discovered that Dr. Thorn had referred Grace to a heart specialist in Dallas named Allen Fletcher over a month ago. Trudy informed her that she was the one who had made the appointment for Grace.

"I don't think she kept it," Hannah said. "Her grandsons would have made sure she kept such an appointment. They would have insisted. Why would Grace break her appointment? Do you think she forgot?"

"Maybe so, but not likely," Trudy said. "A lot of our seniors just don't want to face up to what is going on with them healthwise. It's frightening and so they often ignore the signs. I tell you what. Let me check up on a few things. I'll contact Dr. Fletcher in Dallas and talk with Dr. Thorn. We'll get. to the bottom of this."

"I'd appreciate that," Hannah said. "Call me as soon as you know something. If you need to set up a new appointment while you have the doctor on the line, do so. I'll see to it that she keeps it this time."

"Good. Give me the best numbers to reach you."

Hannah gave Trudy both Grace's number and hers.

"Do you have a cell?"

"No, I never needed one."

"Okay, well I will call you when I know something."

An hour later, Trudy called and told her that Grace had canceled the appointment. Grace told the doctor that she would be calling back to set up a new one. Of course, she never did. Trudy told Hannah that Grace must have given quite a convincing story because usually when a patient breaks a critical appointment, the specialist contacts the family doctor. She told Hannah that her new appointment would be this upcoming Monday at eight o'clock in the morning. Hannah had four days to prepare Grace.

Later that night, when Grace had been put to bed, Hannah made a bed on Grace's couch. She wanted to be near her in case she needed her. She contemplated on which family member to call about Grace. Grace's only living child, John Padgett, lived in Bolivia. He and his wife, Ann, were missionaries there. She would have to call Charlie, Ben, or Andy. Charlie or Ben were the obvious choices. They were, in fact, the most reliable. Ben's schedule was more flexible, but his wife, Careen, and Grace didn't often see eye to eye on things. Grace would feel more comfortable with Charlie's wife, Debbie. Still, Charlie and Debbie were just getting their new business off the ground and

Tyler was about two hours from Dallas. Hannah thought of Andy. He was the logical choice since he lived around Dallas.

Hannah wondered if Andy was capable of taking on a new responsibility. If it were only a one-day visit, Hannah would have no reservations, but she was sure Grace would be hospitalized. She didn't know if Andy could cope with anything else in his life. Hannah thought of Grace. Grace would want Andy. Andy was her favorite. Hannah decided to call him. Then, she'd let the family work out future details.

Hannah called his number. There was no answer. She left a message for him to call her. Two hours later, he hadn't called back, so she called him once more. There was still no answer. She decided she had better call Charlie, but just as she was about to, the phone rang. It was Andy. He was out of breath and Hannah knew he was thinking the worse.

"Hannah, this is Andy. You called? Is everything okay? I mean is Nana okay?"

Hannah was having difficulty breathing, but she managed to speak out. Her voice was soft and shaky, but Andy was too rattled himself to notice.

"She is fine for the moment, Andy. I'm afraid…I'm afraid she's going downhill." Andy heard her sob and try to regain her composure. "I've made an appointment for her to see a Dallas cardiologist. The appointment is this coming Monday. His office is near Medical City. Andy, I wouldn't have been so bold as to interfere in your family's affairs, except I'm scared. I'm afraid she's very ill. I'm sorry, I didn't have any other choice."

Hannah broke down. She heard him let out a heavy sigh.

"Jesus, Hannah, don't be sorry. We are the ones who should be sorry. We should have made her see a specialist months ago. Hell, I thought she had. Charlie said she had. Maybe he thought she had."

Hannah blew her nose and sat down in a chair. Somehow hearing Andy's voice made her feel a little better, a little safer.

"Can you take her, Andy? I mean, can you get off work to have her at her appointment Monday?"

Andy hadn't thought that far. Of course, he would take her. "I can take her, Hannah. I'm off on Mondays. I'll drive to Blossom Sunday and bring Nana back to Dallas that night. She can sleep at my apartment. What time did you say her appointment was?"

"Eight o'clock. I'm glad you can do this, Andy. Do you want me to call Charlie and Ben, or do you want to call them?"

"They don't know?" Andy was surprised that she had called him first. He let out a chuckle. "You sure you called the right Padgett? I'm the screw-up, remember, Hannah?"

She had to giggle. How many times had she heard Charlie or Ben say this very thing? Then she thought of how he handled the boys outside her kitchen door. He was in command. He took charge. No, she had called the right person.

"Grace believes in you, Andy. So do I."

It was true. Grace always said that when the chips were down, it was Andy who would be the first in line to make things right. Hannah was beginning to understand why.

"You sure about that?"

"I wouldn't put my dearest friend in your care if I didn't, now would I?"

Andy knew she was being truthful and something stirred within him. He was beginning to see Hannah in a new light. He was seeing her as a flesh and blood human being, not some fantasy he had conjured up as a teenager, and certainly not some freak who had tipped the scales from sanity to insanity. She was a beautiful woman, who had known more suffering than anyone should be allowed to know. Also, she loved Nana as much as he did, maybe more.

"I appreciate your faith in me, Hannah, but, you're the one who is going to face Charlie and Ben when they find out you called me first."

The tease in his deep voice put her at ease. He heard her laugh softly in response. Her laughter set him back. He was remembering her soft laughter the last time he had seen her on her front porch, and her tears. She was certainly an enigma.

"Hannah, will you come to Dallas with Nana?"

Hannah was suddenly solemn. His was a question she had been struggling with since she talked to Trudy.

"No," she said softly. "Not now. Let's see what the doctors have to say. I'm afraid if I come I will frighten Grace more than she already is."

Something in her tone stabbed at his gut.

"You think she'll be put in the hospital, don't you, Hannah? Are things that bad?"

"Oh, Andy," she sniffed. "I...I...I'm sure she will be put in the hospital. I just don't know for how long. I know they will most likely keep her overnight to run tests and monitor her. I'm thinking longer, Andy. She's so frail and she is almost eighty."

"Jesus," he muttered. "Where the hell have I been? I mean I was just there three weeks ago. Why didn't I see this coming?"

"You are like me, Andy. It is easier to see and believe what our hearts want."

"Oh, Hannah," he choked. Fear and regret sailed through the receiver. "I love her, more than I ever realized."

"She knows this, Andy."

She heard him choke back his tears.

"Andy? Andy, can you hear me?"

"Yea," he said quietly. "I hear you."

"We both have to let go of our fears to help her. If she sees us fall apart, she will lose hope. She can't know we think the worse. She has to know we believe she will get better."

"I do believe it, Hannah."

Hannah smiled again. "You will do just fine, Andy. I knew I called the right Padgett."

"I won't let you down. I won't let Nana down."

"I never thought you would."

She made him smile. He wiped his face.

"Hannah?"

"Yes?"

"About the night I came to your front porch. I'm sorry. I shouldn't have thrown my problems at you like that. I was a bit upset and…"

"Andy, forget about it. Let's concentrate on Grace. She's all that matters right now. I'll see you Sunday."

"Okay, Hannah. You're right. Nothing matters but Nana."

When Hannah hung up her heart was jumping wildly. She hadn't talked so easily to a man like that in well, she couldn't remember when. Andy made talking so easy, especially with so many miles between them. He would be here Sunday, face to face. She would have to talk to him then. Almost three weeks had gone by since he had visited her porch. He and his boys had been on her mind since that visit. Maybe too much. The day after his visit, she was disappointed to see his truck already gone. She let out a heavy sigh. It didn't make any sense. She shook her head. She couldn't worry about Andy's problems, or her own, for that matter. She had to think about Grace.

Hannah checked in on Grace before she laid down on the sofa. The lamplight near her house lent Hannah a small sense of security. She could feel the sand beneath her world shifting and a new fear enveloped her. Change always brought fear. She was restless for some time before falling asleep. She was out of her usual routine. A small, very minute sense of pride filled her spirit. She smiled.

"Sammy," she whispered. "Can you believe all that I've accomplished today?"

And, she had, more than even she realized. For the first time in four years, she had let go of her fear to help another human being. She had made contact with the outside world and didn't fall apart. She made trip after trip, back and forth, from her house to Grace's house and not once did she ever doubt she could do it. When it came time to face Grace's family, she did it like a trooper. Almost always, when she fell asleep at night she dreamed of Sammy, Gabe, or Julie. Sometimes she dreamed of her mother. Tonight though, her mind played games with her. When she closed her eyes, she saw a man sitting on her front porch with his head pressed in the full of his hands. She reached for him and he turned to face her. She heard Andy's pained voice.

"Don't cry for me, Hannah. I'm not worth it."

As she did on that night three weeks ago, she did tonight. She let her tears flow. She recalled the hurt in his voice tonight.

"Andy, I'm sorry I've given you one more sorrow. I will try very hard to be strong for you and for Grace. She's like the mother I lost when I was a child. I must be strong for her, and for you."

Andy called Charlie and Ben and then much later he called Jean. He wanted to arrange for the boys to come to her house Sunday evening instead of the usual time on Monday. When he called, he didn't realize it was after ten. He was weary and tired.

"Jean, it's Andy."

"Andy? What time is it? You sound strange. Have you been drinking?"

He almost laughed. "No, I haven't been drinking, not yet anyway. There is something I have to tell you."

"What is it? What's wrong?" she repeated.

Andy heard a gruff voice in the background. The person with Jean wanted to know who it was.

"It's Andy," she told him. "Something must be wrong."

"Is Frank with you, Jean? I thought sleepovers were taboo."

Andy heard Jean sigh. "Andy it's late. I'll explain this later. Why did you call?"

"No explanations are necessary, Jean. I'm a big boy. I think I can figure out what is going on. Are the boys there?"

"No, they are at mother's house."

"I should have known. Saint Jean wouldn't poison her children's minds. Well, so sorry to disturb you."

Without reason and without thought, Jean blurted out her excuse for having Frank at her house. The minute she spoke the words, she regretted them.

"Andy, Frank and I were married last weekend. Mother and Dad are the only ones who know. Now you know."

A cloud of blackness enveloped him He felt as though his whole being was on fire. He tried to breath. He couldn't. He tried to move. He couldn't. He heard Jean calling out his name, but it was in the furthest reaches of his mind. Then, he gently laid down the receiver. The silence and darkness was so thick, he thought he might suffocate. Too numb to cry, he lifted himself up and went to the refrigerator. He reached for a beer and held it in his hand but didn't open it. He set it down on the table. He could still feel the darkness. The phone rang over and over again. He knew it was Jean. He didn't answer it. He just sat in the darkness, numb and lifeless. An eternity later, there was a knock at the door. He didn't care. He heard the knock again. Still, he sat in the darkness. He heard a key inside the doorknob and the door open. It was Jean and she wasn't alone. He wondered if maybe she had gone mad and brought Frank with her. It wasn't Frank. It was Liz Brewster.

Jean turned on a nearby lamp. Andy looked at her coldly. Liz sat on the couch. She reached for his hand. Andy almost laughed at the absurdity of the situation. His ex-wife had brought his ex-girlfriend, who consequently was a good friend of hers, with her to his apartment to check up on him. Apparently, Jean needed Liz to come with her because Liz still had his key. Jean sat next to Liz. Both looked at him pitiable and frightened. Both were crying. What were they thinking? Did they think he would do himself in because his wife of

fifteen years decided to destroy their family and marry a
burned out computer programmer who had a hefty nest egg?
He lent Jean an icy grin and saluted her, as if to say, *"You win."*
His disdain for her was evident. Whatever hope there was for
his family was now gone. For that, he would never forgive her.
The silence was broken when Jean's cell phone rang. It was
Frank. Andy only heard one side of the conversation, but
understood it well enough to know that he was asking her if
Andy was all right. Would this nightmare ever end?

"Andy, I'm leaving now. I just wanted to make sure you
were all right. We can talk in a few days."

Jean stood and waited for Andy to yell at her or try to stop
her or something, but he didn't. He thought he heard her say,
"good-bye" or *"I'm sorry"*, and then a door open and shut. He
knew she was gone and he didn't care. He just sat motionless.
Liz was still holding his hand.

"Do you want me to stay, Andy?" Liz asked. "I can stay or
leave."

Andy looked at Liz, sweet Liz, who had comforted him the
dark months after Jean had left him. She was always there to
see to his well-being. She had truly been his salvation and
regretfully, he had treated her poorly. For the life of him, he
couldn't understand why she wanted to be near him. In any
event, he was grateful she was here. He knew he couldn't make
it through this night alone. He gripped her hand tightly and
directed her to sit on his lap.

"Stay."

She brushed his lips tenderly as he held her. After a while,
she walked him to his bedroom. He was a defeated man. He
went through the motions of lovemaking, but he was numb,
lost in a cloud of nothingness. Later, after Liz had fallen asleep,
Andy was finally able to release some of his hurt. All night his
tears fell, not like a rush, but softly. He studied Liz as she slept.
She was so beautiful and completely devoted to him. She was
much younger than he was and insecure about their

relationship. She had every right to be insecure. How many times had he let her down? More than he could count? She wanted more than he could give. She deserved more than he could give her. He knew he should leave her alone. He knew he would hurt her again.

Even when he knew he should leave her alone, he reached to hold her. His arm nestled around her waist and he tucked his hand beneath her breasts. It was a familiar position with Liz, holding her this way. He smiled. Her breasts were heavier. She had put on weight. She felt a little like Jean had when she was first pregnant. Suddenly, a shock wave jolted through him. He was cold and clammy, yet sweat dripped down his back. Slowly, he eased his hand lower to feel of her belly. It was soft and round. He always admired what great shape Liz kept herself in, athletic and firm. Her body had changed. All the signs were before him. She heard him stirring and nudged him to hold her again. He complied. They held each other, both aware that the other was awake. Both were aware of the obvious. Liz spoke first.

"Andy," she whispered. "I'm sorry."

Regret wedged its way into his heart. He was regretful that he couldn't love her, not the way she deserved. He would never love that way again. He was repentant that she was carrying his child and all he could feel was a deep remorse that he had put her in this situation. His sorrow deepened when he understood that he would have to marry her.

"No, Liz," he said apologetically. "I'm sorry. How far along are you?"

She turned to face him and conceded to the truth.

"Four months," she answered.

"Four months!" he cried out. "Were you ever going to tell me?"

"I was afraid, Andy. You never answered my calls and I knew you still loved Jean. I was so alone. My life is just a mess. I...I didn't know what to do And then tonight when Jean called and said you had just found out about her and Frank getting married and that you were so upset, I knew I had to see you. I wanted to be here for you."

He looked into her young eyes. He reached for her and held her against his chest. He felt tears fall on him and he tried to soothe her. He kissed her softly.

"Hush now. We'll get through this. You aren't alone. I'll be with you every step of the way."

"Oh, Andy, I never expected you to be so gentle. I thought for sure you would run."

"I'm blessed, Liz. In all the crap that has been my life this past year, this is the most peace my heart has felt. I don't take this lightly."

"Oh, Andy," she cried. "Hold me."

He held her close, letting the realization of new life ease away his despair. She found it inconceivable that he never once questioned whether the child she was carrying was his.

FOUR

Hannah was planning to serve roast beef with new potatoes, fresh green beans and a salad for Grace on her last night at home. Neither Grace nor Hannah had once discussed the possibility of a lengthy hospital stay, but both knew it would more than likely be longer than an overnight stay. There was an undercurrent of tension for Hannah, wondering if she could be alone in her house knowing *her* Grace was miles away in a hospital. What if Grace should need her? What if she should need Grace? To keep her mind off of her own predicament, Hannah busied herself, wanting to make this a special parting for the woman who meant more to her than any other person on this earth. Her plans were altered somewhat when Andy called and said he was coming up a little early and asked if he needed to bring something for supper. When Hannah told him she had already planned dinner, he informed her that he was bringing a friend. This put Hannah in a new tizzy. The thought of entertaining Andy, let alone a stranger, had all but destroyed her nerves.

Hold it together, Hannah. You can do this. You can do this. It's just a dinner.

Yet, even as she tried to convince herself of this, her nerves got the best of her. She ran to her bathroom and let the nausea pass. It was more than entertaining Andy and his friend. It was the fact that her Grace, her rock, was slipping away from her, maybe for a long time. Everything was so uncertain. She looked at her shaky hands and laughed aloud at her own ineptness. She recited a scripture that she said almost daily in an effort to calm her nerves.

"For God hath not given us the spirit of fear, but of power, and of love, and of sound mind."

"Dear Lord, I'm sorry I am so weak. Make me strong. Give me the strength I need to live through this day and do all that I have to do."

When Andy arrived at Nana's around three she was sitting in her living room all gussied up, dressed in her Sunday best. Hannah had fixed her hair up in a twist and had put on her lucky pearls, as Grace called them. She said they were lucky because sixty-one years ago a handsome farmer named George Padgett asked her to marry him. As a gift on their wedding day, he gave her the pearls. She always considered them lucky because she'd been lucky to find a man like George to share her life.

Andy whistled, "Well, look at who we have here. Could be the prettiest sight in Texas."

Grace chuckled. "Not bad for an ex-babe, huh?"

Andy kissed her cheek. Grace held his hand firmly. Their eyes locked. "Thank you for coming, Dear."

"I wouldn't be anywhere else."

Liz stood awkwardly in the background.

"Nana, you remember Liz Brewster, don't you? I brought her here with the boys once."

Nana smiled. "Of course, I do, Andy. My heart's not working right, but my mind is just fine. Hi, Liz. So happy to see you again."

"Thank you. It's nice to see you again, as well."

"What's the occasion, Nana? I feel a bit underdressed."

"Oh, it's Hannah. She's been busy all week going back and forth from my house to her house. The poor dear has worked herself to the bone taking care of me. I don't think my house has been this clean in years. Now, she's got this big meal planned for my send-off. "

"Well, she loves you, Nana. She wants you to know this."

42

"Andy, promise me something."

"Anything, Sweetheart."

"See to Hannah. Call her and make sure she's okay each day."

"Sure, Nana. I can do that."

"Good, now let's get this shindig started."

Hannah's back door was open, so the three walked inside. Hannah was busy in the back of the house, so they sat down in the living room. Andy looked around at the surroundings. He didn't exactly know what he had expected Hannah's house to look like, but it wasn't what he saw. Maybe he was expecting darkness and gloom because of Hannah's condition, but her home was light and airy and all Hannah. The air smelled of home cooking and fresh flowers. Everything was neat and in order, polished to perfection. He heard her footsteps moving toward them and when she appeared, Andy looked at her in disbelief. What he saw, took his breath away. Her green summer dress flowed with every step she took and her long hair that was styled down, turned up slightly at the ends. She looked like she had just come out of a summer catalogue, fresh and tantalizing. It took him two times to stand up and greet her properly. They smiled and shook hands. Some point after that, he introduced Liz to her and as expected, she was gracious to Liz, offering her a drink. Andy noticed Grace's eyes were moist, filled with pride for her Hannah.

As if she knew no anxiety, as if she did this sort of thing every day of her life, Hannah led the three into the dinning room, where dinner awaited. She was using her best china and silver. The table was covered with her grandmother's tablecloth and the centerpiece had been delivered a few days ago from a local florist. Both Andy and Nana looked at each other, amazed at the resilience of this woman. She was poised and versed, and had they not known her condition so well, they would never have imagined that this was a woman who was controlled by fear and anxiety. It wasn't until Andy took her hand to praise her efforts that the reality of her condition come to light. Her hand was shaking like a leaf and she gripped his tightly.

"We are family, Hannah. There's no one here who will hurt you."

Fear threatened to surface and that's when Andy's charm took over.

"Liz, did you know that when I was younger I had a terrible crush on Hannah?"

"Andy," Hannah choked. "You did not!"

He grinned at her and sent her a quick wink.

"It's true," he said reaching for Liz's hand. "But, don't worry. I wasn't alone. So did every other male in Blossom. Just look at her. She's a knock out."

"Andy, stop," Liz nudged. "You're embarrassing her."

Andy looked to see that Hannah was indeed blushing. Her hands shook as she tipped her water glass and drank its entirety. Even in her nervous state, Andy was sure he had never known a woman more poised than Hannah Martindale. He only thought to put her at ease. He looked into her face, so perfectly veiled by years of trained poise. Only now was he able to recognize the difficulty of this night.

"Hannah," he said. "I'm sorry I teased you."

She let out a soft breath. "It's okay, really."

The remainder of the evening was spent with Liz talking about work and Andy talking about the boys. Andy, in passing, mentioned that Jean had remarried and each one wondered just how Andy was really doing. He acted so nonchalant about it. They both knew what a toil this divorce had taken on his life. It nearly destroyed him and today he talked as if he were talking about the weather. Hannah noticed that Andy and Liz were inseparable, holding hands and joking around with each other. She doted on him, even cutting his meat for him. He smiled at her, teasing her and sharing private moments together. Hannah had to guess that they were close, because of their familiarity.

Some time later, Andy looked at the clock and then at Hannah. She nodded knowing that Grace was already tired and that it was time for them to be headed to Dallas. Liz started to help clear up the table, but Hannah stopped her.

"Absolutely not. You are my guests. I'll get this later. It will give me something to do when you leave."

"Are you sure?" Liz asked. "I don't feel right leaving you to do everything."

"Why don't you and Andy put Grace's things into the car? I have everything packed and ready to go. Her things are in her living room by the door. I want some time to say good-bye to Grace."

Liz smiled. "Sounds like a plan."

Hannah watched as Andy and Liz walked back to Grace's house. She liked her a lot. She thought she might be good for Andy. She had an inclination that Liz had something to do with his sudden change of spirit.

After saying goodbye to Grace, Hannah was emotionally drained. She locked her doors and pulled down her blinds. She couldn't watch them as they pulled away. Already the tears were falling down her face. She was sorrowful that her dear friend was so ill, but more than that, she was ashamed of herself. She hated this fear that so consumed her life. She should be strong enough to go with her, to hold her hand. She needed her.

Outside, the wind was blowing and so she didn't hear a knock at the door. When the knock came again, she became alerted. Peering out her curtain, she saw Andy standing on her front porch.

"Hannah, it's Andy. Liz forgot her purse."

She unlocked the door and let him inside. He could tell she had been crying. He thought to hold her, but took her hand instead. He didn't want to upset her more.

"Hannah, don't cry. She's going to be all right."

She looked at him anguished.

"Andy, it's just that I miss her already. I'm such a coward."

"You have more courage than any person I know. You more than proved this today."

"Grace is the one with courage. I should be with her. She would be with me."

"Then come with us tonight. There's plenty of room at my apartment."

"I can't. I'm not capable."

"Yes, you are, Hannah."

She lent him a doubtful smile and shook her head *no*.

"Okay, Hannah. I won't force the issue, but you know my number. You know I'll come and get you."

She smiled. "I appreciate that, Andy."

He smiled back. "Liz said she thinks you put her purse in your bedroom."

"Oh, yes. I put it on my bed."

He followed her down the hallway and into her bedroom. Her room was dark with only the light from the hallway flowing through it. Hannah gave little thought to the fact that they were standing alone in her bedroom. Nor did he.

"So tell me, what do you think of Liz?"

"I think she's lovely, Andy."

As if seeking her blessing or perhaps needing to confide in someone who wouldn't criticize him, he told her about the baby.

"I'm going to ask her to marry me, Hannah. It's the right thing to do. She, I mean we, are having a baby."

Hannah turned to face him so suddenly, she bumped right into his chest. They stood face to face, chest to chest. Her surprise was written all over her face. She thought that maybe she should say something profound or encouraging.

"Oh," was all that came out of her mouth.

He was confused by how good she felt standing so close to him. She didn't have the sense of mind to move away and he

46

didn't have the desire. He could feel her heart racing as she stood against him. She swallowed hard just now aware of her vulnerability. She handed Liz's purse to him.

"You'd better go, Andy. It's getting late."

"Yea," he said clearly rattled. "I'll call you tomorrow."

She watched him walk toward the hallway and put something on her dresser. Then he turned to face her.

"Good night, Hannah."

She couldn't move, adrift in this unsettling moment. He turned away. She heard his footsteps move down the hall to the front door, and then he was gone.

FIVE

Hannah awoke in a cold sweat from the same recurring nightmare that she had been having the past four years. It came less frequent than in years past, but tonight, it invaded her sanity with a powerful vengeance. It shouldn't have surprised her that it came, what with Grace leaving and the anniversary of her family's sudden deaths near. Still, it chilled her to the bone and struck her with terror. She was once again at the mercy of fear.

The sirens were deafening as they cut through the blackness of the wreckage. Hannah was sure her head would explode if they didn't stop. Chaos surrounded her, voices, footsteps, screams, drills, and cars—all rushing through her head like a violent storm. Why wouldn't it stop? She couldn't hear her family's cries anymore. She needed to hear them so she could find them. The weight on her battered body was crushing. She tried desperately to pull it off, but she couldn't.

"Julie? Gabe? Sammy? Where are you? Where am I?"

The stench of burned rubber and flesh filled her nostrils and she began to choke. She could feel a wetness spill through her nose and mouth, and she vaguely wondered if she was choking to death on her own blood. She managed to lift her arm, which felt oddly suspended, unattached from her shoulder. It rested on a mass of something that felt like wet wool or fur. She gripped it tightly. Something like fear flooded through her veins when she realized she was holding someone's hair.

Then, she felt a headband, and as her fingers trailed over it, she knew it was Julie's headband. She felt the tiny roses on the band, roses that matched those in her new dress. Hannah called out to her, but she didn't know if she heard her. She willed her hand to move and felt Julie's small mouth, jarred open and twice its size. She felt inside of her mouth and realized her jaw had been broken. Teeth, bones, and fragments lay randomly in her mouth. Hannah worked frantically to remove them, afraid she might choke on them.

When Hannah's hand fell gently on her baby's tiny throat, that's when she knew she was gone. Her neck had snapped. As Hannah held the precious face of her six-year old daughter, a flood of memories filled her mind. She was remembering the day she was born, her first tooth, her first steps, and her first day of school. She could see her riding her new bike and heard her soft voice singing in the church choir. Hannah wanted to die with her, but then she thought of Sammy and Gabe. She had to find her other baby and make sure he was still alive. She had to find her husband.

Several times she tried to move, but couldn't. Then, by some miracle, the tremendous weight on her was lifted. She felt light and free. Air slapped her face and she saw someone above her reach to lift her. She was being carried away and was crying for her family. Much as she cried, it was no use. Voices around her sounded like hollow drums. She tried to scream, but no one heard her. She cried again for her children, her husband, but no one listened. She was put on a table of some sort and people were putting tubes in her and poking her with needles. She couldn't breathe. She couldn't think. Her mind was whirling. People were talking to her and touching her, people who had no familiar faces. Soon a mass of darkness overpowered her and she lost all sense of life itself. She was sure she was dying.

She didn't die. Ten days later, the first face she saw was not Sammy's or Gabe's, but it was the face of her father. Tony DuJane was sitting in a chair next to her bed. Something was wrong. Dread filled her heart, because she knew her father wouldn't be here if something wasn't wrong. They didn't have a good relationship. A flood of images from the car accident became vivid and she understood too well that her nightmare was real.

She was in a hospital that much she knew. Her arms and hands were bandaged and her leg must be broken, because it was in a lift of some type. She was battered and bruised all over her body. Drugged, she was disoriented and her head felt as though it was detached from her body. She looked at her father for answers. She remembered well the death of her beautiful Julie, still she looked to her father for confirmation.

"Julie's dead, isn't she?"

Tony nodded. He rang for a nurse, because this was the first time she had been conscious since they brought her in the hospital. He moved to hold her bandaged hand.

"She's with Jesus, Baby."

She closed her eyes again and saw Sammy swerving to miss the oncoming car. She would never forget the look on Sammy's face the instant he knew they would hit the other car. His look held all emotions. Their eyes locked as if frozen in time. Each one knew that this was the end. Tears and hysteria threatened to surface, but she had to be strong for Gabe and Sammy. Once again, she looked at her father. He stared at her worn and pitiable.

"Daddy, where's Sammy? Where's Gabe?"

Charlotte, Tony's wife, had been standing in the corner of the room, hidden like the messenger of darkness. She moved toward the opposite side of the bed where Tony was standing. She took hold of Hannah's other hand. Each one gripped the hand they were holding tightly. Panic spiraled through Hannah. Her voice demanded the truth.

"Daddy?" she repeated. "Where are they?"

Tony looked helplessly at Charlotte. She would have to be the one to break the news to her. He was too weak. He had always been too weak.

"They didn't make it, Darling," Charlotte informed, soothing her head gently.

The word *darling* cut through her like a knife. Hannah had never been this woman's darling, not today, not ever. From the time she had come into her life when she was ten, Charlotte and Hannah, at best, tolerated each other. Her mother had only been dead less then a year when her father married Charlotte Burleson. Hannah blamed her for putting a wedge between the special relationship she had with her father. Later, she understood her father's part in this, as well.

With all of the strength she had, she tried to get out of bed, but all she managed to do was pull out her IV. Tony rang for the nurse again. By now, Hannah was screaming, yelling for her family. She was demanding to see them. She was in danger of hurting herself further when two orderlies and a nurse came in the room. They were quick to restrain her, asking Tony and Charlotte to leave. The nurse gave her a sedative as Hannah's cries filled the room. Within minutes, Hannah physically gave up fighting, but her cries still echoed her pain. She looked at the nurse and beseeched her.

"Please bring my family back to me."

Outside her room, Tony stared at Charlotte. His chest heaved in and out from exhaustion. He couldn't bear what was happening to his child, his Hannah. Charlotte gave him little consolation. She told him to pull himself together for Hannah's sake. Charlotte knew that Tony needed a drink badly, so when he left to get some air, she expected him to be gone the rest of the day, maybe longer. It was something Tony always did. When times got rough, he ran. She was surprised that he had lasted this long.

Some time later, the nurse came out and told her she could go back inside the room. She told Charlotte that sometimes in this type of situation the patient might need to be placed in a medical coma so that they could heal without doing more damage. Charlotte told the nurse that they should do whatever the doctors thought best. Hannah was a prisoner, hearing every word, but unable to do anything. She didn't want to be sedated.

She didn't want to heal. She wanted to die with her family. She felt a hand touch her hair. It was Charlotte. She wanted her to stop. She tried to slap her hand away, but her attempts were futile. She heard Charlotte whisper to someone, probably the nurse.

"She's always been so beautiful. Now look at her," she broke down.

The nurse held her gently. "She still is beautiful. She's been through a lot. She's lucky to be here."

"My God," Hannah thought to herself. "Do they really think that I care whether or not I'll be beautiful again? Do they really think I'm lucky because I lived?"

"You should go home," the nurse told Charlotte. "Get some rest. This is going to be a long process."

"How long?" Charlotte asked. "How long until she's well?"

"Physically? I'd say two or three more weeks in the hospital and then about three months of intense rehab, maybe more. Then, there would be out patient care."

"Emotionally?"

"Each person is different. She's lost her whole family. It's going to take a long time."

Hannah's eyes were closed, but she was very much aware. She was aware that her father was gone. She was aware that she was at the mercy of a kind nurse and a manipulating stepmother. She knew whatever happened to her from this point on, would be Charlotte's doing. Charlotte bent to kiss Hannah on the forehead and once again patted her head.

"Don't worry, my darling. I'm here to take care of you. Your father and I are here to take care of our girl."

Hannah was a shell. Her spirit was dead. Nothing mattered. She relinquished her care and will to whoever wanted it. She didn't care. She let her mind drift into the recesses of her memories. She didn't view it as slipping from sanity to insanity. She saw it as a conscious decision, a journey into a new realm of reality. In this world, her family was still with her. In this world, she felt no pain. She would no longer have to fight a world that was cruel and unjust, or a father who had chosen to abandon her. In this moment of acceptance, a peace prevailed. She didn't realize it but this was the beginning of her long road to recovery. There was a power greater than her pain in charge.

Hannah sat up abruptly in her bed. Her sheets and nightgown were saturated. She turned on the lamp next to the bed. It was almost midnight — only midnight. She had a full night to fight her demons. Fear surrounded her — too afraid to lie in bed and too afraid to face the dark house. She felt alone.

"How many times?" she cried out. "How many times must I fight this same battle?"

In the past when she had this nightmare, she would always call Grace, no matter what time. She would talk to her until she was calm. She wanted to hear Grace's voice. She wanted to hear her say that every thing would look different in the morning.

"Grace, why can't I be brave like you? I should be with you the way you are always here for me. How can I ever thank you for all that you've done for me?"

Grace had rescued her from madness and had given her strength these many years, particularly the first year after the accident. Grace made her feel normal amid the madness that surrounded her. She told her that when a heart was in so much pain there really was no right or wrong way to deal with it. She told Hannah that God still had plans for her and that's why she was still on this earth.

Hannah thought they were kindred spirits, because they both knew the pain of losing a child. Grace's daughter, Matilda, drowned in a pond that was within an eye's view of her kitchen window. The day after she buried her child, Grace had some men come out to their farm to drain the pond and fill it with dirt.

"I was mad from grief, just like you," she had told Hannah. "Still, I knew I had to live a full life so I could be a testament for others who hurt."

The thought of Matilda and because of her recent nightmare, Hannah's heart ached for the touch of her own children. She ran to her dresser and opened her jewelry box. Inside were three envelopes, labeled Sammy, Gabe, and Julie. When her family was laid to rest, Hannah was in the hospital. Grace went to the undertaker and told him to cut a lock of each ones' hair for Hannah. She told Hannah that a lock of Matilda's hair had comforted her soul on many nights. Hannah felt of the soft locks, which actually did give her comfort. She tucked the envelopes gently back into the jewelry box. Her recent fear had left, but a new fear was taking root.

"What if Grace dies? Who will love me then?"

She wanted to fall apart. Everything within her was ready to let go. She was close to losing control again. Then, she saw a zip lock bag with something inside of it on her dresser. It was a plastic toy soldier along with a note. As she opened the note and read it, a pouring of something she hadn't felt in years flowed through her — courage.

Hannah,

Nana always told me that you had the courage of an army of soldiers. I saw what she meant tonight. I don't think my son will miss this soldier I found lying around Nana's house. When you become frightened, hold it in your hand as a reminder of your courage and strength. No fear has ever conquered courage, Hannah. We don't always pick our wars, but how we fight them is up to us. This is something I tell myself each day. I know it's not easy, but we have to try. Chin up! I'll have Nana home as soon as I can.

Andy

Hannah clutched the plastic soldier in her hand and felt a peace she hadn't felt in a long time. And there in her room, where earlier demons treaded, a lone soldier slept victorious.

Fifteen hundred miles away from Blossom, Texas, Tony DeJane was lying in bed at his two-bedroom home in Malibu, California. He had recently purchased it and felt a sense of satisfaction that he was finally living his dream—partially. He had always dreamed of sailing the oceans, moving from town to town, country to country. Realizing this wasn't exactly practical, he decided living near the ocean was the next best thing. As he listened to the waves outside of his home, he knew that should the notion strike him, he could rent a boat from the Boat Rental where he worked part time, and sail any time.

He divorced Charlotte several years ago and left Texas shortly after his divorce. At sixty-two, he was a contented man—sober for over a year, retired and working part time. Since boating was a hobby he had dabbled with all of his life, working near boats wasn't really work at all. For the most part, life was good and without complications. He did however, live with one regret—Hannah. What he had done, or failed to do for her, haunted him every day of his life. In her entire life, when she had needed him the most, he had let her down. He missed his baby girl. It had been almost four years since that day he walked away from her. His heart ached to hold her—to tell her he was sorry. Except for her mother, he never loved another soul more.

"Oh, Baby Girl," he mused. "How I wish I could change the past and make things right for you. I was a weak man, but I'm stronger now. I know I wasn't there for you when you needed me, but I'm here now. We could start new and fresh, couldn't we? What would you do if one day your daddy showed up at your doorsteps? There's a hole in my heart for you, Hannah. Say you forgive me. Say that you still love your daddy."

SIX

Andy woke up with his feet hanging off the sofa, feeling like he'd been punched constantly throughout the night. Sleep was hard to come by after getting Nana settled in his room and Liz staying late to talk. They decided that later today, if everything went well with Nana, they would go talk to Liz's parents. They had to be told about the baby eventually, sooner was better, since Liz was already beginning to show. Andy felt like a school kid instead of a grown man. He wasn't looking forward to their reactions, understanding their positions completely. What concerned Andy most were his own intentions. Initially, he knew it was the right thing to marry Liz. Somehow, he just couldn't muster up the nerve to approach the subject to Liz. He was dragging his feet, he knew. But why? The baby wasn't going to wait for his or her father to man up and take responsibility for his actions. The baby was coming. This was reality.

Blessed Consequences.

He finally managed to roll off the coach and put on a pot of coffee. He checked in on Nana, who was still sleeping. The clock on the stove read five-thirty. He decided to let Nana sleep another thirty minutes. He drew open the curtain that covered the sliding glass doors leading out to his patio. When the coffee was done, he slid the door open, stepped into the dark morning, and sat down on a portable swing he'd bought just for this purpose. The moon still commanded the sky and it would be a good hour before the sun took over.

He contemplated what today might bring. To say the least, it would be eventful. He thought of the baby and his boys. What would they say when he told them? Mathew was certainly old enough to understand such things. It would be easier to face them if he and Liz were engaged. He wanted his boys to know that everything had consequences. He also wanted them to know that this baby is loved, just as they are. He decided the same could be true for Liz's parents. Telling them about the baby with a plan to marry their daughter would put them more at ease. He would talk to Liz after Nana's appointment. Why wait a day longer? A thought occurred to him.

"What if she doesn't want to get married?"

He shook his head. One thing he knew for sure. Liz was committed to this relationship. It was time he followed her lead. The love issue had him putting off doing the right thing. He wasn't in love with Liz and he wouldn't fool himself into believing he felt anything close to love. Still, he did respect her and she was a good person. Maybe in time, love would follow. Truth is, he had put off Liz and all other women in the hopes of reconciliation with Jean. With this hope gone, he had no reason not to marry Liz.

The second time around, he guessed, wasn't about love. It was about giving a good life to his new son or daughter. His baby deserved this. His heart stirred and he felt a lump as big as his fist in his throat. He would have a new wife, a new family. Nothing would ever be the same. It was a quandary. He loved being married and having a family. He had prayed to God all of these months to give him back his family. God had other plans. He supposed it wasn't his place to question what God had placed in front of him.

Some time later Andy heard Nana stirring in the back of the apartment and her walker moving down the hallway. He drove away the many thoughts about Liz and the baby to focus on Nana. For now, she was his only concern. What was to happen with Liz and the baby would surely play out. This moment belonged to Nana. He couldn't explain his sudden need to take care of her. Maybe it was his being alone all of these months and knowing that Nana had remained devoted to him, even when he hadn't been to her. Maybe he was remembering his promise to Paps and was mature enough to understand the value of it. Maybe it was because Nana needed him and he hadn't felt needed in months. Or, maybe it was just the plain and simple fact that he had to prove he could get something right for a change. He had to prove that he wasn't always the screw-up. He was a dependable man, who loved his Nana with all of his heart.

He heard her shuffle into the kitchen, and so he went inside, closing the sliding door behind him. Nana smelled of honeysuckles. Andy smiled and thought – *a Nana memory.*

He leaned to kiss her cheek, "Morning, Sweetheart."

"Heaven's sakes, Andy. You're up early."

"I get up this early every day, Nana. Only by now, I've been at work at least an hour. Coffee?"

"I best get all I can. Who knows what that doctor might do? Helen Bledsoe had to give up coffee completely when she had her heart attack."

Andy smiled. "Nana, you haven't had a heart attack."

"Well, I'm seeing a heart doctor, aren't I?"

Her spirit warmed him. Even down, she wasn't going to give into her troubles.

"Andy, mind if I give my Hannah a call? Mercy, I couldn't sleep last night for thinking of her."

Again, Andy had to smile. If she had thought of Hannah last night, it was in her dreams, because as soon as her head hit the pillow, she was out like a light.

"Sure, Nana. Go ahead. Think she's up this early?"

"Probably not, but she wouldn't forgive me if I didn't call her. Andy, would you make the call for me? My old fingers don't seem to be working right this morning."

Andy saw her wrinkled hands shake and he gripped them in his hands to calm her.

"Don't you fall apart on me, Sweetheart. We're just going to the doctor so he can tell us everything is all right. And if it's not, he's gong to tell us how we can make it all right. Understand?"

Nana nodded, almost near tears, but wasn't about to cry. She had never let life get the best of her and she wasn't about to start letting it now. Andy lifted the receiver.

"Call out her number to me, Nana."

Soon, Andy heard Hannah's sleepy voice say, "Hello."

He wasn't sure why he said what he said next, except that it seemed the most natural thing to do after hearing such a voice, and remembering the face that went with it.

"Morning, Beautiful," he said. Realizing what he had said, Andy rephrased his greeting. "Morning, Hannah. It's Andy. Nana wanted to call before she went to the doctor. Here, I'll let you talk to her."

He handed Nana the phone, who seemed less jolted by his choice of words than he was. She took the phone and again, Andy moved by the glass doors and watched the sunrise. As Nana's voice faded into her conversation, Andy was thinking of Hannah and how he had grown to admire her these past weeks. Her sweet morning voice was still reeling in his mind and he wondered why it was affecting him like this. The morning sun rose above the horizon in red and orange splendor.

"Beautiful," he thought. "Like Hannah."

He shook his head, trying to jar his senses. *"Where the hell was all of this coming from?"*

He thought of their last meeting when he had gone back for Liz's purse. They had had a moment, ever so slight, but it was intimate. He looked at Nana, who had seemingly been recharged just talking to Hannah. Maybe that was it. Hannah was one of those people who just naturally lifted a spirit by her presence—by her voice. She was an intangible gift, untouchable, like the sunrise or a bird's song. Andy looked once more to the new morning. Nothing bad could happen today. He thought of Hannah and all that she had been through in her life. He had no sorrows compared to her. He figured God owed Hannah for the rest of her life because of the suffering she'd been forced to endure. He thought of how much she loved his Nana. God willing, between his prayers and Hannah's special grace, Nana would live for a long, long time.

He moved near Nana and wrapped his arms around her from behind. She yelped and he heard her explaining to Hannah why she had screamed. He heard laughter coming through the phone. Yes, Hannah was good medicine for Nana, and for him, too. Just as he was about to walk away to get dressed, Nana handed him the phone.

"She wants to talk to you, Andy."

Andy looked confused, but took the phone.

"Hello," he said.

"Andy," was all she said, but once again, he felt his heart turning flips. Soon, his whole gut was in turmoil. "Andy, I want you to call me as soon as you know something."

"I will," he muttered. "You know I will."

His hands were shaking. *What the hell?*

"I know," she said apologetically. "I guess I'm just nervous. Did Grace sleep at all last night?"

Andy chuckled, relaxing somewhat. "She will tell you no, but she didn't budge from her pillow once she hit it, not until twenty minutes or so ago."

When Hannah giggled, Andy's chest contracted.

"She does this to me all of the time. We will be talking or playing checkers and she'll nod off. Later, I'll tell her, but she argues with me and says she'd been awake the whole time."

"I can picture her now," he smiled. "She's a card."

There was a lull over the phone line as if the two were reluctant to disconnect. Andy barely breathed, but could hear her soft breath flowing through the receiver.

"Hannah," he thought. *"What is happening?"*

She called out his name several times before he realized she was speaking again.

"Andy," she said a third time. "Are you still there?"

"I'm here," he said dry-mouthed.

"I want to thank you for the special gift you left on my dresser. It really did help me."

Andy thought of the toy soldier.

"Did it? I'm glad. I felt awful leaving you alone last night. I still do."

"Don't," she said, trying to sound confident. "Anyway, Grace is only away temporarily."

"That's right," he assured. Again, they lingered, but then Hannah said it was probably time for them to get ready. She told him she would light a candle and say a rosary, even though she wasn't Catholic. Grace had taught her the prayers. He could picture her doing this and it eased his heart immensely.

"That sounds good, Hannah. I promise to call you when I know something. Try not to worry."

Feeling a surge of the strength she felt last night, she uttered, "I won't worry, at least not until we know more."

"Good girl. Try to have a nice day."

"I will. Oh, and Andy…give Grace a hug and a kiss from me."

"Consider it done."

Hannah lay in bed for some time after Grace's call, wishing she were in Dallas with her and Andy. Upset with herself for not going, she tried to rationalize her decision. Grace wasn't a relative.

"No," she thought. "She's more. I should be with her. She would be with me."

Getting to Grace would be impossible, recalling the limited times she had tired to venture outside of her home. She knew Andy, Ben, or Charlie would come get her if she asked them, but then what? She would be an added burden. No one, except

Grace and Andy's parents, Ann and John Padgett, truly understood the depths of her condition. At any given moment she could fall apart, panic, or be so filled with anxiety, she could end up in the hospital with Grace. She always told herself she would die before she would allow a doctor to treat her mental state. These past years, she had fooled herself into believing that she was getting better. She wasn't. She had just become a master of avoidance. If she didn't have to face her fears, she didn't become anxious. So, she limited her life to the perimeters of her home and Grace's home.

She balled her fists in frustration and beat it against her pillow. When she did, she saw the plastic soldier that Andy had given her. She reached for it. Holding it made her think of Andy. His tall, muscular frame filled her thoughts, along with his blue eyes and dark, wavy hair. He was smiling at her and his husky voice was saying, *"Morning, Beautiful."*

Something from the past rushed through her, something she thought had died years ago. She couldn't define it, but she jumped from the bed and looked into her mirror. She studied her image through the harsh light of the morning light. She edged closer to the mirror so that she could truly study her features. She ran her fingers over her nose, her cheeks, and her lips. Could it be that she was beautiful? She suddenly realized what she was feeling. It was raw and fresh, but so real to her. She felt alive again.

Without reason, she slipped her cotton nightgown down her shoulders and let it fall to the floor. She studied her body, a body she hadn't really noticed in years. She let her hands brush over the length of her form, resting her hands upon her abdomen. She thought of Julie and Gabe. Their lives began inside of her. Hannah noted the way motherhood had altered her body. In her situation, it had made her fuller. Before her children, she was thin and shapeless. Children gave her form. Then, for some odd reason, she thought of what Andy had told her about Liz. She would be having a child soon — Andy's child.

Something like envy came over her momentarily. She envied Liz carrying a child. She envied any woman with such a gift. Still young enough to bear children, Hannah knew it was an impossibility. She could barely take care of herself, let alone a child.

She caught glimpse of her long legs and thought of how Sammy loved her legs. He always teased her about how they went on forever. She could almost feel his hands moving up her legs, caressing them. Then, her hands moved to her full breasts and she blushed at the audacity of staring at her own body. She stood for a while, just looking at her vulnerability. She longed to be touched again. The idea was almost laughable. How could a woman afraid of her own shadow even evoke such intimacy? Muddled with feelings of embarrassment and self-awareness, she quickly dressed. She had to erase all such ideas from her mind. They were better left in darkness than to tease her with a foreplay she could never consummate.

Loneliness set in when she glanced toward Grace's house and she became preoccupied by its stillness. The ticking of her clock intensified her alone state. She watched as the second hand made its way around the clock, and then as the minute hand slowly made its changes. Was she going to watch the clock and Grace's empty house all day until Andy called of news? She'd go crazy if she did. She smirked at her own suggestion. Hadn't some claimed that she already had?

For some unusual reason, Hannah found she could not be contained between the barriers of her house, where she generally felt most secure. She had to get out and breathe the fresh air. She had to know there was a world outside of her four walls. She could almost feel her fear suggesting she stay inside, but she pushed it away. In a stupor, she grabbed her cordless phone and stepped outside. Her thoughts moved back to those of Grace and what she was going through today. Grace might be dying, was probably dying, and she didn't have the courage to stand by her side to hold her hand. Instead, she was

was having daydreams of intimacy and feeling jealousy toward a woman she barely knew simply because she was carrying a child. She thought of Andy and felt more shame because her inkling of jealousy was partially related to him.

Hannah felt anger gnawing at her gut, at first slowly, but then it consumed her. She wanted to scream, wanted to throw something or hit something. She laid down her phone and bent to grab a handful of rocks. She threw the rocks in no apparent direction. This action reminded her of the boys who time and time again had thrown mud or rocks at her house while singing their cruel rhymes. Thoughts of the boys reminded her of Andy and he reminded her of a passion she thought had died a long time ago. This cycle of thoughts manifested her anger into rage. In response, she darted toward her weed-infested garden, where she fell to her knees. And there, in the middle of weeds, insects, and cracked earth, Hannah released her anger. She pulled and tugged and tossed away the weeds in such a fury, she could actually feel her heart hammering against her chest.

Her anger was directed toward her helplessness and the hell she lived in because of it. She was angry with God for what he had allowed to be taken from her — first her mother and aunt, then Sammy and her children, and now Grace. She was angry towards a father whose dependency on alcohol had always come before his love for her. She was angry with a town and a people who had branded her and so easily let her die within their hearts. Mostly, she was angry at the betrayal of a passion that had so abruptly invaded her safe world. She didn't want or need such feelings in her life ever again. Hadn't she comfortably tucked such needs away? She would be damned if she would let herself embrace them again, if only in her mind. Especially, since she knew she would be left lifeless, passionless, all over again.

Somewhere between her anger and tears came rationale. Hannah realized she had cleared away a fair portion of the weeds in her garden, and found the task had resurrected her spirit. She looked at her stained hands, knew she should go inside to get some gloves, but she was unwilling to, afraid she might not be able to rekindle this unexpected spell she was under. This spell had left her feeling bold and free. Hannah continued to tug at the weeds, even though her common sense knew she'd be burned by the sun with no hat, and her hands would no doubt be cut and blistered with no gloves.

Still, her spirit was soaring. She was alive and unafraid. She thought of Grace and felt a new hope. When she thought of Andy, she only saw a gentle spirit. She was happy, amid a place she had these past years regarded as too painful to be near. She found herself singing old familiar songs from years past. They were songs of love and hope. They were conspicuously connected to her recently rekindled desires.

In her elated, state, crouched on her knees in the middle of the dishevel of weeds and lost in song, Hannah failed to notice Paul Renfroe standing near her back door. He was staring at her in complete and utter amazement.

Around noon, Hannah's phone rang. It was Andy. Hannah knew by his voice that the news wasn't good.

"Hannah, she's been admitted. Her cardiologist said this wasn't a bad sign or diagnosis, but simply a precaution he likes to take with patients Nana's age. This way, she can be monitored during and in-between tests."

"What tests, Andy?"

"Today, a sonogram, some x-rays, and some blood work. She's already hooked up to a monitor. Tomorrow, she'll have an EKG. Depending on how these tests go, she may have to have a stress test, if her heart can take it."

"How is she, Andy? I mean her spirits?"

"She's up, Hannah, but to be honest with you, I'm glad she's here. The doctors and staff aren't saying much, but I know it's serious. She's always been so strong. Oh, Hannah, I think maybe she might ..."

He was going to say that he thought she might die, but was too choked up to speak. Without his saying, Hannah knew what he meant. He was just now seeing what she had been seeing these past weeks, even months. Clearly, Andy was shaken.

"Andy, are you with Grace now?"

"They are moving her to her room now. I'm in the lobby."

"Good. She can't see you upset. Do you know her room number?"

"718, I think. Yes, I'm sure."

His voice was strained and it quivered as he spoke. He was taking in deep breaths and she knew he was trying not to lose his composure. His attempts failed.

"Dear God, Hannah. What if she dies?"

The word *die* was spoken and he couldn't take it back. The pain of the past months and the stress of his recent news from Liz had all but done him in—and now Nana might die. Hannah gripped the phone tightly. She knew she had to maintain control.

"Andy, listen to me."

"I can't lose her, too, Hannah."

"Andy," she called out more forceful. "Andy, for Grace, you have to get a hold of yourself."

Something in the strength of her voice, so usually docile, caused him to stop staggering. He was able to regain some presence.

"Hannah, I'm sorry. I don't, I mean, I'm all right. I just got scared."

"I know," she said gently. "I'm scared, too."

"Hannah, I think it's just now hitting me that she's so sick. I guess I never saw it before now. Maybe I didn't want to."

"Andy, where's Liz?"

"She's at home. She left my place late last night and I wanted her to sleep in. She'll be here soon."

"What about Charlie or Ben? Have you called them?"

"You were the first person I called. I'll call them when we hang up."

"I just hate the fact that you're so upset and there's no one there with you. Oh, Andy, I should be…"

"You should be here? Is that what you were about to say, Hannah?"

"Yes," she said softly. "I should be. I should have come with you. It isn't fair you being there all alone. I was sure Liz would…"

"I could come get you, Hannah," he interrupted.

"What? When?"

"This afternoon, after Charlie and Ben get here."

"Andy, you must be joking. You are already exhausted. You have so much on your plate to worry about me. Besides, don't you have to work tomorrow?"

"I plan on taking tomorrow off."

"Andy, you're not thinking clearly. You're upset and tired. No. I'll come later if I'm needed, as we planned."

"As you planned," he snapped. "Staying in Blossom was all your idea. Remember?"

His bitter tone cut her deeply, partly because he'd never spoken to her so harshly, but mainly because she knew he had a right to feel bitter toward her. He could hear her sniffles, trying to hold back her tears.

"Hannah, I'm sorry. I'm such a jerk sometimes. You're right. I'm tired and don't know what the hell I'm saying."

She was quiet for some time before she spoke.

"No, you're right. I should be there. I would be if I were capable. I…Andy, tell Grace I love her. Tell her I would give my life for her."

He heard the pain in her voice.

"Forgive me, Hannah."

"Oh, Andy, there's nothing to forgive. We are both scared and we love Grace. We are talking from our grief because we hurt."

"Just say you forgive me, Hannah, so I can deal with this day. Of all the people in the world, you are the last one I want to hurt."

She smiled. Her gentle voice soothed him. "I forgive you, Andy."

"Good," he said letting out a heavy sigh—one less problem solved. "I'll call you with any new news."

"Call me any time. I don't care what time it is. If you don't, I'll call you."

Just as he was about to hang up, he saw Liz walk into the waiting room. Jean was with her. They looked chummy and friendly, too much for his jagged nerves to handle. He didn't want to deal with this now. He wanted to run. Something about their closeness didn't settle well with him. Did Jean know about the baby? He had to guess that she did. Most likely, she knew before he did. In a sense, this left her off the hook. She knew him and knew that he was an honorable man. She knew that he would soon marry Liz. It was almost as if these two women had plotted the recent chain of events in his life. He felt like a puppet in their control. He knew if he didn't get air soon, he'd choke on the ties that had him so bound. Realizing he hadn't hung up the phone, he whispered to Hannah.

"Dear God, the mob is here to lynch me."

"Andy," Hannah called out. "You aren't making sense."

Hannah thought she heard Liz's voice.

"Andy, is Liz there now?"

"Yes," he said shaken, "And Jean is with her."

"Oh, Andy, not Frank, too?"

"No, thank God."

He felt the wind inside of him rise and stop in his throat. He wasn't going to make it. He was suffocating. Liz brushed Andy's cheek and he felt himself blush under Jean's stare. He wanted to shout, "*I don't love her. It's you I love. Come back to me. Give my life back to me again.*"

"Hannah," he whispered. "I've got to go. I'll call you later."

"I'm worried about you," Hannah said.

He laughed cuttingly. "Me, too."

"Will you be all right?"

His reply was unavailing.

"I don't think I'll ever be all right again."

SEVEN

Hannah just finished blow-drying her hair when she saw headlights pulling into Grace's driveway. Her first thought was that someone was turning around, but when the lights went out and she heard a door slam, she ran to see who it was. Andy was getting out of his truck and walking toward her house. Hannah didn't give herself time to think before she darted out of her house to meet him, dressed in only her gown and robe. With just the moon to cast a light on her, Andy saw the look on her face and knew what she was thinking. She was thinking that Grace had made a turn for the worse. Her voice was blocked by dread and all that she could do was stare at him, praying that what she feared wasn't true. Understanding fully, he led her inside the house. Before he could explain why he was there, she was in his arms, crying.

"Oh, Andy, Andy, pl...please tell me...please tell me she's not...worse or..."

Andy held her the way he often held his boys after they had been frightened by a dream. His gentle voice echoing in her ear, gave her reassurance.

"Shhh, no, Hannah. Nana's fine. Just fine. In fact, when I left her she was sleeping like a baby."

He brushed a gentle hand through her hair that smelled like a spring bouquet and he filled himself with her smell. She was breathing hard against his chest and the movement was almost therapeutic to his worn body. Hannah drew only slightly from his hold and questioned him.

"Then, why? Why are you here?"

He lent her a warm smile. "I came to get you, silly."

"You did what?" she called out in disbelief.

"I came to get you," he repeated.

"Oh, Andy," she said slapping softly at his chest and breaking his hold on her. "Whatever are you thinking? I mean, driving all this way for me, when you know I can't possibly go with you."

"Hannah," he said in a solid tone. "Don't even try to sell me your song and dance. You are coming to Dallas with me if I have to carry you on my back kicking and screaming."

She looked into his eyes that were bloodshot from lack of sleep and an abundance of worry. Still, they were dancing merrily. Beyond this, she saw something else. Yes, he wanted her there for Grace, but it was as if he needed her there for himself, as well. She didn't know why, but knew this wasn't all about Grace. Maybe he just needed an ally, someone on his side.

"Andy, you're exhausted. You aren't seriously thinking of driving back to Dallas tonight, are you?"

"You are right about me being tired. Thought I'd crash at Nana's 'till about five and then head out. This would put us in Dallas tomorrow just in time for Nana's first test."

"Andy," she said dazed. "I still can't believe you came to get me."

What he couldn't believe was how good this woman had felt to hold. He took her hand and led her to the sofa, where the two sat down on opposite ends. As they sat in the quiet of her living room, he leaned his head back and closed his eyes, vaguely thinking how nice it would be to sit here forever. She was less settled. He was serious. He was here to take her away from the security of her home. It was absurd to think she could leave with him. He had no idea what he was asking of her. As she watched him resting on her couch, she became more and more anxious by the moment.

"Andy," she said nervously. "Can I get you something to drink or eat?"

With his eyes still closed, he waved his hand to her. "I'm fine. God, Hannah, you have no idea how good this feels."

She propped one arm on the back of the sofa and crossed her legs. She nervously started bouncing her crossed leg up and down against the top cushion, interrupting his catnap. In response, he opened his eyes to see that her robe had slipped open slightly, offering him a view of long legs he had only dreamed of seeing. While he was intent on her, she was preoccupied with thoughts of leaving Blossom and going to Dallas. How could she make him understand that she just couldn't do this? She wasn't capable of functioning in such a setting, especially for the length of time the situation presented.

"Andy," she began her plea. "I appreciate you coming for me but I just can't go back to Dallas with you."

He looked into her face, covered with dread and worry.

"Hannah, if I didn't think you could do this, I wouldn't be here. Besides, you would never forgive yourself if something happened to Nana and you weren't there."

She thought of Grace and what she was going through.

"Andy, is she terribly frightened?"

He scooted closer so that he could reach for her hand and gently rubbed it back and forth.

"She wasn't after I told her how brave you have been and that you are coming to see her."

A look of horror filled her face. *He made a promise to Grace on my behalf.*

"Oh, Andy, you didn't? You shouldn't have told her such a thing! If I don't go now, it will look like I don't care. Now…now I have…"

He smiled in triumph and closed his eyes once more. Again, he squeezed her hand. She began her negotiations.

"You don't need an additional problem with all that you have to deal with. You already have Grace to deal with and Liz. Does she even know you are here?"

Andy sighed heavily at the thought of Liz. She didn't know. He wouldn't lie to Hannah.

"No, she doesn't know I'm here, but she knew it was a possibility that I would come get you. We did talk about that. We discussed you staying at my apartment."

"Oh, Andy, don't you see how impossible this is? It's an uncomfortable situation for Liz and what with the..."

She stopped herself before she said the word *baby*, but he understood fully. Andy let out a breath of despondency. He was tired and weary. He needed sleep, not more debate. He knew that what she was saying held a great deal of truth. He had fought with the rationale of getting Hannah the entire drive to Blossom. He couldn't explain why, but he needed her in Dallas.

"I know you are right on some things, but I know one thing for sure. You can do this. You are a pillar of strength and you don't even realize it. Besides, Nana isn't the only one who needs you. I need you. I need you to be my anchor. I need you to be the calm in my storm."

Hannah let out a mocking, "*Ha!* You must be joking! I'm not anyone's calm. I'm the one who falls apart. Remember? I am the storm! "

Andy felt a piercing jerk in his chest for her. He knew this is how she saw things, but she was wrong. He had witnessed in the past weeks just what a comforting force she had been for his grandmother — and for him. As if he had no control over his will, he moved even closer to her so that he could look directly into her eyes. His fingers were intertwined within hers.

"Come to Dallas, Hannah. Come for me, as much as for Nana."

Why she leaned her head on his shoulder, she didn't know. It just seemed the natural thing to do.

"You don't play fair, Andy."

He let out a sigh of relief. *One less problem solved.* He moved away from her and she thought he was going to get up, but instead, he rested his head on the arm of the other side of the sofa. She stood up realizing that he intended to sleep there. He stretched his long legs and his body filled the space in such a way that all she could do was stare at him. In the scope of less than an hour, he had managed to invade the sanctity of her world and change all of the rules. She should be angry with him, and she was, but when she saw the way he was hugging his chest, he seemed small and lost. He was as he had declared on her front porch weeks ago, a broken man. She went to the hall closet and got a blanket to cover him. Already, he was in a sound sleep. She locked the door and turned out the lamp. Instead of going to her room and packing, she sat in a nearby chair and watched him.

The fear of leaving her home and surviving in a new environment suddenly looked like a picnic compared to the problem she now faced. The problem, of course, was Andy. He had somehow pierced through her world, and at a very fast rate, became part of it. The earlier thoughts she had had this morning surfaced. Roused by a fleet of emotions, she couldn't keep up with them. She thanked God for the darkness, as it wouldn't give her away. She had never known a man so completely uninhibited with his emotions as Andy. This left her uneasy and vulnerable. Each time he confided in her, she became more and more exposed. He said she was a pillar of strength.

It's all a façade, Andy. I may look in control, but on the inside, I'm a shattered wreck.

She wondered how long it would be before he figured this out and regretted the decision to come get her.

In a bedroom several blocks from Hannah's house, Paul Renfroe watched his wife sleep. Yet, his mind was on another woman. He was thinking of Hannah. After seeing her this morning in her garden, instead of speaking to her, he left unnoticed. Even now, hours later, his heart was still unsteady.

74

He was close enough to touch her. She looked like an angel, beautiful like she used to look. She seemed strong, working in her garden. Her demeanor suggested that she was getting on with her life, letting go of her past. He wished he could.

Paul decided to get up and fix himself a night-time snack. Just as he was about to walk down the stairs, he passed by Paul Jr.'s room and heard him laughing, and then he heard a girl's voice. He stood in front of the door, wondering what would be the best approach in handling the issue of his having a girl in his room way past midnight, especially on a school night. He decided the best approach was to confront him, so he knocked on the door. When Paul Jr. answered the door, it was clear he had been drinking. His breath and room reeked of cheap wine. The girl with him was lying partially unclothed on Paul's bed and giving no indication that she might be the least bit embarrassed by the fact.

"What's going on, Son?" Paul asked nervously.

"Oh, you know, Dad," he whispered. "Just getting me some."

Paul pushed his son into the room and shut the door. His anger soared through him, but his voice was cool and held low in an effort to spare Sue from this scene. He turned on the light and the girl covered her face. Paul turned from her disgusted.

"The two of you have five minutes to dress. Then, we are going downstairs as quietly as we can. We are going out to my car and use my cell phone, so I won't wake up your mother. Then, we are going to call this young lady's parents and deliver her to them. Have I made myself clear?"

Paul Jr. grinned," Whatever you say, Dad."

Paul could feel his blood boiling. "Wipe that shitty smirk from your face or my fist will."

Paul Jr. turned solemn. In his sixteen years of life, his father had only hit him twice. Once was when he had run out into the street and was almost hit by a car. The other time, he had told his mother to *shut-up*. Even half-drunk, Paul Jr. knew his dad wasn't to be reckoned with tonight. Paul Sr. closed the door behind him and went to the bathroom where he had hung a pair of jeans and a t-shirt. He dressed and when he went back into his son's room, both Paul Jr. and his girl were dressed. Paul Jr. had to prop Denna McKenzie, his gal, to keep her steady. Together, the three managed to make it outside and to the car without waking Benny or Sue. After calling the girl's parents, the three were on their way to her house.

The ride was silent and few words were exchanged. Paul Sr. and Denna's parents spoke briefly when he dropped her off. Within ten minutes, Paul was driving his son home. When they got there, Paul grabbed his son by the collar and warned him.

"I'm too angry to discuss this tonight, and frankly, you are too drunk to hear me. Rest assured tomorrow we will talk. I'm driving you to school and I'm picking you up. I'm taking your car and keys. There will be no weight lifting or cruising about town. You will be coming straight home."

Paul Jr. didn't argue with his father. He was, as his father had said, too drunk to hear or care. Paul walked his son to his room, where he immediately crashed on his bed. In the darkness of the hallway, Paul Sr. cried. This wasn't the first time he'd seen his son drunk, but it was the first time he'd been so blatant as to drink at home and bring a girl to his room. Sue was awake when Paul went back to bed.

"He's been drinking, hasn't he? I know because when I went to his room while you were gone, I could smell it."

"We'll talk about this tomorrow."

"Where did the two of you go this late at night?"

"Not tonight, Sue. I can't deal with it. I'm too angry."

"He's a good boy, Paul."

"I know he is, but he has a serious problem. The sooner we accept this, the sooner we can get help for him."

"You could be more understanding, Paul. Kids today have a lot of pressures. I don't like the way you're turning against him. I think you're being too hard on him. I mean, all boys drink, or at least try it. You did."

"Is this what you think? You think I'm turning against him? It's a school night, Sue, not a weekend. Your son is drunk off his butt and he had a girl in his room. That's a problem in my book. I may have drunk a six pack once in a while, but never before I was eighteen."

"A girl? Denna?"

"You know about her?

Sue nodded. "They've been talking."

"Well, they were doing a hell of a lot more than talking tonight."

Sue's eyes moistened. "Oh, my God. No wonder you are so angry."

Paul let out a deep breath and held his wife.

"I can't accept this behavior, Sue," he said more calmly. "He needs help. We are his parents. We have to find him help."

She broke into tears. "It's just been so hard on him since Gabe…he blames himself because Gabe was supposed to stay at our house that night, but Paul Jr. got sick. He thinks if he hadn't been sick, Gabe would be alive."

"I know," Paul whispered. "It's been hard on us all. But, we can't let him throw his life away."

"Maybe it's a phase, Paul."

"Maybe," he said, but really knew differently. "Sue, I think we should check out that rehab facility in Dallas. You know, the one Reverend Barnett's grandson went to."

"Rehab? I won't hear of such talk. My son will not be put away in some institution. Look what happened to Hannah. No, I won't hear of it."

"That was different, Sue. Her family abandoned her there. We'd never abandon our son."

"No," she spat. "Never!"

"Sue, Darling, listen to me."

She rolled over turning her back to him. "Leave me alone."

"Sue, I'm not saying we should definitely send Paul Jr. there. I'm just asking you to consider the possibility. Maybe we could go to Dallas and take a look at it."

"We will help him. We are his parents. He just needs our understanding. No, Paul. I won't consider it."

"You know," he said angrily. "You need to wake up and realize just how serious a problem our son has. It's not just drinking. He says he only smoked pot once, but how can we believe him? Sooner or later, you have to face the problem he has."

"My son is not a drug addict."

She lay defiant with her back against his. Both stewed in their own anger. He was thinking she could at least try to understand his position. She was thinking she could never lock her son up in an institution.

"Sue," she heard him call out through the night. "At least think about it."

"Good night, Paul," she said flatly.

For the first time in their marriage, he didn't like his wife. He wanted to be as far away from her as he could. He got up and grabbed his pillow.

"So, you're going to run off to the couch and pout, aren't you?"

"Yea, Sue. I think I'll do just that."

"I won't change my mind."

"I didn't think you would. Listen, I'm tired. I'm hurt. I'm upset. I really don't want to say something I'll regret. So, I think it's best for both of us if I just walk away for a while."

Before she could speak, he was halfway down the hall. He checked in on Paul Jr. and Benny. Both were fast asleep. He made a bed on the couch and he could almost picture Sue upstairs crying. Right now, he didn't much give a damn. He closed his eyes and the idea of spending one more week, one more day without seeking help for his son struck fear in his gut.

78

It was the same fear he'd felt when he saw Paul Jr. high on marijuana. It was almost like a death. He understood Sue's fear of having him in rehab. He wasn't crazy about the idea either. He just knew the problem was bigger than he or Sue. He thought of Hannah the first time he and Sue had gone to visit her in the hospital.

"Sue," he cried. "I do understand your fear. But, I won't allow the same thing to happen to our son that happened to Hannah."

He stopped his own thoughts. *Can I be certain I won't — indirectly? Who knows what really happens in such a place when no one is around?*

Paul remembered Hannah's bedraggled state every time they would go to visit her. She was a far vision from the woman who possessed his dreams, both night and day. She was a lost soul, lifeless, but for a body that sustained her. Her spirit was buried with her family and she lost the will to live life. At first, when he and Sue had gone to visit, she would beg them to get her out. After a while, she stopped asking and when they came to see her, she barely spoke to them. She had resigned herself to living the rest of her life there. Every time, he would leave after speaking with the staff and accept that this was *normal* for a woman who had survived what she had survived.

"Hannah, forgive me for not taking you out of that place when I knew I should have."

He closed his eyes and he saw her face, the way it looked today. She was giggling, like her old self and whispering in his ear, "I forgive you, Paul because I love you. I've always loved you."

EIGHT

Andy looked at Hannah, who was sleeping. They had left Blossom just before dawn. It had been difficult for her to leave and he was having second thoughts about his decision to bring her. Her condition, he was learning, was far more complicated than he realized. It was deceiving to those who didn't understand it because Hannah appeared so perfect, so together. He knew she was torn in a million pieces inside, but when he watched her sleep, she was the picture of everything right and beautiful. She was amazing to watch. He reached to touch her hand that had fallen limp in her lap, but stopped short of touching her.

He couldn't explain, even to himself, his protectiveness toward her. Maybe it was because he had promised Nana he would watch over her. He intended to keep this promise, where he hadn't kept his promise to Paps to watch over Nana so many years ago. Hannah shifted somewhat and was now facing him, still sleeping. Her hair fell over her face and he was remembering how good it smelled last night. That's when he noticed that around her neck was a gold chain and hanging from the gold chain was the plastic toy soldier he had given her. A lump made its way to his throat and he swallowed hard, as he caught a further glimpse through the window of her vulnerability.

Hannah, I'm sorry for your pain.

He noticed his gas gauge was getting low and he needed coffee, so he looked for a rest stop or a service station. He saw a sign for some fast food places and gas stations, so he pulled into the right lane. When he exited the highway and parked at a gas station, he nudged Hannah gently. She stretched lazily and tried to adjust to her surroundings. She understood they had stopped for gas. She looked at Andy anxiously.

"How far have we traveled?"

"Half way. You've been asleep about an hour."

"An hour! My goodness, I can't believe I dozed off. Usually, I'm too tense to sleep."

"You needed the sleep. You didn't get much last night."

"Neither did you. I imagine you're exhausted."

"Me? I always run on second wind."

She smiled. "Poor, Andy. You came all this way to get me and then I behaved so badly before we left. I'm sorry."

"You didn't."

"I did. You were so sweet to let me go back and check on things — twice."

He grinned. "Yea, thought I was going to have to hogtie you to my truck. You know, like Uncle Jed had to do with Granny when they left the cabin."

Hannah laughed. When she did, Andy felt that lump again. She pulled out a brush from her purse and as she moved it through her hair, Andy could feel the electricity. Streams of hair shot out in all directions and when she turned to him, the same sparks shot from her eyes. Andy wondered if he had ever known a woman more alluring. The thing that got to him was the fact that she had no idea of the impact she had on him or others. She dabbed some lotion on her hands and up her arms. He could see her hands were shaking as she tried to unfasten her seat belt. She was braving a good front. He leaned over to help her and she let out a nervous giggle.

"Restrooms and coffee inside," he said. "Should make us both feel better."

She let out a deep breath. She tried twice to get the nerve to open the door. She looked at him apologetically.

"You'll have to be patient with me. I get a little nervous in public places. Well, a lot nervous."

He smiled warmly. "I don't blame you. Some public places are scary as hell."

She knew he was trying to make light of what he knew to be an ordeal for her. He walked around the truck and opened her door.

"Let me get the gas pumped and then I'll walk you inside."

She nodded and sucked in a deep breath. She willed her shaky legs to get out of the truck, while Andy pumped the gas. Since it was around seven, the place was busy with people stopping before work. She could feel her heart racing, but was determined to do this without making a spectacle of herself. She didn't want to behave the way she had at home. Before she lost her nerve, she headed toward the front door of the store. She called back to Andy.

"I'm okay, Andy. I can go by myself."

"You sure?"

No, I'm not sure. I'm on the edge.

"Positive."

She dashed into the store and immediately saw the sign for the women's room.

Please, no one be inside.

There wasn't. She was grateful too that it only allotted one person. When she closed the door behind her, she felt her nerves betraying her. Her entire body was trembling and she was breathing heavily. She splashed water over her face in an effort to gain back her composure. She scolded herself in the mirror.

You will not fall apart in this restroom.

Hannah heard a knock at the door and vaguely wondered if it were Andy. Then she heard a woman's voice ask if anyone was in there. Hannah answered softly and once again, she let her thoughts take her to that dark place called fear.

Stop! There is nothing to fear. Andy is outside waiting for you. In an hour, you will be with Grace.

She happened to look at the walls and saw messages carved or written all around her. To divert her thought process and fear, she started to read them. Hannah gaped at the graffiti. Some of the messages and implications were downright raunchy—certainly diverting her thoughts. It was then she remembered a seventeen-year-old girl and her friend carving messages in a bathroom stall at the Seven Eleven in Greenville. Hannah and her longtime friend, Elaine, had done this after drinking a few too many cups of cheap wine. They were out with their future spouses and they stamped their everlasting love for them in the ladies' room. Hannah could still envision the writing on the wall—*Hannah ♥'s Sammy*. A lifetime away, she smiled, feeling the courage of that young, impulsive girl on the brink of being a woman. She heard Elaine's outgoing voice telling her that Bob, her boyfriend, had asked her to marry him. Elaine imprinted the date of her engagement on the wall. The two jumped up and down, with Hannah secretly wishing Sammy would propose to her. Little did she know that a few months later he would propose. Their lives together had seemed as immortal as their etchings.

Somewhat calmer, Hannah could still feel her stomach rumble. She refreshed her makeup and mustered up the courage to face the day. Andy was waiting for her at the counter near the front of the store. His smile warmed her. She didn't know why, but she trusted Andy completely, even though his life was a mess and he had no concept of how to deal with a person with chronic anxiety. She had to guess she trusted him because Grace had such faith in him.

"Do you want something, Hannah? Coffee? Doughnuts? Anything?"

She felt of her rumbling stomach. "Just coffee."

Inside the truck, she leaned her head back against the seat and cracked her window slightly. She had done it. She couldn't help but to feel somewhat proud of herself and the significance of this moment. She hadn't been in public for years and she managed to pull it off without falling apart. The closest she had come was the lobby of her bank in Blossom. This event had taxed her nerves more than today. Maybe it was because she knew so many people in Blossom. She always measured how well she coped on a scale from one to ten—ten being complete panic. While this hadn't been pleasant, she certainly had experienced much worse. In fact, given her track record, this had been a good encounter. She gave it a five.

She thought about the day ahead—the week ahead. Was she really on her way to Dallas? The reality was setting in and she didn't know how long she could maintain the façade of normalcy. She was as displaced as a fish on land. She knew Andy was watching her, but she couldn't face him. She didn't want to fall apart, not in front of him—and not after accomplishing what she had just accomplished. Of all people, she never wanted him to see the depth of her condition. As they rode down the highway, the old fears and doubts began replacing her short moment of victory. Thoughts of *"what if"* prevailed and Hannah wondered what had possessed her into believing she could exist in the outside world after so many years of isolation. It was then that she felt Andy reach to take her hand.

"Hannah, you are doing great!"

You have no idea what you've gotten yourself into.

"Am I?"

"Yea, you are. I'm proud of you. I don't exactly know what I was expecting to happen, but you did great back there."

She let out a chuckle and played down the situation. "Why? Because I didn't fall apart in a public bathroom?"

"No," he said kindly. "Because you are putting yourself out there. You are facing your fears. The fact that you are here is a testament in itself."

His kindness was almost too much to bear. She wanted to crack. She could almost feel the tears forming, but fought them adamantly. She braved a smile and faced him.

"Thank you. I appreciate your thoughtful words."

"I'll tell you a little secret, Hannah. I've fallen apart in many public places—more than I care to admit. You'd be surprised what too much drinking can do to a person."

"Nothing about drinking surprises me, Andy." She turned to face him directly and disclosed a piece of her troubled soul. "My father drank a lot—after my mother died. It changed him. So, I do know a little bit about the subject."

She offered no more information. Andy always wondered about her family, her parents and Sammy's parents. Where had they been all these years? They certainly seemed to have abandoned her.

"Does your father live near Blossom, Hannah?"

She shook her head. "He lives in Houston with my stepmother, or at least that's where they lived the last time I heard from them."

The coldness in her voice told Andy under no uncertain terms how she felt about her father and stepmother.

"I take it by your tone that you aren't on the best of terms with them."

"We don't speak to each other."

"Man—what did they do?"

"For starters, they institutionalized me. This was their way of handling my condition."

"So you could heal, right? I mean, after your accident. Maybe they thought they were helping you. I mean, like what we are doing with Nana."

His words cut so deep, she wanted to jump out of the truck. He had no idea what he was saying. It wasn't the same as Grace—not even close. Hannah was the first to admit she had needed help after the accident. She was out of control and she didn't blame her father for having her committed. It was what happened afterwards. He rarely visited her. On the infrequent occasions he did visit, he never held her, but rather stood in the background while others pretended to be doing what was in her best interest. He allowed her stepmother to invade the sanctity of Gabe and Julie's rooms and taking it upon herself to box up their belongings. She had even gone into her room and discarded Sammy's clothes and personal things, so that when Hannah did come home, she had nothing left but memories of her family. Thankfully, Grace Padgett insisted the photos and albums remain in her care, else Hannah seriously doubted she would have even them to comfort her. Also, had it not been for Paul Renfroe, Hannah was certain her stepmother would have drained her financially—more than she already had done. Paul convinced a weary Hannah to give him legal power of attorney and he managed to maintain the integrity of her remaining estate, primarily her home. While she was in the hospital, he rented her home to a young couple.

Hannah was suddenly silent. Andy realized he had struck a nerve that led to the heart of her pain. On her face, he saw her battling with her emotions. He saw her beginning to withdraw, alienating herself from the world. She was shutting down. Her past demons were taking control.

"Hannah, don't go back to that dark place," he said softly. "Your father isn't here to hurt you. You're safe with me."

This time the tears couldn't be contained. She dropped her head down. When she did look at him, she looked so helpless that he decided to stop the truck. He took the next exit and pulled on the side of the service road. Before he knew it, he was on her side of the truck and holding her in his arms. She was pleading for her dignity.

"Andy, please take me home. I'm not ready for this. I don't want you to see this part of me."

He let out an exasperating breath. Nana's test was in two hours. If he took Hannah back now, he would be late for her test. He knew Charlie and Ben were there, but that wasn't the same. He wanted to be there—and with Hannah. Yet, as he held her, it almost seemed heartless to put her through this. He would leave it up to her.

86

"Hannah, I'll take you home if you really want me to, but I don't think that's what you want. You would never forgive yourself if I did."

Please God, give me strength.

"Andy, you can't always be here to take care of me when I fall apart. What happens when you aren't around?"

"My gut tells me that you are strong enough to handle any situation. Christ, you've already survived more than any person I've ever known. But just in case, I have an idea. I don't know why I didn't think of it before."

Andy reached into his glove box and pulled out a cell phone.

"See this? It used to belong to Jean. I kept it in case she ever—well, anyway, then I was going to give it to my son, Mathew, but I think right now it would be better served by you having it. It's still in service, but not charged. When we get to Dallas, I'll fix you up. You can put in your own personal numbers and call me anytime."

"Andy, why are you putting yourself through this? I mean, you have so much on your mind already. You don't need me. I'm just an added burden."

"I don't see you as an added burden. I see you as someone who's going to help Nana get well. I see you as a friend. Believe me, a good friend is hard to come by these days. When I needed you, you were there for me."

"When did you ever need me? When was I there for you?"

He frowned. "You trying to embarrass me?"

"No," she said truthful. "I just can't remember how I ever helped you."

"Well, let's take last night, for example. At the hospital, when Jean and Liz came walking toward me, I felt as though I was suffocating and there was nothing I could do. I wanted to run to the nearest bar so that I could forget everything about my life—cause that's what I do, I run. But, I'm tired of running.

I have my boys to think of and now the baby. I can't be running away from my life anymore."

"I don't understand what this has to do with me."

"I was talking on the phone with you when I saw them. This made me think of you and how much courage it had taken for you to let Nana go. I needed your courage and I thought if I were near you, I could get a dose of it. It made sense then."

"It made sense for you to come to me for courage?"

He had to smile at the irony. She smiled, too.

"You helped me twice, actually. Last night and that first night on your porch."

Hannah was amazed that anyone should seek her out for courage. She felt immensely lifted.

"When I was little, my mother used to tell me that helping someone was like being a lamplighter. You give light to someone when you help them, someone who has little hope."

"That's right. I guess that last night you were my lamplighter. You were my hope."

"I can't believe I'd be anyone's hope."

"Well, I didn't take a drink, did I?"

"No, you didn't."

"One day at a time, Hannah, just like your fears."

"I guess we are alike in that respect. I mean, when fear overwhelms me I want to run back to the security of my safe world."

"We all get scared, Hannah. I'm scared as hell about my future. Talking to you helps me."

She reached for the cell phone and stared at it. It would become her lifeline to Andy and the handful of people she had allowed in her world. She looked at him committed to try.

"It works both ways, Andy."

"What?"

"I promise to call you, if you do the same."

"Does this mean you are coming with me?"

She wiped the wet from her eyes and nodded. He pinched her cheek.

"That's the spirit."

He let loose of his hold on her and moved behind the wheel. She could see that his hands were shaking, too.

"Two misfits," she thought.

"Too damn wonderful to be near," he thought.

As they began their journey again, he almost laughed at this present situation. She was, in fact, an added burden to a life that was already completely full of drama. On the other hand, she was also someone he could speak freely with, someone who didn't judge him. She was someone who needed him as much as he needed her. He turned to see her watching him. She lent him a weary smile and then she laid her head back and closed her eyes.

I won't leave you alone, Hannah. I promise.

Hannah was surprisingly calm when they entered the hospital and took the elevator to Grace's room. Andy guessed that she was just doing what she always did when confronted with her fears—hiding them. A nurse was tending to Grace when the two entered the room. They were her first visitors and Andy thought this amazing given their morning. He had made it before Charlie or Ben.

"Well, well," the nurse said. "You have some company, Mrs. Padgett."

The nurse looked at Andy. "She's been asking about her family. I'll give you a few minutes alone together before we'll have to take her for her test. We are taking her a little earlier than expected."

"Glad we got to see her first," Andy noted.

Grace smiled when she saw Andy. He leaned and kissed her cheek.

"Morning, Sweetheart. Brought you a surprise."

Grace caught her breath as Hannah came into view. She couldn't believe her eyes. She looked at Hannah and then Andy and then back at Hannah. Hannah was quick to reach for her dear friend. The two held each other for some time before breaking their embrace.

"Mercy me," Grace said. "If the president of the United States had walked into this room, I couldn't have been more surprised. Tell me I'm not seeing things. Tell me it's really you Hannah. Oh, my Dear, I can't believe you are here!"

"That makes two of us," Hannah declared and smiled at Andy. "Make that three of us."

As the two women shared small talk, Andy saw a spark in Nana's eyes that he hadn't seen yesterday. He knew he'd been right to bring Hannah to her. He looked at Hannah, who stood strong and composed. He thought that even as close as he had been to Nana, it couldn't measure up to the bond these two women shared. He wasn't jealous, but simply aware of the fact. It was the same kind of bond Nana shared with his dad. He sat in a nearby chair and listened as Hannah replayed the morning for Grace.

"I couldn't have made it here, if not for Andy."

"He's a special one, my boy is. I just wish he knew how special."

"Hey," he teased. "I'm here. I can hear you talking about me."

Just then, the nurse reappeared along with two aides. Hannah edged away from Grace toward Andy. The aides moved Grace onto a gurney. The nurse explained the procedure to Andy.

"She is going to have a procedure called an echocardiogram. The test will take pictures of her heart and give a clear description of its history. Depending on the results, we may have to do a more advanced stress echocardiogram. She would be sedated and it can take anywhere from one to two hours to complete. You can wait in the outside waiting room."

Hannah and Andy made brief exchanges with Grace just before she was wheeled to radiology. As they sat in the waiting room, both were silent, exhausted from lack of sleep and worry.

"It's the damn waiting that kills me," Andy said, interrupting the silence.

"I know, but I believe she is in good hands, Andy. I have a strong feeling about this."

"Yea? Well, that's something anyway."

Andy's phone rang. It was Charlie. She heard Andy tell him that she had just been taken in for testing and not to rush. It would be a good hour or maybe longer. When the conversation ended, Andy looked at Hannah.

"I need to call work, but the reception inside the hospital isn't too great. I need to step outside to make the call. You want to come with me or stay here?"

She contemplated the best scenario. She felt uncharacteristically safe in this niche of the hospital, probably because she had just seen Grace, and too, there was a restroom a few feet away—a safe spot. Still, she did have to make some calls herself.

"Andy, does your cell phone accept calls out of your area code without charging you? I have a few calls to make and if it's going to cost you extra, I'll use a pay phone. Leaving so unexpectedly, I left some loose ends at home. For sure, I need to call my boss and let her know what's happened to me."

He sat staring at her with his mouth wide open. He was taken back by the fact that she had said *boss*, indicating that she was employed.

"You have a job? I wasn't aware that you worked."

"I can see that. Money doesn't grow on trees, Andy. I do have to eat and pay the light bill. I work out of my home."

Yea, but how is that possible?

He had to admit that he'd been curious as to how she lived. He guessed that she had gotten some big insurance claim from the accident and that's how she lived. In actuality, what Andy thought was partly true. She had received a claim, but most of it had gone to pay off the debts she'd been left with and to pay off her house. She kept a tidy little bundle in an IRA for her retirement, but knew if she didn't make some money now, she'd soon be dipping into that.

"So tell me," he said curiosity peaked. "What kind of work do you do?"

"I'm a typist for a law firm in Greenville"

"Whoa, a law firm? But you never leave your house."

"I have an arrangement with the firm. Either my work is mailed to me via e-mail or standard mail, or it's delivered to me by UPS. Or, sometimes someone from the office delivers and picks up the work."

"What do you type?"

"Whatever—contracts mainly or I interpret court data-anything they ask of me."

"But how- I mean, how did you get the job?"

"My best friend since middle school, Elaine Greene, well, she manages the firm. She discussed my situation with her bosses and they agreed to my conditions on a trial bases. I guess they like my work, because I've been with them for two years."

"You never stop amazing me."

"A lot of people work out of their homes, Andy."

"I know. I just didn't know that you did."

"Most people don't know anything about me."

"Yea, well you've made it real convenient for people not to know anything about you, Hannah. I promise I'm not being mean or anything like that—well, it's just that I'm seeing this whole other side of you. I like it. You need to let other people see it, too."

"Easier said than done."

"There's nothing easy about it. I just wish you could see yourself through my eyes. You'd be surprised what I see."

She looked at him, humbled by his words. Once again, he had touched the nerve of her heart. She thought she might cry, not because of her anxiety. Now she was calm. It was his mannerisms—the way he could take a *nothing moment* and make it significant. She smiled warmly at him and nudged his arm.

"Go make your calls, Andy. I'll be fine. I have some knitting to do in my bag to keep my mind and hands occupied. I'll make my calls later."

"Well, if you're sure."

She nodded. He smiled that gentle smile of his and walked off. She watched him until he was out of view. He was a gift, an unexpected friend who had stumbled into her life. He was less secure than he pretended to be and more compassionate than any human being she had ever known.

Across from Hannah sat a stately gentleman. He was reading, but every once in a while, she caught him looking at her. The more he stared, the faster she knitted. When he walked toward her and sat down next to her, she dropped her knitting on the ground. As her ball of yarn rolled across the room, he was quick to retrieve it. While he was the picture of decorum, she was jumbled, set off by this unexpected encounter. He handed her knitting to her and smiled.

"Someone you love is here?" he probed

She nodded. "A friend, but she's more like family."

"Me, too," he said. "My mother had a triple Bypass yesterday."

"Oh," she heard her shaky voice say. "I'm so sorry."

"I appreciate that. The doctors tell me she'll recover nicely. They say she's a fighter."

"I know your mother will be fine. It's very difficult to keep a fighter down."

"I'm Alex King," he said offering his hand to shake.

"Hannah," she said shyly, barely able to make physical contact and removing her grip almost as soon as their hands had touched. Still, she forgot herself in the moment and offered her support to this stranger. They talked about his mother and Grace. She became more at ease. They made small talk about their homes and soon discovered that they had both once lived in Greenville. His voice was soothing and gentle as he made a confession to her.

"It's strange being on the receiving end. All of my life I've always been the one to give advice, to comfort. Now, I find that I am in the same position my patients and their families have been in time after time."

"You're a doctor?"

He nodded. "And it's much easier to give advice than take it."

A surge of courage allowed her to smile and touch his hand again, giving him encouragement. This slight gesture she had given lifted some of his burden, and perhaps hers, as well.

"I wish you and your family the best."

"Thank you, beautiful Hannah," he said to her. "The same to you."

From the corner of his eye, he saw Andy moving toward them. Alex had seen them together earlier and guessed they were probably married or involved. A woman as beautiful as this woman was bound to be in a relationship. He gave her a quick wink, standing tall before her. Reluctantly, he let go of her hand. Then, he looked at her kindly.

"I hope your friend is a fighter, too."

When he walked away, she noticed Andy moving toward her. He was carrying two doughnuts in one hand and a cup of coffee in the other. A paper was tucked under his arm. He sat down where Alex King had just been sitting.

"I leave you for twenty minutes and already you've found someone to take my place."

94

She saw the tease in his eyes, but was in no mood to play along. She tugged at his shirt slightly.

"His mother just survived heart surgery. He asked about Grace, that's all."

Andy stuffed the jelly doughnut in his mouth and offered her the other one. She shook her head. When she looked at him, cherry filling was dripping at the side of his mouth. He wiped it off with his arm.

"He was flirting with you, Hannah."

Her cheeks grew a shade of bright pink, glowing pinker as Andy's smile grew wider.

"Don't be ridiculous," she spat.

"I can't say I blame him."

"He was just being kind, that's all. We were the only people in the waiting room. I think he felt obligated."

"Whatever you say, Hannah."

He finished off the second doughnut and he could see that she was in somewhat of a tizzy.

"Don't be upset with me. I was just having some fun with you."

"I just don't know where you get your ideas sometimes, that's all."

"Hannah, you are a beautiful woman. Men are going to look. Lucky for you, I'm not the jealous type."

"Just be quiet, will you?"

He couldn't resist one more rib. "You know, Honey. I believe we've just had our first official quarrel."

"Oh," she puffed. She grabbed her purse and darted toward the restroom with no concern or fear, but simply to rid herself of his teasing. She could hear him laughing even as she reached the door. He studied her until she was out of sight, knowing he had embarrassed her. He shouldn't have teased her, especially when she was trying so hard to be strong. He just couldn't resist.

Oh, Hannah, thank you for giving me a reason to laugh today.

Inside the protective walls of the restroom, Hannah leaned against the wall. Her heart was racing wildly. She went through her usual self-talk and rituals, trying to maintain her composure.

Why does he have to be so irritating? I'll never make it at his apartment.

Then, she thought of Grace and focused on her. She was here for Grace. She would have to find a way to deal with the rest.

You can do this, Hannah. You must do this.

She willed herself back to the waiting room. She found Andy crouched inside a corner chair with a newspaper covering his face sleeping like a baby. As she watched him, irritating wasn't the word that came to mind—more like incorrigible. He was an incorrigible mess—a wonderful, incorrigible mess. She sat down next to him, listening to his slight snoring, thinking she hadn't heard such a comforting sound in years. She saw on the table next to him, two cell phones being charged. A slight peace prevailed in her heart.

My lamplighter.

.

NINE

Once Grace had been taken back to her room, Hannah never left her side. Throughout the afternoon and into the evening family members came in and out of Grace's room. Hannah tucked herself quietly in the corner as the hours passed, watching the familiar faces of Grace's family, listening off and on to their conversations. Sometimes, she was even a part of these conversations, always feeling a bit detached and awkward. She constantly struggled for comfort and yet there were times when she felt almost free from her anxiety, particularly when she was visiting with Grace or when Andy was in the room.

Andy, Hannah thought, was a natural conversationalist. As each new family member came to visit, he explained the little he knew of Grace's situation with calm and patience. There was very little to tell. The doctors would be in either this evening or tomorrow morning with the results of Grace's tests. Grace slept off and on throughout the day. Her mood tethered between joy to see her family and anxiousness about what was to happen. She never let on to her family how nervous she really was, but Hannah knew better. She knew the look of fear when she saw it. She saw it every time she faced herself in a mirror.

Each member stood over Grace, joking around and giving her encouragement. In truth, they were staggered that she was even there, fearful of the unknown. Charlie, more than the others, had been closest to Grace the past few years. Recently though, he had started a new business and let Ben and Andy carry most of the load. He came over to Hannah and sat beside her, reaching for her hand to comfort himself more than her. She listened to him speak about how he knew she really hadn't been right and blaming himself for not doing something about her condition sooner. Hannah told him they were all feeling the same, but that they shouldn't because Grace had been so good about covering up her condition, even to her, and she saw her almost every day.

"I just wish we knew something," Charlie said.

Ben just shook his head and held onto his son, Tom. "You heard what Andy said. They might not make their rounds until later tonight or even tomorrow."

Ben looked at Hannah and thanked her for all that she had done. Neither Ben nor Charlie questioned her presence at the hospital. They never really thought about how she had actually gotten to Dallas, or the fact that she rarely left her home. They just thought it natural that she was there. Because Grace was limited to just a few guests and they had already exceeded the limit, Ben and Tom left the room to go to the waiting area so others could visit. Soon Charlie and Debbie followed, leaving Hannah alone with Grace. She took this time to rest and soon she was sleeping along with Grace.

A lone figure came inside the room. It was Jean, Andy's ex-wife. Her footsteps alerted Hannah. She must have jerked up suddenly. She saw Jean smile warmly.

"I'm sorry for startling you, Hannah. How's Grace?"

"Sleeping, but good. The tests wore her out."

"I imagine," Jean said. "And all of the company."

Jean looked lovingly at Grace. "I've always loved this woman. She has been so good to us, Andy and me, and the boys."

Hannah thought Jean might break down, but instead she took the chair on the opposite side of the bed to where Hannah was sitting. Hannah had seen Jean maybe a handful of times and these were only brief encounters. At the same time, Hannah felt as though she knew her well, through stories from Grace and Andy. Physically, Jean had aged well, slightly fuller now, than the thin teenager Andy married. Hannah couldn't help but study her, as she reached for Grace's hand and gently held it. The three sat quietly for some time before Jean stood and kissed Grace's forehead. She looked at Hannah.

"Would you tell her I was here?"

"I will, but you don't have to rush off. She might wake up."

"That's okay. I just needed to see her, just for a moment. Besides, I have three very anxious boys who want to see her. Andy thought they might feel less worried if they did. He's going to bring them in shortly."

Before she left, Jean turned to face Hannah again. She wanted to choose her words carefully as not to insult Hannah.

"Andy told me how difficult it was for you to leave your home to be here. I just want you to know that we, all of us, appreciate the fact that you are here for Grace. She loves you so and it's different than with her grandsons. I think women have a bond that men just can't understand."

Hannah looked at her and smiled. She was beginning to see why Andy was having such a time letting her go. For some reason, Hannah was compelled to walk around the bed toward Jean. The two women embraced for one slight moment. Jean took one final look at Grace.

"Hang in there, Nana," she said and then looked at Hannah. "I'll get the boys."

Hannah nodded and watched her walk away as quietly as she came into the room. She thought about Jean and Andy — and their situation. Earlier that day, Hannah had met Frank. Physically, he couldn't match up to Andy's strong physique. Frank was shorter than Andy, almost Jean's height and ten or so years older. Full around the middle and balding, Hannah could see why Andy never suspected Jean might have an interest in him. He wasn't your usual *leave your husband for me* type of guy. Yet, what he lacked in physical charms, he compensated with diplomacy. There was a definite chemistry between Jean and

Frank. They boys seemed to get along with him, especially their youngest, Bobby. This was to Andy's disdain. Her thoughts were interrupted when Andy came into the room with Mathew and Jeff. Bobby stayed with Jean. The three stood next to Grace's bed. Hannah smiled.

"Boys, this is Mrs. Martindale. She lives next door to Nana."

"We know that, Dad," Mathew said. "We've met at Nana's"

"I don't remember her," Jeff corrected.

"Well," Hannah began. "It was a long time ago. I doubt that you would. It's nice to see you again."

Andy had one arm on the shoulder of each one of his sons. He looked directly at Hannah.

"Still sleeping, I see. That's good. I wish the doctors would come and tell us something tonight."

"Me, too. The later it gets, my guess is that it will be tomorrow."

"Yea," Andy said worn-out. "If it were their grandmother…"

Jeff looked at Nana and then at his dad. "Dad, is Nana going to die?"

"Die?" Andy said, caught off guard. "No, no, Son. She won't die. Well, we're doing everything we can to make sure she doesn't."

Mathew slid his hand in Andy's when tears threatened to fall. "We prayed for her, Dad. Me and Jeff and Bobby."

"Yea? Good. I'm sure God heard you."

"I know he hears us, but mom says he doesn't always give us what we pray for. She says that God knows more than we do and that sometimes He doesn't answer our prayers the way we want."

"Mom's right, but this time I think it's going to go our way."

"Dad," Mathew said. "Mom and Frank are leaving soon. Thought I'd hang around for a while. You could take me home on your way to the apartment tonight. If that's all right."

"Tomorrow's a school day."

"Mom says it's okay with her. My homework's all done."

"Yea, sure, no problem. I'd like that."

"I want to stay, too," Jeff whined.

"Not tonight, Jeff. Mom might need you. This is hard on her, too."

"I guess."

"In fact, I'd better get you back to her. It's almost nine already. Hannah, do you mind keeping an eye on Mathew?"

"Not at all."

When Andy left, Mathew sat in the same chair Jean had sat in earlier. He just kept staring at Grace. Hannah thought he looked like he was carrying the weight of the world on his shoulders. She wanted to go to him, but she also knew he was trying to be strong for his dad. Mathew understood little about Hannah, except that she was Nana's friend and she was shy. He liked her because she always treated him like a grown-up. Maybe that's why he felt comfortable unburdening his heart to her.

"I heard my mom and Frank talking. My dad is getting married to Liz. They are having a baby."

Hannah looked at him startled, mesmerized by his dark hair and blue eyes. He looked like Andy and bore his heart like Andy. She walked over to him and took his hand. She wanted him to feel free to speak, but this wasn't the place for this discussion.

"You know, Mathew. I've been in this room all day and I could use a walk. Your Nana is sound asleep. I don't think she will miss us. Would you like to walk with me?"

He could feel her hand shaking as he squeezed it. He remembered his dad telling him that hospitals made Hannah nervous. He guessed she was nervous.

"Yea," he said. "Dad gave me some money for a drink. I'm thirsty. You want a soda, too?"

"I'd love one. Let's check in with your dad first, though. We wouldn't want him to worry."

They walked the hallway hand in hand, looking for a vending machine. Just like Andy, Hannah felt at ease with his son. He was gentle and kind.

"This is cool, staying up late — being with Dad."

"You and your dad are close, aren't you?"

"He's the best."

"I think he shares the same opinion of you."

They talked about school, friends, and baseball — his favorite sport. They talked about his brothers and how they sometime fight, but mostly get along. He talked about how his mom and dad would fight when they were together and that's why they got divorced. He said Frank was okay and made his mom happy. He said he liked Liz.

"Don't tell Dad I know about him and Liz having a baby and getting married and all. I was being nosy when I heard Mom and Frank talk."

"I won't tell, but you should talk to your father."

"I will. I think maybe now Mom and Dad will stop fighting."

"It's hard on you when they fight, isn't it? It kind of puts you in the middle."

He didn't answer her, but she could see by the look on his face that it was true. When they reached the vending machine, he groaned.

"Oh, man, they don't have any grape."

Hannah smiled tearfully. "You know, my son, Gabe, loved grape soda when he was your age."

"I didn't know you had a son, Mrs. Martindale."

"What?" she said taken back.

"I mean, I never saw any kids at your house. Does he live with his dad?"

"Oh, Mathew, that's because Gabe was killed many years ago. You were too young to remember him."

"He died?"

She nodded, turning her head away. Mathew tugged at her arm slightly.

"I'm sorry. You must miss him a lot."

"Yes, I do, and his little sister, Julie. They were both killed in a car accident."

When she saw the pained look on his face, she didn't have the heart to tell him she had lost her husband, as well. Before she knew it, Mathew had planted his arms so that he was hugging her waist and she could tell he was crying. She guessed he was crying as much for himself as he was for her. She ran a gentle hand through his hair and let her own tears fall. She swept a hand over her wet eyes.

"Hush now, Sweetheart. No more tears tonight. Let's go and find you a grape drink."

The two walked side by side, as they made their way around the corner of the hallway and down a new corridor. Hannah was empowered with courage, courage derived from the kindness of an eleven-year-old boy — Andy's boy, her newest friend.

Andy and Liz were sitting together in the room when she walked in with Mathew. All of the other family members had said their *goodnights* and gone home. Mathew stood next to Andy. He and Liz both looked bone tired. Andy looked at Grace, sleeping soundly. He knew it was time to leave, but he didn't want to leave. Liz was slumped down in the chair and her shirt had lifted somewhat, exposing the part of her pants that covered her abdomen. The life inside of her was beginning to swell. In response, Andy unconsciously moved a gentle hand over her girth.

My Dad and Liz are getting married. They are having a baby.

Andy happened to catch Hannah watching them. He moved his hand away in response. Hannah was embarrassed that she had interrupted such an intimate moment. He cleared his throat.

"The doctor came while you were out."

Hannah alerted. "What did he say?"

"He said that Nana's heart is weak. The left side is functioning at barely thirty percent. The right side is stronger, maybe working at seventy percent. She has a workable blood flow and that's good. He doesn't want to operate on her, not at her age. The risk is too high. He's giving her medicine to make her heart stronger. He wants her to stay here a few days to monitor her. If she responds to the medication, she will be home within the week."

"This is promising, right?"

"I guess. They are suggesting that someone take one of those hospital training courses. You know, how to work with patients in Nana's condition. He said with a bit of luck, medicine and good care she should live another ten years. No guarantees though."

"Nothing is guaranteed, Andy."

Andy looked at her drawn. "He told us to notify Mom and Dad."

Hannah sat down at this news.

"John and Ann? Of course, they should be called. Did you...?"

"Charlie talked to him. Dad's arranging to leave. Mom is staying for now. She's tying up loose ends."

"Oh, Andy, I wanted different news, too. It could be worse."

"Yea, I guess."

Again, it was silent in the room. Andy looked to see that Mathew was sitting in Liz's lap, half asleep. Liz's head was propped back and her eyes were closed.

"Liz tires so easily these days. I guess I should be getting Mathew home, too. I just hate to leave Nana alone."

"She won't be alone. I'm staying here with her."

"Oh, Hannah, no. I promised you that I wouldn't leave you alone. I know what an ordeal this day has been for you."

"It's been an ordeal for everyone. I won't be alone, Andy. I'll be with Grace."

"Yea, but..."

"I'll be fine, Andy. Besides, I have my handy little cell phone if I need you."

He smiled, remembering how he had to give her a lesson on how to use the phone.

"Where will you sleep?"

Hannah slapped the chair. "It makes into a bed."

He looked at her skeptical. "Are you sure you can do this?"

No, I'm not sure of anything.

She nodded—fear filling her entire being. She lent him a weary smile.

"Yes, I'm sure. I've been psyching myself up all day. It's what I want."

"Call me—anytime. I mean it."

"I will."

He stood, unwilling to leave. He wanted to stay with Hannah. He felt safe with her. He had to laugh at the irony, feeling safe with a woman who was so consumed with self-doubt, a near recluse. Still, she was strong and with each passing moment, he admired her more.

"Hannah, I asked Liz to marry me today."

I know.

"That's wonderful, Andy. I wish you much happiness."

He moved around the bed, pulling a single chair next to hers. He whispered as not to be overheard. He couldn't explain why he could speak so freely to her. His heart was so torn and he knew she would listen and not judge.

"I wasn't planning on asking her today, especially not here, not today—with Nana still in the hospital. I can't even tell you how or when it happened. I just think it's the right thing to do—you know, with the baby and all."

"Andy, you don't have to explain yourself to me."

Hannah looked into his sorrowful eyes. Today had been a rollercoaster for him—for both of them. He was so tired. Remembering how her touch felt so warm and secure, he took her hand.

"I should go, but I don't want to leave her."

Something in his helpless tone released her own pent up sorrow. From now on, Grace's condition was a waiting game—waiting for her to get better or worse. Hannah was caught up in a moment of darkness at the prospect of losing her dear friend. She clutched Andy's hand tighter.

"Andy, she will be okay, won't she?"

"I hope so, Hannah. I hope so."

The tone of his voice rekindled her previous doubts. She moved closer to him. They were embracing, with only the arms of two chairs between them. Her head rested on his chest for comfort. His hands nestled on her back, soothing her. She could feel his mouth brush the side of her face and the top of her head. Was he kissing her? His breathing sounded like a roar in her ear and when he spoke her name, it sounded as if he were praying. By accident, Andy's hand touched the flesh on her back. They both felt it at the same time. Quickly, he moved his hand away, but refused to let go of their embrace.

Beautiful woman

"Andy, you should go," she barely managed to speak.

He knew that he should leave—knew he had held her much too long. Inside, the conflict of his emotions left him confused and uncertain.

"I want to be here with you—with Nana."

As he held her, Hannah happened to glance over toward Liz. Her eyes were still closed. Reality left her skin cold.

Mathew was waiting for him. Liz was waiting for him. Liz was carrying his child. Andy was a friend — only a friend. That's all he would ever or could ever be in her life. She drew away from his hold and reluctantly he let go of her. He stood and moved toward Nana, kissing her goodnight. Without facing Hannah, he spoke to her.

"Take good care of her. Remember, I'm just a phone call away."

Hannah watched him nudge Liz and Mathew and the three lagged toward the door. Liz mumbled *goodnight* and Mathew said something like *I'll see you*. Hannah met Andy's eyes for the last time that night. Words were not enough, so they didn't speak. He simply waved at her and the last thing she saw was Liz's arm draped around his waist.

Do you know how fragile he is, Liz?

Hannah stared at the door for some time before she was able to let out a breath. The nurse came in shortly after to take Grace's vitals. She helped Hannah unfold the chair that made into a bed and got her a pillow and blanket. Grace never stirred. Soon, the room was quiet again

Hannah listened to Grace's heavy breathing and reached to touch her hand. A flow of tears fell silently down her face. In the darkness of the room, instead of the usual fear that always managed to invade her nights, Hannah was experiencing a new flow of emotions. She looked at Grace's sleeping form once more.

"Grace, my Darling, can you hear me? I made it through my first day away from my home. I was afraid almost the entire day, but I made it. Andy helped me. I met Mathew and we shared a grape soda together. He's wonderful, just like..."

She was about to say *just like his father*, but she bit her tongue. She squeezed Grace's hand one final time before releasing it.

"Good night, Grace. I love you."

Through the cracks of the door in Grace's room, a stream of light flowed through like a ray of hope. Hannah closed her eyes, clutching her plastic soldier. She felt Andy's strong arms around her. His breath was rushing down her neck. She knew it was wrong to think of him, but she didn't have the desire to stop. She understood something else as she lay there with him in her thoughts. Even though she would never be able to realize her unexpected feelings for Andy, the secluded life she had been living was ending. A flicker of excitement touched her soul as she began letting go of her past. With hope and determination, life would be good again.

TEN

Kelly Roberts, the owner of *Your Way Floral Designs* had taken Andy Padgett's order, an assorted arrangement to be delivered to his fiancée, Liz Brewster. The message on the card read: *To my beautiful fiancé and the mother of our child. You will be a wonderful wife and mother. Andy.*

Kelly Roberts was left dumbfounded. She looked at the address where the flowers were to be delivered. It was Liz's. She had been at that house more times than she could count. She couldn't believe the bombshell that had been thrown in her lap. The odds of her taking this call were beyond remarkable. She took care of the business side of the floral shop and left the operating part to her partner and shop manager. Today, she just happened to be in the area and had dropped in to say *hello*. It was a long shot that she had even taken the call. It was an even longer shot that Andy Padgett had selected her shop out of all the florists in Dallas to send flowers to his fiancé. It was surreal to say the least.

Liz, is this true? Are you engaged? Are you going to be a mother?

Kelly shook her head in disbelief She pondered what to do. Liz had been a part of her life since she was in middle school and her brother, Doug, and Liz became high school sweethearts. They broke up in college and Doug married less than a year later. Kelly knew he still loved Liz. His marriage lasted a year. The divorce lasted much longer. Before she had time to think any more, she was calling Doug's cell.

"What's up Kel?" His cheery voice asked.

"Well," she said. "You're in a good mood."

"I should be. I'm officially divorced—well, at least I will be when I stop by the judges chambers and sign the papers."

Another surreal moment

"That's good. Now you can get that witch out of your life once and for all."

Doug laughed. He was feeling free.

"Doug, I got a very strange order today –at the florist. I thought you might want to know about it. It concerns Liz."

"Liz? What about her?"

"Doug, she's getting married. Her fiancé ordered her flowers. I know it's our Liz because of the address where he wanted the flowers delivered."

"Her finance…who?

"Some guy named Andy Padgett."

Doug knew all about Andy Padgett from Liz. He knew Liz dated him, and she had told him she loved Andy. He also knew he treated her badly, so badly she had turned to him for support. Kelly wasn't able to see the gut-wrenching pain on Doug's face. He was torn apart, remembering the last times that he and Liz had been together. These times had been a promise of better days to come for him, or so he thought. She was coping with her breakup with Andy. He was suffering through a nasty divorce. Doug thought he read more into it. He was wrong. He rubbed his forehead. Suddenly, today was spiraling downhill.

Andy Padgett, you are one piece of work, you know it.

Kelly thought the fact that Andy had picked her floral shop was a coincidence. Doug knew better. No doubt, Liz had at sometime or another mentioned Kelly's business in passing and Andy wanted to capitalize on the opportunity. He was rubbing it in his face that he had Liz and not him. What he didn't know was if Liz was part of this cruelty.

"There's more, Doug."

"It gets better?"

"Liz is going to have a baby, or at least that's what the message Andy sent her implies."

Kelly read Andy's message to Doug. He was silent. A million thoughts went through his head. Without realizing it, he was gathering his things—his suit jacket and brief case.

"Doug," Kelly asked. "Did you hear me?"

"I heard you. Liz is getting married and having a baby."

"Aren't you just the least bit curious—I mean about the baby? The two of you were together not too long ago."

"I know what you are thinking, but we weren't together that way."

After he spoke the lie, he wondered why. Kelly was on his side, always had been. He just couldn't bear another let down. He wasn't going to let his heart hope. Yet, it had a will of its own. It was already stirring. Suspicion consumed him.

Liz, what's going on?

"Oh," Kelly said disappointed. "I'm sorry I called and ruined your day. I just thought you might want to know."

"Don't be sorry, Kel. We take care of each other, don't we? Truthfully, I hope she'll be happy. She deserves it. I had my chance. I blew it."

"That's very gracious of you considering things."

"I'm not gracious, I'm real. Liz has moved on and I have to move on, too. In less than an hour, I'll be free. I'm leaving the past behind me."

He heard himself say the words and for a second, he meant it. Yet, the situation got the best of him. He couldn't let it go. He had to know. After talking with Kelly, he searched for Liz's number, still on his phone.

Is it possible that I'm the father of your baby?

Before common sense prevailed, he sent her a text.

Liz, we need to talk – Doug.

When Andy arrived at the hospital early that next morning, he found his grandmother and Hannah laughing and carrying on like old times. Of course, Nana was complaining about not being able to eat real food and that she didn't think she could stay one more day in the hospital.

"A person can't get any sleep around here, what with them poking and prodding you all the time."

"They are just taking care of you, Nana," he said.

"That's what I told her, Andy. Maybe she'll listen to you."

Andy smiled at Hannah. It was amazing to him that she looked so good after spending the night sleeping in a hospital chair. Her spirits were high and her smile bright.

"The doctor was in already, Andy. He says Grace is doing wonderfully. She's not too happy about the fact that he wants her to stay a few more days."

"It's not necessary," Grace grumbled.

"Sweetheart, play along, please. It will make us feel better."

He pinched Nana's cheek lovingly. She sent him a playful grump. An aide came in with breakfast. Grace was about to complain again about the food when Andy sent her a cautionary gaze.

"Be nice," he whispered, kissing her on the cheek.

"Mrs. Padgett," the aide said. "How would you like a bath after breakfast?"

The thought of a bath lifted her spirits immensely.

"Now that's the best news I've had since I've gotten here. That would be wonderful, Dear. Too bad I have to wear these awful hospital gowns."

"I brought you some from home," Hannah said. "They're in my suitcase. Andy, is it still in your truck?"

He snapped his fingers. "It's at my apartment. I didn't want to leave it in the truck over night. Sorry."

"That's okay," Grace said disappointed. "You can bring it later."

"Tell you what," he said. "I can go get it now. I don't have to be at work until three."

112

"Mercy, no, Andy. You can bring it later—and your checker game. Hannah thinks she can beat me, but she never does."

"That's because you cheat," he laughed.

"I do not. And if you can't be nice to me, you can leave."

"Who's going to make me? You?"

"Humph, if I weren't in this bed, you wouldn't be so brave."

Andy put up his hands as if to shield himself from her wrath. Hannah laughed aloud at the two sparring, knowing how much they loved each other. Grace was certainly full of herself this morning and Andy wasn't letting her get by with anything. The aide was laughing, too.

"You'll feel better after your bath, Mrs. Padgett. Maybe between the two of us, we can take him on."

"He's always been a handful. He's been over my knee more times than I can count."

Hannah looked at Andy. She was picturing him as a young boy, looking a lot like his son, Mathew. Grace had told her stories of Andy and his Paps on their farm. She said he was always full of life and couldn't be contained. He was happiest when he was outside working with his hands and getting rid of all his energy.

"Andy," Hannah suggested. "Let's step out while Grace has her bath. Maybe get some coffee."

"I have a better idea," Grace suggested. "Why don't you take Hannah out of this hospital for a while? She's been here since yesterday and there's no reason for her to wear herself out."

"Grace," Hannah interceded. "I'm fine."

"When was the last time you ate?" Grace asked.

She couldn't remember and so she shrugged her shoulders.

"I'm not hungry, Grace. You know I'm not a big breakfast eater."

"Nana's right. You need a break."

"Andy, I...I'm staying."

"We won't be gone long. We can go to my place. You can clean up and eat. Just a few hours, Hannah, and then I'll bring you back on my way to work."

"But...who will stay with Grace?"

"I talked to Charlie and he's coming by this morning. She'll be okay."

"Of course, I will. Now go. I want you alert for checkers. I don't want anyone saying that I'm cheating."

Hannah would have laughed, but she was suddenly a bundle of nerves. The new comfort zone she had built was crashing. She looked at Andy and made one final plea.

"I really want to stay."

He took her hand gently. "I know you do, but you really need a break. It will be fine. You trust me, don't you?"

Grace looked at Andy and Hannah. He had a way with her. He was one of just a few people that could convince her she was capable of doing more than she thought she could. Even Grace sometimes couldn't do it. Hannah gave Grace a hesitant look.

"If you're sure...I want to stay."

"Go, Dear. I'll be here when you get back. In fact, I'll probably take another nap. Seems like that's all I do these days. Wouldn't hurt you to get a few winks yourself."

"Well," she hesitated. "I guess I can."

"Get your purse, Hannah. We're going to my place."

She let him know under no uncertain terms that she was coming back.

"A quick shower and something to eat. Then, I'm coming right back."

"Hannah," Andy coaxed. "A rest..."

"No, Andy," she said in a near fit.

"Okay, okay. Whatever you want. I'm a sucker for a lady with beautiful brown eyes."

A strand of hair had fallen in her face and Andy brushed it back gently. His touch calmed her and they stared in each other's eyes forgetting that Grace and the aide were even in the room.

"My eyes are hardly beautiful, Andy, especially today."

They are to me.

He felt a surge of panic at what he was feeling. It was something he couldn't quite define, but it scared the hell out of him. He stared hopelessly at Hannah. She reached for her purse and kissed Grace goodbye. Andy followed her lead. Unaware that he had taken Hannah's hand, the two walked out of the room together. Grace was left to wonder exactly what or if something was going on between the two of them.

Hannah let the hot water from Andy's shower ease away weeks of fear and worry. For the moment, the past no longer existed. Her concern for Grace had lessened. Only the moment and the utter luxury of steamy water trailing down her was relevant. Vaguely in the background, she could hear Andy moving about the apartment. Several times, she heard the phone ring. Once, she heard the doorbell. Yet, as far as she was concerned, she was removed from any place other than where she was. There in the shower, she let her mind wander.

Andy's small apartment was completely male, void of the frills and niceties of a woman's touch. It felt safe to Hannah and she couldn't explain why. It was, as Andy had said, a neglected hole, a place to store his things and catch a few winks at night. Never had he considered it home. Still, it was all Andy, too. Hannah opened the lid to the shampoo bottle Andy had in the shower and took in its smell, an expensive brand, probably a gift from Liz. Andy wouldn't have picked out such a trendy item. Yet, because Liz had given it to him, he used it. Hannah already associated the essence to Andy, remembering how it lingered on his neck. Quickly she scolded herself and twisted the lid back. When she removed the cap from her own shampoo, something floral, she compared it to Andy's woody scent.

What are you doing?

Reluctantly, she drew herself from the shower and dried off, draping the newly bought towel, forest green, around her. She turned on the sink faucet to brush her teeth and realized she had left her toothpaste inside her purse, which was on the kitchen table. She reached into Andy's cabinet to look for some and when she did, an open box of condoms fell into the sink and onto the floor. Hannah stared mortified at the singly wrapped prophylactics scattered about the floor and in the water-filled basin.

Oh, my goodness!

She examined the soaked container. Nervously, she plucked up the packets from the floor and in the sink, dabbing the wet ones dry. She took her blow dryer and made a fruitless attempt to salvage the cardboard container. Realizing she couldn't, she stacked the loose packets neatly inside the cabinet. She stared at them for some time, feeling like she had just invaded a private aspect of Andy's life. When she caught a glimpse of herself fretting in the mirror, she realized the utter ridiculousness of the situation and laughed aloud.

If he doesn't ask, I won't tell him.

Andy had pizza warming in the oven, pepperoni with extra cheese. It wasn't exactly breakfast, but it wasn't exactly lunch either. Groceries in the house were scarce and he hoped she didn't mind. He was sitting at the table reading the paper and finishing off a cup of coffee when she came into the kitchen. He knew she was near even before he looked up to see her. Her scent gave her away. His eyes inconspicuously trailed the long line of her slightly fitted jeans. She was slim, but full in the right places. The red in her blouse brought out her dark features, her eyes—her hair. The top button of her blouse was tempting to come loose and Andy swallowed hard, thinking she looked good enough to devour.

"Well, well," he teased, dropping his paper. "I thought I was going to have to call the fire department to get you out of the shower."

"I indulged. I'm sorry, but it felt so wonderful."

"Well, you deserved it. Sit down. Your food awaits you. What can I get you to drink? I've got coffee or water."

"Water please."

Andy pulled the pizza from the oven and placed the hot pan on a cooling rack on the table. Hannah sat down and saw that two plates were already set. He filled a glass of water for her and refilled his coffee, before sitting down next her.

"Thank you," she said.

"You're welcome."

He slapped two slices of pizza on each plate.

"Andy, you shouldn't have waited for me. I feel badly about taking so long in the shower."

"It's not a problem. I had some things to do around here. Besides, it was time well spent. You look great."

"Better," she said biting into the juicy slice and slurping up the cheese. "I wouldn't say great."

"You don't take a compliment very well, do you?"

She laughed. "I just know I've looked better."

"Well then, I've got something to look forward to."

She blushed, which only made her more attractive. He was a charmer, for sure. Hannah wondered sitting next to him, where her anxiety had gone. She watched him as he sprinkled more cheese on his pizza. He caught her watching him and smiled.

"How about Nana, huh? She's always been a pistol."

"That's what I love about her. She is so strong and self-assured."

"I know someone else who is strong. She just doesn't realize it."

Again, she blushed. Again, he smiled that smile that made her believe everything he was saying. She looked at him. Her mind was swarming with thoughts she had no right thinking—scattered condoms, wavy dark hair, and soft blue eyes. She wanted to run into the bedroom and close the door so that she wouldn't give herself away. As it was, he didn't notice her staring at him. He was too busy fighting off his own feelings.

"How's the pizza. Good?"

"Mmm, I didn't realize how hungry I was."

"I'll bet."

"I used to make pizza, you know, for my family. It was my grandmother's recipe. Her mother gave it to her. The secret to a great pizza is the crust and sauce. If you love pizza, you'd love mine."

"My mouth is already watering," he said licking his lips. "So when are you going to make one for me?"

"Oh, Andy, I haven't made one in years."

"Yea, but you will for me, won't you? I mean, knowing how I love pizza so much."

She had to smile when she saw his dancing eyes. "Well, you have been awfully nice to me."

He fluttered his brow and gave her such a grin, she burst out laughing and so did he. Sauce was smudged in one corner of his mouth and she instinctively took her napkin and wiped it off. Her touch was almost intimate.

"Thank you," he said in a not so calm voice.

He saw her blush again, but knew he probably was blushing, too. They didn't speak for some time. They couldn't. A knot was lodged in his throat and she was shaking so much, she knew she would make a fool of herself if she did speak. They happened to catch each other's gaze and she smiled so sweetly at him, he felt his heart stop. He wasn't exactly sure what was going on, but only knew that something was. He opened his soul to her, as if she could change the course of his life.

"Hannah, I'm afraid. I'm afraid if I marry Liz, I'll regret it for the rest of my life."

118

"Andy, this is very personal. I'm not sure I'm the right person..."

His voice trembled. "Please listen, Hannah. I need to tell someone. You're the only person I trust."

She reached to take his hand that lay limp on the table. "All right," she said softly.

"I don't love her. If it weren't for the baby..."

"Andy, that's saying something. Besides, you must feel something for her, I mean, to be with her the way you were."

He ran a hand through his hair, filled with regret. She just might be naive enough to think that sex and love went hand in hand. How could he make her understand that sometimes one was a diversion for the need of the other? She lent him a bittersweet smile, trying to be supportive. He continued talking.

"Sure I feel something for her. Liz is a great girl, but she deserves more than what I can give her."

"Things could change, I mean, once the baby is born. Your feelings could change."

"And if they don't?"

She didn't have an answer. Suddenly, the pizza in his belly soured. He stood up and took their plates to the sink. He stared out the window and was remembering what his father had once said about being married and accepting the pain as well as the blessings. Would he have to suffer the rest of his life for one mistake?

"Andy, I'm sorry. I didn't mean to upset you. I..."

She got up and stood next to him. He turned and moved closer to her. They were so close, they could feel each other's breath. He coursed over her face, timeless with beauty and so delicate, he was sure she would break before his very eyes. He leaned his head down lower and brushed her mouth so gently, their lips barely touched. Still, he had crossed a line. She tried to speak his name, but the word never got out. They kissed a second time, long and passionate. He whispered to her.

"Beautiful Hannah."

She did find her voice. "Andy, we can't."

He knew that she was right—knew that he should end this right now. He might have drawn her in for one more kiss, had his cell phone not jolted him back to reality. The call was ironically from Liz. He edged slowly away from Hannah and leaned against the sink for support. Hannah heard him say *hello*. She listened to bits and pieces of their conversation—his and Liz's. She had to get away. She edged slowly from Andy, slowly from his sight. She walked into the living room and settled on the couch—dazed. With her head in her hands, she let out a cumbersome breath.

Oh, this can't be happening.

Andy hung up the phone and watched Hannah struggle with what had just occurred. She was shaken. He was none too steady himself. He sat next to her on the couch. He took her hands.

"Hannah, look at me."

She couldn't. She couldn't do anything but go over what had happened moments earlier.

"Hannah, please look at me."

When she did, he saw that tears filled her eyes.

"Hannah…"

"Oh, Andy, I'm so confused."

Once again, she tucked her head down. He was quick to lift it back up.

"I know, I'm confused, too."

She threatened to cry once again.

"I think you should take me home, to Blossom."

"Would that change what's happening here? I doubt it."

"Nothing's happening, Andy"

He touched her cheek softly and ran his hand through her hair.

Hannah, I'm sorry, but something is definitely happening here.

He smiled at her wearily, unable to discuss the matter with her because he was just as torn as she was. This was just one more complication in his life. Hannah crossed her arms to her chest and drew within herself. The old fear she knew so well had suddenly surfaced. She wanted the security of home, far away from what she was feeling. She knew it was just one kiss—two kisses. Unknowingly, she touched her lips. She knew they couldn't turn back. That's why she had to leave.

"Andy, you will take me home, won't you?"

He looked at her injured. His disappointment was mounting. He was angry with her and couldn't explain why. Maybe it was because deep down inside, he knew she was right. Or, maybe he wasn't angry with her at all, but at himself for allowing his heart to move in this direction.

"If that's what you want, Hannah, yes I will. It won't be today or tomorrow, because of my work schedule. I can take you home Saturday."

"Thank you," she said softly.

"Not a problem," he returned cuttingly.

Tired and hurt, he stood abruptly and started walking toward the kitchen, in an effort to keep his emotions in tact. She could hear him from where she sat—tossing dishes and mumbling under his breath. A few minutes later, he was back in the living room. His hands were tucked inside his front pockets and his face was clearly torn. He was straining to remain calm

"I'm sorry I upset your day, but I'm not sorry I kissed you. I admit that I'm confused about what's happening and a lot of other things, but I wasn't a bit confused that I wanted to kiss you. I was damn sure about it. And if you think I feel safe about what's happening, I don't. It scares the hell out of me."

He turned away from her again and went to the back of the apartment. He came back carrying a game of checkers, the bag Hannah had packed for Grace, and his work jacket. She was taken back by his emotional honesty. She remembered what Grace had once told her. *He wears his heart on his sleeves.* Hannah understood what she meant now. Tears threatened to surface, but she refused to cry. Her eyes followed him as he moved closer to her. He was calmer, but still agitated. Then, he stood directly in front of her.

"And another thing," he spat. "You were kissing me, too. Don't even pretend you weren't."

She was so lost, so out of her element. He knew he had interrupted a life so completely filled with torment and now he was adding more to it. She was trembling so badly, his heart broke. He squatted in front of her so that their faces were at eye level, forcing her to look at him.

"Hannah," he soothed. "You are the last person I want to hurt. But please, please, I beg of you. Don't deny that something is happening here. Back there—back in the kitchen when we were kissing, it was the first time since I can't remember when that I felt so…alive, so full of hope. This has to mean something."

She looked at him so overwhelmed. She knew she had to get away from him, where she could be safe. She didn't trust herself, not with him so close.

"Andy, I…please take me back to the hospital."

He let out an exasperated air.

"Okay," he surrendered, but offered one last spar. "I'll take you now. Just promise me one thing, Hannah. Don't close your mind to us. Trust your heart."

She broke out into tears and fell helpless in his arms. Before she realized it, they were kissing again. She couldn't fight this, even when she knew she should. It was a long, tender kiss that could have escalated into a storm, had Andy not stopped it. Instead, he sat down and led her to sit on his lap. She laid her head on his chest for security. One of his hands fell casually within the waves of her thick hair, where it nestled safely. The other hand settled on the small of her back. These subtle touches eased away their uncertainty as they put aside the complexities of their lives for this momentary happiness. A gentle peace overcame both of them and they slipped into a soft lull, faintly recalling that she needed to get back to the hospital and he needed to get to work.

ELEVEN

Doug Chasey was already sitting at a corner table when Liz arrived at the restaurant Saturday around noon. It was a quaint Italian Café built within a tourist cultural center in Weatherford. He chose a secluded table away from the main entrance and traffic. He was nursing a tea, dressed in a pinstriped gray suit. His blonde hair was clipped short, impeccably styled, as always. From a distance he looked as good as he ever had, too handsome, too overpowered with charm. When she saw him up close, his face told her that life hadn't been going his way. When he saw her, his green eyes flashed and he smiled, perhaps for the first time since the last time he had seen her. He stood and pulled out a chair for her. She sat down, demurely crossing her hands in her lap. She knew he was studying her all the while he was motioning for the waiter.

"The lady would like ice water with a twist of lime."

She had to smile. "Still assuming, huh?"

He smiled too. "No, I just know some things never change."

To Doug, she looked amazing. Motherhood looked well on her. She was trying to conceal her condition, he could tell. She couldn't, at least not to him. He knew every inch of her body. That's why he knew it was different from the last time he had seen her. His heart couldn't rest until he was certain the life she carried wasn't part of him.

"Liz, you look beautiful."

She opened her menu. "So do you. Did you have trouble finding the restaurant?"

He shook his head. "It's nice, far from home—far from anyone. It's the kind of place you might pick if you have something to hide."

She gave him a chiding glance, and then went back to studying the menu.

"I'm here with Mom for the weekend. It's Aunt Betsy's birthday."

"I see. Does your mom know that you're meeting me?"

"No. She went to the movies with Aunt Betsy. I said I wanted to rest."

"Ah."

A temporary lull fell between them. Then, Doug recanted.

"Does the song that's playing do anything for you, Liz?"

She stopped to listen and smiled. "You know it does. Please tell me you didn't ask them to play it."

"I'm good, but not that good."

Once again, the two were silent. The waiter brought their drinks. Doug said they needed more time before ordering. The waiter left. Doug stared at Liz, who was still looking at the menu. A million memories swept over him.

"Liz, look at me."

She moved her eyes from the menu. "What is it?"

"How are you? I mean, really?"

"What's this about, Doug? Let's get to the point of this meeting, I got your text and agreed to meet with you because you seemed, well, so adamant. What's going on?"

His stare severed through her.

"I know, Liz."

"What do you know?"

"I know about the baby. Don't ask me how, I just do."

She let out a nervous laugh. "I'm not keeping my pregnancy a secret, Doug."

He continued. "I also know that you plan to marry Andy. You know, the cad who dumped you—the one you came running to me for comfort when he broke your heart."

125

She let out an exasperating breath. "Doug, what do you want from me? Why did you want to see me?"

"Well," he said. "Since you asked, I'll tell you. You're pregnant. We had a heated reunion not too long ago. I may just have an investment in what's going on with you right now. I'll get straight to the point. Am I the father of your baby?"

She stared at him boldly mustering up the lie she had practiced, knowing he had texted her for exactly this reason. Her legs were limp and her heart was pumping furiously. The waiter came to take their order. Doug waved him off once again.

"No, Doug. You're not. If you were, I would tell you. You should know me that well by now."

"Oh really," he said doubtful. "I have a gut feeling about this, Liz, and my gut tells me I just might be."

Fear rushed through her. She tried to take control of the situation. She tried manipulation.

"What about your wife? Does she know you're calling me? She hates me, you know."

"There is no wife, Liz. I'm divorced."

"Oh, I knew that you said you were in the process, but that she wanted to reconcile."

"Yea, well, that didn't work out too well. What she really wanted was my money."

"I'm sorry, Doug. Really, I am. Maybe that's why you are calling me. Maybe you are just lonely and you are remembering what we had. I don't know. I've moved on, Doug. I'm with Andy and we are getting married. Yes, I'm having a baby. It's Andy's baby, not yours. I'm sorry, but that's the truth."

He looked into her eyes for a long time before he dropped his head in concession. He raised his head and she saw eyes of regret for a love he would never have. In a class act, he lifted his glass to her and held it up as a final toast to their relationship. She knew he believed her and that he wouldn't be bothering her again.

"Well then," he choked. "To Liz and her baby. May you both be happy and healthy."

She tipped her glass and smiled wearily, already feeling the weight of her lie.

"Thank you," she said before taking a drink. "This means a lot to me."

"And you mean a lot to me, Liz. If you ever need anything ..."

Don't fall for this, Liz. Remember what he and his family did to you.

Hannah's plans to go home on Saturday were nixed, mainly because she couldn't bear to part from Grace –or Andy. As it turned out, she and Andy spent the better part of the morning getting things ready for Grace's release from the hospital. She was doing so well that the doctors were discharging her tomorrow. Because she had two doctors' appointments the following week, Andy made plans to have her and Hannah stay at his apartment. He would put Nana in his bed and move Mathew's bed into his room so Hannah could sleep near her. It made more sense for Grace to stay at his apartment than at Charlie's or Ben's houses because they lived so far from the hospital and the cardiologist. When the apartment was ready for Grace's arrival, Hannah made them a quick lunch—tuna sandwiches, her favorite, and macaroni and cheese, his favorite. Andy had one hour to shower, dress, and take Hannah to the hospital before he had to go to work.

Andy's heart felt lighter. He had a new bounce to his step that he hadn't had since his divorce, maybe even earlier then that. He found himself singing in the shower, excited about life and the hope of sharing his with Hannah. He knew things were a mess in his life, but the muddied waters were beginning to clear. Since the day they first kissed, he found himself thinking about her every waking minute. He made it a point to find any opportunity that he could to be with her, to steal a kiss or a hug, or just to be near her. She was his solace and he looked forward to the day when they could really be alone.

While he showered and dressed, Hannah busied herself by doing the dishes and odd jobs around in the kitchen. She was cleaning some vegetables when Andy finished dressing. She didn't see him standing at the kitchen entrance. He was studying her every move, so graceful, so beguiling. She was humming a soft tune and it made him smile. He couldn't believe he had fallen so hard for her and each time they were together, each time they kissed, he moved closer to surrendering his heart completely. He moved behind her and wrapped his arms around her waist. He whispered in her ear.

"I guess all this healthy food means you won't be making me your famous pizza any time soon," he teased.

"You probably wouldn't like it anyway—all that rich cheese and mouth-dripping sauce. Not to mention a crust worth dying for."

"Stop," he begged. "You're killing me here."

He nestled his face on her neck and kissed it softly.

"Sweet," he said.

She turned around to face him. She reached to move her hands through his hair. She couldn't resist. He couldn't resist kissing her. When they kissed, it was a lingering kiss, thorough and intimate.

"Hannah," he said softly. "Just don't tell me I have to give this up."

"You might have to—at least long enough to take me to the hospital and yourself to work."

He blew out a deep breath and glanced at his watch. "Ah, work."

Still, they held each other. They didn't move. She plucked at his shirt.

"Andy...do you have an extra key to your apartment?"

"Key?"

She nodded. "I was thinking maybe I could sleep here tonight. You know, instead of at the hospital. I don't think Charlie would mind bringing me back here on his way home. That is if it's all right with you."

He closed his eyes and felt a rush of excitement fill his being. He couldn't believe what she was suggesting. Or was she? He'd have to wait and find out. In any case, it would be a time for them to be alone. She was a woman of many surprises.

Alone tonight with Hannah. Oh, the blessed possibilities.

He reached into his pocket and took a key from his key chain. Suddenly, his hands were shaking and his voice along with them. He lent her a nervous smile as he handed her the key.

"Here's mine. I don't have an extra one. This way, you can't change your mind."

She took the key. Then, she took his trembling hands and stilled them with hers.

"Don't be afraid, Andy. I'm here to protect you."

Andy was grateful that work tonight was busy, so the time would pass quickly. Not quickly enough he thought considering what was waiting for him at home. He couldn't stop smiling. He could still feel Hannah's kiss and smell her smell. Several times, he picked up the phone and called her just to hear her voice. He even called Charlie to make sure he could give her a ride home. He was acting like an adolescent on his first date, he knew. He didn't care. It wasn't every day that a man like him had a woman like Hannah waiting for him at home. His thoughts were interrupted when he heard his name paged over the loud speaker.

"Andy Padgett, you are wanted in your office."

Jean was waiting for him at the door and he could see that she had been crying. Within minutes, he had her inside his small office and she was in his arms. She whimpered and carried on so emotionally, he couldn't understand what she was saying. When he finally managed to calm her down enough so that her words made sense, he led her to a chair and kneeled down in front of her. His first thought was that something had happened to the boys.

"Jean, what is it? It's not the boys?"

"No, Andy, the boys are fine."

"Well, that's a relief? What is it?"

"Andy," she cried. "I know it's wrong of me to come to you like this. I don't deserve your sympathy. If you send me away, I'll understand. You have every right to do that. I've been so stupid."

"Jean," his heart skipped. She was squeezing his hands so tightly she was hurting him, but he didn't complain. "What is it?"

"It's...it's Frank. We had a terrible fight. He...He..."

Andy's mind went to a dark place.

"He didn't hit you, did her?" he asked forcefully.

"No, Andy. He would never do anything like that."

Being with her this way was so familiar. His knees almost gave way, so he sat down in a chair next to her to ease his nervousness. What could have happened? What had she and Frank fought about to have her come running to him? Jean looked at his confused face.

"Andy, can you take some time for us to go some place private and talk? This isn't something we should discuss at your work."

An earthquake couldn't keep him from talking to her. He managed to stand and left her alone long enough to tell his manager he'd be taking an early lunch. He led Jean out a back door where his truck was parked. Her car was parked next to him.

"Where should we go?" he asked anxious.

"I don't know. Your apartment?"

He thought of Hannah. He wasn't sure what time she would be there.

He shook his head. "Not a good idea."

"Just some place where we can talk privately. Some place where no one can see us."

They got into Andy's truck and he drove to a neighborhood park where he sometimes took the boys to fly kites. It was thickly secluded with trees and he parked his truck off the main road. He looked at her and could tell she was a bundle of nerves. Before he could speak her name, she was on his side of the truck in his arms, crying her heart out.

"Andy, do you love Liz?"

"Liz? Is this about Liz?"

"It's about us, Andy. It's about me making a mistake. Frank and me, well, we're not working."

He closed his eyes. Tears surfaced. This moment was so surreal and so full of irony, it left him depleted. His Jean, the love of his youth and the mother of his children, a woman he was certain he could never live without, was suggesting they should still be married. How many times had he prayed for this moment? He couldn't count. Now that it was here, he could only look at her in complete shock.

Why Jean? Why after all of this time? Why when I've finally found some happiness?

She saw the look of disbelief on his face. He had every reason to be skeptical. Then, she reached for him, placing her mouth over his. To save his heart, he drew her away, looking into her eyes that clearly read regret.

"Let's talk first," he said shaking.

Not wanting to mess things up, she stopped. His heart was beating out of his chest.

"Jean," he said trying to restrain himself. "I'm listening."

She wrung her hands and tears fell softly down her face. She was struggling to speak, but Andy knew whatever she had to tell him, she had to do at her own pace. After several attempts to speak, the words finally came out.

"Andy, Frank's been offered a job in Austin with the company. It's several steps up and a substantial raise for him. If he accepts, he starts in two weeks."

The sympathy he felt moments earlier had turned suddenly cold. Fear filled his gut.

"Austin? That's four hours away."

"I know," she said upset. "I told him we couldn't move. I told him that my family was here, my mom and dad, my sister, and you, Andy. The boys need to be near you."

Andy swept a hand through his hair. A heavy pressure tugged at his chest. He wanted to scream, but he maintained his composure. Inside he was a seething volcano ready to erupt.

You may have taken Jean, Frank, but you can't take my boys. I'm their father.

"What did Frank say when you told him you didn't want to leave?"

His voice was shaking as much as his hands.

"He said we could come back to Dallas often to visit. He said we could meet you halfway when it's your weekend to have the boys."

Yea, that would work.

Jean saw the bitterness on his face. It stung at her heart. She knew how much he loved his children. She reached for his hand, but he withdrew it—something he had never done. She stared at him, pained by his sudden coldness.

"Frank thinks I want to stay because of you. He thinks as long as you're near, there's always the chance that you and I might..."

"Might what, Jean?"

"You know," she blushed. "Get together again."

He looked at her and he saw longing in her eyes. He reached to kiss her, but when he did, he felt unemotional, as if she had taken everything he had to give. He was empty. She

132

wasn't *his* Jean anymore. She was this stranger, who used to hold his heart in her hands, one who had cruelly disposed of it and now she thinks she wants it back. She ran her hands over his face, a face that had aged five years in one.

"I'm sorry, Andy. Sorry for hurting you so much. I've never stopped loving you."

"Jean," he choked. "Stay. Don't take my boys."

"Andy, I don't want to leave. I want…"

"What? What do you want?"

She sat silently, wanting to revive the passion she had known with this man. This wasn't going exactly how she had envisioned. She ran her hands up and down the front of his shirt. She could feel his heart beat wildly, but he made no move to kiss her again. His eyes were unreadable.

"Oh, Andy, I don't know what I want. I thought I wanted to be married to Frank, but now I'm not so sure."

"I see. So you thought if we slept together, it would help you decide. Is that it?"

"You make it sound so — cheap. I'm confused, Andy."

He lifted her chin and saw regret in her eyes. Tears fell freely down her face and he knew in his heart that she was here to say goodbye. Exhausted from months of uncertain heartache, he also knew he would always love her because of what they had once shared, but something had shifted inside of him. She wasn't the same Jean he had fallen in love with years ago, nor was he the same Andy. They had moved in different directions, just as she had been trying to tell him all along.

"We were good together, Jean," he said in a voice of finality. "Weren't we?"

"Yes."

Just as he leaned to kiss her on the cheek, his cell phone rang. It was Hannah.

Sweet salvation

"Hey," his weary voice answered.

Hannah's voice was hysterical, alerting Andy.

"Hannah, calm down. What is it?"

"Andy, Oh, Andy. Grace has had a heart attack."

"God, no. When?"

"About twenty minutes ago. She was alive then, Andy. That's all I know."

"I'll be there as soon as I can. I have to call Charlie and Ben."

"Just hurry, please!"

When he hung up, he saw the look on Jean's face.

"Grace?"

He nodded. "A heart attack."

"Is she...?"

He shook his head. "I don't know."

He reached for her, distraught from today's roller coaster of emotions.

"Oh, God, Jean, — a heart attack. What if I lose her?"

She took his hand and held it firmly.

"You won't. People have heart attacks every day and survive."

He started the truck and drove Jean back to her car. He checked in at work and told them he'd be off for a few days. Jean waited for him, following him in her car to the hospital. The ride was silent — no radio, just the humming of his motor. Nana weighed heavy on his heart. He pressed the gas pedal down hard. He had to make it in time to see her. His hands were shaking. Why couldn't he make them stop? He looked in his rearview mirror and Jean was still behind him. She was always the one he ran to when life got to him, at least she was until his divorce. Today though, it wasn't her arms he wanted. It was Hannah's arms. She would stop his hands from shaking.

Jean met Andy at the entrance of the hospital. They walked in together. She reached for his hand.

"I'm going to call mother and see if she can keep the boys longer. I'd like to stay here, if that's all right."

134

He nodded. "Sure, Jean. I'd like that."

"Did you get a hold of Charlie and Ben?

"Charlie is here. Ben's on his way."

"What about Liz? Did you call her?"

"Damn," he sighed. "I forgot about Liz. No, I'm going to wait to call her. She's in Weatherford this weekend with her mother and Aunt. It's her aunt's birthday. I hate to ruin her weekend."

"She would want to know, Andy."

"Maybe, I'll see."

"You go on up, Andy. I'll make my calls and join you."

He leaned to kiss her cheek.

"God, you're beautiful."

"Andy," she blushed.

"You will always be beautiful to me."

"Go," she nudged him gently.

He watched her move outside to make her calls. Before he had time to dwell on today, he caught an elevator that took him to the seventh floor I.C.U. waiting area. He found Hannah sitting in the corner, lost and probably scared to death. Her head was leaned against the window next to her chair and she was looking out the window at the view of the rooftop. An evening rain had created puddles and the exhaust from a nearby vent manufactured smoke clouds. Andy could see in the distance a small park. A lone swing swayed empty back and forth lending an eerie premonition that stabbed at his heart. The gray sunset added to the mood. He gripped Hannah's shoulder causing her to jump. She looked up at him and he was searching her face for an answer she couldn't give. He sat down next to her and draped his arms across her shoulders. She let out a sigh of relief.

Andy is here.

He leaned closer to her and kissed her softly, his hands unconsciously playing with her hair—less shaky now that she was near.

"Anything?"

"No," she said. "Nothing since they took her inside."

"Maybe the nurses know something."

"Charlie already asked."

"Where is he?"

"I think he's making some calls."

"Well, then. I guess we wait."

"Andy, she can't die. She can't. One minute we were talking and laughing and the next minute she was staring at me with eyes that were saying the saddest farewell. Her hands were like ice and then...then...she slumped over... and then..."

"Shhh...don't. We have to be strong. She needs us to be strong."

Inside, he was feeling the same fear she was feeling. He lazed back and stretched his long legs in front of him, nervously swaying them back and forth, so that they brushed against her leg. She shifted closer to him and they fell into a comfortable sync, with his arm still wrapped around her and their eyes never losing contact with each other.

Vaguely Hannah noticed that Jean had walked in and sat down beside Andy. She might as well have been sitting across the room for all Andy had noticed. It wasn't until she reached into her purse for a Kleenex and blew her nose, that he even realized Jean was there.

"I hate waiting," Jean said. "I'm going to get something to drink. Can I get you some coffee or a soda?"

"Thank you, not me, " Hannah said.

"I'd love some coffee, Jean."

Andy saw a look of penitence in Jean's eyes. Jean brushed his cheek with a quick kiss and walked off. Andy watched her until the waiting room door shut her out of his view. Hannah could see him battling with his emotions. A new threat challenged her.

"Andy, does Jean's being here mean anything?"

"Absolutely nothing," he said flatly.

"I thought maybe…"

"It's over, Hannah. We've both moved on."

He kissed her softly. Even in their sorrow, he smiled.

"I thought about you so much today."

"Did you?"

"God, I'm so glad you're here. How are you holding up?"

"I'm pretty much a wreck, " she said on the edge. "From the looks of you, I'd say I'm not alone."

"A hell of a pair, huh?"

His smile was so sad, she wanted to hold him, but she didn't. Instead she took his hand and the two sat in silence, lost in the realities of the day. She leaned her head against his arm and his chin rested on the top of her head. He knew he should get up and call Liz. He owed that much to her. He didn't want to leave the security being near Hannah gave him. It was a defining moment, sitting near Hannah, dazed, but feeling comfort from another woman with Jean so near. A prevailing peace came over him. He knew he was going to be all right—without Jean.

TWELVE

Jean called Frank to let him know about Grace and that she would be at the hospital for a while. He had been waiting for her call—fearful of the reason for her delay. She had been gone so long, he thought that maybe she was rethinking her life with him. They had only been married a short while and his job offer really threw her for a loop. When he heard her voice, Jean could almost see the relief on his face.

"It's me," she said.

He laughed. "Did you think I wouldn't recognize your voice?"

"Listen, Andy's grandmother, Grace, had a heart attack. I'm at the hospital now with Andy. Mom has the boys. I'm going to hang out here for a while."

"I could watch the boys."

"It's okay, Mom didn't mind."

"How is Grace?"

"It's a waiting game right now."

There was a moment of silence before he asked her about her meeting with Andy.

"Did you and Andy have a chance to talk? You were pretty upset when you left me to talk with him."

"I still am, Frank, but yes," she answered softly. "Andy and I talked."

Jean could feel her heart racing. She was afraid, afraid of letting go of the life she once had. She loved Frank, but everything and everyone she ever knew belonged here—in Dallas. She also knew that so much had changed. She couldn't believe she was encouraging him to accept the job. Yet deep down, she knew it was the right thing to do.

"Frank, I think you should take the job in Austin."

He swallowed hard. "Will you and the boys be going with me?"

Until that very moment, Jean hadn't been certain just what she was going to do. When she heard her own voice say *yes*, she knew she wanted to be with Frank. She had turned to Andy because he had always been her strength. She also turned to him for closure.

"Yes, we're coming, but Frank, we have to be fair to Andy. He and the boys are so close. They always have been. We have to make a strong effort to make sure this works out for everyone."

"Of course, we will, Jean. I don't have any children of my own, but I've grown to love yours. I can only imagine how difficult this will be for him."

"Frank," she paused nervously. "Nothing happened between Andy and me."

He felt his entire body fall limp in relief. He had taken a gamble sending her to talk to Andy, but he knew for the sake of their marriage, he had to let her get this *goodbye* out of her system.

"I trust you, Jean. I have faith in us."

"Frank, can you come to the hospital? I know how difficult it is to be around Andy's family, but I need you to hold me."

"I'll be there in fifteen minutes."

Hannah felt Andy's thumb move up and down her neck in beat with her heart. The steady movement was soothing and she let herself fall into a semi-conscious state, moving in and out of the moment. She closed her eyes and took in the feeling of being held again after so many years. She felt Andy's warm breath circle the top of her head as if he were breathing needed strength into her soul.

Stay with me forever, Andy. I always want to feel this safe.

"Hannah," she heard him whisper, and so she turned to look into his blue eyes. "I've got to call Liz. She's been texting me all evening. She has to be worried."

She nodded. When he moved his arms from around her, she wanted to cry out for him to come back, but she didn't. She simply watched as he stood before her, arranging his clothing, tucking in his shirt, readjusting his belt. He ran a hand through his hair and sent her a quick smile. She watched him leave the way he had watched Jean leave, until he faded behind a closed door. Some time later, she was being paged by the volunteer sitting in the I.C.U. room.

"Hannah Martindale — Hannah Martindale — phone call for Hannah Martindale."

Hannah walked nervously up to the desk where the volunteer sat. Her body was shaking uncontrollably. She was sure the call was about Grace, but why would they talk to her instead of the family?

"I'm Hannah Martindale."

The attendant held a warm smile and handed her the phone receiver. Hannah heard her own voice say, *hello.*

"Hannah," a deep voice spoke. "It's me, it's Paul. How are you, Hannah? How's Grace Padgett?"

"Paul?" she asked surprised. A momentary pause kept them from speaking, but then he did.

"I've been so worried about you, and of course, Grace. I'm not sure I should be calling you, but I had to know that you were holding up okay. I must say I was surprised when my receptionist told me you had left Blossom. Is Grace in I.C.U.? I didn't realize things were that serious. I understood she was having some tests."

"She had a heart attack this afternoon, Paul. I don't know anything else yet. Of course, you should be calling me. I'm glad you did."

"I was hoping you would be."

Paul's voice was strong and caring—a final link to her past. For an instant, she wished he were there by her side. "How have you been, Paul?"

"Me? Busy with work and the boys."

"How are they boys? And Sue?"

He got quiet and almost lost his composure. "Things haven't been well with Paul Jr., Hannah."

"I'm sorry. What's wrong?"

"Hannah, it's not something I want to talk about on the phone. I'd like to come see you, if that's all right. I have to make sure that you are really okay and...I could use a friend right now."

"Paul, I'm fine. I promise. Grace's family has been wonderful."

"I'm in Dallas, Hannah," he blurted out.

"Oh," her voice cracked. Paul's face filled her mind and she suddenly wanted him with her. "Of course, I want to see you. Maybe you could come to the hospital."

"I'd like that. Where have you been staying?"

"Mostly, I've been staying here, at the hospital."

She didn't offer more and he didn't ask.

"Oh, Hannah, I still can't believe you left Blossom. You must be, well, you must be getting stronger. I'm so anxious to see you. Maybe I can convince you to slip away for a few hours, for dinner or a drive."

"It all depends on Grace."

"Yes, yes, of course."

"I can't wait to see Sue, Paul. It's been so long."

"Sue couldn't come, Hannah, but she does send her prayers for Grace."

"Oh," Hannah said disappointed.

Paul's heart was in his stomach.

"So," he said, getting his thoughts together. "Let Grace's family know we're thinking of them, Sue and me. I'll call you tomorrow."

"Paul, let me give you a cell number to reach me. This way you won't have to go through the hospital."

"You have a cell? Since when?"

"It's a borrowed one. One of Grace's grandsons lent it to me."

Hannah gave him the number.

"Okay, well, I will definitely call. Good-night, Hannah. It was so good to hear your voice."

"You've been a good friend, Paul. I can always count on you."

"I care for you, Hannah."

More than you will ever know.

When Hannah hung up, her hands were shaking so uncontrollably, she ran to the nearest women's room to catch her breath. Paul's voice had sounded so wonderful, and yet, floods of emotions were surfacing within her—longing, excitement, regret, dread. She stared into the mirror and saw before her a tired, frightened woman. Paul could do to this to her, make her feel both wonderful and frightened. He was indeed, her last link to Sammy.

She was always afraid to break away from her past, but also reluctant to face it. When Paul was near, everything became too real again. Hannah dabbed some base across the dark circles under her eyes and then put on some eye shadow. She brushed over her cheeks with some blush and added gloss to her lips. Her hair was a fright. She ran a brush through it and tried as best as she could to make it look decent.

Her head was pounding and so she took some Tylenol. Taking in two deep breaths, she went back to the I.C.U. room. Her phone indicated she had a text from Elaine. She played around with the darn phone for a while before she figured out how to read the text. She said that the temporary help was working out and for her not to worry one bit about work. Hannah thought about calling her, when she saw Andy walk

142

back into the waiting room. Without saying a word, he took her by the arm and the two sat down.

"Anything from the doctors?"

She shook her head.

"Damn," he said. His face was pale and his hands were shaking. Hannah reached for them. They were like ice.

"Andy, she's a fighter, remember?"

"She has to be, Hannah. She just has to make it."

As they settled down for a long wait, Hannah told Andy about her phone call from Paul. He told her about his phone call to Liz.

"She wants to come home — to be with me."

"Of course, she does, Andy. She cares for you."

She saw him wince and he let out a deep breath.

"Oh, Hannah, I'm not looking forward to the conversation I'm going to have with her. I think the sooner I break off the engagement, the better things will be for everyone concerned."

"Andy, I've been thinking a lot about, Liz — Liz and you."

"What were you thinking, Hannah?"

"Maybe it's better if...I mean, think long and hard before you do something you'll regret."

He looked at her unbending. "Don't go there, Hannah. I've already done something I regret. I can't change everything, but I can do damage control."

He took her hand to his lips and kissed it. He knew the next few days would be difficult for her, concerning Nana and Liz. The walls she had built were so high, it would take a lot of reassurance to convince her that they would be good together. Swallowing hard, he closed his eyes and imagined them in his kitchen holding one another.

"You can't give up on us now, Hannah. You took my key."

They stared at one another, lost in an unpredictable tide, first low and then high. A tear fell down her face and landed on his hand. He didn't bother to wipe it off. She was crying for Grace, for Liz, for herself. She didn't know if she was strong enough to withstand the many scenarios that might come her way. What if Grace died and she was left to live in that big house in Blossom alone? What if Grace lived and she had to watch from a distance Andy and his new family? What if she and Andy allowed their feelings to be fulfilled? Could she actually live with the consequences? Worst of all, what if Andy came to regret his decision to stay with her and couldn't deal living with a woman so limited in life? Andy watched as the inner demons in her world were at war. He might have kissed her, but saw Charlie and Debbie moving toward him. Hannah and Andy both stared at him alarmed.

"We talked to the doctor, Andy. Nana's awake. She pulled through. Debbie and I just saw her. She's talking and complaining about everyone fussing over her because of a little heart attack. Ben and Careen are in there now."

Charlie and Andy hugged. Debbie reached to give Hannah a quick hug.

"Give Ben about ten minutes and then you two can go see her. She's in recovery room 6 here at I.C.U."

"What did the doctors say?" Hannah asked.

"Not much. They are monitoring her tonight, keeping her comfortable. Tomorrow, they want to meet with the family to discuss options."

"Did they operate tonight?" Andy asked.

"I'm not exactly sure what they did. I only know she's alive. Andy, Debbie and I are headed to the airport. I got a call from Dad earlier. His plane lands at DFW around midnight. Call me if anything changes with Nana."

"Dad's coming? This soon? God, it will be good to see him. Yea, Yea, I'll let you know if things change. I'm staying here tonight, Charlie — Hannah and me."

"There's a smaller, more private waiting area across the hall. It's got those nice recliners — better for sleeping. Debbie and I may be joining you."

When Charlie and Debbie left, Andy and Hannah made their way to the recovery room where Grace was. She was hooked up to monitors, oxygen and IVs. She wasn't exactly sleeping, but she was dazed. She did manage a smile when Andy kissed her hand. She looked over toward Hannah.

"I'm sorry I frightened you today, Little Bird," her weak voice barely managed.

"Just don't do it again," Hannah sniffed, trying desperately not to break down.

"We can't stay long, Sweetheart," Andy said. "We just wanted to see you. Get lots of rest. Do what the doctors tell you. We'll be right outside if you need us."

"I love you, Grace," Hannah managed to say.

Grace only nodded and closed her eyes. Andy clutched Hannah's hand.

"She looks so helpless," he barely got out.

Hannah led him away. Just outside the room, they fell into each other's arms. Neither one cried, but just stood there and held each other. After one more look at Grace, they made their way back to the waiting area. Andy looked around for Ben, but he wasn't anywhere to be found. He remembered Charlie telling him about the smaller waiting room, so they went to look for it. There, he found Ben and Careen, along with Jean and Frank. They were chatting to fill in the time. Andy gave Ben a hug and then Careen. He took Jean's hand and kissed her cheek softly. He barely acknowledged Frank. They made small talk and Hannah edged away from the group. Andy watched her from the corner of his eye as she found a recliner near the wall, where she sat down. Already she had settled in with a pillow and blanket. Sometime later, he moved toward her.

"I'm going to take Jean in to see Nana. Think you'll be all right?"

"I'm fine, Andy. Go."

He patted the chair next to her.

"Keep my bed warm, Hannah."

She watched him take Jean's hand and lead her to the door, brushing by Frank without as much as an excuse me. Vaguely she heard Ben and Frank talking. Careen was on her cell phone. The television was on, but no one was watching it. Her eyes were heavy and she felt herself drifting off. Sometime after that, someone had turned out the lights to the room and the only light left was that from the television. She thought she heard footsteps moving near and when she opened her eyes, Andy was sitting next to her. He was making his bed, when she spoke to him.

"Andy?"

"Yea," he said softly. "I was trying not to wake you."

"It's all right. How's Grace?"

"The same."

Hannah closed her eyes again, still groggy. Then, she felt an arm move around her waist. Andy, leaned in to kiss her. She did little to resist his touch. She felt his kiss move up her neck and down to where her blouse opened in the front. He gave her one more kiss before moving to his chair, where he covered himself, closing his eyes. Just before drifting off himself, he sent her a playful innuendo, causing her to smile.

"I hope you'll be able to control yourself sleeping next to me tonight."

THIRTEEN

When Hannah woke up the next morning, the small waiting room was empty and dark, with only a slightly opened blind to bring in the morning light. There were no signs of Andy or his brothers—or anyone. This brought her new anxiety about Grace. She looked at her watch and it was almost eight. She jumped up, eager to know how Grace was doing. Her fear mounted when she went to find Andy or one of his brothers in the waiting area across the hall. No one was there.

Dear God, she has to be okay!

She found a nearby restroom and tidied up as best as she could—brushing her teeth and refreshing her deodorant. When she pulled out her brush, her hair was so unruly, she decided to pull it up in a ponytail. After blotting some lip gloss and a few dabs of perfume, she knew she'd done all she could do to make herself presentable. She walked down the hall to the recovery room where Grace was. No one was there so she walked in and found Grace sleeping soundly. Hannah thought it was eerily silent and this added to her anxiety. When a nurse came in, Hannah questioned her.

"Did she have a good night?"

"She had a very good night considering everything. She's a fighter this one."

Hannah let out a heavy sigh of relief. "Did they operate on her already? She looks almost like she's in a coma."

"No, Ma'am. We're just monitoring her right now. She's sleeping a lot because we are medicating her and that's so she doesn't wear herself out fighting to live. Are you family? The doctors are having a meeting with the family this morning."

"When? Where?"

"It's in the conference room just down the hall. Dr. Fletcher and Dr. King are both here, so it may be going on right now. Would you like me to take you to see?"

"I, no, I think I'll just stay here with her. Are we still limited to our time?"

"Stay as long as you'd like. Things have been quiet around here. If it gets to be too much, I'll let you know."

When the nurse left, Hannah sat in a chair next to Grace's bed and watched her dear friend sleeping. It seemed that all she had been doing this past week was watch her sleep and wait for the doctors to tell her something. She was restless and anxious. This morning, her nerves were especially on edge. She guessed it was because things had been going so well and then this bombshell happened. She noticed Grace's feet were hanging out of the blanket and so she moved to redo it, tucking her feet in and rearranging the blanket to cover her completely. She was humming one of Grace's favorite hymns when she noticed a tall, distinguished man walk into the room. Upon his entering, she smiled, knowing his kind face anywhere. Within minutes, they were in each other's arms.

"I thought you might be here," he said.

She studied his warm smile, his kind blue eyes, and dark wavy hair slightly sprinkled with gray. As she looked at Andy's father, she couldn't help but to compare the two men. Both were much too handsome for their own good. So many memories of this man and his wife came to mind. John Padgett and his wife, Ann, along with Grace, had nurtured her both physically and emotionally back to life so many years ago.

"John," she embraced. "It's wonderful to see you."

"And you, Hannah. Just look at you. I can't believe my eyes."

"How long has it been, John?"

"Over two years. You look amazing, Hannah."

She smiled. "Thank you. It's day to day—you know. Is Ann with you?"

"No, she stayed behind to finalize the details of our mission. We decided to end our work in Bolivia early. We are moving back to Texas, so we can be close to Mom."

"Grace will love that. I'd like to hear more about your work in South America sometime, you know, when Grace is better. The last time you wrote, you were expecting a new teacher for the school in Cochabamba so that Ann could focus more on the new mothers there."

"We've actually recruited two."

"That's wonderful," she said turning to Grace. "John, the nurse said that you and the family were meeting this morning to discuss options with the doctors. How did it go?"

John pulled her aside. "Let's go to the waiting room and talk."

John explained to Hannah that Grace was scheduled to have an Angioplasty at two o'clock that afternoon. It was the less invasive procedure opted by the physicians—the other being open-heart surgery. Dr. King, the cardiologist who would be performing the procedure, told the family that he would most likely be placing stents inside of Grace to provide support in her arteries. These will keep the arteries open so that blood can flow more freely to the heart.

"I thought they already did something like this," Hannah commented in frustration.

John shook his head. "They didn't want to until it was necessary. While it's a common procedure, it's still quite risky, given Mom's condition and age."

"Five hours," she sighed. "We have to wait five hours until the procedure and who knows how long after that."

She was so tired of waiting. She was also hungry and needed a shower. She looked at John and wondered how long it had been since he slept. He had just traveled from one continent to another.

"John, you must be exhausted. When's the last time you slept?"

"I slept a little on the plane, but I have to admit it's all catching up with me."

"Why don't you try to get some sleep now? The chair I slept in last night wasn't too bad."

"I know," he smiled. "I slept next to you and Andy after I got to the hospital early this morning."

"You did? I didn't know. I must have been really out of it."

"Well, Andy tells me that you've been keeping a close vigil on Mom this week. He said that you've scarcely left her side."

What else has Andy told you?

Hannah looked around the waiting room. Just a few people were there. She was looking for Andy.

"Where is everyone? I mean, where's the rest of your family?"

"Ben and Charlie are in the cafeteria eating breakfast. Andy left to take care of some things at work and to pick up someone named Liz Brewster to take her to a doctor's appointment that she has this morning. It seems that I'm going to be a grandfather again."

He's with Liz.

Hannah caught John's eye. She was struggling with this recent news. He was looking at her for some kind of answer to this latest development in Andy's life. When she didn't say anything, he continued talking.

"Charlie tells me they are going to be married, although Andy didn't tell him or anyone else for that matter. Charlie said he learned about it from Liz. I guess in light of her pregnancy, marriage is the next logical step. Of course, in my days, we married first and then had the baby."

Hannah gave him a guarded smile. Everything was such a mess. She wondered what John would think when he found out about Andy and her. Or, did he already know? She was

150

suddenly overcome with guilt and shame. She had opened her heart to a man who clearly was at an emotionally crossroad. When she was away from Andy, she knew she had no business being in his life for anything other than a friend. Yet, when he was near, all rationale went out the window.

How did this ever happen?

"Hannah," John said interrupting her thoughts. "I have a suggestion. It's going to be a long day. We are both running on second wind as it is. Let's you and me go check in on Mom one more time. After that, what do you say we leave the hospital for a while and go to Andy's place? He told me you have a key. We can clean up and maybe get a little shuteye before Mom's procedure. I think we could both use the break. What do you say?"

She wanted to say *no* and stay in the comfort of the hospital that had become her safe haven away from home. She wanted to be near just in case Grace had another episode. Also, she didn't know if she could bear being at Andy's place again, remembering the promise of their show of affection there. Still, she was in desperate need of a shower and she was bone weary, so she agreed to go. All the while, her mind kept wandering back to Andy and Liz and the baby. Her heart felt threatened— a probable circumstance.

Andy is going to do the honorable thing and marry Liz. He will for the sake of the baby.

Already, she was rebuilding her walls.

Andy was in the waiting room sitting next to Liz, when John and Hannah arrived back at the hospital around one o'clock. He watched as his father led Hannah to sit across from them and next to Charlie and Debbie. Ben and Careen, along with their son, Tom, were sitting next to Liz and Andy. Tom moved to an empty seat next to John so that he could be close to a grandfather he hadn't seen in years. Tom was the only grandchild there. Andy decided not to bring his boys, since they were in school and they didn't handle waiting too well. Charlie and Debbie's only child, Nicolle, was away at college. Nine souls waited — patiently at times and impatiently at others for word from the doctors that would tell them of a mother, a grandmother, a great grandmother, a friend's fate.

Andy looked at Hannah, so outwardly poised and looking more beautiful than ever. She looked rested and refreshed. He was less put together, spent from sleeping a night at the hospital and then later, taking Liz to her doctor's appointment. It didn't appear that rest was in the cards for him today. Hannah was quiet, unwilling to look Andy in the eyes. Instead, she studied the interactions of the Padgett family. The gathering spoke in sporadic conversations.

Ben was telling Andy that he hired some boy from Blossom to mow Nana's yard. Andy suggested that he mow Hannah's, as well. Charlie and his dad were discussing Ann Padgett and all that she had to do to prepare to come home. It might be months before she actually did, but she wanted John to be here and so she didn't mind. Tom asked his grandfather about fishing. Debbie was asking Careen and Liz about a new Asian restaurant she had heard about in Dallas and wondered if either one had been there.

Hannah could see that Andy's heart was torn. He tried on several occasions to strike up a conversation with her, but she evaded his attempts, shaking her head emphatically as if to say that this wasn't the time or place. He knew she was right. He wanted to scream out, especially when Liz retold the details of her earlier appointment at the doctor's office and how Andy almost cried when he heard the baby's heartbeat. John, it seemed, was clearly taken by Liz's devotion to Andy and joy about the baby. He was patient with her as she told John how she and Andy met and how she had fallen head over hills in love with him on their first date. It was almost more than Andy could handle. He held his tongue, telling himself repeatedly that later, when the time was right, this deception would finally end.

Hannah stood up and walked aimlessly toward a window near the corner of the waiting room. Always protective of her, Andy gave little thought about following her and standing behind her. He rested his head slightly on the top of hers, with one hand on her shoulder and the other hand tucked inside a back pocket. Panic burned through Hannah and she knew that if she didn't get away from Andy, from his family, she would lose control. That was the last thing she wanted to do.

God, please maintain my dignity, please!

"Hannah," Andy apologized in her ear. "I'm sorry. I didn't know Liz would be here. I can only imagine how you must feel."

"Andy, don't talk, please, not now."

So, he didn't, but neither did he move back with the rest of the group or Liz. Instead, he remained with Hannah. His casual deportment seemed so natural it eluded the eyes of those around them. Even Liz, who had always been jealous of other women around Andy didn't question his actions. She knew Hannah had a difficult time in public and that Andy was her friend. Liz looked at Hannah as someone who needed taking care of and she never assumed there could be anything between him and her.

John Padgett on the other hand, had an unnerving instinct about their closeness that brought him concern. He shook it off almost immediately. After all, this was Hannah, a woman as close to family as anyone, one who cared for his mother daily and was bonded to her as no other person was. She was scared, worried, and so out of her realm of comfort. Andy would do the same for Debbie or Careen, if Charlie or Ben were not here. Besides, he and Liz were engaged and from all indications, they seemed a good match. He would be a father soon. Still, when he saw Andy brush the top of Hannah's head, his suspicions resurfaced. He vaguely wondered why no one else could see how familiar these two stood together.

Around four o'clock, Dr. King came out to talk to the family. He spoke directly to John as Andy, Charlie, and Ben listened from a distance. Hannah stood in the same corner alone and the others remained seated. Unexpectedly, Liz came up to Hannah and took her hand.

"She's going to be fine, Hannah. I've got a good feeling about this."

Hannah looked into her eyes. Her concern was so genuine, she had to turn away.

Don't be nice to me, Liz. I don't deserve your kindness.

"Thank you," was all she could say.

Liz was right. Grace had survived the procedure and was resting comfortably in the recovery room. The doctor said she would be able to go to her own room in a few hours. They had put three stents in where most of the blockage was. The family rejoiced as families do when good news like this comes their way. They were hugging, kissing, and laughing. Hannah was celebrating alone. She happened to catch Andy's eye and he lent her a smile so emotional, it almost broke her heart. She wanted him to take her in his arms and celebrate with him, but he remained reserved. Instead, Liz held his hand. Dr. King broke away from the group and happened to notice Hannah standing in the corner, looking tentative and needing reassurance. He moved toward her.

"Hannah?" Dr. King asked.

She looked at him as if she should know him, but couldn't quite place where. He helped her to recall.

"We met several days ago. My mother was having open-heart surgery. Your friend was having some tests done."

"Of course, I remember you. You're Grace's doctor?"

"Dr. Fletcher and I are associates. I did today's procedure for him. Hannah, your friend is doing wonderfully."

She took his hand without realizing it, squeezing it tightly.

"Thank you so much—for everything."

"You're so very welcome, Hannah."

"Dr. King, how is your mother? I pray that she's doing well."

"She's doing remarkable, Hannah, I'm pleased to say. You were right. She's a fighter. I anticipate that with two or three more days in the hospital, both my mother and Grace will be ready to go home."

"Dr. King, this is wonderful news. How can I, we, ever repay you?"

She wanted to hug him and almost did, but instead she gave him her brightest smile.   She was looking at his kind face. He was looking at her beautiful smile. He took off his surgical hat and she noted that he was a handsome man, probably around forty-five. He was close to crossing the line of professionalism, he knew, but she was so captivating, he found he couldn't help himself.

"Call me Alex, Hannah," he said. "Perhaps at another time, we can celebrate together."

His could have been a rhetorical remark, much like *keep in touch* or *let's get together*.   She had to guess it was. Before she could further interpret the value of his words, Alex King took her hand and led her to where Andy and his family were. He told the family that it would be best for them to wait to visit with Grace in her room instead of the recovery room. He suggested they take a couple of hours to eat something or get away for a while.

"Let the nurses and staff do their jobs and in a few hours Grace will be alert and feisty as ever."

He turned to Hannah, still holding her hand.

"Duty calls, I'm afraid."

In the corner of his eye, he could see Liz holding Andy's arm and leaning her head on it. He had guessed wrong that day in the waiting room. Hannah wasn't with this man. This made him smile even more. Reluctantly, he let go of Hannah, taking this moment to shake John's hand one more time.

"Thank you, Dr. King," John said. "Thanks for everything. I know this is routine for you, but it's not for us. You have no idea…"

"I do as a matter of fact," he commented. "Hannah can tell you."

He turned and gave Hannah one last smile and then he dashed off, leaving her blushing from the obvious attention he had given her. She looked at Andy. He was threatened by jealousy. Liz teased.

"Hannah, Dr. King was flirting with you big time."

"No," she stuttered. "He, he was just being friendly."

"You sure about that?" Andy shot out, halfway teasing, mostly serious.

She was so far removed from her comfort zone, she had no idea what to do or say next. This, in Andy's eyes, made her more beautiful than ever. She couldn't help but to stare into his eyes. He was smiling, but his smile suggested something like envy. He was envious of a doctor who had just saved his Nana's life, simply because he had gotten closer to Hannah today than he had. It was irrational, he knew, but he was just human enough to let it get to him. It also helped to reinforce what his heart was feeling. He didn't want to live his life without this woman in it.

His gaze pierced through her and she thought she might faint. Instead, she turned away from him and excused herself from the group. She walked out into the hall and found a nearby seat, where she sat to try to catch her breath. It wasn't working, so she went in search of a different waiting area, because the one across the hall was too close to Andy. She couldn't find one. Feeling her panic mount even more, she continued to walk aimlessly down the hallway until she found the elevators. Without thinking, she got on and hit the button for the bottom floor. There were half a dozen strangers standing next to her, but she didn't care. She had to get away. She needed air.

Just before the elevator door closed, she looked up and saw Andy. He was alone. Both relief at finding her and fear that she would send him away, covered his face. He got on quickly and stood next to her, where he inconspicuously took her hand. The two watched the door as it slowly closed. They were together again with a million emotions stirring in every direction. She thought she might choke on all that she was feeling. When the elevator door reached the first floor, Andy took her down a narrow hallway that led to some medical offices. At the end of the hallway was some kind of giant pot with a tree inside of it—a décor for the hospital. He backed her in the corner behind it. There, without thought or consequence, he kissed her. His kiss was intense and desperate, as if he might never kiss her again.

"Andy," she said. "We can't do this anymore."

He looked at her with his heart clearly written all over his face. She was never to forget this look, nor this time and place, because this was the moment, he declared just what she meant to him.

"Hannah," he whispered. "I love you."

"Love...," she barely said before he reached for her kiss again. He gripped her firmly against him and she could feel his heart pulsating against her. He was pressing his mouth over hers in such a way, her breath caught in her throat. He lifted her face so that she had no choice but to look at him.

"Say it, Hannah. Say that you love me, too."

"It doesn't matter if I love you or not, Andy. I'm not strong enough for this relationship. I'm not strong enough to come between a father and his child."

"Hannah, you wouldn't be doing that."

"Yes, I would be. This is wrong, Andy. You know it in your heart, too. That's why you're struggling so much with it. You belong with Liz—and the baby."

157

He let out a heavy sigh at the mention of Liz's name. Already, she had worked her charms on his father and family, making what he had to do more difficult. Now, one afternoon around Liz and Hannah was ready to throw in the towel.

"No Hannah, we aren't wrong. Marrying Liz just because of the baby is what is wrong."

"Andy, I can't cope with this, not now. My only focus is Grace. She's all I have the energy to deal with right now."

Andy let go of his hold on her. He stepped back and gave her a forceful statement.

"You win, Hannah. I'll leave you alone—for now. But Hannah, I can't pretend anymore. I can't pretend I'm in love with Liz, not for my family, not for her—not even for you. I'm sorry, but that's just how it is."

Hannah looked into his face. What she wanted to do—what her heart told her to do was to hold him and never let him go. What her sense of propriety told her was to back away from this relationship for the sake of what was right and decent. She didn't know what power allowed her to walk away from him, but she did. His eyes remained on her until she turned the corner and walked out of sight. He sat down in the middle of the floor and let his tears flow quietly down his face.

Hannah, we will be together. I don't know how or when, but some day we will be together.

Hannah took her time regaining her composure before going back to the waiting room where John Padgett and his family were. She made a detour at a restroom on the first floor, far away from the eyes of anyone who knew her. It was a small room, suitable for one person. She locked herself behind its protective four walls. Here, she was able to release the anxiety and pent up emotions of the afternoon. She ran the water in the sink wetting a paper towel and wiping it across her face, neck, and down her cleavage. A heavy pressure crushed so strongly against her chest, she felt her breath leave her. Had she not been through this so many times, she would have surely thought that she was having a heart attack. She knew she wasn't. However, her recent contest with Andy had taken such toll on her, she could almost feel herself blacking out.

She sat in the middle of the floor and let her back rest against the wall. Because she was so hot, she opened her blouse and unzipped her pants. She let the coldness from the tile floors seep through her until the darkness slowly began to drift away. As the spinning subsided, she began to think more clearly. How many times had she been on the verge of losing control? She thought of Andy. What would he think if he saw her now? He was better off with Liz, better off without her.

You think I'm beautiful, Andy. This isn't beautiful. I'm not the woman you think I am. This is the real me. I can't take you here, Andy. I won't take you here.

The thought of Andy brought on a sudden surge of sadness. Her heart ached for him to touch her again. She wanted to run back to him and tell him she was wrong, but her lack of courage kept her pinned against the wall. She let her heart feel the loss of a man who had shown her how to love again. She cried and cried until she could cry no more.

Then, another voice reeled in her head. It was the voice of conviction. This voice had taken her from near death to where she was today. It had comforted her in her darkest hours and loved her unconditionally when the world had so cruelly abandoned her. It was gentle and powerful at the same time. It was commanding her today. It was her voice.

Get up, Hannah. Get up and face your fears. Do you want to spend the rest of your life hiding behind doors? Do you want to spend the rest of your life alone? You are the woman Andy thinks you are — and so much more.

Hannah sat up slowly and adjusted her clothing. As she stood to face herself in the mirror, she felt empowered— something she hadn't felt in years. She looked at her reflection and instead of the usual dread, she smiled. She heard another distant voice.

Hannah, I love you.

Peace prevailed through her soul and she accepted this gift of love that God had given her, even knowing she could never see it fully realized. She looked completely beaten, lost, with bloodshot eyes, and smudged make-up, yet inside she knew she was at peace.

Andy, I love you, too – more than you'll ever know!

Hannah reached into her purse to find some lipstick or blush, anything to bring back color to her face. When she pulled out a handful of items, Andy's apartment key fell to the floor. She reached down to pick it up and held it close to her heart.

I sill have your key, Andy. This has to mean something, doesn't it?

FOURTEEN

The day that followed Grace's surgery was grueling for Hannah. On the up side, Grace was progressing nicely and getting stronger by the hour. No one was surprised. She had always been a fighter. On the down side, Hannah hadn't been near Andy since the last time he had kissed her. She spent most of her time with Grace and John, trying to avoid Andy as much as possible. He was of the same mindset. He went to work, visited Nana, and slept wherever and whenever the opportunity arose. Last night, he slept on the couch in his apartment, letting his father have his room. Hannah insisted on sleeping at the hospital with Grace, mainly to be with her, but also to avoid any contact with Andy. Several times, John and Grace tried to convince her to sleep at the apartment to get a good night's rest. She told them that she got plenty of rest at the hospital and that it was just a temporary arrangement.

"Don't bother arguing with her," Andy finally told his father. "She doesn't listen to me and she won't listen to you."

The distance they had placed between one another was having an ill effect on their dispositions. Hannah withdrew and rarely talked to anyone, except for Grace and sometimes John. She missed her time with Andy. So much, she longed to talk to him or just to have him sit by her side. She wanted to reclaim their friendship, but knew that she was too emotionally invested to let it remain a friendship. She also knew that at least for today, he was still with Liz. She heard some tidbits about her and Andy from Debbie and later, Jean, who came to visit that morning. Before she had time to feel too sorry for herself, she heard footsteps come in the room. Her heart stopped. She knew any minute that Andy or Liz might walk through that door — or both. Thankfully, it wasn't either one of them. It was a nurse's aide, who had come to give Grace a bath.

While Grace was bathing, Hannah excused herself and walked down the hall to the nearby waiting area. When she came into the room, Andy was sitting next to John. She thought about turning around and leaving, but John saw her and waved for her to sit next to them. Slowly, she edged closer, knowing this moment had been a certainty. Even so, she wasn't prepared for how her heart felt when she saw Andy. It was racing so fast, she knew it had to be showing. She sat next to John. Andy sat across from them.

Andy knew he would be seeing her at the hospital today and he had psyched himself that he was going to keep his promise to her. Come hell or high water, he was going to keep his hands off her. He rationalized that with his father so near, he could trust himself around her. Andy looked into her brown eyes, red from lack of sleep and most likely worry because of him. She was in disarray from sleeping in her clothes and he thought to rib her about it to break the ice between them. Then, he changed his mind and simply acknowledged her presence.

"Hannah," he said detached.

She lent him a weak smile, "Hi, Andy."

"Hannah," John interceded. "We were discussing Mom's care when she leaves the hospital. Andy thinks she should stay at his place for a few days when she gets out or maybe longer. He thinks the long drive to Blossom may be too much for her right now."

She looked at Andy staggered. Did he also expect her to stay at his apartment? Worse yet, would he send her back to Blossom and not allow her to stay? She turned back to face John.

"I don't know, John. What do the doctors say?"

"Nothing yet. We are just speculating. I think Andy has a valid point though. Don't you? Both Ben and Charlie live almost as far as Blossom, so Andy's place is the most logical one if traveling is too difficult."

"Of course," she said shaking. "I, I want what is best for Grace. I was just hoping…"

"What?" John asked.

"Well, I was just hoping that I could help you…you and the family, take care of Grace when she gets out of the hospital."

"We're counting on you, aren't we Andy?" John said. "Hannah, you've been such a gift to Mom, to all of us. We would be honored for you to help care for Mom. Who else could do the job as well? I must warn you, though. It will be more like me helping you take care of Mom."

She looked at Andy. "I don't want to impose."

He spoke to her directly. "Hannah, you could never be an imposition."

She couldn't bear the distance between them any longer. She let her emotions fill the gap.

"Andy," she spoke softly. "I'm so sorry. I…"

Andy looked at the anguish on her face. He didn't mean to make her cry. His heart broke at the sight of her vulnerability. Her eyes spoke volumes. They said *I love you. I miss you. I'm dying without you.* Had John not been there, she would have broken her reserve and he would have broken his promise. Instead, he only touched her long enough to still her hands, smiling warmly. Then he looked at his dad.

"Looks like this matter is settled."

Paul Renfroe showered, shaved, and dressed in new trendy clothes. When he finished dressing, he phoned Sue in Blossom. She was compliant, but still upset with him for the reason he had gone to Dallas. Their son needs love and understanding, not some cold rehabilitation center. Her anger soon turned to regret when she heard Paul's voice telling her about the center he had visited earlier that day. She should be with him, if for no other reason than to support his choice. After all, he wasn't exactly putting Paul Jr. in rehab, he was just checking out options.

"Paul," she said and then paused.

"What is it, Sue?"

"I love you. You know this, don't you? Even though I don't agree with you, I love you."

"I know," he said truthfully. "I love you, too."

Then, he reassured her.

"I only inquired about the place, Sue. I have my reservations, too. We can talk about it when I get home tomorrow."

"I missed…miss you."

"I miss you, Sue. Whatever we do to help Paul Jr., I promise, we will do together. We're a team. We always have been."

He could hear her sobbing on the phone.

"Sue, don't cry. We've brought him up strong. He will be all right."

"I know. I just miss you, that's all. I don't like arguing with you. Please promise you'll hurry home."

"Honey, I'll be home tomorrow," he promised. On a happier note, he brought up Hannah. "Hey, I do have some good news. I'm having dinner with Hannah tonight. I was beginning to think I was going to leave Dallas without seeing her. She wasn't answering my calls and her cell phone kept going to voice mail. I finally got in touch with her again at the hospital. It seems as though she had lost the charger to her phone and it wasn't charged. She's new at this cell phone business."

"Dinner? My goodness, she is doing better. I can hardly believe…I mean, I don't believe it. This is wonderful, Paul."

"I know, Sue. This could mean we're getting our Hannah back."

Suddenly, Sue wished she were with Paul, feeling nostalgic about her lost friend. It would be so good to see Hannah—and know first hand that she was getting better.

"So you haven't actually seen her yet?" she asked Paul.

"No, I haven't, but the few times that I've talked to her, she sounds good, Sue. She sounds strong."

"Paul, please tell her that I wish I could see her. Tell her that she still means the world to me."

"She knows, Sue, but I'll tell her anyway."

Paul thought of Paul Jr. and how he had been affected by Hannah's tragedy. Hannah was getting well and so there was hope for Paul Jr. Paul checked his watch. It was almost seven. Dinner reservations were for seven-thirty. It wasn't actually Hannah who had extended the dinner invitation to him, but John Padgett. When he had talked to Hannah earlier, he invited her to dinner. She said that she already had plans with Grace's family. They were celebrating Grace's recovery and the fact that she would be leaving the hospital soon. John told her to call Paul back and invite him to join them. Of course, wanting to see Hannah, he jumped at the opportunity.

"Paul, call me when you get back from dinner. I want to hear everything about Hannah."

"Of course, I will."

"Paul," she said hesitant to let him go.

"Yea, Sue?"

"Nothing, have a good time. I love you."

"I love you, too."

When he hung up the phone, Sue sat down at her kitchen table. A flood of memories poured over in her mind and heart—memories of a friendship that she thought had faded into obscurity. She had let Hannah go years ago because it was too painful to be her friend. Now, it seems she had been given a second chance to redeem this relationship. An old fear resurfaced in the pit of her stomach—one she had also buried into obscurity. With Hannah getting well, it took on a fresh new meaning.

Hannah, I know Paul harbors feelings for you. What I don't know is if you feel the same towards him.

Liz dressed in about five outfits before she decided on the one to wear. It was a new style in tunics—long and loosely fitted. She was running late and thankfully, she had already warned Andy she might be late and to go ahead and order for her, especially since she was picking up the boys on her way to dinner. Everything in her closet was getting too tight to look decent. Soon, she would need to buy maternity clothes. She studied her tummy in the mirror, moving her hands over it gently. Her life would be perfect if only...if only her baby was Andy's.

She was grateful yesterday that Andy's mind had been preoccupied with thoughts of the boys moving to Austin and Nana's procedure. At her doctor's appointment, Dr. Minton congratulated them both on a healthy baby. He said everything was normal and on target for a growing, healthy baby just slightly over fourteen weeks. He had said it so nonchalantly that Andy never questioned the baby's timeline. Why should he? Already the deception was grating on her conscious. It didn't help that she had two text messages from Doug Chasey for her to call him.

Leave me alone. I thought I convinced you at our last meeting that you weren't the father. What do you want from me?

She thought of Andy and how much she loved him. This love would have to sustain her during these dark moments. Once they were married, she had convinced herself, she would calm down. She knew Andy was prolonging the wedding until his mother was in the states. But, that could be as long as two months, John had told her. She couldn't wait two months. She would have to persuade Andy into an earlier wedding. Just then, she got a third text from Doug.

Call me. We really need to talk.
Frustrated, she sent him a text back.
Leave me alone!

Hannah sat on the passenger side of Andy's truck on the way to the restaurant, a family steakhouse that everyone had agreed on earlier. Few words were spoken and even fewer glances were given. They were alone, but not by their own suggestion, but John's. He drove his rental so he could swing by the hospital one last time before dinner. Andy and John decided to take two vehicles because of Hannah. If she and Andy had gone with John, Hannah would begin making her excuses not to go to the restaurant and why she should stay at the hospital. As it was, it had taken both Andy, John, and Grace to convince her earlier this afternoon. The decisive factor was Paul Renfroe. Hannah had invited him to join them for dinner and she knew she had to go because of him.

As they rode, Andy did manage to slip in a few momentary looks at her. He couldn't help himself. She was wearing the only dress she had brought with her, a white summer shift, fitted and chic. The front on it was embroidered and it had a studded border. Only someone with a figure like Hannah's could pull off such a look. It was classic, just like her. With every move she made, the dress rode up, displaying the line of her long legs. It took every ounce of self-control Andy possessed not to stop the truck and take her in his arms.

No one should look this damn good!

Andy and Hannah were the first to arrive. The host led them to a large table near the back of the restaurant. They sat quietly next to each other, with a chair beside her for Paul and one beside Andy for Liz. Hannah was jittery for a sundry of reasons—Paul, Liz, being so near Andy. Without thinking she took his hand. He rationalized this wasn't breaking his promise since she initiated the move. Just this once, they dared to look into each other's eyes. They were lost. He squeezed her hand. It was shaking uncontrollably.

"Don't be nervous, Hannah. I'm here."

She let out a short laugh. "You're the main reason I'm so nervous."

He smiled. "No need to be. I promised to be good and I will be. By the way," he paused. "You look ravishing."

She knew she was blushing. Her face was hot from his compliment, but more so by the undertones in his voice. What she didn't know was that his heart was jumping all over the place. Keeping a promise had never been so difficult. He reached for a menu and pretended he was reading it, all the while focusing on Hannah.

"Tonight, after dinner, I'm breaking off the engagement."

His words were a whisper, but she was certain the whole world had heard. Before, she could contemplate what he had just disclosed to her, she saw Paul Renfroe moving toward her. Hannah looked at Paul and then at Andy as if to gain confidence. As he got nearer, Hannah tired to stand, but couldn't. She looked at Andy anxiously.

"Help me up," she said softly.

Andy guided her up and she stood within inches of Paul's smiling face. Paul reached to shake Andy's hand first.

"Hello," Paul said. "I know you must be John's son. The family resemblance is obvious."

Andy nodded. "Andy Padgett."

"Paul Renfroe."

Paul turned to Hannah. She looked into his face and years of friendship and a heart full of love for this man shrouded her. Time stood still and she was lost in a surge of memories. She couldn't help but fall into his arms, where she remained for some time. Then, Hannah did a remarkable thing. She kissed Paul fully on the lips.

"Paul," she cried. "I've missed you so much."

"Hannah," he soothed. "I've missed you."

Her legs gave way and she sat down again. Paul sat next to her. Andy, feeling a bit like the fifth wheel excused himself, but she was quick to grab his hand.

"Stay, Andy, Please."

Andy cleared his throat. "Okay."

A lull fell between the three before Paul spoke

"Hannah, I'm so glad you called me back and invited me here tonight."

"Paul," she said. "You have no idea how good it is to see you."

"I might," he smiled. "Hannah, you look beautiful."

Andy breathed a little easier, when he saw his father walk in with Charlie and Ben. Paul and John made their exchanges and John introduced Paul to Charlie and Ben. All the while, Hannah held tight to Andy's hand. John sat at the head of a long table, next to Paul. Charlie and Ben sat on the opposite side of the others.

"The girls are ten minutes away," Charlie informed them. "They said to go ahead and order if we want to."

"Let's just get drinks," John suggested. "By the way boys, tonight is my treat. You too, Hannah and Paul. No arguing."

Andy watched Paul through the corner of his eye. He had his arm on the back of Hannah's chair and his fingers were nestled slightly within her hair. His hand remained there as they discussed Paul's family, Blossom, and other topics exclusive to the two of them. His constant fawning and pawing all over Hannah was annoying to say the least. Andy wasn't jealous, as he had been with the doctor yesterday. This was more of a curiosity. He was curious as to what he wanted with Hannah after all this time. From what Hannah told him, they hadn't seen each other in ages. Why did he want to see her now? Why here in Dallas? Why not in Blossom?

"Hannah tells me that you've been friends for a long time," Andy cut in their conversation.

Paul nodded. "We've been friends for years. How many, Hannah? Sixteen? Seventeen?"

Hannah smiled, "Almost eighteen."

"Eighteen!" Paul pretended surprise, even though he remembered the exact day, the exact hour he first met her.

Andy let out a quick whistle. "That's a long time. It seems like Nana has mentioned your name a time or two."

"I live a few blocks from Grace and Hannah. I know your grandmother well—just as I do your parents."

"Well, glad you were able to join us tonight. I think you made Hannah happy."

She looked at Paul. "He's right. It's good to see you. I just wish Sue could be here, too."

"Oh," Andy said, raising a brow. "You're married? Hannah didn't mention that."

"Yes. My wife's name is Sue. We have two sons, Paul Jr. and Benny."

"I have three sons," he said making small talk. The more he chatted with this Paul character, the less time he could spend talking to Hannah. Even as they talked, Paul couldn't keep his hands off her. He knew that Hannah was unnerved, because the more he twisted her hair the more she twisted his hand. The fact that they had this long history did tug at Andy a bit. His speculations about Paul were interrupted when Debbie, Careen, and Tom arrived. Andy looked at his watch.

Where's Liz?

He dreaded what he had to tell her, but also wanted to get it over with as soon as possible. Just when he thought she'd never get there, she did, along with two of his boys. She was dressed in such a way, her condition was clearly accentuated. She moved about the table, beginning with John, kissed, and hugged everyone present, even Paul. When she sat down next to Andy, Hannah finally let go of his hand. Andy was sure he would choke on the entire situation. Resentment set in and he

170

knew he shouldn't blame her, but he did. It was clear that his father had already accepted her as part of the family.

Mathew and Jeff both ran up to their grandfather, hugging them and giving him high fives. Mathew sat across from Paul, next to his grandfather, while Jeff plopped down in Andy's lap.

"Where's Bobby?" Andy asked Liz.

"He was asleep and Jean said that he hadn't been feeling well today. She knew you would understand."

"Bobby's sick?"

"Just a little, Honey. Jean thinks he got too much sun."

"She could have called me."

"Andy, he's sunburned and tired. It's nothing. Is this how you're going to be with our baby? Overbearing and overprotective?"

"I just want to know how my kids are doing, that's all."

"A father has a right to know," John agreed.

"Says one great father to another," Liz boasted.

John gave Liz the thumbs up sign. Andy noted the bond already forming between Liz and his father.

How am I going to look my father in the eyes tomorrow when he finds out I've broken it off with Liz.

He let out a breath of condemnation. Hannah couldn't help herself. She touched Andy on the leg gently. He put his hand over hers, drawing strength from her.

"Andy," she said calmly. "Why don't you go see Bobby after dinner? It will make you feel better."

"That's a great idea, Hannah. I think I'll do just that."

As the waiter took the last of the dessert plates, Andy had just about had enough of this night. He could only imagine how Hannah was feeling. Outwardly, she appeared strong, but he knew better. How could she be okay? All night, everything that came out of Liz's mouth was in some way connected to the baby—and all night Paul kept pawing and hovering over her as if she was some sort of pet. He had a thing for her. Anyone with eyes could see it.

"I know I'm babbling," Liz apologized to the gathering. "But, this baby means everything to Andy and me. Andy's been so wonderful."

Liz squeezed Andy's hand and gave him a quick peck on the cheek.

"Eventually, we'd like to be married in the church, but as you can see that's really impossible right now. Some things can't be put off. Did Andy tell you that I'm Catholic, as well?"

Andy balled his fists. He watched Liz with utter amazement. He could feel his temper begin to flare.

Where is all of this coming from? What are you trying to prove, Liz? You've already won them over.

Inside, Liz was battling her own demons. She was desperate, grasping onto this moment wondering if after talking with Doug, this might be her last night with Andy. She knew she was being a chump, but she seemed to have little control over her actions.

"Andy wants a girl. A girl would be wonderful, but confidentially, I want a boy. I want a boy just as sweet and kind as his father."

Andy felt as though his head was on fire. He knew he had to get out of here before he said something he would regret. He looked at his boys. They would be his way out. Then he looked at Hannah. He couldn't leave her here with his family—and certainly not with Renfroe. He happened to look over and he saw Paul moving his hand up and down Hannah's arm. Andy doubted if had touched his wife as much throughout his entire marriage as he had touched Hannah tonight.

Andy stood up to excuse himself. "I need to run out to the truck for something. Be back in a minute."

When he left, Liz confided in John. "Andy isn't himself tonight. He's so quiet and withdrawn. He's usually more excited about the baby."

"He's been through a lot this week with his grandmother," John offered. "He loves her very much."

Hannah thought of Grace lying alone in the hospital while they were eating and drinking and celebrating. It wasn't fair. Hannah looked at Liz, who was now discussing Andy's fatigue with Debbie. She wondered where Andy was going to find the strength to end his relationship with her. She wondered if he really should. Her thoughts were interrupted when she felt Paul's strong hand press over hers.

"Everything all right, Hannah?"

"I'm fine, Paul, just tired. I was thinking of Grace. She's still so weak, so…"

As if sensing she needed him, John Padgett got up and sat down in the chair where Andy had been sitting. He took Hannah's hand. Without reservations, she leaned her head on his chest for comfort. The strain of the day had caught up with her. She drew comfort in John's hold. Minutes later, she raised her head and smiled. She knew she would be all right.

"Thank you, John. I guess I'm more tired than I realized."

"We all are. I was thinking of dropping by the hospital for a little while and checking up on Mom. I'll let you tag along if you promise to leave with me and get a good night's sleep at the apartment."

She nodded. "I promise."

"I could take her," Paul offered.

"No need," John said. "But thank you."

Paul was feeling disappointed, left out, knowing that Hannah was far more connected to this family than with him. It hadn't always been that way. He was also a bit let down because he knew his time with her tonight was nearing an end. John stood to go back to his seat just as Andy returned. He looked into his son's face, grimacing with pain.

"A headache?"

"Splitting."

"How about we wrap this night up and all get a good night's sleep?"

"Okay by me," Andy said relieved. Liz stood and took hold of Andy's arm.

"Andy, your father and Hannah want to go back to the hospital for a while. How about I take the boys to Jean? You can go on home and try to get rid of your headache."

"Actually Liz, I want to see Bobby, just to know he's all right. I'll take the boys. You go on home. If it's ok with you, I'd like to come by your place for a while. There's something I want to talk to you about."

As everyone was leaving, Paul asked Hannah for a few private moments. She walked with him to his car. When they reached the driver's side, he took both of her hands in his.

"Hannah, I don't want to let you out of my life now that I have you back in it."

"Paul, you've never been completely out of my life, not really."

"You know what I mean, Hannah. I know Sue feels the same way."

"I know. Please forgive me for avoiding you. It was just too painful. It was easier to let everything and everyone go so that I didn't have constant reminders of what I had lost. I hope you understand."

"I do understand, but now that you're healing…well, now we can move forward."

"Paul, it never goes away. It's just more manageable at times."

"It's the same with me, Hannah. Sammy was like a brother."

"Paul," she choked. "Not tonight, please."

"All right, but I plan on calling you when you get back to Blossom. Maybe the three of us, you, Sue, and me, can get together — maybe dinner or just to hang out at home."

174

"I think I'd like that. Just don't expect too much. Tonight was almost too much for me."

"We'll take it in increments, but I won't allow you to be isolated again."

"I need to go now, Paul. John's waiting. But, please, do call me."

He moved her closer to him. Surprisingly, she did little to resist when he leaned in to kiss her. He held the kiss perhaps longer than he should have, but he didn't want to let her go. She was more beautiful than he ever remembered. His heart was already feeling the weight of his desire for her. One thing he knew. Now that they had rekindled their relationship, he wasn't about to let her hide behind four walls ever again.

Andy got to his apartment around midnight. His father and Hannah were already asleep. His father was sleeping in his bed and Hannah had taken the boys' room. He stood in the doorway and watched her sleep. She was lying on her back, with her arms over her head. Her long hair fanned across the pillow and he could hear her slight breathing.

So beautiful. So vulnerable.

A rush of desire flowed through him. He knew he had fallen way too fast and at the worst possible juncture in his life. This didn't change the fact that he wanted to be near this woman forever. Even with the situation he now faced with Liz and the arguments his father would be giving him about postponing the marriage, he couldn't contain the joy he was feeling. It was so damn incredible. He was a man who swore he would never love again, yet here he was — head over heels. God, he loved this feeling — loved her.

He and Liz had talked tonight. They didn't exactly throw out the idea of marriage, but they postponed it — for now. Liz told him that she knew something had been troubling him. She knew he was overwhelmed with the happenings in his life — his Nana being sick, Jean taking the boys to Austin, and Jean's recent marriage to Frank. Liz told him that she thought he still loved Jean and that this was really at the heart of his decision not to get married now. Andy tried to convince her otherwise, but she only heard what she wanted to hear. Even when he was leaving, she was still holding onto hope. She kissed him at the door with tears trailing down her face. Her parting words still pierced at his conscience

We belong together, Andy. I love you enough for the both of us.

Andy took one more glance at Hannah before making his way to the living room to make his bed on the couch. The weight of his situation overpowered him. He fell to his knees and buried his head within his pillow. He wanted to be a good man. He wanted to do the right thing. Did this mean he had to give up Hannah and a chance to love again? Andy knew how rare this kind of love was. He thought of his three boys and how much he loved them. He thought of his unborn child. He wanted to be the kind of father they could honor and respect — like his father.

God, this is too much! I can't do this alone! Help me to be a righteous man.

A certain peace prevailed in this moment of submission. He wasn't alone. Someone had been guiding his footsteps all along. Andy had only to believe. He began to pray.

Our Father Who art in Heaven…

FIFTEEN

Andy jumped up from a dead sleep when he heard a loud knock at his front door. It was a local florist delivery for a Ms. Hannah Martindale—a dozen pink roses. He signed for the flowers and lagged toward the kitchen, where he put them on the table. They were from Paul Renfroe. Andy let out a grunt of disapproval. *He's probably letting her know for the hundredth time how wonderful it was to see her last night and how beautiful she was—blah blah blah.*

What a chump!

As he was making coffee, he happened to notice that it was almost ten o'clock. He hadn't slept this long in years. The way he felt, he could probably sleep that much longer. Instead, he dragged himself down the hallway to the bathroom and realized that his father and Hannah had already left. He laughed to himself. He never heard a thing this morning. He also noticed that Hannah had left her cell phone charging on the dresser in the boys' room. He shook his head.

What am I going to do with you, Sweetheart?

He smiled thinking of her. She was too sweet and delicious to be real. He wanted to be alone with her. They needed to talk. It would have to be later. He only had two hours until he had to be at work. He couldn't let himself indulge in thoughts of her for too long. As it was, he was going to have to rush in order to swing by the hospital to see Nana for a few minutes— and Hannah. He could smell the coffee brewing as he jumped into the shower. There was nothing like a shower and coffee to get a tired body moving. As he was drying off, he heard Hannah's cell phone ring, most likely Hannah telling him to bring it when he came to the hospital. He dressed and before he would forget, he grabbed her phone and slipped it into his pocket. It rang again, so he answered it.

"You've got to take your phone with you, beautiful lady, or how else can I get a hold of you?"

"I don't know, but I'm sure we can figure out some way," a brassy voice on the other end of the line said.

Andy stuttered. "I'm sorry. I thought you were someone else."

"Who? Hannah?"

"Who is this?" Andy asked curious.

"I'm Elaine Greene. Hannah's boss, I guess you could say."

Elaine Greene was a brassy, loud-mouthed, and often opinionated woman, who cared little about people who didn't like her or found her character just a little too out there to be the center of an established law firm. She was however, the heart of the Campton Brothers' firm and had been from the time she started working there over fifteen years earlier. She had short, bleach blonde hair that was styled with a spiked flair. Her dress was bold, sixtyish and her make-up extreme. She cut no corners when it came to the outlandish way she dressed.

Yet the firm Elaine managed, the one she affectionately called her firm, was run with the utmost efficiency and competence. She was completely devoted to those she worked with, from her top-notch bosses to the maintenance crew hired to retain the upkeep of the building. She never forgot a birthday or an anniversary, or any other monumental celebration that might come up in an employee's life, especially the life of an employee who happened to be her best friend since middle school. That's why she was calling Hannah. Today was her birthday.

"I'm sorry, Ms. Greene, Hannah's not here."

Elaine let out a rowdy cackle. "Please, call me Elaine. Ms. Greene is a bit too formal for my blood."

"Well, Elaine," Andy repeated. "She's at the hospital visiting my grandmother. She's not real good at keeping up with her phone."

"You must be Andy."

Andy was a bit taken back that she knew who he was. Then he realized that Hannah had probably discussed him with Elaine, the same as she had talked to him about Elaine.

"So Hannah told you about me, huh? I hope good things."

"She might have mentioned you, on an occasion or two," Elaine teased. "And yes, definitely it was all good."

Andy smiled. On a more serious note, Elaine asked Andy about Hannah.

"How's our girl doing? Really? I mean, I can't believe she just jumped right out there and went to Dallas with you. You must have something I don't have, 'cause I've been trying to get her out of that house for years."

"I do. It's my secret weapon. I have my Nana. Nothing but my grandmother could have pried her away."

Elaine let out a genuine laugh. "She does love her Grace. How's Grace doing Andy?"

"She's good and getting stronger each day."

"That's wonderful."

Andy looked at the clock. He didn't want to be rude, but if he didn't leave soon, he was going to be late.

"You want me to tell her that you called, Elaine?"

"Give her the message," she said. "And tell her Happy Birthday. I wanted to catch her before I left the office, since I'll be out all afternoon. You can have her call me this evening if you wouldn't mind."

So, today is Hannah's birthday.

"Sure Elaine, I'll do that."

"Oh, by the way, Andy, were flowers delivered to your house for Hannah from a man named Paul Renfroe? I swear he's called me twice asking me to find out from Hannah if they got to the right apartment. Lord."

"They were delivered," Andy said annoyed by the fact.

"He told me that he had dinner with Hannah and your family."

"Yep, he had dinner with us. What's with this guy, anyway? He had his hands all over Hannah."

Again, Elaine laughed aloud. "Oh, he's been sniffin' around Hannah ever since she married Sammy. You'd think he would have gotten the message by now."

I guess I'm not the only one who thinks this Renfroe character likes Hannah a little bit more than a friend should.

"Andy, I'm having a hard time wrapping my head around the fact that our Hannah actually went to a public restaurant. This is amazing."

"Well, Hannah's pretty amazing, Elaine."

"Oh, you don't have to tell me. I'm hoping this trip to Dallas will be a catalyst for things to come."

"That's my hope, too. She means a lot to me—to my family."

"Hannah's a special one, that's for sure. I love her like a sister—even more. She's been through a lot. I wouldn't want her to get hurt any more than she's already been. You know, by something or someone."

"Okay, "Andy said unsure of where this was going. "I wouldn't want that either."

"Good," Elaine said satisfied that she had gotten her point across to him.

"Listen Elaine, I really need to scoot. I have to get to the hospital and then go to work. I'll be sure and let Hannah know you called."

"I'd appreciate it. Oh, Andy, just one more thing before we hang up."

"What is it?" he said losing his patience.

"Are you as sexy in person as you sound on the phone? I'm not interested, mind you. I'm happily married to a middle-aged stud. It's just that my best friend has been spending a lot of time with you."

What do you think you know, Elaine?

"I'll tell you what, Elaine," he said matching her wit. "I don't think I'm qualified to answer that question. Why don't you ask Hannah? I'd be curious to know what she tells you."

It was close to noon when Andy arrived at work. He usually didn't come in on Mondays, but he was making up some hours that he had missed due to Nana's illness. He never made it to the hospital but did talk to Nana on the phone. She was cheery and this lifted his spirits. He told her that he might be able to swing by after work around four-thirty or five. He called his Dad's cell to talk to Hannah, but no one answered. He left a message and headed out to work.

When he got there, he went directly to the back and walked into his tiny, cramped office. He'd come to know it as his *home away from home.* Cramped as it was, he felt energized by the sight of it. It had been his constant haven over the past fifteen years. Work had been his therapy after his divorce. Behind his work desk and on the floor of the store, he was transformed. At work, he wasn't a screw-up, but someone who could be relied upon, someone who knew the store's business probably better than anyone who worked there. Andy knew and understood the people who worked under him, and they had the deepest respect for him. He was their favorite boss and workers were always fighting to work on his shift. He knew his customers, too — most by name and if not, by face. When Andy ran the store, things came alive, things happened. He was the only assistant manager who didn't have a college degree. He had gotten his position by sheer determination and hard work. At least this was Andy before his divorce.

For these reasons and because Andy was completely loyal to the store, Joe Broughton, the manager and Andy's closest confidant, had overlooked his many shortcomings this past year.

No one knew better than Joe did just what Andy had been through with his divorce. Joe knew what family meant to Andy. He knew that Andy had been as faithful to Jean as he had been to the store. Yet, his work habits had deteriorated this past year. Andy had let his personal life affect his work in such a way that Joe had no choice but to take some sort of action.

The past year, Andy had been late for work at least once a week, maybe more. He had broken company policies continuously, such as making too many personal calls and taking too many extended lunches. Others had to cover for him while he ran down the street to run some sort of errand, only to be gone for hours. When Andy brought his boys to work because he couldn't find a sitter, they ran around unsupervised. Girls contacted him at work by phone and some even came by to see him. More times than not, Andy was hung over when he came into work. Now, Andy had been missing a lot of work because of his grandmother. Ordinarily, this would be a legitimate excuse, but given Andy's track record this past year, this was just another check to add to Andy's already mounting list of misdeeds.

Joe popped his head into Andy's office. "Hey, how's it going? How's Grace?"

Andy smiled. "I think she's going to make it. She's good."

Joe shut the door behind him and moved inside Andy's small office. "I'm glad."

Andy noted his serious tone and a rush of something like dread came over him.

"Andy," Joe said. "We need to talk."

"I figured this was coming. Look, I know. I've been pissing off my job for a while now, but I'm finally getting my life on track. Things are starting to fall into place."

"I hope so," Joe said earnestly. "I really do, but I have to make this official."

Andy looked at him feeling somewhat betrayed. "You're documenting it? Can't you consider this a warning?"

"I'm sorry, Andy. You've dismissed all of my warnings. If I had another choice…"

"You do."

"No, Andy. You've backed me into a corner."

"I see," Andy said confrontational. "What's it going to be? Probation? Termination?"

Joe looked into his eyes.

God, I hate this.

"You know that I'm not firing you, Andy. I'm not even giving you probation. I have an alternative."

"An alternative?" he asked skeptical.

"A leave of absence."

Andy let out a disgruntled laugh. "What's the difference?"

"The difference is your slate is clean and when you are ready to come back to work, you will…"

"What, Joe, have a job waiting for me?"

Joe nodded. "Well, yes."

"We both know that's bullshit, Joe. How many times have I read an employee this same line of crap?"

"Andy, you're like a brother to me. You're godfather to my son. You're my best friend. Do you really think I'd jack you around? I'd give my life for you. It's not what you think, Andy. I can give you three months pay. Maybe by then…"

"What?" Andy asked bitter. "I can get on welfare? File bankruptcy? I'm barely making ends meet now and you know it."

Joe held his hands up. "I was going to say that maybe in three months your life will be more stable."

"Right and my slate will be clean. Sure, Joe, whatever you say. So, tell me, when does this official leave begin?"

Joe lowered his head. "Today. You can store your things in my office if you don't want to take them home. They'll be waiting there for you when you come back to work."

"Thanks, but no thanks, Joe. I believe I'll take my clutter with me."

Joe reached for Andy's arm, but he pushed him away. Joe let out a sigh of resignation.

"Andy, it's only temporary."

Joe stood and walked toward the door, half expecting Andy to respond. He never did. Already he was gathering his things.

"Call me, Andy, when your head is together."

He looked at Joe angry and hurt. "I wouldn't hold my breath."

Andy's first instinct was to go to the nearest bar and release his anger the way he'd been accustomed to doing since the day Jean told him she wanted a divorce. He wanted a drink so badly, his hands were shaking. He parked his truck in front of a dive called *Renko's*. It was a run down pool house outside of Dallas near Garland. He had been here a few times when he was low on money and couldn't afford the more reputable bars. It was also far enough from his realm of the world that no one he knew would be there. It wasn't much to speak of, but the drinks were cheap and the pool free so long as you were drinking. He guessed old habits never really died, especially when a person was down on his luck. He was about to get out of his truck, when his cell phone rang. It was his dad. He couldn't talk to him right now. He threw the phone on the seat.

Not now, Dad. Right now, I can't take another lecture on all of my shortcomings.

There were only half a dozen souls in the bar when he walked inside, including the bartender. He nodded at Andy when he ordered a large draft beer. Andy paid the man and walked toward the pool table where two men, probably in their late twenties were in *a winner takes all* match. One of the two men was clearly out of his league.

When the game was over, Andy threw a ten on the table, challenging the winner. His challenger laid a ten down next to Andy's and ordered another drink from the bar. When the game began, Andy noticed from the corner of his eye that a cute little waitress sat down on a chair next to the pool table to watch the match, primarily to get a good look at Andy. It wasn't often a man like Andy walked into *Renko's*. She threw Andy a bold smile. He smiled back.

"You haven't touched this yet," she said handing Andy his beer, after his first turn.

He took the tall glass and lifted the mug her way as if to say *Thank you*. Just as he was about to take a sip, she said something to him that made him stop dead in his tracks.

"My name is Hannah. What's yours?"

Andy couldn't think. He only knew he had to get out of this place before he choked on this turn of events. He laid the beer down where it had been and handed the cue stick to his opponent, along with the winnings.

"I've had a change of heart about playing. I need to be getting home."

When he walked out of *Renko's*, he didn't look back at anyone. He just fled. Inside his truck, he laid his head on the steering wheel. A million thoughts filled his mind. He had almost lost sight of his priorities, because he was feeling sorry for himself. Fate, or something like it, had saved him. He thought of Hannah sleeping so peacefully last night, like a beautiful promise.

Hannah consumed him—her tragedy, her courage, her caring heart, her warm smile. He thought of Nana and how she was fighting so hard to live. No doubt, she would be letting him have it about now. He thought of his boys and his unborn child. All of these people were blessings in his life. All of them were depending on him. How could he have disregarded them so easily? He had lost a job. Losing a job wasn't like losing someone you love. It certainly wasn't worth losing his soul. He started his truck and pulled away slowly. As he drove down the road, it occurred to him. Last night he had prayed for guidance and today his prayer was answered. God made his message loud and clear.

Okay, we do it Your way. My way hasn't been working out so well.

Sixteen

It was nearly three in the afternoon when Andy arrived at his apartment. When he walked inside, the first thing he noticed were the flowers on the kitchen table, reminding him that it was Hannah's birthday. He rubbed his throbbing head, so he went to the medicine chest for some aspirin. He looked at himself in the mirror and didn't much like what he was seeing. He wanted to rid himself of any memory of his recent near mishap earlier this afternoon. Twenty minutes in a bar and he reeked of alcohol and smoke. He reeked of guilt, but more exact of regret for his temporary lapse in judgment. He thought he had passed this point of behavior. He stripped himself down and threw his clothing into the washer. Then, he jumped into the shower, letting the water massage him, all the while rubbing tiny circles over his temples in an effort to rid himself of his self-imposed migraine.

The rumbling in his gut came next. Rapidly, it moved up his gut to his throat. He was going to be sick. He made a running leap from the shower to the commode just in time. Dripping wet, he cursed his stupidity. His nerves had gotten the best of him and for a moment, he understood completely how Hannah felt when she was experiencing anxiety. The water in the shower was still running. He waited a few minutes just to make sure this wave of sickness had passed. His eyes caught sight of Hannah's clothing hanging on the door hook.

Hannah, I'm sorry. Nothing happened.

He was humiliated by his behavior today, even though he tried to rationalize that he hadn't really done anything wrong, nor would he have. Still, he had placed himself in a vulnerable situation. When the nausea left, he finished his shower. Some time later, wrapped only in a towel, he went into his room and rested on his bed to try to regain some of his strength—some of his dignity. He clicked on the answering machine next to his bed and listened to the messages. The first one was from Liz.

"Andy, it's me. Would you please call me when you get in?"

Andy thought of Liz and how broken up she had been last night. Once again, the tightness in his stomach surfaced. He held tight to it as he listened to the next message.

"Andy, it's Dad. I tried to call you on your cell with no luck. I'll check back with you later. Not to worry. Everything is fine. Nana says *hi* and for you to hurry back to see her."

Nana, what a royal butt kicking you'd be giving me now.

He winced at the next call.

"Hi, this is Paul...Renfroe. I'm calling for Hannah. Just wanted to wish you a happy birthday, Hannah. We were wondering if your flowers arrived. If you can, Hannah, give Sue and me a call. We'd love to hear from you."

Andy let out a sarcastic laugh. *We? Who are you kidding, Renfroe?*

Joe's message cut him deep. He fast-forwarded it.

"Andy it's me, Joe. I'm worried about you, man. You know I care..."

Like hell, you care.

Andy's heart sank when he heard his mother's voice. He missed her deeply, and suddenly longed to have her close.

"Andy, John, it's mom. It's about two p.m. your time. I was calling about Mother. John, I'll try to call again tomorrow, but I can't promise anything. My prayers are with you and Mother. I love all my guys."

"I love you, too," Andy whispered.

The next message blared through the machine.

"Andy, this is Elaine Greene again. Guess Hannah's not in yet. Please have her call me."

Andy forced himself up even though his body was begging him to stay in the bed and recover from the recent fit he'd put it through. It had left him emotionally exhausted. He stood to dress. His jeans came on none too easy. He struggled with a t-shirt that had the inscription *World's Best Dad* on it. He suddenly felt very shallow. In the background, he could hear another message from Liz. He gritted his teeth.

"Andy, it's me again. Where are you? Listen, Mom wants to take us out to dinner some time. I didn't have the heart to tell her about our talk last night. Call me. I still love you."

The last message was from Jean, The boys had been pleading with her all day to let them spend some time with their grandfather.

"Andy, it's Jean. The boys have been driving me crazy to see your dad. I called the hospital and got a hold of your father and he said it would be all right for me to bring them there for a while. I'm only letting Mathew go, because I think all three would be too much. Maybe later, you could get Jeff and Bobby, or bring your dad here to see them. What do you think? Call me."

Before Andy had time to reflect on her call, the phone rang, grinding at his headache. It was his dad.

"Andy, it's Dad."

"Yea, Dad. I'm on the way."

"Listen, that's why I'm calling. Don't bother to come by the hospital this afternoon. Nana had a busy day and I'm afraid we wore her out. The nurse gave her some pain medicine and I think when we leave she'll be pretty much done for the night. Hannah and I are about to leave. Thought anything about dinner?"

"Man," Andy said. "I really wanted to see her. No Dad, haven't thought much about dinner."

"Charlie and Ben are talking about eating out for dinner again. It's probably easiest. Personally, I don't think Hannah is up to it. I wouldn't mind just bringing something back to your place."

"Dad, I found out that today's Hannah's birthday. I was sort of thinking we could throw her a small party. Nothing fancy, just family. Thought I'd get a cake and some balloons— maybe get the boys to help me decorate the place up. I'd like Charlie and Ben and everyone to swing by just to let Hannah know how much we appreciate what she's done for Nana. What do you think? She doesn't have family to speak of, Dad."

"She definitely deserves a celebration. You get the cake, Son, and whatever else you want for the party. I'll figure out something for supper. It'll probably be pizza if Mathew has his say about it."

"Is Mathew with you? I got a message from Jean saying she was going to drop him by the hospital."

"She brought him by about thirty minutes ago. Jeff and Bobby are at home though, and I'd sure like to see them."

"I'd like them to be here tonight, Dad. Tell you what. I'll pick them up, get the cake, some gifts and the three of us can get this place ready for a party. Can you manage to stay away till about six-thirty? I figure it will take me at least that long to get things set up."

"Sure, we'll hang around here for a while and then pick up the food."

"Great! And, Dad, I'd like this to be a surprise."

"It will be."

"Well, I'd better call Jean. I've got a lot to do and little time to do it in."

"Andy, I'm glad you and Jean are finally able to set your differences aside. For the boys, it's best."

"I know, Dad. I'm trying to do what's best. It's just sometimes I get distracted along the way."

"I know we haven't really had the chance to talk much since I've been back, but...well, I'm proud of you, Son."

"Proud of me? Why, Dad?"

"You've come a long way. You've overcome so much."

Don't be proud of me. Not today.

He spoke from a heart weighed heavy with remorse. "I appreciate your saying so, Dad."

Jean was touched by Andy's thoughtfulness toward Hannah. When he asked her for some ideas for gifts, she offered to go to the mall and pick out the gifts herself.

"She's been so wonderful with Grace. And despite everything, I love Grace like she was my own grandmother."

"All right," Andy allowed. "If you really want to. Get something feminine, you know frilly, something you'd like."

She laughed. "I'll do my best. How about I get the gifts and then drop the boys off at your place?"

"Thanks, Jean. That would help me out a lot. Sure it won't be a problem?"

"I'm going to The *Galleria*. It's close to your complex. I'll have them at your place around what? Six?"

"Yea, great." Andy paused for a moment, hesitated and then blurted out, "I'd like you to come, too. That is, if you want to come."

"Oh, Andy, I wasn't expecting..."

"I know. I know. But, the boys need to see us united, and...hell, you can even bring Frank if you want."

"Oh, Andy," she choked. "I don't know what to say."

"Just come. And Jean...later, we have to talk. Frank, too."

"What is it, Andy? Is it about the move?"

"Partly. Listen, I don't really want to get into it now. Later, okay?"

"All right. And Andy thanks. I...well, I wasn't sure we'd ever reach this point."

"Well, life does go on."

Andy's apartment was cramped with people scattered on the couch and chairs and any place on the floor where there was a spot to sit. Charlie and Debbie brought chicken instead of pizza, along with all the trimmings. Debbie and Careen spread the food on the stove and a nearby cabinet top. Jeff, Bobby, and Jean had strung balloons and crepe streamers across the ceiling in the dinning area. Frank had composed a computerized banner that read Happy *Birthday, Hannah. We love you.* Everyone had signed it, except John and Mathew, who were keeping Hannah detained until the right moment. Tom signed their names for them while Ben spread a paper tablecloth over the table. Andy placed Hannah's cake in the middle and silently marveled at how perfectly it suited her.

He knew it was Hannah the moment he saw it. It was as if it had been decorated especially for her, even though it hadn't. It was chocolate, Hannah's favorite, smoothed over with white icing. The edges were lined with pink roses and on one side of the cake, there was a garden of flowers artfully crafted from pink, yellow, blue and green icing. On the other side of the cake was a birdbath where two blue birds flew nearby. The scene reminded him of the many times he had looked out his window as a young man and saw Hannah working in her garden, where a similar birdbath nested. The lettering, done in pink icing as well, expressed the usual birthday greetings, except nothing was usual about this birthday at all. It was the first, Andy hoped, of many that Hannah was celebrating with him.

As they waited for Hannah's arrival, Andy went back to his bedroom and drew out the black velvet ring box that he had earlier tucked inside the top drawer of his chest. He'd been shopping, too. He opened up the case to look at the ring one last time, silently wondering if he would really have the courage to give it to her. It wasn't an engagement ring, though God knew he had thought about it. No, an engagement ring wasn't appropriate for today. Maybe, if he were a lucky man, an engagement ring would come later. He ran his thumb over the delicate rose-shaped ring designed from gold and sprinkled with black gold. A small diamond was set within the heart of the rose. It was a beautiful selection, messianic and chic, much like Hannah, herself. A plain card with the handwritten words of a man who viewed himself as a simple man was tucked within the opening of the velvet case. The card simply said *With all my love, Andy.*

"They're coming!" Andy heard Bobby shouting. "Let's hide!"

Andy was shaking, partly, he knew, because his body was protesting his recent stupidity, but also he was anxious about Hannah's reaction. He wanted everything to be perfect for her. He wanted her to know that she was part of this family, heart and soul. As the doorknob twisted and eager faces waited to bid her birthday wishes, Andy impulsively moved into the kitchen where he would be hidden from her view. He backed into a corner. Fear overwhelmed him and he was acutely aware of what Hannah went through each day.

Be happy, Hannah. You're part of our family. You're part of me.

The door opened and the deafening shouts of *surprise* echoed throughout the small apartment. Andy remained hidden within the safe bounds of the kitchen. His throat was on fire. He managed to move toward the faucet and drew a glass of water that he drank in one gulp. He felt his gut rolling. Beads of perspiration covered his forehead.

He heard his dad and Mathew's voices, but not Hannah's. Minutes later, he saw her standing near the walkway that separated the living area from the dining area. He couldn't see her face. He saw John get a kitchen chair for her to sit on and that's when he could see her from the side. She didn't say a word. He imagined faces staring, waiting for a signal for something to begin. Andy caught his father's face as he walked into the kitchen, apparently looking for him. He gave his son a quick wink.

"Good work, Son. Everything looks great."

Andy found his voice. "I had help."

Then, Andy walked to where Hannah sat. He squatted next to her and she turned to face him. Tears filled her eyes and she barely had the presence of mind to smile. With everyone watching, he gently brushed her cheek with a kiss.

"Happy Birthday, Hannah."

"Andy," she barely managed. "Thank you."

He squeezed her hand. "You're welcome."

Turning to the others, he stood and clapped his hands once. "Okay, gang. Let's get this party rolling. First thing, chow time!"

He fixed Hannah's plate and everyone else followed his lead. Soon the room was buzzing with small talk and laughter. Andy's boys and Tom took their plates to the boys' room. Ben, Charlie, and Frank sat on the couch. Careen, Debbie, and Jean sat around the coffee table. Andy and John moved two chairs next to Hannah. Neither Hannah nor Andy ate much, nor did they have much to say. Thankfully, John did most of the talking, filling in details of Grace's recovery.

"I swear," John said. "Mom will outlive me."

In passing, everyone made his or her round with Nana stories.

"Talking about her like this," Hannah said. "Well, it makes it seem like she's here with us."

"She is, Hannah," John said. "She's in our hearts."

Time passed and Andy looked at Hannah. She hadn't eaten much from her plate in the past twenty minutes. He looked at his own plate. He hadn't eaten much either.

"Finished?"

She nodded. He took her half-full plate along with his half-full plate and threw them in the trash.

"God bless paper and plastic," he said to no one in particular. John moved into the living room. Jean sat down where John had been sitting to wish Hannah a happy birthday. She noticed Hannah's drink hadn't been touched.

"Oh, Hannah, would you rather have something else to drink? We brought soda."

"Oh, no. Tea's fine. Thank you. I'm...I'm..."

Jean took her hand and squeezed it. "I know. I hate being the center of attention, too."

Jean had a crooked smile and one eye was slightly crossed, but Hannah understood Andy's attraction to her. It was her style. She was natural and not a bit pretentious. Hannah liked Jean. Andy sat back down just in time to hear Jean's comment. He considered what she had to say and looked at her as if her were understanding her for the first time. After so many months of fighting, it was nice to let go. It also gave him a new perspective into Jean.

"I never knew that," he told Jean honestly. "I mean, about your not liking to be the center of attention. Why didn't I? I should have known that."

"What?" she asked, taken back. She blushed, but not from embarrassment. She was remembering a shy, young boy who'd stolen her heart with his deep sensitivity.

"It's all right," she said with perhaps the same fresh perspective he was feeling. "Now you know."

She stood to go back where Frank was, but before she left, she looked at Andy with a heavy heart. It was as if she were recapturing the essence of the man she'd fallen in love with, always thoughtful and always intuitive. She lent him a smile that touched his heart. He watched her until she sat next to Frank. Hannah was watching him watching her. Andy smiled at Hannah.

"Jean and I have reached a crossroad. We've decided to be human to each other again."

Hannah smiled meekly. "I'm glad."

He swallowed hard and leaned toward her hopeful. "Glad of what, Hannah? Glad we're being human, or glad there's not something going on between us?"

When she turned to face him, she half expected him to be teasing, but he wasn't. He was completely sincere.

"I...I, well," she sputtered. "Both, I guess."

He spoke almost as if he were an outcast, as if he really didn't have the right to say what he was saying.

"Hannah, I promise you. There's only one woman who has my full attention and you know who she is."

When she looked at him, for a moment she forgot they weren't the only people in the room. He closed his eyes and let out a crumbling breath as if everything that he was or would be depended on her. At that moment, she understood fully the something she couldn't identify earlier about Andy's behavior. He was struggling with the same pith she'd seen her father struggle with when he'd let her down, when he'd broken promises. Sammy had given the same look after he'd lied to her about other women. She snapped her head toward Jean, but Jean held no shame. Hannah gripped the leg of the chair she sat in and prayed.

Please let me be wrong.

She studied him with both misgiving and promise. When he looked at her, clearly regret was there, but was remorse? Had guilt shown its face? She smiled at him warily.

"Andy, thank you again for the party. I..."

She cried more for fear of what she thought she knew was true. Had Andy succumbed to his past demons?

"Hannah, don't cry."

"I'm just a little overwhelmed. That's all."

She noted his shaky hands and sunken eyes, tell-tale signs of a fall from grace.

Andy, say I'm wrong.

As if reading her mind, he took her hand and signaled to the others.

"Present time."

She must have looked frantic because he laughed out and upbraided her tenderly.

196

"Don't look at me that way Hannah Martindale. What do you expect? It's your birthday after all."

Everyone stood around the small table where Hannah sat. Jean had done well in her selection of gifts. From the boys she gave her a journal, remembering Grace once telling her in passing how Hannah liked journals. From everyone, she was given a long, floral robe, made of silk, similar to those worn by Geisha women, yet more practical and durable. The last gift was also from everyone, as well. It was a picture of Hannah and Grace together. Jean had framed it in an oval antique casing. Andy looked at Jean pensively as if to say, *how did you manage this on such short notice?*

Later, after cake had been served and everyone was gathering things together to leave, Andy pulled Jean aside and asked her about the picture.

"Actually," she confessed. "It was going to be a gift for Grace. I already had it framed and wrapped. When you called, I knew Hannah should have it."

"Well, you're full of wonders tonight."

Again, she was taken back by his sentimentality, having her feeling slightly uncomfortable.

"Andy, Frank and I need to be leaving soon. So Mathew can stay?"

"Yea, and Jeff and Bobby if they want. Dad has sleeping arrangements all figured out."

"Oh, Andy that's too much. I think..."

She stopped herself from ending her statement.

"Whatever you think, Andy."

"I'd like all three, if it's no trouble. I'll bring them home early. Will someone be at the house?"

"Mom will be."

Andy thought of his ex-mother-in-law. "She'll love that."

"Won't do her any good not to," Jean said flippant. She motioned for Frank. "Andy, what did you want to talk to us about?"

"Yea, I'll walk you to your car."

He walked them outside, with the darkness to clothe his insecurity. He hated telling him his news, once again letting Jean down in front of Frank. As the three stood by Jean's car, he told them about his job.

"Don't worry about the boys and support. I'll pay it. If I have to beg, borrow or steal, I'll pay it."

"Andy, we'll work it out. Remember, we all want what's best for the boys."

"If there's one thing I am, Jean, it's a good father. I'm not about to screw that up like everything else."

"Andy, you weren't the only one who messed up."

He looked at her a bit stunned. "Yea, but I'm the one who got blamed for it."

"I accept my part. Frank accepts his part."

"Well, I guess it's really water under the bridge now when you think about it, huh?"

"Yea, I guess," she cried. She blew her nose. "Andy, about the house."

"What about it?"

"We'd like to sell it, unless, well, you'd like to move into it."

He let out a bittersweet snort. "I believe I'll pass on that offer. That's a little more than I could chew. I see no reason why you shouldn't sell it. How soon do you think you'll be leaving?"

"Frank leaves in two weeks. We'll leave when the house sells."

Andy swallowed hard, twice, before he could speak. "Well, I guess that's that."

She reached to kiss him, even with Frank watching.

"Andy, do what Joe suggested. Get your life together."

He lent her a potent grin that expressed both concession and determination.

"That's exactly what I intend to do."

198

After saying good-bye to Charlie and Ben and their families and making tentative plans to meet at the hospital sometime around nine tomorrow morning, those left at Andy's prepared for bed. John supervised baths while Andy made pallets on the floor in Andy's bedroom. The three boys would all sleep near Grandpa. Hannah would take their room and Andy the couch. Hannah was busy cleaning up the last bit of dishes when Andy caught her red handed.

"Here, here," he scolded. "No one in this family works on their birthday."

"Oh, Andy. It's only a few dishes."

"I don't care. Scoot."

She conceded and watched as he finished the dishes.

"Tell me how you knew, Andy? I mean about my birthday."

"Honestly?"

She nodded curiously, "Honestly."

He held up a finger, "Hold on then. I'll be right back. And so help me if you touch a dish..."

"I won't! I won't!"

She watched him disappear down the hallway and return with a vase that held a dozen pink roses. Her hand went up to her mouth in surprise.

"Oh, Andy, you didn't?"

"No," he said agitated. "Someone beat me to it. They're from Paul and Sue Renfroe. That's how I knew about your birthday. These and your friend, Elaine, called. By the way, she wants you to call her back."

"Oh," she said taking the roses. Her downcast eyes were unreadable. He was getting pissed all over again with Renfroe's nerve.

"So, are you going to?"

"What?"

"Call him."

"Paul?"

"He's the one that sent you flowers."

"His wife sent them, too, Andy."

Andy said, "Yea, right," under his breath. She said, "What did you say?"

He shrugged. "Not a thing."

She studied the roses. "They send them every year. Well, not roses, but flowers."

"For eighteen years!"

"No," she stifled a laugh. "Just four."

"Oh," he said less agitated. "That's a little different. Wanna know what I think?"

"I'm not sure I do."

"I think..."

His words were interrupted when Bobby came storming in the kitchen. "Daddy, Grandpa's gonna tell us stories about Bolivia and Grandma and all that stuff."

Andy picked up his youngest son. "Oh, yea? Bolivia and Grandma and all that stuff, huh?"

Bobby kissed him on the cheek, squirmed from his arms and headed for his bedroom.

"'Night, Daddy," he hollered.

"Whoa, back the horse up, little buddy."

"What?" he asked impatiently. "Grandpa's waitin'..."

"Did you scrub those teeth?"

Bobby flashed his shiny, clean teeth.

"All right," he said kissing his son one more time. "See you in the morning."

Bobby was halfway to his room and he reared back into the kitchen and kissed Hannah smack on the lips.

"Happy Birthday, Hanny."

"Thank you, Bobby, and thank you for my gifts."

He smiled. "You're welcome. 'Night."

"Good-night, Bobby, and enjoy your stories."

As quickly as he'd come in the room, he left. Andy laughed as he turned back to finish the kitchen work.

"Damn, if only I could bottle that energy. Now...what were we discussing?"

"I forget."

"You forget, huh? Convenient."

She blushed. He grinned. She rapped her fingers on the table. "No, I don't believe I will."

"What?"

"Call Paul and Sue."

"You mean, Paul," he corrected

"And Sue," she stressed.

He dropped the dishcloth into the sink and moved toward her, consciously checking to see if any eyes might be watching.

"I'm glad. I don't much care for him. You know he has a thing for you, don't you?"

"Andy, it doesn't really matter. We both know I don't feel the same."

"You should tell him to get lost."

"He and Sue have been good to me since...the accident."

His mood changed from jealousy to protective.

"You miss them, I know."

He was referring to her family.

She took his hand. "I miss them every day. Most especially..."

He took her in his arms and held her tenderly.

"I know, on your birthday."

"Andy, you gave me such a gift tonight."

"Did I?"

"I'll never forget this birthday, the cake, the gifts, and your family. For as long as I live I'll remember it because it was you who..."

"Can we go and talk on the patio, away from...?"

He didn't say his father and his boys, but she knew. She nodded. He led her outside, closing them out from the world with a glass door. They leaned against the railing. Darkness had set in and they stood close enough to touch. He let out a breath of defeat.

"Hannah, I lost my job today."

She reached for his hand, "Andy, no."

Inside she was relieved that this was the cause for his mood and it wasn't what she had feared. Her relief was short lived. He spoke to her pointedly.

"That's not all. Today, after I left work...I went to a bar."

She closed her eyes tightly. "I had a feeling."

He didn't have the inclination to ask her why she had a feeling. When she withdrew her hand abruptly from his hold and put distance between them, he understood exactly what weighed on her mind.

"Hannah, I'll say this once and I pray to God you believe me. I bought a drink, but I couldn't drink it. I left without taking a sip. Nothing happened."

"You're free to do what you want, Andy. If you want to drink or anything else, it's your own business, not mine."

"Hannah, in fifteen years, I was never unfaithful to Jean. Not once. I couldn't be to you, either."

"I don't have the right to expect you to be faithful to me, Andy."

"The hell you don't! You don't get it, do you? I love you. And in my book, that's right enough."

"Andy, I don't know what to say."

He studied her face. He could tell she was putting up her defenses again. He couldn't blame her, but if it was the last thing he did, he was going to convince her just how much she meant to him. He reached for her and held her in his arms so tightly, her breath caught in her throat. He broke his promise not to kiss her, pressing his mouth over hers, lost in passion. In this stolen moment, hand and lips never stopped moving, reaching, exploring.

"Oh, Hannah, I know one thing for sure," he panted. "Tomorrow we're going to have to find a way to be alone. Either that, or I'm going to go absolutely out of my mind."

She smiled into his chest.

"Tomorrow," she said faintly. Then, she reached for him in the dark and kissed him one last time before she pulled herself away. With distance between them, he questioned her.

"Hannah, do you love me?"

She smiled. "Kiss me again and I'll tell you."

Once more, he drew her near. He kissed her so long and hard, pressing her back against the brick wall. She was kissing him back, lost in this unexpected love that had swept over them like a storm.

"Yes," she whispered. "I love you, even though I shouldn't."

He stopped kissing her and held her tight against his chest. She could feel his heart racing.

"Hannah, I called off my engagement last night."

"Oh," she cried out. "Does she know?"

"About us?" He shook his head. "She thinks I'm still in love with Jean."

Hannah closed her eyes.

"This is such a mess, Andy."

"Oh, Hannah, I..."

His words were stopped when John Padgett slid open the glass door. They weren't exactly in a lover's embrace, but the picture was painfully clear. He made no attempt to condemn their behavior, although his silence spoke volumes. After what seemed like an eternity, he cleared his throat to speak.

"Andy, Liz is on the phone."

SEVENTEEN

The day after her birthday, Hannah woke up before dawn. She hadn't slept all night remembering John's dull reaction at seeing Andy holding her and understanding fully what was occurring. His silence was a powerful message, but she blessed him for it. She doubted seriously if she could have faced his words. Andy was quiet too, even though he had tried to reassure her misgivings just before going inside to take Liz's call.

"Hannah, I'm glad it's in the open now. Tomorrow we'll discuss this like three adults. Try not to worry. Try to get some sleep. I love you."

She couldn't even fake a semblance of assurance for him. When he brushed her forehead with a kiss, she simply turned from him and walked inside the apartment. John was standing over the kitchen sink staring at nothing in particular, and for the slightest of seconds, their eyes met. She heard her voice say something like, *goodnight,* and then she disappeared down the hallway, retreating behind the closed door of the bedroom where she was sleeping.

The dawning of a new morning did little to ease her concerns. Around eight, Hannah listened as Andy and the boys were busy preparing for the day. Water ran in the hall bathroom and small feet thumped across the floor. She heard Bobby complain when Mathew tried to comb his hair, and then, Mathew hollered down the hallway to his dad that Bobby wasn't cooperating. Andy quietly chided the two, reminding them that Grandpa and Hannah were still sleeping. She heard dishes clanging and chairs sliding as the boys chatted and laughed around the table eating breakfast. Jeff must have started clearing the table because Andy's voice excused him from a duty Hannah was certain was as routine to him as brushing his teeth.

"Don't worry about the dishes, Son. I'll get them later."

"You sure, Dad?"

"Yep. We're running late. Everyone have all their things?"

Hannah imagined them nodding or something of that nature for moments later Andy was opening the front door.

"Okay then, let's get rolling."

Then, a hush fell over the entire apartment. Hannah waited for some time to make certain John hadn't gotten up before she opened the door and left the security of the bedroom. The small apartment was in an upheaval from the everyday habits of a family preparing for the day. She instantly started tidying up the place, folding blankets, picking up bits of trash and making her way into the kitchen where she filled up the sink to do the morning dishes. That's where John found her when he walked into the kitchen. She felt his presence, but still quenched when he spoke.

"Oh, Hannah Dear, I must be suffering from jet lag. I just can't seem to get myself up in the mornings."

She remained guarded, but managed to talk.

"I could make some coffee if that would help."

His voice, his mannerisms, they were so much like Andy's, or rather, Andy's were like his. She dried her hands and looked in a cabinet for some coffee. She opened almost every cabinet in the kitchen before John came behind her and opened up the freezer door to pull out the coffee. She glanced up to see him smiling.

"An old family secret."

He handed her the can, but her hands were shaking so badly, she dropped it on the floor. Luckily, the lid held. Still, she couldn't stop her tears. As she leaned down to pick up the can, she made her apologies.

"I'm sorry. I'm so clumsy this morning."

John took the can from her.

"The coffee can wait, Hannah."

She lent him a despairing look and turned her back to him. "Oh, John. I'm so sorry about last..."

He turned her around gently and wrapped his arms around her. "Shhh, now. No crying. Let's dry those eyes and then we can talk about it."

She wiped her nose with her hand and nodded. He led her into the living room where they sat on the couch. He spoke first. His air was gentle, but steadfast.

"Hannah, here's what I think is happening. Andy's been going through a lot, first coping with his divorce and then dealing with being a father again. He's scared. Once a marriage crumbles like his, one that a person like Andy has put his whole life into, it's not easy to bounce back up. He took the hard road. Then, his Nana got sick. Hannah, you remember how close he was to his Paps. It almost killed him when he died. He's afraid of losing Nana, too.

"And through all this confusion in his life, he becomes friends with you. You're beautiful. You're familiar. You love Nana as much as he does. You don't threaten him like Jean or Liz. And you're attracted to him for the same reasons. He understands what you've been through because he's lost his family, too. It's not really the same, but similar. You're scared, too. You're afraid of getting back out into the big world because it's hurt you so much. Andy takes away some of this fear. He's a safeguard. It's only natural that you've turned to each other."

She closed her eyes, taking in John's words. "I told Andy almost the same thing just days ago. Only coming from you, it sounds so sensible, so rational."

"There's nothing rational about it, Hannah. Don't get me wrong. There are a lot of emotions flying around here, and it won't be easy to let go."

"I...," she lowered her head. "I...oh, I didn't mean for this to happen. I've been fighting this all the way. Oh, God, I have such feelings. I never thought I'd feel like this about another man."

He blew out a heavy breath. "Hannah, I can see that you're struggling even now. I can see how much you care."

She looked to him for guidance, for understanding. "Help me, John. Every time I look at Liz, I think of the baby...and, oh, it all seems so impossible. But when I'm so near Andy, I, I, lose myself. I get lost in the moment, the way we're feeling. I can't seem to help myself."

He rubbed his face with both hands, and then, he turned to face her. His expression was somber. His tone was firm.

"Hannah, please forgive me if I come on too strong, or if I sound cruel. But you mentioned the baby and the baby must come foremost. You know how Andy is about his boys. He'd die for them. This child will be no different once he sees and holds him or her for the first time. Everything will change."

He took her hands in his, gripping them resolutely.

"Hannah, you know how hard life is. A child deserves the opportunity to grow up in a secure and happy home with both a mother and a father, if it's at all possible."

She drew her hands away from his grip. A new kind of fear emerged, a mistrust that this man was going to take her happiness away.

"You're saying it's wrong for me to care. You're asking me to let go of Andy, aren't you?"

"What I'm asking is that you consider the repercussions if you and Andy continue with this. He'll eventually be forced to choose between you and the baby, because Liz will be resentful, and because that's the way of things when a father and mother separate. Be honest. Will you be able to live with the consequence of either choice?"

She leaned against the back of the couch, closing her eyes. She gripped the blankets she'd folded just minutes earlier, the blanket that had covered Andy last night. Tears fell quietly down her face. A sense of concession overcame her as she listened to John. He was only saying what she'd been thinking all along, but coming from him, it was so final. The truth was, she had no choice but to fall in love with Andy, and, there was no choice in what she had to do now. Pain burned inside of her, an inferno she knew only time could diminish. She'd lost love before. This was no different. Losing Andy was like a death.

"It hurts so much!" she cried.

John reached to hold her. She leaned against his chest. "Hannah, if I could spare you this..."

She made one final plea to him. "Ask me to do anything, but don't ask me to let him go. Not now, when he's brought life back into me."

"Hannah," he said none too steady. "Be brave."

She grabbed his shirt and held onto him so strongly she heard a button pop off.

"I'm not brave. I can..n't le...let hhh...him go."

"You are brave. I've witnessed your courage time after time. Think of how much you love him. This will make you strong."

"No. God..." She cried until her body wore out. She found herself once again in the dark hole she'd known so well, depleted, and hopeless. Any hope she'd felt yesterday was now lost in the thought of never holding Andy again. With her tears gone, she lay motionless against John. He stroked her hair over and over as if this was somehow easing her pain. His heart was torn as well, silently fearing she might not be able to pick herself up again. She had suffered so much. And Andy...Oh, God. Anger soared through him. He wanted to hit something, but didn't. Rather, he just sat there stroking her hair, trying to understand the inhumanity of their situation. Sometime later, she lifted her head. With all emotions drained, she spoke to him.

"John, will you do me a favor?"

"Anything," he scarcely managed to say.

"Take me to see Grace. If she's still doing well, I want you to take me home."

He cleared his throat. "Home? Maybe a separation is all that's needed here."

When Andy got back to his apartment after taking the boys home, his father and Hannah were already gone. He found a note on the table from his father.

Andy, I've taken Hannah to the hospital, but I'm coming right back. I'd like you to stay. I think we should talk. Dad.

He crumbled the note, but left it on the table.

"I guess now's as good a time as any."

He made more coffee. From his pocket, he drew out some antacids for his unsettled gut. He flipped on a radio that sat in the windowsill above the sink. Some country sound was playing a song about heartbreak. He switched it back off.

"Oh, no. No lonely heart songs today."

To kill time, he finished the dishes that someone hadn't gotten around to finishing. The water was cold now, but he didn't bother replenishing it with hot water. Time still ticked away, so he decided to shower. He wanted to be near Hannah, so he showered in the boys' bathroom, knowing she'd done the same thing this morning. Her soap and shampoo scent still filled the air and he drew in a deep breath as if this were bringing her closer to him. She looked so lost, so frightened last night. What was she thinking now? He was afraid that facing his father would be too much for her. He wanted to be with her when she did, but no doubt, they had already spoken. He dried and shaved. As he dressed, he heard his father come in. He prepared himself to face the piper, determined that his father wasn't going to get the upper hand on this issue. There was no negotiating here, even though he knew his dad would put up some valid arguments. But Hannah was something that just happened. There was no argument against such fate. John was sitting at the table drinking vender coffee and reading a paper when Andy walked into the kitchen. Andy touched his shoulder gently.

"Dad."

John never looked up, but offered, "Son."

"I made coffee, but I see you bought some."

He laid down the paper and handed his cup to Andy. "It can stand a little freshening up."

Andy refilled his dad's cup and then poured his own. He sat down in the chair next to his dad.

"How's Nana this morning?"

"She's good. They're talking about letting her come home tomorrow or the next day."

Andy squeezed his eyes shut and whispered, *fantastic.* Then opening them again, he met his father's solid stare. "And Hannah. How is she?"

"Not well, Andy. Not well at all."

Andy winced. "Damn it!"

"She wants me to take her home today."

His chin dropped. "Oh, no."

"I told her I would."

"Well," Andy gritted. "That's a matter we can argue about later."

"You want to argue, Son?"

"No, I don't. I'd like for you to let me and Hannah work this out on our own."

"I see. And what about Liz? What about my grandchild?"

"My child," Andy pressed, "will be as loved as the rest of my children. I don't take my responsibilities lightly. As for Liz, we've already broken our engagement."

Andy got up and walked toward the patio door. He opened the curtains and brought morning into the room.

"Dad, please don't fight me on this. Can't you be happy for me? I'm finally getting my head together."

John slapped his hand on the tabletop. His coffee spilled over his paper. He didn't bother clearing it up.

210

"Your head is any place but together, Son. Have you any idea how many lives your recklessness is affecting?"

Andy let out a bitter laugh. "I knew you'd see things this way."

"How else can I see things? You've got to face some realities here. You're playing a dangerous game with other people's hearts, not to mention your own."

"Game? You think this is all a game to me? It's my life, Dad."

"Then you'd better get a grip before you destroy it and others along with it."

"Look, I know you're worried about the baby..."

"You're damn right I am! But the baby's not the only one I'm worried about. I'm worried about Liz and you, and how you just might be throwing away a rare chance for a good, solid relationship. I'm worried about Hannah and what all of this could do to her in the long run."

"All right, Dad," he said calmly. "Say what you have to say. I'll listen because I love you. But I'm giving it to you straight, just because I'm listening doesn't mean I have to agree with you. I just might disagree."

"Well," he had to laugh out. "I have no doubts about that."

John was more in control now. He sat back down and began talking, praying to God that Andy would really hear what he had to say.

"In the beginning when Jean left and you covered up your hurt by going to bars and drinking heavily and doing so many things that went against what you'd been taught was right, I understood why. As time passed, though, and these habits continued, they started affecting the people and things in your life you valued most...the boys, your family, friends, and your work. It was as if there were no consequences to your actions. The world owed you because you'd been wronged."

"Dad, you..."

"Please, Andy. Let me talk."

"All right. Go on."

"Well, part of this recklessness caught up with you and kicked you in the butt. I'm talking about Liz and the baby, of course. Suddenly, there were real consequences to your unrestrained habits. You couldn't hide behind your pain and bad fortune by drinking. You had to face what you'd done. So, you did what you knew was right and took responsibility for your actions. But, then you saw a way out—Hannah."

"My God, you think I'm using Hannah to run away from my responsibilities?"

"Maybe you are and don't realize it."

"Do you actually think that little of me, Dad?"

"Andy, it's a natural thing to run when you're cornered."

He looked at his father disgusted. "Believe me. There are easier ways to run from your problems."

John conceded. "You may be right." He paused and then posed a question to him

"Andy, how well do you really know Hannah?"

"If you're asking me if we've slept..."

"I'm not. I'm referring to her heart, her mind."

"I know I love her, and when I'm with her I'm a better person."

John had to smile. "Well, that's not a bad start now is it?"

Andy let down his guard somewhat. "Look, Dad. I know what you're saying is true, but believe me I can feel myself moving past my destructive habits. I'm not running away from life, I'm running to it. Hannah has helped me to realize just how much I have and how much I have to lose if I continue my life as it's been. I know you see Liz as my chance for happiness, but I see marrying her as another mistake. How can I marry Liz when I don't love her and give up Hannah when I do? It doesn't make sense."

"Andy, even without the complications of Liz and the baby, a relationship with Hannah won't be easy."

"You're talking about all of her problems, aren't you?"

212

He nodded. "I'm not sure you're fully aware of how deep they run. Andy, I've known Hannah for fifteen years. She's not the same woman she was when I first met her. Then, she was the heart of her family, and maybe even of Blossom. Her spirit, oh her spirit, well, it was like a contagious ball of energy everyone wanted to be near.

"When Hannah lost Sammy and Gabe and Julie, this spirit died. The person she was no long existed. I tell you, I still haven't recovered from the shock of what she looked like when your mother and I went to pick her up at the institution. She was as near to walking death as I've ever seen. Her hair had almost completely fallen out. She was wand thin, emaciated. I honest to God didn't think she'd live, but she did.

"Survival wasn't easy for her. She had to have help at first. Mom stayed with her, slept in her house for almost a year before she was able to stay alone. She had nightmares and flashbacks. Mom had to feed her, dress her and Hannah fought her all the way."

John looked to see that Andy's face was covered with his own tears. "Oh, Dad, she's been through...pure hell."

John let out a heavy sigh. "My point exactly."

Andy looked at him with new awareness.

"You think I'm going to add to her hurt, don't you?"

"Andy, without knowing it, you already have."

Andy stood with his hands in his pockets. He looked forlorn, and perhaps for the first time understood that he could possibly hurt her, if not today, tomorrow.

"There's something else you need to know, Andy."

"What?" his voice squeaked with emotion.

"The man, Tolbert Dole, who hit Hannah and her family head on, was drunk. He walked away with only minor injuries, but he might as well have died with her family. You see, the accident drove him completely out of his mind. About a year after it happened, he ran his car into a tree and killed himself."

Andy closed his eyes and shook his head. "Jesus."

"Hannah came to learn that drinking can kill a person in more ways than how her family was killed, like it had killed Tolbert Dole."

Andy thought of his own problem with alcohol. He knew his dad wasn't making comparisons, but he couldn't help but to do so, himself.

"I'm not like Tolbert Dole," he rationalized. Yet deep down, he knew that people didn't become Tolbert Dole overnight and that he really wasn't much different at that.

"I've slowed way down on my drinking, Dad. Honest. It's been weeks."

"I just wanted you to be aware that it's a sensitive issue with Hannah."

"I already knew that because of her father."

John nodded. "Well, now you know it goes deeper than that."

"She's come so far, Dad. Every day she takes one more step. Every day she gets stronger."

"She has come far, Andy. I won't argue that. I'm just afraid that she's not strong enough to deal with taking a child away from his or her father."

"She wouldn't be. I plan to be a big part of this baby's life, just like my boys. Hannah knows this."

"Hannah believes in family as strongly as you do. It's killing her to think she's coming between you and this baby. She told me so herself. And God help her if you do resent her some time down the road, if and when the baby should somehow drift from your life. Hannah won't be able to live with the fact that she took from you and your child the opportunity to build a real family with Liz."

"I'd never resent her," he snapped.

"Can you really be sure?"

"Yes."

"Well, you just might be human enough to where you might not have a choice but to resent her someday."

214

"What do you want from me, Dad? Do you want me to give up Hannah? Is that it?"

"I only know that emotions are running high right now. When this happens bad decisions are made, and in this situation, these decisions could be irreversible. I'm asking you to stop and step back for a while. No, marrying Liz at this point isn't the course of action you should take. But neither is diving into the fire with Hannah. Take time, Son. Concentrate on what's at stake. Truthfully, I think you should distance yourself from both Liz and Hannah. You just might lose both if you don't."

"I broke it off with Liz because it isn't fair for me to lead her on, Dad. She deserves the chance to rebuild her life without me."

"Andy, Liz isn't totally innocent in all of this. She's done some gambling herself. Tell her you've done some thinking and that you want to spend more time with your boys before the baby comes along. In truth, Andy, that's not such a bad idea. Jean told me about the move. This time with your boys is important."

Andy's tone was drawn. "So the madness continues."

"No, Son. It's ending."

Andy felt something like bitterness rise within him. He brushed past his father without as much as a glance, swiping up his keys off the table. Just before walking out the door, he stopped and requested to his father.

"I'm asking you not to take Hannah back to Blossom until I've had a chance to talk to her."

"All right, Son. I won't."

Andy waved a hand, but didn't look back. When the door separated him from his son, John Padgett lowered his head and cried.

Andy and Hannah said *good-bye* at a park near the hospital. It was private, and safe enough to where their emotions wouldn't lead them to do something foolish.

"I went back to the store and talked to Joe Broughton, my boss. I told him I was taking his advice, you know, getting my life together. He has a cabin near Hot Springs, Arkansas. He offered it to me. I'm taking the boys there. We can do some fishing and boating. I think it will be good to spend some time...Oh, Jesus, Hannah, I'm dying. I feel like someone's taken a knife to my insides. I don't want to leave you. I want...but Dad thinks we should distance ourselves for a while. Maybe, he's right. I don't know. I only know leaving you is tearing me apart."

"Andy, this time away will be good for us. I can take care of Grace without you distracting me."

He nudged her gently and gave her a vernal grin, teasing her, because it was too painful not to. "You know, I think you like my distractions."

She laid her hand against his arm, clutching it tightly in an effort to keep from falling apart. "Andy, don't tease me. I don't think I can bear your teasing today."

He kissed the top of her head. "I'm sorry. It's a bad habit I have, joking around when my heart's falling apart."

She kissed his arm.

God, help me to let him go. I can't do it alone.

He slipped her cell phone in her hand. "Keep this. Call me — when you need me."

She looked at him lost, "I do need you."

He inhaled with an air of determination. "Hannah, don't think for one minute that this is a final good-bye. It isn't."

You really believe this, don't you?

The idea that he couldn't see this for what it was broke her heart.

"Andy, I'll be all right without you."

"I don't want you to be all right without me!" he snapped angrily. Then more calmly rephrased what he was feeling. "Hannah, don't you dare give up on us. Time and distance will only prove to make us stronger, bring us closer. You'll see."

"Oh, Andy, if there were another choice..."

He stood up, clutching his fists. "Damn it, Hannah. One round with my dad and you're ready to throw everything away. Don't you think I might just be worth a little more fight?"

"Oh, Andy, I'd fight to my last breath, if..."

He leaned to draw her up to her feet and into his arms. "If what, Hannah? What?"

"If..." And because she couldn't bear the agony on his face, she turned from him. "If," she finished, "it were the right thing for us to do."

He wanted to shake her, but he simply held her tighter. "It is the right thing, Hannah. Our being together is right."

"Andy," she sobbed. "I think maybe you're wrong."

"No," he whispered. "Don't let me go. Don't believe we're wrong. I can't go on without the hope of us."

"Hope," she muttered. "I guess there's always hope."

He knew she was slipping away and he was out of his mind with fear. He could fight his dad's opposition, and Liz's, so long as Hannah was fighting alongside him. But, she was letting go. He felt it. He held her face in his hands and looked directly into her eyes.

"I love you, Hannah. I'm not letting you go. Please, I beg you, don't you let me go either."

"Andy, I..."

He pressed his mouth harshly on hers, desperate. He kissed her as if he might never kiss her again. His uncompromising kiss reflected his pain. Once again, his heart had opened up to love a woman, and once again, it bled from rejection.

"I'm taking my boys on a fishing trip, that's all, Hannah. Don't let go of us."

Yet even as he spoke, he could feel her slipping away.

EIGHTEEN

Grace came home one week after her surgery. John and Hannah fussed over her like two mother hens, but Grace was determined to return to the normal life she'd lived. She didn't stay at Andy's, but insisted on going home.

"I'm not in my grave yet," she sparred.

"Oh, Grace," Hannah doted lovingly. "It's so good to have you home."

Each day Grace grew stronger, and so did Hannah. Having Grace around put life back into perspective. When Grace was around, the loneliness she felt from Andy's absence seemed less painful. Their lives became routine again. Every day was the same. Hannah would cook all the meals and John cleaned up. Breakfast was at seven, lunch at noon, and dinner at six. Every morning after breakfast, they would take a walk, sometimes around the block, sometimes to a park that was about three blocks from their houses. And every evening after *Wheel of Fortune*, they would take their nightly stroll, which usually ended on either Grace's front porch or Hannah's. At this time, they would discuss everything from the weather to Ann's coming home to Debbie's and Charlie's new business. Rarely, did they discuss Andy, except when Grace brought him up in passing. Both John and Hannah were quick to change the subject if she did. If Grace suspected anything, she never let on.

Later, they would move into Grace's living room where John presented them with a nightly concert on Grace's out of tune piano. While John played, usually the classics or old gospel tunes, Grace knitted. Sometimes Hannah did too, but usually she'd doodle on a sketchpad or let herself get lost in the music, imagining what life must have been like growing up in a family headed by John Padgett. These were difficult times for her as well. Some time halfway into John's playing, Grace would begin to nod off, signaling Hannah to run Grace's bath. By eight-thirty or nine Grace was tucked in her bed. Hannah and John said goodnight and then Hannah would make her way back to her house.

During these evening hours and while Grace took her naps, Hannah worked for Elaine, working sometimes well past midnight. She did this to keep herself from thinking, for it was at this time when loneliness got the best of her. Often, she thought of Sammy, but more often, Andy. This fact disturbed her, for she felt as though she was somehow betraying Sammy. Yet, rationale and constant self-talk did little to keep her from thinking of Andy. Somehow, her thoughts always found their way back to him. Somehow, her dreams were always filled with his laughter, his presence. More times than not, she awoke with an emptiness so deep, she wondered if she would ever fill it.

Andy called her every night and they talked for hours about nothing—and everything. They talked into the late hours of the night and when it was time to part, they reluctantly let each other go, living for the next time they would talk. They were lonely, but hopeful. He was confident they would be together forever. She was certain they wouldn't, but never said the words, secretly longing for them not to be true. She knew if she spoke the truth, it would become too real. For now, reality was a million dreams away.

Since Hannah had returned to Blossom, she was less contented staying in the house, and she looked for ways to escape it, where she'd always found reason to stay bound. At these times, she would piddle around the yard, pulling weeds, cutting grass, tilling the garden, painting the trim of her house. When John would offer his help, she'd brush him off saying that working outside was therapy for her soul. He would always walk away, understanding that Hannah was like a caterpillar breaking free of its cocoon, moving at an unyielding pace. The fear that had always plagued her was replaced somewhat with restlessness. It almost seemed foolish to her to spend any more time in her house than she had to, for she'd already lived an eternity crippled within its boundaries.

One morning she knocked on Grace's door full of energy and self-determination, declaring she was sick and tired of looking at her forsaken garden.

"John, there's a nursery on the highway going into Greenville. I was wondering if you might take me there today."

So, the three piled in Grace's car and spent the better part of the morning picking out flowers, plants, soil and accessories for Hannah's garden. When they were finished, they broke their routine and had lunch at a country cafe they spotted along the way, one that had a menu with a section for the *healthy heart*.

"We should make it a point to eat here again," John said.

"It's wonderful, isn't it?" Hannah fairly sang, and then proceeded to ramble on about plans for her garden.

"Mercy me, child, something happened to you while I was in the hospital, something that might have made being sick worthwhile. Hannah, I never thought I'd see you, well, so much like your old self."

Hannah smiled warmly. "Something did happen. I learned there are many people who care about me. I've learned how to reach out to them."

Reaching out became a motto to her. On her daily walks with Grace, she became reacquainted with her neighbors, leaving most astonished. Some asked them in to visit, while others extended invitations to dinner or church functions. Always, she declined. She'd come far, bust wasn't ready for socializing on such a scale quite yet. John took her and Grace to the local grocery where Hannah was like a child exploring the world as if she were seeing it for the first time. When anxiety threatened, and it usually did, she focused on how far she had come. When that didn't work, she retreated. On the occasions where she reverted, she was hard on herself and often withdrew into her old habits. John was quick to pull her out and reassure her.

"Baby steps, Hannah. It's just like Mom. You can't expect to bounce back to one hundred percent overnight."

"I know, John. My common sense tells me this, but I want so much to be *normal* again. I want my life back."

"Hannah, we all change with time. Some, like you, have more dramatic changes, but we all have them. You do have your life, Hannah. You're moving at full speed. Why, you're the buzz of Blossom."

"I couldn't find the courage without you and Grace."

"You give us courage. Why your determination has helped Mom to recover more quickly than we ever dreamed possible."

Hannah lent him a playful gaze. "Do you ever feel like you've gotten a raw deal here?"

"A raw deal?"

"You know, having to deal with a cantankerous old woman and a crazy lady who's afraid of her own shadow?"

"Oh, Hannah," he laughed out. "I guess we all have our crosses to bear."

"Well," she said slapping on a pair of gloves and moving toward her garden. "Don't look for yours to get much lighter any time soon. Your only hope is that Ann rescues you quickly."

He laughed all the way to Grace's back door. When he looked back at her, she was already busy in her garden. Clearly, she was in her element moving about the many flowers and plants that so reflected her resurrected spirit. As he watched her, he thought of Andy. An inkling of doubt pinched at his soul, doubt that Andy would be able to let her out of his life, especially now that she was becoming so strong.

Liz got off work at two p.m. and decided to make a stop at the *Pampered Mom*, a quaint second hand shop she'd heard about that wasn't too far from her house. Big shirts and oversized stretch pants just weren't cutting it any longer, and she decided to buy some maternity clothes. She selected three casual short outfits and a couple of dresses and took them into a dressing room. As she tried the clothes on, she caught perhaps for the first time, a true image of her swollen self. She was feeling what she guessed were the maternity blues, because she could see nothing beautiful and wonderful about the way her body was changing. She moved her hand over her abdomen and vividly recalled how it used to be, flat and firm, along with the rest of her body. She sighed, wondering if Andy had called off the engagement because he didn't find her attractive any more.

They hadn't made love since the night they had driven to Blossom and picked up Nana. This thought concerned her greatly, because she knew Andy was a man who enjoyed sex and had never had a problem expressing his needs and desires, or showing them for that matter. Lovemaking had always been good with them, but it had abruptly stopped. Liz harbored doubts inside. She wondered if Andy was still holding on to his feelings for Jean. A more threatening thought occurred to Liz. It had to do with the notion that maybe Andy had found someone other than Jean. She shook the idea off, since Andy spent most of his waking hours at work or with his family—and Hannah. She shook off this thought almost as quickly as she had thought of it.

It wasn't possible. Hannah was, well, indisposed somewhat by nature, and too, she was a bit older than the women Andy usually dated. Still, Liz had to admit Hannah was a striking woman, who looked like she was in her twenties rather than her thirties. Liz thought of Hannah and almost laughed at the idea. She was, well, too prim and proper. Even if she were attracted to Andy, Liz knew her sense of morality would never allow her to follow through on any such thoughts. She smiled for the first time, brushing the notion of Andy and Hannah from her mind.

One thing she had going for her was the fact that Andy was absolutely crazy about the idea of the baby and so was his family. Andy was a good father and this thought gave Liz the security of knowing her baby would have a strong father figure. She knew she could search forever, but would never find a more devoted man. Suddenly, Doug was in her thoughts. She was musing as to the kind of a father he would be. She shook her head.

Oh, no you don't, Liz. His parents wouldn't let him be a father to any child he had. They would control them, just as they did Kelly's children. I'm sure, if the truth were known, they had a big part in the ruining of Doug's marriage. No way any child belongs in their clutches, especially mine.

After trying on half a dozen more outfits, she decided on two pair of shorts and matching tops, a summer dress, and a casual pantsuit. She left the store slightly lifted from her previous mood. Maybe Andy would call today, or maybe she'd have a text. If she didn't, she decided, she'd call him. While they weren't engaged, she had something that would bring him back to her. She had the ace in the hole.

She got in her car and headed for home. Interstate 75 was under construction as usual so she took a shortcut to her house. She exited on Mockingbird Lane and before she knew it, she'd bypassed the construction, but was stuck in a traffic jam. She was hot from the early July heat and hungry as a bear. She knew where there was a fast food drive-through near and made the necessary turns to get to it. She ordered a burger and some fries, parked, let her engine idle and ate as she waited for her hunger to subside. That's when she saw Doug's black BMW pull up beside her. He got out looking like the devil himself coming to disrupt her life again. He didn't bother asking, but opened up the passenger's door, got in and sat down. Sweat trickled down her spine. He reached for a French fry and popped it in his mouth.

"I'm not sure these are good for you. I mean, for the baby."

"Let me worry about me and my baby," she snapped.

He held up his hands and smiled that sinfully handsome smile of his. "All right. But, I'll always worry about you. You know that."

"Don't," she said flatly. "What are you doing here, Doug? Are you following me?"

He laughed. "Surely you didn't forget that my law office is right over there. You know I come to this joint almost every day. Maybe you're following me."

Her tone was short and curt. "Wishful thinking."

"Liz, can't we be cordial? I mean, we just might run into each other from time to time."

"In a city the size of Dallas that's pretty doubtful. Besides, we play in different ballparks."

He rued, remembering the past. "Not always."

She stopped short of biting into her burger. "Doug, don't do this, not today. Not when I'm feeling..."

He reached to touch her hair. "What, Honey?"

She dropped her burger into the sack. Her appetite was gone. "Nothing. I just went shopping for clothes and I'm feeling very pregnant, that's all."

"Well, if my opinion counts, I think you look..."

"Don't say wonderful, or I'll box you."

He choked on his laugh and looked into her rearview mirror, pretending vanity. "And risk you scarring this pretty face. No way!"

She couldn't help but to stare. It was a pretty face and he was only half teasing. He was fully aware of his looks. She vaguely wondered if her baby would inherit them. Disgust ran through her.

Don't you dare pine over this man. Not after what he and his family put you through. Don't you dare.

"So, Liz. When's the big day?"

She reached for her abdomen and held it.

"Not soon enough," she sighed. "I'm ready for this baby to come out."

Again he laughed. "Actually, I was talking about your wedding. When are you getting married?"

"Oh," she blushed and then presented him with a lie. "Andy's mother is in Bolivia now, but will be coming back to the states soon. Andy wants her at the wedding."

"And you're still happy?"

"Except for feeling fat and ugly, I'm very happy."

"Well," his voice became strained. "I'm glad. You deserve happiness." He looked at his watch. "Guess I should go. I'll be late for my date. Can't keep a beautiful girl waiting."

"Don't worry, Doug. If I know you, you've got another one waiting in the wings to take her place," she said sarcastically.

Something caught in his throat. "Is that really what you think of me, Liz?"

"No," she said regretfully. "I had no right saying what I did. I'm sorry."

He made a swishing sound with his mouth and reached for the doorknob, but stopped before he opened it. "Liz, if you need anything..."

"I don't," she whispered.

He turned to her and studied her for some time, hair, eyes, lips, swollen belly. Then, he leaned toward her, resting one arm on the back of her seat and one arm on the steering wheel. Their faces came within inches of each other. He moved his mouth over hers slightly. Then, he drew himself away.

"If you're lying to me, Liz, I'll never forgive you."

She was trembling. "I'm not."

Once again, his eyes trailed her girth.

"I wouldn't let them hurt you like they did with our first..."

"Hurt?" she whispered bitter. "Doug, they had us give up our baby up for adoption. I wasn't sure I'd be able to face myself again after that. I know I'll never get over what they forced us to do. It's a nightmare I live with every day of my life."

"Oh, God, I know. But you aren't the only one who relives this nightmare. Oh, Liz, we were too young to fight them. But, we're older now."

"The baby's not yours to fight for, Doug."

He nodded woefully in concession. "I know."

He opened the car door and once again turned toward her. "That beautiful woman? My date? It's Allison."

"Allison?" Liz envisioned Doug's niece, Kelly's daughter. "How is she?"

"Beautiful, like Kel. She's growing up so much you'd never recognize her. Why she's almost..."

His words were stopped by grim reality. They stared at each other, remorseful of a past so accursed, it had changed their lives forever. Each one knew what the other was thinking.

"Our daughter is seven years old, too."

"Well," he cleared his throat. "I just wanted you to know I don't have women waiting in the wings. I keep a low profile these days."

He got out without saying good-bye. She watched him get into his car and start it up, and then back out of his parking place. Just before he drove away, he tapped on his horn lightly. She gathered up her courage and held her head up high.

Just drive home and call Andy.

She only prayed that Andy was there to make things right.

Paul laid out his bed on the couch for the fourth night in a row. It was better this way. At least he and Sue weren't in constant battle with each other. Since he'd gotten home from Dallas, Paul found out that when he was gone, Paul Jr. had been out every night drinking and God knows what else. Last night he had been drinking and driving. Paul was ready to send him for treatment in the Dallas Rehab. Sue was adamant that her son would not go there, even after Paul had talked to her at length about the center. Paul was just about to lie down when Sue came in the room and sat down in a chair next to him. She looked distraught, overworked. Her voice trembled as she talked.

"Come to our bed tonight, Paul."

"Sue, we'll just end up arguing. You don't want that, do you?"

"I prefer it over this silence."

"I'm sorry, but I don't."

"Paul, let's talk about Paul Jr."

"Unless it's about treatment, I don't want to discuss it. Especially after he pulled what he did two nights ago. He could have been killed driving that fast and being so high."

"It is about treatment, Paul."

His eyes lit up. "Oh?"

"Deacon Nelson says there is a church center for troubled teens near Austin. It's Christian oriented and follows the guidelines of the church, but also uses tough love. They've been very successful breaking teens from destructive habits."

"Go on."

"We could stay with my sister when we go to visit him and save on that expense. The only problem is Deacon Nelson isn't sure it's covered by insurance. We'd have to check it out. Otherwise, it would be too expensive."

"You do realize, Sue. This is the first time you've admitted that our son has a major problem."

She fell into his arms. "I know he does. It was just too scary to admit. Saying the words makes it so real, like there's no turning back."

He held her gently. "There, Sue. I know. And don't you see? There is no turning back."

She wiped her wet face. "So, you'll go visit this place with me?"

"Yes, and if we don't like it, we'll look for another one. We'll look until we find a place we're both comfortable with."

"I'm sorry I didn't go to Dallas with you. I should have."

"It's okay," he said kissing her forehead. "At least now you're willing to look for help."

"Come to our bed tonight, Paul."

"All right," he conceded. "I'm sorry, Sue. Sorry I've been so distant. I just had to make you see."

"Me, too," she said as she followed him up the stairs.

She slipped off her clothes and laid them in a chair next to their bed. He took off his robe and underwear. They held each other for some time before he reached for her. Yet, even as they made love, Sue understood that Paul Jr. was only part of their problems.

"I'm sorry, Sue. It's been so long, over two weeks."

"Don't apologize. I'm happy just to have you here."

He held her close. "I don't deserve you."

"Why do you say that, Paul?"

He thought of Hannah, wishing she were lying beside him right now. No, he didn't deserve Sue. She deserved someone whose mind wasn't two blocks away in another woman's bedroom.

"No reason, except you're very special, Sue."

She kissed him. "So are you, Paul."

She tried to initiate a second bout of lovemaking.

"Sue, I'm really bushed."

She withdrew her drive and kissed him on the cheek.

"All right, Honey. Good night."

He rolled to his side, feeling like a world-class jerk, but couldn't force himself to make love when he didn't have the desire.

"Good night, Sue. See you in the morning."

"I love you, Paul."

"I love you," he said honestly.

Paul and Sue made plans to go to Austin that weekend. The Saturday they were to leave, he went to the office and put in a couple hours of work. On a whim, he called Hannah. He'd only spoken with her a few times since she'd gotten back from Dallas. He just had to hear her voice, and maybe, if he were lucky, she'd let him swing by her house for a visit.

"Hello," she said. Her voice was raspy, low, and incredibly sexy.

"Hello, yourself. I hope I didn't catch you at a bad time."

"Actually, I'll tell you a secret if you promise not to think badly of me. I'm still in bed."

His mind was in somewhat of a spin imagining her in bed, sensual, beautiful.

"So that's your beauty secret. It's almost ten."

"Ten! I can't believe I've slept so late!"

She laughed and he did, too, pretending they were a couple, sharing an intimate joke.

"Paul. How are you?"

"I'm good. At least I try to be positive."

"How's Paul Jr.?"

"God, not good. But Sue and I are going to look into some church program in Austin this weekend. It's designed to help teens with his type of problems. We leave today."

"Oh, Paul. I'll be praying that it works out."

"I appreciate that, Hannah," he said and then, changed the subject. "I drove by your house the other day. It looks great."

"I've been working hard. I like keeping busy."

"Do you know how wonderful it is to have you back so much like your old self? You're remarkable, Hannah. By the way, did you get the mimosa I left for you? I remember how you always loved the smell of mimosa."

"I still do. I'm just not sure it will root this late, but I can try. Thank you, Paul. That was thoughtful of you."

He got quiet and she assumed he was thinking of Paul, Jr.

"Hannah, are you busy? I mean, I'd like to talk to you about something, something personal. It won't take long."

She stretched. For some reason, she thought of Andy. His words echoed in her mind.

You know, he has a thing for you. You really should tell him to get lost.

Then, she thought of Sue. Andy was right in the sense that it was mainly Paul who had kept their friendship connected. Sue had let go years ago. Hannah didn't know if Paul clung onto their friendship because he had a thing for her, as Andy suggested, or if she was her final link to Sammy, a man he loved like a brother. Hannah always believed the latter, but now, in light of their last meeting where he kissed her with such longing, she had to wonder. In any case, she knew it was time, time to put a stop to his interpretation of their relationship. She would let go quietly. She would do this to honor the friendship the four had shared—Sue and Paul, and her and Sammy. Letting go would not be easy.

"Actually, Paul, I do have plans today, but please, you and Sue stop by anytime when you get home."

"Sure," he said disappointed. "We can do that."

"Paul," she said delicately. "See to Sue. This situation with Paul Jr. has to be hard on her and she's going to need you more now than ever. It won't do for her to worry about matters that have little significance."

NINETEEN

Andy came home to discover that the home he and Jean had lived in for ten years had been sold. Jean and Frank were in Austin looking for a place for them to live. Andy would have the boys another week. Tired, cranky, and needing a break from each other, Andy and the boys made plans to spend the weekend with Nana and his dad.

"You sure Nana's up to it, Dad?

"We'll keep the boys out of her hair when she's tired. I'm glad you're coming. There's some property I want you to look at with me. It's not too far from Greenville, about thirty miles or so."

"What kind of property, Dad?"

"Andy, do you remember Dennis Larkin? We were in sales together at IBM?"

"Oh, sure. You took me horseback riding on his dad's ranch—a nice setup as I recall, cattle, horses. You're not thinking of buying a ranch, are you, Dad?"

"Only part of it. Dennis' dad wants to scale back. Dennis' grandfather has recently passed away and his father's not in the best of health. It's just gotten to be too much for him and he's relying on Dennis to help him manage things. Well, Dennis does what he can, but he's a salesman, not a rancher. His dad is particular about his property and doesn't want it to go to just anyone. He heard I was back in Dallas to stay and called me up. Wants me to look at it. If I'm interested, I'll show it to your mom when she gets here. She may not want something with such a vast amount of upkeep."

"Mom thrives on upkeep, Dad, and you know it. Out of curiosity, how many acres are we talking about?"

"Somewhere around twenty acres right now, along with his grandfather's house. He said it's a sturdy house, but needs quite a bit of work done to it. He got too frail to take care of it himself and too proud to ask for help."

"Sounds like someone we once knew, huh?"

Andy, of course, was referring to his Paps.

"I had no idea you'd be interested in living so far out, Dad."

"Well, before I was city folk, I was raised on a farm."

"Yea," Andy mused. "It was great."

A lull fell between them as they remembered Paps.

When they resumed their conversation, it was merely to pass the time. Andy was dying to ask his dad about Hannah, but didn't dare. John wanted to ask Andy if he'd seen Liz yet, but he didn't dare. They ended their call with John telling Andy about his mother's plans to come home.

"Oh, Andy. I almost forgot the most important news."

"What's that?"

"Mom will be here in less than a week."

"I can't wait, Dad. I know you can't either."

"I do miss her."

"Me, too. Mom has a way of making everything right."

Andy called Liz before Hannah, because he wanted to save the best for last. He left the boys with Jean's mother for the night and went by Liz's figuring this was as good a time as any for them to talk. She couldn't have been happier to see him. When he saw her, he was taken aback by her appearance. The baby had grown so much in the three weeks he was away.

"Liz," he teased. "I think we're having a linebacker."

She blew out a breath. "I feel like I'm ready to deliver already."

Andy noticed she was a bit pale and swollen. He got a pillow and put it on one arm of the couch.

"Come here," he ordered. "Put your head on the pillow and your feet in my lap."

232

Liz did as he told her. Andy took her shoes off and began rubbing her feet gently.

"Andy, do you have any idea how good this feels? In a minute I'll be purring."

"You should quit your job, or at least slow down."

"Oh, yea. And who's going to pay my bills?"

"Me," he said flatly.

"Andy, you can't afford..."

"Don't you worry about money, Liz. What bills do you need me to pay? Give them to me. I'll pay them."

"Andy, I was only speaking in generalities. But thank you for offering."

"I guess we should start thinking about a crib and stuff for the baby."

"My sister is letting me have her crib and her high chair. I think she even has a car seat."

"What about bottles and diapers and clothes?"

"Well, we'll have to get them. I'm breast feeding, Andy."

"Yea? That's cool. Jean never did. I always thought it was the most natural thing a mother could do."

"But don't think you're getting out of feedings, Andy. That's what breast pumps are for."

"You mean they have pumps that...oh, don't tell me."

She laughed. "How can you be so green with three children?"

"My job was diapers and baths. I'm great with diapers and baths."

"Oh, Andy," she smiled as he continued to knead her feet. "It's so good to have you here. I missed you."

"Liz, don't," he said somberly.

"Just because we postponed the engagement, Andy, doesn't mean I've postponed my feelings. I still love you."

"Liz, I can't pretend…"

She held her stomach abruptly. "Oh, my God!"

"What is it?" he asked jarred.

"The baby moved. Put your hand on my stomach."

He stopped massaging and placed his hand on her abdomen.

"Move down lower, Andy. Can you feel it? He's kicking."

Andy felt a slight kick and then a more distinct one. He laughed out and then moved his hand around to feel the baby kick once more. He was moved beyond words, recalling similar intimate moments he'd shared with Jean. His heart soared with pride and joy and something like immortality. He lay next to her on the couch with his head resting on her abdomen.

"Oh, Liz. Thank you for this moment."

She ran a hand through his hair. "Oh, Andy, there will be so many more."

The revelations of feeling the life of his unborn child brought tears to his eyes. Still lying beside her, he prayed for another moment. It never came. Liz dared to ask him what her heart feared.

"Andy, do I turn you off physically?"

He raised his head. "No, Liz, you don't turn me off. You're a beautiful woman."

"But, you never touch me. I mean, you don't...come to me, not like you used to, anyways."

"Liz, I thought I made it clear to you. I don't want to give you false hope."

"Is it Jean? Andy, do you still care for her?"

"Liz, stop," he said. "Don't do this to yourself. Can't you accept...?"

"'Cause if it's Jean, I guess I understand. I mean, I don't like it. But, I know how much you loved her and I'm not fool enough to believe you can turn your feelings off just because I love you so much. We were very active, Andy. It was good. A man doesn't give up good sex unless, well, unless he's uninterested. Either my being pregnant turns you off or there's someone...else. Is it Jean, Andy?"

"Liz, Jean and I are finished."

234

"I know. I know. But, that doesn't mean you don't still care."

"Of course, I care. She's the mother of my boys."

He stood up and walked toward the window staring out at nothing in particular. She watched him struggle with what he had to say. Then, he sat back down next to her and took her hand.

"I am in love with someone else, Liz, but it's not Jean."

She closed her eyes and let out a breath. "Oh, God, it's someone other than Jean. Who, Andy? No, I already know who. I just didn't want to believe it. It's Hannah, isn't it?"

Shock registered on his face. "Liz, how...?"

"Call it intuition. Fool as I am, I thought it was just a passing phase you were going through because the two of you were so near each other."

"Liz, I never meant to hurt...I plan to be here for you always, through everything."

She swallowed hard, trying not to cry. "Does she lo...love you, too?"

He nodded. "Liz, nothing's happened between us."

"You mean sexually?"

"Yea, sexually."

Something like determination surged through her.

"Andy, is she worth giving up the chance to be with your child always? If you don't love me now, Andy, at least know that we get along. Love could happen later. And, we have our baby to bond us. That's more than most couples ever have."

"I won't deny we get along, Liz. You're a terrific person. It just doesn't seem fair to you, or the baby, to start off with only half a heart in the arrangement."

She placed his hand over her abdomen once more. Then, she drew him toward her. He lay over her with his arms outstretched, careful not to press down on her. She pulled his head up and lowered hers to meet his. Their mouths touched. It wasn't a passionate kiss, but it was endearing.

"Give us a chance, Andy."

He could feel her belly contract under him.

She reached for one more kiss. "I love you, Andy. Your child needs you. And Andy, there's one more thing I found out while you were away."

"What?"

"We're having a boy."

"A boy...I had a feeling."

He dropped his head into her hair. His outstretched arms were shaking as he hovered over her. He conceded to the rightness of their being together. He cried in her arms.

Hannah, forgive me.

"I'll try, Liz," he whispered. "But, I have to tell Hannah in person."

"Andy, are you strong enough to do that?"

His arms gave way and he rolled off the couch and sat on the floor, uncertain. He caressed her girth and then her face.

"I don't know if I am, Liz. Maybe you should go with me to Nana's. Knowing you're there will remind me of my promise to you and the baby."

She moved to sit on the floor next to him.

"Andy, we'll be good together. You'll see. Hannah's a beautiful and gracious woman. She'll find love again."

He buried his face in his hands. "Don't say anymore, Liz. Don't. I can't bear to hear it."

She moved his hands and turned his head to face her. She leaned to kiss him. His lips were salty and cold.

"Time, Andy. Time is all we need. I love you enough for the both of us. And for now, that's enough."

Hannah was working in her garden and Grace was sitting in a lawn chair watching her when Andy and Liz and the boys arrived. Bobby ran straight for Grace.

"Nana!" he yelled. "We're here! We're here!"

He washed her wrinkled face with kisses.

236

"Let Nana have a look at you. My goodness, I believe you've grown a foot since I last saw you."

Bobby went to where Hannah was and knelt down beside her.

Andy's home!

"What you doin'?"

"I'm trying to get these fern plants to spread. They're being stubborn, I'm afraid."

"Do you talk to them?"

"You know, I do. But, maybe you'd have better luck.

"Okay, little ferns, you'd better grow or Hannah will be yanking you out with the rest of the weeds."

Hannah laughed. "Now why didn't I think of tough love?"

She looked up to see John and Mathew in an embrace. Jeff walked up to Nana and brushed her cheek with a kiss, far more reserved than his younger brother. He smiled at Hannah.

Where are you, Andy?

"Your garden's nice, Hannah. It's pretty like you."

She looked at him both touched and somewhat surprised.

"Why thank you, Jeff. You're awfully sweet."

He blushed. "Maybe I could water it for you while I'm here."

"That would certainly help me out. I have more flowers on the side of my house, too. The weeds go crazy. I could use some help there, as well."

"Sure," he smiled widely. He stayed fixed by his Nana, staring starry-eyed at Hannah.

From behind her, Hannah heard Liz call out to her.

"Hello, Hannah. It's good to see you again."

Hannah stood and slowly turned toward Liz. Her heart gave way and her insides were flipping around, but outwardly, she was composed. Liz's presence could only mean one thing. Andy was going to try to make a go of their relationship. While she knew it was the right thing to do, she was human enough to secretly wish it wouldn't happen. She pulled her glove off her right hand and extended it to Liz.

"Good to see you, too."

The two shook hands. Liz felt jealousy. Hannah felt fear. From the corner of her eye she saw Andy standing next to John near Grace's back door. She knew he was watching them and this fact unnerved her. She could feel her self-composure betraying her and so she made an excuse to go inside.

"Liz, would you mind seeing Grace to her house. I've got a million and one calls to make before the day's over. I can't believe I've let time slip by me like this."

"Of course, I will, Hannah."

Hannah turned to Jeff, who still stood by Grace.

"This evening when I water, I'd sure like your help."

"You got it," he burst out, and then ran off like a rookie who had just made the big league.

Hannah walked as quickly into her house as dignity and her legs would allow. She closed the door behind her and leaned against it, unable at first, to catch hold of her breath. The moment of reckoning had slapped her so savagely, she hadn't had time to prepare. Why hadn't Andy warned her Liz was coming? Why hadn't John? She slid to the floor, emotionally drained.

You could have warned me, Andy. I wasn't prepared.

Tears flowed down her face, first slowly, but then, like a rushing stream. Her heart ached and she felt as though she might faint there on her kitchen floor. She sat there for some time before she heard the knock on her door. Minutes went by before she had the courage to answer it, already knowing it was Andy. She let him in and he quietly shut the door. One look at her and his heart was broken. He let out a cry of agony.

"Hannah, I'm sorry."

She couldn't speak just yet, couldn't look at him. She walked to the sink and stared out the window.

"Liz looks wonderful, happy...maternal."

"Hannah..."

"Don't! Don't look at me with that pitiable, cow-eyed stare. Don't you dare pity me!"

"It's not pity, Hannah. It's regret."

"That's almost as bad."

"It's not for you. It's for me."

She doubled over with agony.

"What do you want from me, Andy? You've made your choice. We both knew it would come to this. Please, leave me alone."

He sat down at her kitchen table and laid his head down. He didn't bother holding back his tears. His cries echoed throughout her house and her heart. In a minute, she would go mad. She walked toward him slowly, this broken man she loved so desperately. She ran a hand through his dark hair, so wonderfully Andy. Her voice hushed his cries.

"Don't cry, Andy. I can't bear it. I don't hold you accountable. You're doing what's right. Don't cry, Darling."

"I love you, Hannah. I don't think I can make it without you, without touching you, without hearing your voice. This is even harder than with Jean. With Jean, I knew it was over. You're my soul mate, Hannah. You have more of my heart than anyone else will ever have."

Her legs buckled up and she sat on a chair next to him. She could lend him no comfort because she was as broken as he was. They sat there, he crying outwardly, she crying silently. The sound of her clock ticking throbbed in her mind. As if frozen in this black moment, both were at a loss for words. He finally lifted his head and his eyes told his heartache. Without speaking, they said their good-byes. He stood, zombie-like before her, making the automatic motions of a man leaving a room, only it was as if he were removed from himself. He walked to the door and just as he was about to leave, he lowered his head.

"Hannah, I need to feel your arms around me one last time."

Still sitting at her table, she looked at him as if his request was as normal as waving. She stood slowly and moved toward him. She noticed that her blind was drawn down over the window and she felt slightly secure by this fact. This would be their last, private moment. She stood before him and wrapped her arms around his neck. He lifted his head to face her. She was the most beautiful person he had ever held in his arms. Conflicting emotions such as anger and love took over the moment. Recklessly, their lips met.

They kissed so hard, so passionately, they fell to their knees. Not once did they break from their kiss, but rather took in air through their open mouths. Tongues explored mouths and necks and faces. Hands moved in a heated rush, afraid they would never experience such passion again. He came to know the shape of her body as his hands moved over her clothed body rashly. She felt the extent of his desire as he pressed himself hard against her. They took as much from this moment as their sense of decency would allow. Love soared in their hearts, and fear in their souls. No woman, even Jean, had filled him with so much passion, so much desire. Numb lips parted, but hearts still raced. He rested his head against her breasts.

"I will always love you, Hannah. Always."

His parting kiss was gentle, tender. She leaned her head against the wall and listened as he opened the door. Fear suddenly consumed her and she called out his name. Once more, he was by her side.

"I just wanted you to know that you showed me how to love again, Andy."

His throat and eyes and heart were on fire.

"You did the same for me."

She smiled warmly. Her eyes shut. They caressed each other, cheek to cheek.

"You're my lamplighter, Hannah. You give me hope."

He leaned to kiss her forehead without looking into her eyes. Then, she heard her door click shut and knew he was gone for good.

TWENTY

Hannah withdrew from the Padgetts, but not from the world. She turned to others for support, in particular, Elaine. She went to see Grace less frequently since Ann had arrived, knowing Ann was more than capable of taking her place, at least, with the physical duties of taking care of Grace. Hannah still stole moments to be with Grace, because she couldn't bear the thought of letting her go completely. She loved Grace and letting go of her would be like letting go of Sammy and Gabe and Julie — and of course, Andy.

She worked longer hours for Elaine. Her garden and yard became more of an obsession than it had been. She worked on things in the house that she'd neglected for so many years, like painting and striping the hardwood floors and wallpapering. When her restlessness could not be satisfied with her usual activities and she had exhausted Elaine of work and energy, Elaine's nephew, Nick, made an unexpected visit and dropped off three undisclosed, sealed boxes, courtesy of his aunt.

"Here," he huffed. "Aunt Elaine says to get busy on this and not to call her until you've used everything in these boxes, or at least a week."

Nick left, almost as abruptly as he'd arrived. Hannah cautiously opened the boxes. When she saw what was inside, she sat bewildered over the mass assortment of art supplies Elaine had sent. There were brushes, oils, water paints, canvases, sketch pads, charcoals, pastels, dry powder for ceramics, just to name a few. She had no idea where to begin first, so impulsively, she called Elaine, even after being warned.

"You forgot the kiln, Elaine."

"I forgot the what?"

"The kiln, for ceramics. How am I supposed to do ceramics without a kiln?"

"You're talking a foreign language to me here."

"It's an oven, Elaine, and I'm only joking. I'm overwhelmed by what you did. I just had to call. And, I'm sorry I've been such a pest. I promise to do better."

"Oh, baby girl, you're not a pest. You're just sprouting and I can't keep up with you. I'm not complaining, mind you. I've got all kinds of things in store for you."

"Oh, boy, you're making me nervous."

"Don't worry. I'm not throwing anything at you that you aren't ready for."

"What kinds of things?"

"Oh, like maybe working at the office a day or two during the week, and maybe renewing your driver's license and getting back out on the road."

"Oh, Elaine, you're crazier than I am."

"Well, now, that's not too crazy. You're one of the sanest people I know. Now, would you get to painting or drawing or whatever, and leave me alone? I've got an office to manage."

"Elaine, you're like a sister to me. I don't know what I'd do without you."

"Don't you dare get mushy on me. I'll cry and the way I wear my make-up, that wouldn't be a pretty sight."

"Oh, Elaine, I do love you."

"Who doesn't? Now, bug off!"

"I'm going! I'm going!"

Just as she was about to hang up, Hannah heard Elaine's brassy voice choke up. "Listen, Sweetie. I'm proud of you and the way you're pulling through this Andy business. I have the feeling you're doing better than he is."

"Why do you say that, Elaine?"

"Honey, look what he had to let go."

Hannah transformed her dining room into an art room. Her spirit was flowing at full speed as she engaged in a talent and a passion she'd long ago let slip away. She became absorbed in her sketching. So absorbed, she worked through lunch and up to nightfall. She made rough sketches of ordinary things that surrounded her—her garden, her birdbath, a vase her mother had given her, her clock, her wedding band, her porch swing. By nightfall, she looked upon her work with the scrutiny of a perfectionist, always her worst critic. By midnight, after sketching a half a dozen more pictures, she went to bed declaring she'd lost her touch and that returning to art was a waste of her time. Yet when she awoke the next morning, she was drawn to her newly made studio and her recent sketches, admitting that her initial appraisal may have been premature. They weren't so bad after all, especially for someone who'd been in a four year hiatus.

As she did her morning dishes, she happened to notice that Jeff Padgett was walking aimlessly about Grace's backyard. He looked lost, and Hannah was remembering Andy and the first time she'd seen him after so many years. His son had that same look of discontentment. Suddenly, her heart roused, alerted by the possibility that Andy might be next door. She couldn't face him yet. Her pain was too raw. She looked for his truck, but didn't see it. Jeff stared in the direction of her house and walked toward her garden. He searched around, and she had the suspicion he was searching for her. He moved toward her hose that rested near her back door. He turned the spout on and began to water the garden, careful not to disrupt or harm any part of it. She watched him from a distance. He was so much like Andy, like John. His hair was dark. His eyes were blue. He loved the outdoors. She was entranced, bewitched as she watched him lovingly examine the garden, pulling a weed here and there, lost in the scope of duty. As she watched, the phone rang, temporarily interrupting the moment. It was John.

"Hannah, I'm sorry about Jeff. Is he bothering you?"

244

"Not at all, John."

"We've been worried about him. He's not taking the move well, and so Andy's letting him stay with us for a while."

"I see," she said cautiously.

John immediately understood her apprehension.

"Hannah, Andy's not here. He's in Dallas. I brought Jeff back with me last night."

Relief flowed through her. An uncomfortable moment fell between them, but then John asked, "How are you, Hannah? Really?"

"I'm, I'm ….all right."

"If you need anything…"

"I know where to turn," she finished. "Thank you."

"Well," he said sympathetically. "I wanted to remind you."

When she hung up, she was shaking. How could the mere mention of Andy's name send her into a tailspin? There were so many reminders, she wondered if she would ever be able to escape them. Once again, she looked out to watch as Jeff dallied in her garden. She remembered the unplanted mums she'd bought a few days ago and had an idea. She reached for her hat and two pairs of gloves and went to her utility room where the plants were. She grabbed them and walked outside.

"Well, good morning, Jeff. How fortunate of me to find such a helper when I need one."

"Hi, Hannah. Hope you're not mad at me."

"Don't be silly, Jeff. I'm glad you're here. I was just about to find a home for these mums in the garden. Have any suggestions?"

Jeff looked around. "How about over there by those green plants, the ones with the fuzz on them."

"That's hazel alder, and you're right. I think that's the perfect spot for the mums."

She threw him a pair of gloves.

"How would you like to plant them?"

"Me?"

She nodded. "I'll show you how."

She showed him how to carefully part the soil and moisten it so that it was ready for the plant and it would accept its new home. She gently took the plants from the pots, careful not to tear the roots that had already formed. They set the plants in their new home and covered them with topsoil, gently packing the dirt over their roots.

"You don't want to water them too much for at least a day. The shock might be too much."

"You know a lot about plants."

"Not really. I've sent my share of plants to plant heaven, usually from over watering and over feeding, or planting them too early or too late. But, I go with my instincts. If you're lucky, they accept the home you've chosen for them and bless you with a beautiful showing."

"You want me to water the plants and bushes around the yard, too?"

"You know, I do. I've really neglected them these past few days. There's another hose on the side of the house."

He nodded. "I could water your grass if you want."

"Well, now. Isn't that nice of you to offer, but I couldn't impose on you."

He kicked the ground. "You aren't. I want to."

"Well, all right. The sprinkler's in..."

"I know, in Nana's shed."

"I have one, too, Jeff."

"I'll get both of them and do Nana's yard, too."

"You sure that's not too much for you to do?"

He waved his hand up, so much like Andy. "I can handle it, Hannah. Honest."

She held her heart. "All right, but come by for some lemonade when you need a break."

"Yes, ma'am," he beamed. "I'll be sure and do that."

246

He disappeared around the side of her house, and she could do nothing but cry.

Hannah sketched Jeff using pastels. She captured the innocence of a young boy as he bonded with nature on a summer's day. His hair was matted, his clothing wet from sweat. His eyes were the color of columbines and his lips rosy red. She detailed his pudgy cheeks and childlike nose, semblance of his toddler years, yet formative enough that the eye could see a budding young boy. When she drew his smile, it was a reflection of generations of Padgett men's smiles, free, slightly tilted, and honest. What she failed to capture was an eight year old's growing crush on the garden lady who lived next door to his Nana, a lady with startling brown eyes, ruby lips and long, ebony hair.

They drank lemonade and made peanut butter and jelly sandwiches. He talked about Austin and his brothers. She talked about drawing and flowers and Grace. She showed him her sketches and he became her biggest fan. He told her he was going to have a new baby brother and she said she knew. He said his dad was thinking of buying a farm. Hannah seemed surprised.

"A farm? Where?"

"Near Greenville. The house is big and junky."

"You mean it needs a lot of work?"

"Yea, but dad's really excited."

"I can imagine. You'd like it, too, wouldn't you?"

"Yea, I just wish I could live there with him."

"I'm sure he'd like that, too. You'll see your dad a lot. He'll make certain of that. Besides, your mom would be very sad if you weren't with her."

"Dad needs someone, too."

Loyalty

Jeff looked at her as if he might cry. "Hannah, Dad won't forget me, will he?"

"Oh, Jeff, no. He'd never do that. He loves you too much."

"But the new baby and…"

"It doesn't matter. He has enough love for all of his children. Oh, Jeff, wipe that idea from your head. Your dad will love you forever."

He smiled proudly. "I know. My dad's the best."

"Yes," she had to agree. "He is."

He blurted out. "He's getting married next Saturday."

A whirling blackness crashed through her. She knew it was inevitable, but actually hearing the words was so, so damn real. She lost control of her speech and so she just sat there, staring at Jeff as if he'd just sentenced her to death.

"Hannah, can I ask you something?"

She nodded, because the words still wouldn't form.

"Are men supposed to cry?"

"Cry?" she managed.

"Yea. I caught Dad crying last night. He said he was just sad because his boys were going to be so far away."

"What else could it be?" she said none too easily.

"Maybe he misses you."

"Me?" her jaw dropped.

"Maybe. He has your picture in his wallet."

Her hands went up to her mouth. "Oh, Jeff…"

He stood up and hugged her from behind, patting her shoulders gently.

"It's okay, Hannah. I guess you miss him, too."

It had never been John Padgett's intention to buy the Larkin's property, but merely to entice Andy into doing so. His plan worked like a charm. The moment Andy saw the worn down house and the mass of rich farmland that surrounded it, he was sold — hook, line and sinker.

"It would be a great place to raise a family. Don't you think, Andy?" his father had coerced.

"Your family's raised, Dad."

"The boys could each have a room to stay in when they came for visits. The baby could sleep downstairs with you and Liz."

"Why you old snake. You planned this all along, didn't you, Dad?"

John only grinned. The rest was a matter of negotiating. Andy was able to get a loan to buy the house, along with twenty acres, because Joe Broughton verified that Andy was still a full time employee at the Grocery. With John lending him the down payment, it was a done deal and would only be a matter of time before Andy would have the farm he'd always dreamed he'd have. The farm, his boys, and the baby were all that kept him going. They were his primary concentration. Even though his farm wasn't officially his until the loan went through, Dennis let him go ahead and begin the repairs. Andy bought a used tractor and bulldozer at an auction and his first line of business was to clear away the brush and weeds that overtook the property. That's what he was doing when his dad and Dennis came by for a visit, the Friday before he was to be married.

"Now, I don't know about you, John," Dennis teased. "But riding a tractor the day before I got married wasn't top on my list of priorities. Boy," he scolded Andy. "What the dickens are you doing here? Go back to Dallas and get yourself ready for that pretty gal of yours."

Andy checked his watch. It was almost four p.m.

"Damn, time ran away from me."

"You don't want to be so worn out you don't enjoy the honeymoon," Dennis continued his teasing.

John Studied Andy's drawn face. "Pack it up, Son. You've done enough for one day."

Andy nodded. "Yep. Guess it'll be here when I get back."

Dennis and John assessed the work Andy had done already and Dennis was pleased. "You know, Andy. Any time you need work, full or part time, I've got enough at my place to keep you busy until this place is paid for."

"Oh, yea? If you're serious I just might be interested."

"Oh, I'm serious all right. And I'll make it worth your while. A strong hand like you, one who knows the land and animals, isn't easy to come by. I'd be generous, knowing you've got three boys and a baby on the way."

"I appreciate that, Dennis. Let's talk after…"

"Yea, I know. You gotta confer with the Mrs." He looked at John. "Guess he's already whipped."

Andy played along with Dennis. How the hell was he to know how miserable he was? Liz got along with him. Hell, she got along with everyone. Everyone loved her, everyone except him. He was really a sorry bastard. Liz was going out of her way to make him happy, even knowing about Hannah. She'd actually been great and a life with her wouldn't be a bad life. It just wouldn't be the same as a life with Hannah. He tried to brush Hannah from his thoughts and concentrate on the wedding. He had a lot to do before tomorrow. To rally up some excitement within himself, he thought of the baby. Soon, his new son would arrive. That was excitement enough. He looked at his father.

"Guess I better get back to Dallas. So, I'll see you and Mom tonight at the restaurant?" he reminded.

"Yea, Andy, but if you've got a moment, I'd like to talk?"

"Sure, Dad. Sure."

"Sounds like a father and son thing," Dennis said. "Andy, can you give your dad a ride back to his car?"

Andy nodded. "I mean it, Dennis. I'd really like to talk later."

"You got it," Dennis said as he walked back to his truck. "Good luck, Andy. Liz is a terrific gal."

Andy waved. "Thanks, Dennis—for everything."

When Dennis left, John stood still staring at the horizon.

"It's a nice setup, Son. It suits you."

250

"I do love it, Dad. I appreciate your helping me get it."

He shuffled his feet in the dirt. "I'd do anything for you, Andy. You may not believe this, but I want you to be happy. Can we talk about tomorrow?"

"Not much to say, Dad. I'm getting married."

"I know, Son, but, I'm so worried about you."

Andy laid his hand on his dad's shoulder. "Don't be, Dad. It's like I told Hannah once. It really doesn't matter how I feel or how she feels. What matters is the baby. In a way, Liz is sacrificing more than any of us. She's marrying a man she knows is in love with another woman. I'd say we're all living our own little hell, wouldn't you?"

Liz and Andy were married at Liz's family home the last Saturday in July. They married at two in the afternoon and afterwards, the bride and groom and their families went to the party room, at the restaurant where Liz worked, for a quaint reception. Liz was radiant, wearing a satin white, mid-length dress that did little to disclose her pregnancy, but she didn't care. She was reeling as she floated around the room chatting with those who came. Andy was more upbeat than he anticipated. His sons were with him, and Jean. Frank hadn't come because of work and Andy thought it was just as well. When Jean came up to congratulate him, he couldn't help but notice how lovely she was.

"You look wonderful, Jean. Thanks for bringing the boys."

"I wanted to. Andy, Jeff is going to fight going back to Austin with me."

"I don't think so, Jean. We had a long talk last night. He's willing to give Austin a chance. We did some negotiating."

"Oh, yea, what?"

He closed his eyes, ready for battle. "Christmas."

She burst out laughing. "You got it."

He opened his eyes in surprise. "What? No arguing?"

251

"I think Christmas is the least I can do after uprooting them and separating them from their father."

He kissed her cheek. "You know, if we weren't married to other people, I just might suggest we tie the knot again."

"Oh, Andy," she smiled through tears. "Sometimes I wonder how I ever let you go."

"Yea," he pretended smugness. "Me, too."

They smiled at one another, fully knowing there would always be bonds between them — first love, the boys. Liz and Andy's mom, Ann, walked up to them. Liz took Andy by the arm.

"Is this a private party or can anyone join in?"

Andy put his arm around Liz's shoulder.

"Any party I'm at you two are welcome to join."

Liz kissed him fully on the mouth. Andy was only slightly embarrassed. Ann Padgett was studying her son with great concern, for she knew firsthand of his situation. Tall and lean, with a head of silver hair that was styled short, Andy considered his mother the epitome of grace and beauty. Her voice almost sailed when she spoke. As a child, he rarely remembered her raising her voice, even to discipline her sons. Rather, she took them calmly to the side and taught them the lessons of life through example. Andy looked at his mother with loving eyes, imagining that Hannah might look the same when she was sixty. He quickly pushed thoughts of Hannah away. So much he wanted to keep Hannah from his mind out of respect for Liz, especially today. Jean kissed his cheek and took Ann's hand, leading her away. This left Andy and Liz alone to mingle with their other guests. He made a conscious effort to be doting and devout. He noticed that she had banished her shoes along the way and he laughed.

"I guess you'll want another massage tonight."

She leaned closer and whispered seductively to him.

"Tonight, I want it all."

252

Liz and Andy spent their first night as husband and wife at Andy's apartment. Family and friends had all gone home and they were alone by ten o'clock. Andy ran Liz's bath water and filled it with some kind of bath bubbles he knew she liked. He decided that since he was married, he'd give everything he had or it would be a mockery to what he had sacrificed, which was Hannah. In his room, he took her and held her tightly. His kiss was full and honest. He unzipped her dress and was about to slide it off her shoulders when she stopped him.

"I'm a little self-conscious these days."

He smiled. "All right. Your bath is ready."

She kissed him again. "I won't be long."

While she bathed, he showered. When he was finished, he lay on the bed waiting. He was feeling a little self-conscious these days, too, so he slid on his briefs. As he waited, his thoughts naturally turned to Hannah, just as they always did at night. He wondered if he'd be able to pull tonight off. There was only one woman he wanted and he was feeling like an adulterer, even though he wasn't married to Hannah. Liz was his wife. He sat up to rid his mind of her. What kind of a heel fantasizes about another woman when his wife was getting ready for him in the other room? He decided to hurry Liz along before he lost his nerve. He knocked on the bathroom door.

"Liz?"

There was no answer.

"Honey?"

Still, there was no answer. He opened the door slightly. Liz had fallen asleep in the tub. He almost cried. It was the first time he'd felt anything close to love for her. She was exhausted, he knew, and she was exhausted because the baby had taken all of her energy. He reached for the towel on the hook and nudged her gently.

"Liz, wake up."

She stirred slightly.

"Andy? Oh, I must have fallen asleep."

"Come on, Mama. Let's get you out of here."

She stood and he wrapped her in the towel. Then, he lifted her into his arms and carried her to the bed.

"Pretty soon, you won't be able to carry me."

He smiled and then helped her in her gown.

"Andy, would you get me a glass of milk."

He kissed her forehead.

"You got it."

When he returned to the bedroom, she was already sleeping. He set the milk down and walked to the other side of the bed. When he lay down, she barely moved. He watched her sleep for some time before he attempted to do so himself. He thought this was an appropriate way for them to spend their first night together as man and wife, considering the circumstances. His loneliness was somewhat eased by the fact that he'd done the honorable thing in marrying Liz. She was, after all, the mother of his unborn son.

Elaine wasn't about to let Hannah dwell in self-pity on the day Andy got married, so she dragged her out of Blossom and the two went shopping. For the first time in over four years, Hannah went to a mall.

"Elaine, I'm going to panic."

"So panic. Someone will lend you some Prozac. It's prescribed like it's water these days."

"Elaine, I'm serious. I'm dizzy. I need to leave."

"Look, Honey. I figure the worst that can happen is that you'll keel over and I'll have to call the paramedics. Who knows, maybe one will be tall, dark and handsome."

She rolled her eyes. "I've had two tall, dark and handsome men. The next one's going to be a blonde, maybe a Swede."

"That's the spirit. Off with the old and on with the new."

"Help," Hannah cried. "I'm being kidnapped by a lunatic."

They went to every store in the mall that had clothing for women. Hannah ended up with half a dozen outfits she didn't need. Throughout the day, men were constantly giving her the once over, some smiling, some were even bold enough to speak. Always their advances sent her into a panic and she declared that she just had to leave, and every time Elaine would brush her off until they had been shopping all day. Exhausted, Hannah sat down on a bench.

"I'm not going into one more store."

"Oh, yes, you are. Just one more. You'll love this one."

She led her to a lingerie shop, clearly more intended for men than women.

"What are we here for, Elaine?"

"This one's for me, Honey. You don't need this stuff. You'd look sexy in a straight jacket. It's for me. Bob loves anything leopard."

"Please don't tell me anymore."

As Elaine shopped, Hannah haphazardly shuffled through some very revealing underwear. A male customer happened by and smiled at her appreciatively. She felt bold enough to smile back.

"So this is what women like?" he said grinning.

"Actually, I think we buy this because men like it."

Abruptly, she turned her back to him, mortified that she had just said what she did. She was halfway out of the store when she realized she was carrying a pair of black, sheer panties with red roses at the crotch. She stopped dead in her tracks and slowly turned to see if the man was still there. He was, and was watching her with immense pleasure. A clerk happened by and saw Hannah with the panties.

"Would you like to purchase those, Ma'am?"

"Purchase?" She looked at the panties and then the man. "Yes. Yes, I would."

The clerk rang up eight dollars and thirty-two cents. She wanted to yell out, *for a pair of underwear,* but she didn't. She paid the clerk and walked out of the store, where she sat on a bench to wait for Elaine. As she waited, the gentleman in the store came up to her and leaned down to whisper in her ear.

"A nice selection. You gave me something to dream about tonight."

Then, he walked away. She was still jumbled when Elaine walked out of the store.

"Hannah, what happened? Why did you leave so fast?"

Hannah grabbed her by the arm and dragged her toward the mall exit.

"We're leaving, Elaine, and I'm not taking any arguing from you."

"I'm coming! I'm coming! You mind telling me what's got you so riled up?"

She stopped and looked at Elaine frustrated and confused.

"You want to know why I'm so upset? I'll tell you. I just paid eight dollars and thirty-two cents for a pair of underwear."

Hannah dreamed of Andy that night. They were lying under the moonlight on a quilted blanket. He was holding her and telling her that he loved her. He was kissing her and moving his hands into forbidden places. He was undressing her garment by garment and when he reached to slip off the final article of clothing, he slid off a pair of black, sheer panties. He smiled and spoke in a sensual voice as he examined the garment.

"Hannah, My Love, how did you know that I have a thing for red roses?"

TWENTY-ONE

Andy drove home deciding that the only way to keep his life on the straight and narrow path was to keep himself as busy as possible. He fought daily the impulse to pick up the phone and call Hannah, just to hear her voice. So many times, he wanted to make up some excuse to go to Nana's so that he might catch a glimpse of her. Three weeks into his marriage, he was now able to control these impulses, but thinking of her was something he had little control over, although he did manage to drive thoughts of her back when they surfaced. At these times, he thought of the baby and the things that needed to be done at the farm. He was driving himself, literally, into physical exhaustion, so that when he lay his head down, he was too tired to think.

Liz and Andy remained in his apartment until the loan to the farm was finalized, even though Dennis had told him he could move in anytime. Andy wanted everything just right for Liz and the baby, and too, Liz was still putting in four hours a day at the restaurant. The apartment was more convenient for her. He worked for Dennis the better part of the day and then he'd go to his place and work at least four more hours. Today, he was running past his usual time. He looked at his watch as he turned into the apartment complex. It was almost nine. Liz had his dinner warming in the oven. He ate, showered and then joined her in their bedroom, where she was reading a book in bed. When he lay down next to her, she placed her book to the side and cuddled close to him.

"Andy, you're wearing yourself out. Can't you slow down some?"

"Not if you want a house anytime soon."

"I wish I could be more help."

"Your job is to stay healthy."

"Andy," she spoke in a possessive tone. "I want you."

"You got me, Liz."

"No, silly. You know what I mean."

He turned to her. She'd been good not to force the issue. During their three weeks as husband and wife, they had never actually consummated their marriage. They had done a lot of heavy kissing and touching, and this had seemed to satisfy them both. Now, as she was getting closer to term it seemed likely to him that they should wait until after the baby was born. He almost laughed at his own hypocrisy, remembering that he and Jean had enjoyed a full sex life up until the month she delivered. He knew what was really going on here, and he doubted he was fooling Liz. He reached to kiss her hard and passionately.

"I'm sorry I haven't been a good husband," he said sliding his hand up her gown. "I promise to do better,"

"You're a great husband,' she murmured as he drove his hand inside her "Oh, Andy. It feels so good to have you touch me this way."

"Does it?" He continued. He rolled her on top of him.

"You're a beautiful woman, Liz."

She kissed him and reached to touch him. He was having a difficult time responding and she became increasingly frustrated. To compensate his inadequate performance, he moved his hand inside her once more so that at least she would be satisfied. She edged off him more frustrated.

"Liz, I'm sorry. I've never had this problem. I guess I'm more exhausted than I thought."

"It's not the lack of sex, Andy. It's the reason behind it."

She rolled over and turned her back to him. He moved his hand up her gown again in an effort to initiate a second chance. "Let's try once more, please."

She turned to face him with tears in her eyes.

258

"I'm sorry I'm not her."

"Oh, Liz, stop. I chose you."

"Are you sorry?"

"No." He covered his lie with a gentle kiss.

"I can wait until you're ready, Andy. I won't bother you again until you are. When you've dealt with your feelings, then we can begin our marriage."

"Liz..."

She placed her hand gently over his mouth.

"I'm not angry, just hurt. And I won't be the kind of wife who has to beg her husband."

She kissed him softly.

"Good-night, Andy. Remember that tomorrow I have a doctor's appointment. I'd like for you to be there."

"Okay," he whispered, regretful that he'd hurt her. "Liz, I am trying. I want to be a good husband."

"I know," she said honestly. "I know."

She fell asleep almost instantly. She could sleep so easily these days. He wished he could. He lay awake until way past midnight reliving tonight's fiasco.

"God," he prayed. "Get Hannah out of my mind. Please, get her out of my mind."

Dr. David Morton, Liz's obstetrician, and Nancy Clark, his nurse practitioner, sat Andy and Liz down to discuss recent complications in her pregnancy.

"Liz, you've developed a condition medically known as preeclampsia, or in layman's terms known as toxemia. Your blood pressure is consistently high and you have an unusual amount of swelling. Also, there is protein in your urine," Dr. Morton informed.

"All right," Andy said cautiously. "So what does all this mean?"

"At this stage, Liz needs to stay off her feet most of the day. No more working, Liz. You need to cut down on your salt intake. Also, I want you to take some extra calcium. Nancy will supply you with some samples before you leave. If you do this, hopefully, the toxemia won't progress any further and you'll go full term and deliver a healthy baby."

"Back up a little, Doc. Are Liz and the baby in danger?" Andy's voice rang out in alarm.

"Not at this stage. What can happen, and I stress can happen, is the disease can prevent the placenta from getting enough blood. This prevents the baby from getting oxygen and food. In the most serious scenario, the baby might move outside the placenta and immediate delivery would have to occur, for the baby's survival as well as Liz's. However, right now I'm watching Liz's condition with concern, that's all. I anticipate for her to carry the baby full term. Should her symptoms become more serious, we may have to discuss hospitalization."

"What kind of symptoms?" Andy asked.

"Severe headaches, vomiting, ringing in her ears, unusual pain in her tummy area, and blood in her urine. But, if Liz follows my instructions, she should be perfectly fine."

"Oh, she will. I'll make sure of that."

"Try not to worry. The baby's strong and healthy. Everything's progressing normally for a twenty-nine week old fetus."

Andy nodded. "I'll watch her like a hawk."

Dr. Morton shook his hand. "I just bet you will."

After they left the doctor's office, Andy called Dennis and told him he wouldn't be working today. He called Liz's mom and arranged for her to be with Liz during the daytime while he worked. Liz called her boss and told him she had no choice and asked that she be put on maternity leave. Andy catered to her, cooking, cleaning, and running her bath. He insisted she go straight to bed, even though she argued it was only eight o'clock.

"You heard what the doctor said," he ordered.

"He said rest, Andy. He didn't say I was an invalid."

He kissed her.

"Liz, indulge me in this. I don't want anything to happen to you or the baby."

He massaged her abdomen gently, and then kissed it.

"Oh, Liz, I love this little man so."

"Andy," she said, rubbing his hair as he rested his head on her stomach. "Sometimes you leave me speechless."

He closed his eyes and prayed that God wasn't somehow punishing the baby for something he'd done. She closed her eyes and prayed that Andy hadn't noticed the significance in the age of the baby.

Three weeks to the date of her doctor's appointment, Liz was hospitalized at Baylor in Dallas. A day later, on September seventeenth, Patrick Ryan Padgett was born by cesarean section, weighing three pounds and six ounces. Little Patrick was hooked up to a respirator, IV's, a heart monitor, a vitals' monitor, and a dialysis machine, all used in an effort to keep him alive. Liz's condition, that had been critical before delivery, began to improve the moment Patrick was delivered. When Patrick was born, only Andy and Liz were allowed to see him, but not hold him. Andy watched helplessly as the hospital staff worked to save his small son's life. When he was six hours old, Andy held him for the first time. He was amassed with tubing and wires, and Andy shook when the nurse handed him his son.

"It's all right, Mr. Padgett. He looks like he might break, but he won't. He actually needs the touch of his father and mother. Touching will help him respond sooner."

Once Patrick was in his arms, the wires and tubes fell from sight and all he could see was the vulnerability of this precious life. Though he was nothing but skin and bones and scarlet colored flesh, Andy thought he was the most beautiful baby he'd ever seen. He was fighting against great odds, and surviving them with more spirit than he'd ever imagined possible.

"Hey, buddy. It's your Daddy. Now why'd you go and give me and your mommy such a scare? Mommy's been so worried about her little linebacker. I tried to tell her you were tough, but she still worries."

Andy kissed him through his face protector. He gently rubbed his little feet and hands and belly.

"Ah, you like that, huh? Well, Daddy doesn't mind."

The nurse smiled at Andy.

"You take to fatherhood like a duck to water."

He smiled. "Well, I've had a little practice. Patrick's my fourth son. But, I have to tell you. All this," he said looking at the wires and tubes, "well, it's all so new, and scary as hell."

"I know it seems overwhelming, but we deal with premature babies every day. Patrick's actually doing very well for an infant so small."

"I can almost hold him in the palm of my hand."

"He kind of puts life in perspective, doesn't he?"

Andy nodded. "Amen to that."

He closed his eyes and willed Patrick to fight. "Live, Son. Live. Daddy loves you so much."

Three days after Patrick was born, Liz was dismissed from the hospital. Patrick would remain until he weighed at least five pounds and until his lungs were stronger. Already, the dialysis machine had been taken away. He was kept on the respirator every two hours. Liz stayed with him during the day, taking shifts with Beverly, her mom, and Ann and John. Andy stayed at night, sleeping next to Patrick in a hospital chair that folded out into a bed. He was allowed this arrangement until Patrick's status improved and he was moved to a different section of the nursery. Then, he stayed until the late hours of the night, always reluctant to leave.

"He's so small, Liz. What if he should need us?"

"Andy, I feel the same. If he does, we're only ten minutes away."

When Andy awoke each day, he and Liz both went to see him, sharing in his morning feeding and cuddling and treatments. Andy learned how to suction his nose and give him breathing treatments. He read him books or sang him songs, always holding him close to his chest. Liz would have to push Andy out the door to get him to leave.

"Go. Get to work. Make some money to support us. Get that house finished."

He'd reluctantly leave, kissing Patrick and Liz goodbye. Before leaving, he always said the same thing to the attending staff.

"Take good care of my boy while I'm gone."

Andy pulled into Nana's driveway around six-thirty a.m. on a late, crisp September morning. Already, the foliage was changing its colors. In less than a week, it would be October. Where did the time go? The first thing he did when he got out of his truck was to look toward Hannah's house. It was still and quiet. He knew she was probably asleep, but he couldn't help but to look, hoping he might get a glimpse of her. He hadn't seen or heard her voice in almost three months. It seemed longer—an eternity. It was a bittersweet desire—wanting to see her, but not wanting to see her. When he went to the back door, he waited for some time before going inside, starring aimlessly at her place, her lush garden, her freshly painted house. She was transforming her life, just as his dad had said. Inside, Ann Padgett greeted her youngest with hugs, kisses and breakfast.

"Thanks for coming by on such short notice to watch Nana this morning. I know how difficult it is for you to be here. Charlie was going to, but at the last minute…"

"It's not a problem, Mom. Glad I could do it. I can't avoid my family forever."

She smiled even knowing his heart was torn into pieces. She changed the subject to Patrick. Patrick was the light of his life.

"Your father and I are so excited to go see little Patrick today."

"He's grown so much you might not recognize him," Andy beamed. "The doctors say if he continues to progress the way he has been, he'll be home sooner than expected."

"Oh, Andy, I know you're so anxious to have him home."

"You bet. So tell me, Mom. What's this big surprise you have for Patrick?"

"I'm not telling you. It's as much for you as it is for him."

"And it's so big that you need to borrow my truck, huh?"

"You don't mind, do you?"

"I don't mind, but she doesn't ride as smooth as Nana's car."

She only smiled and hummed as she fixed Andy's plate with eggs, bacon, and homemade bread. Her surprise was a rocker. Nana had rocked John and his sister, Matilda, in the rocker and she passed it on to Ann for her three sons. It had been tradition in the family that all the Padgett grandchildren would be rocked in the same chair, from Nicolle all the way down to Bobby, Andy's youngest. When Bobby was born, he was to be the last Padgett grandchild. Once, Andy brought the chair up in passing at the hospital, but Ann told him that she had sold it years ago. In truth, she had gotten it out of storage to have it repaired and refinished.

John walked into the kitchen and sat down next to Andy, laying his hand over his arm. They looked at each other and smiled.

"Dad, you look good."

"So do you, Son. How's Liz?"

"Oh, you know, busy. She's all pumped up about Patrick. She's a terrific mom."

"She was working on a baby blanket the last time we saw each other at the hospital."

"She's been working on it for months," Andy teased. "Patrick will probably graduate before she finishes it."

"Leave her alone," Ann chided. "She's had a few things on her mind these days."

Andy smiled. "Yes, she has. She's held it together better than me most of the time."

"You make a good team, Son."

Once again, Andy stared at his dad. He let out a deep breath.

"I'm trying."

Ann kissed the top of Andy's head.

"You're doing wonderfully."

Then, she looked at John.

"We really need to be going soon, so we can do what we have to do and get Andy's truck back to him."

John nodded. "Just a few more bites, Mother. Besides, it's not every day I get to have breakfast with my youngest son."

"So tell me, Dad," Andy elbowed him, all the while watching his mom. "What's this big surprise that Mom has for Patrick?"

"Well," he said, pretending to spill the beans.

"Don't you dare, John Padgett!" Ann warned.

All three started laughing. John cleared his plate and went to the sink where Ann was doing the dishes. Andy wondered if he and Liz would be sparring like this when they were sixty. He watched his dad wrap his arms around his mom's waist. This made him think of Hannah and the afternoon at his apartment when he had done this exact thing. Suddenly, his heart felt empty. He had an inclination to run next door. He said a silent prayer that he wouldn't do anything stupid today—for Hannah as much as for himself. He stood up and nudged his parents along.

"Get out of here, you two," Andy said. "I'll do the dishes."

"Oh, okay," Ann said. "Now remember, Nana will try to talk you into eating and doing things she's not supposed to eat or do. Don't give into her."

"Nana and I will do just fine."

"Why do I get the feeling that you will give into Nana?"

Andy kissed his mom.

"Maybe because I always do."

Andy lay on the couch after tucking Nana in for her morning nap. He decided it would be a good idea for him to get a little shuteye while he could. When Patrick got home, he knew those days would be few and far between. The clock on the wall cuckooed signaling it was ten o'clock. Nana woke up shortly after his parents had left and so he fixed her breakfast and then the two of them talked. She told him all about her special diet, her medicines, and how Ann was making her do some kind of exercises with weights that she didn't much like. She talked about every thing under the sun—except Hannah. Andy thought this was sad, because she always talked about Hannah. He knew that he was the reason she didn't.

He was consumed with thoughts of Hannah today. He knew it was because she was only a few feet away from him. He could literally have her in his arms in less than five minutes. He wanted to hold her so badly, he could barely contain himself. The only thing that saved him was blessed sleep. He was so bone tired, he couldn't keep his eyes open. Still, when he closed them, he saw Hannah.

Will I ever get you out of my mind?

As he dozed, he could hear cars passing by through the open window and some dogs barking in the distance. In the cedar near the side of the house, he listened as some mocking birds sang their songs. All were faint noises, lulling him to sleep. He heard the screen door in the back flapping back and forth, not quite shut and knew he should go shut it. He couldn't will his tired body to get up, so he didn't. Then, he heard the sweetest voice and he was sure he was dreaming. Yet, when he heard it again, he knew he wasn't. His heart jumped to his throat.

"Grace, Ann, John? Anyone here? Grace?"

Andy's eyes popped open.

Hannah

He stood abruptly, straightening out his attire as best he could. She was moving in his direction, calling for his parents and Nana. When she reached the living room where he was, she stopped the minute she saw him. Their eyes locked and they could do nothing but stare at each other. After what seemed like hours, he moved closer to her. She leaned against the doorway between the kitchen and the living room, because her legs threatened to give way. He tried twice to take her hand, but never quite managed to, only slightly touching her fingers. He smiled at her nervously. She let out a short breath and then smiled back. They were so close they were almost touching — almost.

"Andy," she managed. "I didn't know you...I mean Grace didn't tell me you were coming."

"She didn't know, Hannah."

"I didn't see your truck, or I wouldn't have ..."

"Mom and Dad have it."

"Oh," she barely said.

John, you could have warned me.

Andy viewed her like a work of art — so beautiful. He studied every detail about her, knowing that the possibility of their ever being this close again was remote. He wanted to touch her so badly it hurt. Somehow, he had the sense not to do this.

"You look...beautiful, Hannah."

She closed her eyes. "Do I?"

"You always look beautiful to me."

I love you, Andy. I miss you.

He was lost in her face. She was more toned now, darker from the sun. Across her face was a small trail of freckles that hadn't always been there. He guessed it was from working so much in the sun. Her hair was full, flowing down her back—lustrous. He lowered his eyes and they fell on her lips. He swallowed hard.

Why do you have to be so damn beautiful?

She knew it would be hard to see him again, but what she didn't know was that it would be impossible to stop the flow of emotions. Tears fell down her face. When he was able to look up at her again, he saw them. He watched her struggle to maintain her composure.

"Hannah," was all he could say.

Every fiber in her being told her to hold him—and she actually did reach for his hands. She was holding Andy's hands, staring at them through her tears. That was when she saw it—his wedding ring. It slapped her like a cold wind. In the realm of this reality, she quietly dropped his hands and moved toward the back door. He was quick to follow.

"Don't go," he said reaching for her arm.

She turned to face him. Her eyes were ablaze with pain. Her heart was broken in a million pieces. This was worse than their last goodbye. At least then, she had the slightest glimmer of hope that he would some day come back to her. That hope was gone. She knew how Andy viewed marriage and what its vows meant to him.

"I have to," she whispered.

Andy wanted to take her in his arms. It would be so easy. A vision of his small son with tubes throughout his body came to his mind. He looked at Hannah, now so strong and vibrant. He was remembering a frail, scared woman, who couldn't leave her very home because of tragedy. She had come so far. Both his son and Hannah had taught him what true courage and strength really were. He thought of Liz—his wife.

God, give me the strength to let her go.

268

He leaned and kissed her softly on the cheek. He could barely speak.

"I'm not sorry I fell in love with you, Hannah. You made me a better man."

"Andy..."

"Let me finish. Before you, I was lost, broken."

She closed her eyes. His voice quaked

"I will always love you, Hannah."

She opened her eyes and saw honesty in his.

Cruel fate

She looked at his wedding ring for strength. She didn't say *I love you, too,* because she knew if she did, they would be lost forever. Instead, she turned away.

"Good bye, Andy."

She opened the door. Her heart begged him to stop her, but he didn't. He watched her as she ran toward her back door, never looking back. When she was out of sight, he fell to his knees and cried.

By the time, Patrick was one month old, he weighed almost five pounds and was moved to a smaller hospital in Plano that was more convenient to their apartment. Friends and extended family were now able to visit with Patrick for short periods of time. Except for his breathing treatments, his major organs were functioning on their own and all medications had been withdrawn. Patrick was having difficulty accepting Liz's breast, although he'd been drinking her milk through a nipple. Every day, Liz tried to nurse, but Patrick couldn't manage the task and he'd become frustrated. One day, Andy came in the nursery and found Liz bottle feeding Patrick and crying.

"He won't nurse, Andy. I wanted him to nurse."

"Oh, Liz. He's worked so hard to survive. Why not give him a break and yourself. Besides, he's still getting your milk, which is what counts."

"I guess you're right."

He kissed her cheek and then Patrick's.

"Of course, I am. Liz, you look worn. Go home and get some sleep."

"I guess I am tired. Andy, come home early tonight. I miss you."

"Okay, I'll try. Now scat. When Patrick comes home, I want you as strong and healthy as him."

"How's the house coming?"

"The downstairs is almost finished. The boys' rooms will have to wait. I'd say by the time our little guy is ready to come home, his house will be ready."

She smiled weakly. "You've worked so hard."

He took Patrick from her arms.

"I've done nothing compared to what you've done. Oh, by the way, I bought you a present. It's on our bed."

"A present? Oh, Andy, what?"

"You'll see when you get home."

She kissed him. "Remember, come home early."

Liz was almost to her car when Doug Chasey drove in the hospital parking lot. She saw him almost immediately. Her heart fell as she watched him park and walk toward the main entrance. She thought to leave without acknowledging him, but he had seen her, too. He called out her name and she stopped. He changed directions and walked toward her car. When they were face to face, he smiled broadly at her. She was jittery, fearful as to why he was here. His tone was cordial, but not overly as it had been in the past.

"Liz, I gather by looking at you, that you've had the baby."

"Yes, a boy."

"A boy, huh? Is he here?"

She nodded. "He came early. He gave us a scare."

"I can imagine."

"Why are you here, Doug? Tell me it's not to see Patrick."

"Patrick? That's a nice name, Liz. But no, I'm not here to see your son. I'm here to see a client."

"A client, huh? And this client just happens to be at this hospital?"

He nodded. "You look pale, Liz."

"I guess I'm still not fully recovered from having Patrick."

"I guess." He studied her nervousness, her wringing hands, and her trembling lips. "Liz…you look like a woman who has a lot on her mind."

"Why?" She burst into tears. "Why can't you leave me alone?"

He walked her to a more private place in the parking lot because she was beginning to attract attention.

"Honest, Liz. My being here and your being here are purely coincidental."

"I don't believe you at all!" she spat tearfully.

"Call room 432. Thomas Burns will answer it."

She turned from him. "Stay away from me and my family!" Her voice was stern and filled with panic.

He watched her make several nervous attempts at getting into her car, before she managed to open the door and sit behind the wheel. When she backed out, her tires squealed and she erratically drove off, leaving him to wonder about what had just happened.

After Doug was certain Liz had left the hospital, he made his way to the nursery. He casually glanced through the glass to view the babies. All the cribs were empty. Doug waited idle for some time in a nearby waiting room. Liz's strange reaction to his being there could mean either that she'd had enough of him and his family's interference, or that her anxiety implied something else.

His gut contracted. "Dear God, is Patrick mine?"

He walked rashly back toward the nursery. A few of the babies were now in cribs. Doug saw Andy Padgett standing next to a crib, talking to a nurse who was changing Patrick. Doug observed Patrick, hair so light it could almost be considered white, full plump cheeks, fair skin. He had a strong suspicion that he just might be looking at his own flesh and blood. His thoughts were abruptly interjected when Andy Padgett picked up Patrick and for the slightest of moments, their eyes connected. Andy smiled and Doug lent a subtle nod. When Andy walked away with Patrick, Doug made a vow to himself.

I'm sorry, Liz. This is one matter I can't let rest.

Liz went back to the apartment shaken and frantic as to the direction in her life. If Doug suspected, even if only slightly, that he might be the father of Patrick, he'd never back off until he knew. She fell on the bed, exhausted from the weight of her lie. Her arm fell over a beautifully wrapped box. It was Andy's gift to her. A card was taped to the box. She read the card first.

To my wife, who has given me the gift of a son. No words are adequate to express what my heart feels, so I won't even try. Wear this and know, my heart is completely dedicated to us as husband and wife, and to our little family. I have been blessed, I know. I open up my heart to you. Andy.

Liz fumbled with the wrapping. Inside the box was a locket. On one side was a picture of Patrick. On the other side was a picture of her and Andy that had been taken on their wedding day. Liz burst into tears.

Forgive me, Andy. Forgive me.

TWENTY-TWO

Several days after her encounter with Andy, Hannah sat at her kitchen table feeling lost and defeated. She felt like she was back to square one. Andy was on her mind night and day. She could still feel his touch and smell his scent. She was always on the verge of tears. For two days, she had been in bed. Today was the first day she had gotten dressed. She didn't answer her calls, not even from Grace, which sent John knocking on her door. She told him she had the touch of the flu and didn't want to get anyone sick. She didn't know if he bought her fib. She didn't care. She just wanted the hurting to stop.

She didn't go outside to work in her yard or in her garden. She looked around at her four walls. So badly, she wanted to escape them, but she was once again held captive. So long as she lived here, she would always have to worry that she might run into Andy. Her heart could not bear another encounter like the one she had. It was too painful. Mindlessly, she picked at the tablecloth and fiddled with her cell phone that was on the table—the one Andy had given her. She knew it was ridiculous for her to hold on to it and even more so, to allow him to continue paying for it. She knew she should get her own phone. Somehow, she felt that it was her last link to him. She wondered how long it would be before Andy disconnected it. Maybe he never would. Maybe, he felt the same as she did.

Call me, Andy. I need to hear your voice.

Once again, the tears began to fall. She knew she couldn't continue like this. She had to make some changes, but change was always difficult for her. She opened up her texts and saw she had eight missed ones. Most of them were from Elaine. Two were from Paul. He wanted her to call him and talk about

Paul Jr. She knew she wouldn't be any help to anyone right now. Paul's call would have to wait. There were two from Alex King, Grace's doctor. She knew it was personal. He, at a very fast rate, was becoming a focal figure in her life—mainly because of his insistence. She wished she could be more excited about it, but she couldn't. At least today, she couldn't. Today, she didn't want anything to do with men. She opened up the ones from Elaine. Three had to do with work, but the last one was personal. Coincidently, it had to do with Alex King. Hannah read it with only slight interest.

Have you decided what you are going to do about the cute doctor?

For some reason, Hannah thought about how jealous Andy had gotten over the attention Alex had given her at the hospital after Grace's procedure. She didn't know why, but this somehow made her feel a little better, wondering what Andy would do if he knew that Alex King was presently in touch with her. On several of Grace's follow-up visits, she had gone with John and Grace. Alex King was there. In the span of these short visits, he had managed to get her phone number. He called her regularly and they were getting to know each other via phone calls and texts. On one occasion, while Grace was having a test done at the hospital, the two had lunch in the cafeteria. He was aware of her limitations, or at least as much as Hannah was willing to share with him. He knew she didn't drive and he knew she hadn't been out much since the death of her family. She learned he had recently lost his wife and they shared this common bond. They were both hesitant about dating—Hannah far more than Alex.

Elaine had received four promo tickets through her firm to the symphony, where there was going to be a tribute to the *Beatles*. She knew of Hannah's involvement with Alex and thought it would be a good idea for Hannah to invite him to go. Elaine would take her husband and the four would go together. Alex could meet them there and Hannah wouldn't have to worry about him picking her up or leaving alone with him. It would be a date, but it wouldn't be a date.

I don't want a man in my life, Elaine. Leave me alone.

Elaine wouldn't let it go, especially when Hannah finally called her and told her about the incident with Andy. Elaine listened patiently for an hour before she made a decision.

"Here's how this is going to play out, Hannah," Elaine voiced. "I'll be at your house in two hours or less. Have your little bags packed. You're coming home with me for a few days."

"Elaine, no, I can't. I have..."

"Hannah, you've known me long enough to know that I don't take *no* for an answer once my mind is made up about something. You're coming to my house and that's that. Oh, by the way, pack a nice sexy dress for the symphony. Either that, or we'll go shopping tomorrow for one."

"I'm staying at your house, Elaine. I'm not going out with Alex. I've already decided."

"We can talk about it when you get here, but you need to see that there are more fish in the sea than Andy Padgett. Alex is a catch and a half."

"How do you know, Elaine? You've never met him."

"Well, I'm about to, right?"

"Elaine, you push too hard. I'm not ready."

"Humph, you weren't ready for Andy either, but you dove right into the fire. Maybe Alex is the one to make you forget all about Andy. Did you ever think about that?"

When they hung up, Elaine got Hannah to thinking. She was wrong about Alex.

He's not the one, Elaine. Anyone but Andy would only be a substitute.

The symphony was magical and Hannah had a better time than she ever imagined she would. When it was over, the four went out for coffee and dessert at an off-the-wall café near the east side of Dallas. They laughed and talked, reminiscing the music of the Beatles. Each shared their favorite stories about their connections to the fabulous four. As the midnight hour approached, Alex reluctantly brought the night to a close. Tomorrow he was taking a trip to Houston for a three-day conference. He asked Hannah for a private moment. She walked him to his car, while Elaine and Bob went to theirs.

"Hannah," he said taking her hand. "I had a wonderful time tonight. I'm so glad we finally took the leap. It wasn't that bad, now was it?"

"It was nice, lovely actually."

He smiled. "If I'm lucky, when I get back to Dallas, we can see each other again."

For the first time tonight, she felt anxiety. She tried to calm her nerves by telling herself that Elaine and Bob were just a few feet away. And too, Alex was a perfect gentleman.

"I'm still pretty new at this, Alex."

"Me, too, but I think I could learn to like it. You make it easy."

"Alex…I…"

Before she could protest, he leaned down to kiss her. It was soft and gentle, like Alex. He took the liberty of kissing her again, this time longer, but with the same tenderness.

"Hannah, I'll call you when I get back from Houston."

He got inside his car and rolled down the window. He had his hands on the steering wheel and she noticed he still wore his wedding ring. She touched it softly.

"It took me four years to take mine off."

He twisted the ring slightly.

"I know it's foolish," he said. "I just can't make myself take it off."

"It's not foolish at all. You'll know when you are ready."

He lifted his hand to touch her cheek. He was about to say something, but she stopped him.

"Don't," she whispered. "No sad memories tonight. It was too beautiful of an evening."

He smiled. "I don't want it to end. I wish..."

"What?" she asked.

"I wish we were alone."

When she didn't reply, he took her hand and kissed it.

"I'll probably call you tonight, Hannah. I'm not sure I can wait until I get back from Houston to call."

She gave him a nervous smile. She should be excited that this man who was so open with his feelings wanted to get to know her more intimately. She should be, but all she wanted to do was run, run to the security of Elaine's car. There, she wouldn't have to face the reality that he wasn't Andy and that his kiss left her empty.

Alex called her almost every night and each time she let him know a little bit more about herself. When she hung up from talking to him, she vowed she would tell him the next time that she was only interested in him as a friend — which was the truth. Then, loneliness would set in and she realized that affection and tenderness actually eased the pain of a broken heart. Tentatively, they made plans to have dinner at Hannah's house and then to go to a movie Saturday night. He told her about an old movie house that had been restored just twenty minutes from Blossom and on a good night, maybe two dozen people patronized it. He was sensitive to her condition and wanted her to be as comfortable as possible. As it got closer to Saturday, she knew she couldn't go through with it. It would officially be a date and she wasn't ready for that.

Long after dark, she sat on her swing watching the crescent moon as it dipped behind a cloud. It was cool outside and she had to wear a sweater. She heard activity going on at Grace's but couldn't bring herself to go over there. She missed them so much and they were concerned because she had so abruptly put distance between them. She couldn't completely distance herself because of her deep love for them. As she sat, she realized that she hadn't checked her mail in a few days. She couldn't help but smile at her own progress these past months remembering that nighttime had once been the only time she would dare to venture out of her house. Now, she couldn't be contained.

She shuffled through her mail putting aside the usual commercial ads and bills. As she continued to thumb through the mail, she stopped short when the light from the moon cast a glow on a postcard that had a picture of a sailor standing next to a brightly painted sailboat. Her hands were shaking, but she had an inclination about the postcard. She ran into the house so she could see the card better. Her mouth gapped open when she saw the name of the sailboat on the postcard. It was called *The Hannah.* Even before she turned the card over, she knew it was from her father. She felt an excitement beyond measure and at the same time, a sense of loss for what had once been but could never be again.

Tony DeJane, her father, had owned a similar sailboat he had coincidentally christened *The Hannah* the summer of her tenth birthday. She remembered vividly the many times that summer they had sailed the waters of the Gulf of Mexico near Galveston Bay. The two fished and swam and Hannah learned to sail. He taught her about the ocean and the life in it. She learned sea life by name and that every living thing in the ocean relied on other living things to survive.

"We're like the ocean animals, Hannah. We all need each other to survive."

"But not all the animals are strong enough to survive, Daddy."

"That's true, but you are. You are as strong as they come. Remember this, Hannah."

They often sailed until sunset, sometimes watching it surrounded by nothing but ocean. They told stories and they sang songs of the sea, and Tony never touched a drink while he sailed.   It was a magical summer, a father and daughter, bonding and learning about life, learning about each other.   The last time she'd been on a boat of any kind was the last time she and Tony had sailed *The Hannah*.   It was the time he'd told her about her mother's cancer and that she wouldn't be with them much longer.   Hannah could still feel his arms around her as he explained to her about her mother's journey from this life into another.

"Mommy is like the hermit crab, Hannah, whose home has gotten too small, too worn down.   She's moving on to a bigger, more peaceful home, where her spirit can thrive and live forever."

"Is she taking us with her?"

"She can't, Honey.   We have to stay and build our own lives, separate from Mommy."

"You won't leave me, will you, Daddy?"

"Never.   Even when we are not together like we are today, just close your eyes and think of me."

Hannah thought about the irony of that time.   It was the summer that she'd found her father, but also the summer she had lost him.   She dared to turn the card over and read his words.   Almost three years had gone by since she'd last heard from him –almost four years since she'd last seen him.   She traced his sketchy handwriting.   As she read, she was once again ten years old and in the arms of her father.

Hannah, I know you told me you never wanted to see or hear from me ever again, but when I saw this postcard, I had to send it to you. Fate was calling out to me. I think of you all the time. Not a day goes by when I'm not reminded of you. I do love my Hannah girl. If you remember anything of me, remember that. Charlotte and I have been divorced two years now. I'm now living near Malibu. Here's my new number and address if you should ever want to get in touch with me. Always, Daddy. P.S. I'm in my twelfth month of sobriety.

She read and reread his card so many times she had memorized his words. She held back the tears that so wanted to surface with great difficulty. It wouldn't do to fall apart. Falling apart wouldn't bring back the lost years, nor would it fulfill the many years of his empty promises. She wasn't going to let one little postcard tempt her into starting a relationship back up with him. She knew it would only end up broken as before, with him running away when times got tough and her being left to pick up the shattered pieces.

Hannah was putting the finishing touches on a vase she had made for Grace when she heard a knock at her front door. She looked out a side window and saw a female figure through the glass. She heard her knock again.

"Just a minute. I'm coming."

Hannah's heart stopped when she opened the door and saw Sue Renfroe standing before her. Her hands automatically covered her mouth in utter surprise. Then, tears streamed down her face as the two women locked eyes with each other. Hannah instantly held out her arms to embrace Sue and Sue fell limply within her hold. She was gripping Hannah with equal emotions and the years that had separated them crumbled away with this one embrace. Reluctantly, the two released their hold so that they could look up at each other. Sue talked first

"Paul was right," she declared. "You do look wonderful."

"Oh, Sue. You are the most blessed sight. I'm so glad to see you."

They sat on the couch, surface chatting, touching faces and hands, as if to assure themselves that the other was really there. When the initial shock of seeing each other again faded, the consequences of their long separation and the toll it had taken on them surfaced.

"I never really thought this moment would ever come," Hannah said, biting her lip in an effort to hold tears back.

Sue lowered her head. "I should have come by years ago. I was the one who let us down."

"Oh, no, Darling. I pushed you away."

Sue looked at her as if seeking absolution.

"Still, I should have. It was just easier to let you go."

Hannah gripped her hands tightly.

"You're here now. That's all that matters."

Sue tried to brave a smile and Hannah knew no matter what she said, Sue would always feel a certain blame that she had let her dearest friend down in her greatest time of need. Truthfully, Hannah would always secretly harbor bitterness that in her years of complete isolation, Sue had somehow abandoned her. She brushed away her deepest fear and asked Sue about Paul Jr.

"How's Paul, Jr., Sue? I understand he's in a treatment center near Austin. Paul tells me he's doing very well."

"He's doing much better than we expected. Actually, every day we pray his recovery continues."

"Sue, I just know it will. My heart says he's going to be fine. He has you and Paul in his corner."

Sue studied Hannah fully. She was as Paul had described — beautiful, perhaps more than she remembered. Today, she was wearing a pair of fitted jeans that brought to the eye her long legs. She had on a red blouse that highlighted her dark features and a fresh rush of fear impended over her, as she realized she could not hold a candle next to Hannah. If Hannah truly wanted Paul, Sue had little doubt as to which of them he would choose. She lowered her head, fully shamed by what she was about to request of Hannah.

"Hannah," she said wringing her hands. "I came to talk to you about…about Paul."

She looked at Sue's pale face. "What about Paul?"

Sue's voice shook.

"He's in love with you, Hannah. He always has been, I guess. In the past, he managed to keep his distance. He never acted on it. Now, I think he's planning to confront you."

"Oh, Sue, I think you're wrong. Paul loves you and the boys. He doesn't love me."

"Hannah, surely you know how he feels. It's so obvious."

"Sue, do you honestly believe I'd ever betray you like that? My God, Sue, can you, after all that we shared, believe this?"

Sue fell apart in front of Hannah, weeping like a child. "I only know that he loves you and I let you down. You just might..."

"You think I'd betray you out of some kind of vendetta?"

Somehow, when Hannah said the words, they sounded so petty, so ugly. But yes, that had been her fear and it would have been justifiable for Hannah to turn to a man who had not abandoned his love the way her best friend had.

Sue's jaw twitched. "I'm sorry, Hannah. I, I, just don't know what else to do. "I'm so afraid of losing him."

Tears formed in her eyes and she walked away from Hannah moving toward her kitchen. Hannah followed her. A pain so bitter against her earlier joy at seeing Sue flowed through her. She looked at Sue, so broken, and she saw a reflection of herself the way she had been four years ago. Death was not the only thing that stole a husband from a wife. She touched Sue's shoulders gently.

"We shared such precious moments together. We loved, cried, fought, made up, shared intimate secrets. I could never, ever betray such a friendship, for me, if not for you. Let your heart rest, Sue."

Memories of yesterday flooded Sue's mind—Sammy and Paul's friendship, Gabe and Paul Jr.'s inseparableness, little Julie's eyes, Benny's smile, Saturday night card games, Sunday dinners, holidays together, a bond so close, they could have been blood. Sue fell into Hannah's arms.

"Oh, Hannah. I'm sorry I let you go. I'm so selfish. I was more lost than you were. As long as Sammy was alive, I always felt safe, knowing Paul would never cross the line. When Sammy went, you became too much of a threat. I'm weak and self- absorbed. I let fear control me."

That statement abridged the moment, for no one knew better than Hannah did what fear could do to a soul. Hannah wrapped her arms around Sue tightly, just now understanding that Sue had lived a marriage similar to hers, only hers had been far more insufferable. When Sammy had gone to other women, she always had the comfort of knowing that deep down, he loved her and would always come back to her. But Sue, she lived with a man who had been faithful to her physically, but never in his heart. It was a sad realization and Hannah had to wonder if she'd talked to Sue like this years ago, things might have been different.

Hannah knew as certain as she loved this woman she held, that she was saying goodbye to her and her family forever. Yet, the moment was far deeper than letting go of Paul and Sue. She was letting go of a past, so precious, so safely tucked within her heart. She never imagined reaching such a crossroad. She kissed Sue's cheek softly and for the longest time, they held each other. When Sue left, she left perhaps lighter of heart with the assurance that Hannah would no longer be an obstacle in her marriage, but also regret. She was regretful for the loss of a friend as beautiful as Hannah Martindale.

John waited until it was almost eight in the morning before he knocked on Hannah's door. He was anxious to talk to her and figured this was a respectable amount of time to wait. She wasn't asleep, but she hadn't dressed just yet. When she answered the door, she was taken aback, not because he was there, but because of the serious look on his face. His face was so serious, in fact, she feared that Grace had perhaps had another episode.

"John?" she asked hesitantly. "Is everything all right?"

"May I come in, Hannah. I know it's a bit early, but this is important. I wanted to catch you before you began your day."

"Is it Grace?"

"No, Dear. It's not."

"Of course, come in, please. Do you mind if I dress real quick?"

He shook his head. "Go on."

While she dressed, he looked aimlessly around, wondering what would be the best approach to tell her what he had to say. It wouldn't be easy. No matter how he said what he had to say, it would cause her pain. Minutes later, she came out dressed in jeans and a t-shirt. He smiled remembering something Andy had once told him.

No matter what she wears, she always manages to look beautiful.

John had to agree. She was one of those rare women who bore a natural beauty. She sat in a chair across from where he was sitting.

"John, What is it? It isn't Andy, is it?"

He shook his head. "No, it's not. It's about a friend of yours."

"Elaine?"

Again, he shook his head. "It's about Alex King."

"Alex? Has something happened to Alex?"

He looked at her directly and spoke. It seemed all he did these past months was deliver bad news to this undeserving woman. He figured just giving the truth without sugarcoating it was the best way to go.

"Hannah, I know you've been talking a lot to him these past weeks. I know you've been out with him several times. Mom told me. She also told me that you told her that Alex was someone you might want to get to know better. Ann and I were pleased that you were seeing someone and getting on with your life. That was until Mom told us something about Alex, something I'm sure you aren't aware of."

"I know what you are going to say, John. It's about his wife, isn't it? You're afraid I'm going to be hurt again, because he isn't ready to let her go."

He looked at her curiously.

"You know about his wife, Hannah?"

She nodded. "Alex told me about her the first time we really talked. He's been so lonely."

"Lonely? Is that what he calls it?"

"Well yes. I think that's why we get along, John. We have that common bond."

"What bond is that, Hannah?"

She looked at him strangely. "We've both lost a spouse."

"You've both lost a spouse?" he repeated her words.

"Yes, his wife died less than a year ago, with cancer."

John let out a breath of exasperation. He took her hands and held them firmly. He was angry and he felt like punching Alex King.

"Hannah, Alex King is a married man. His wife is alive and well. He has two children."

She stared at him disbelieving. "He's not married, John. He's a widower. His wife died less than a year ago. She had cancer."

"Do you think I would have come to you if I weren't certain? After what Mom told me, I checked around. Mom told me that she was sure she had met his wife once. She was upset that he was calling you and when she found out you were dating, she made me find out for sure."

She was in a swoon. "Married? Alex? Oh, this can't be true."

Alex had been so convincing. He had an answer for all of her questions. She never once felt that he was lying. In fact, she often believed that she was the dishonest one and that maybe she was leading him on by giving him false hope.

"From what I understand, his reputation as a ladies' man is well known."

"I guess to everyone but me. Oh, John, I just can't believe this. Are you absolutely sure? I mean I would hate to accuse..."

"Call him. Better yet, call *The Women's Clinic* near the hospital and ask for a P.A. named Rene King. That's his wife."

"Oh, I'm such a fool," she berated herself.

"No, Hannah, you just have a trusting heart. I'm just sorry I'm the one who had to tell you this. I don't want you hurt any more than you've already been."

She appealed to his sense of trust.

"John, you have to promise me something."

"What, Hannah?"

"Don't let Andy know about this. I couldn't bear it."

"Do you think I would? No, Hannah, you've both been through so much. If I could have spared you..."

She put her face in her hands and cried.

"I love him so much it hurts."

John stood and moved to sit on the arm of the chair where she was sitting. He could do little to comfort her. He also knew these tears were for Andy and not for Alex.

"I only went out with Alex to forget how lonely I am without..."

"I know," he soothed.

"John, it's been so difficult living so near the people he loves and wondering if he might show up and that I might run into him. Or worse, knowing that he avoids coming to see you and Ann and Grace because of me. This breaks my heart."

"Time will ease the pain, Hannah—for both you and Andy."

She looked at him hopelessly. "That's what I'm afraid of, John. I'm afraid he'll forget me. Why shouldn't he? He has everything—a wife who loves him, a new son, his farm."

"Hannah, you aren't someone easily forgotten. Yes, Andy has been blessed, but he sacrificed a lot when he let you go. More than I ever realized."

286

Hannah stood and stared out the window. Her mood was dejected. Her soul was empty. She had to get away—away from the pain and lost dreams.

"John, I've been doing a lot of thinking."

"About what, Dear?"

She turned to him wearing a look so melancholy, it cut through his soul.

"I'm leaving Blossom."

He couldn't speak, but looked at her in disbelief. She continued.

"Except for you, Ann, and Grace, there's really nothing left for me here."

He finally found his voice. He bargained with her to stay.

"We're your family, Hannah. You're like a daughter to Ann and me. Mom loves you as she loves no one else. She's mourning the times you used to spend together already. It will break her heart if you leave."

"It breaks my heart, too. But, I can't stay. Surely, you understand this. I know you love me and that you're sensitive to my situation, but Andy is your son. It's inevitable that we will run into each other. Right now, my pain is too raw to face this possibility. Maybe later I'll come back. I don't know."

"I do understand. But Hannah, Blossom has been your home for years. Your house is here, your belongings. What will you do with them?"

"I haven't thought that far yet."

"I'll take care of them. They will be here when you come home."

She smiled a tender smile.

"I can't, John. Don't you see? If I'm going to make it, I have to break away from him. And that means breaking away from you, as well."

"Where will you go?"

"To begin with, I'm going to mend some bridges. I'm going to spend time with my father."

"You and Tony have been communicating?"

"A little. It may turn out to be a disaster, but I have to try."

"Hannah, I know you've been making great strides these past months, but moving is such a tremendous change, even in the best of situations. You're making a decision on pure emotions. This makes me frightened for you."

"I'm frightened for me, too, John. If I had another option, don't you think I'd take it?"

He took her hands and squeezed them tightly.

"A visit with your father may not be such a bad idea, Hannah, but I need you to promise me something."

"What, John?"

"Don't do anything rash about your home and belongings. Think about this long and hard. You don't want to do something you'll regret later."

"Okay, John, I promise. And now, will you do me a favor?"

"What is it, Hannah?"

"Will you take me to see my family?"

"Are you sure that you're up to it?"

"No, but I need to go just the same."

He lowered his head and she could tell he was almost in tears. She reached for him.

"John, don't. I need you, of all people, to be strong for me. I need you to have faith in me, so I can have faith in myself."

He looked at her full of remorse that she had been given little choice but to leave.

"I have immense faith in you, Hannah. I'm worried about us — Ann, Mom and me. I don't think you quite understand just how much we will miss you, how much we cherish you."

"It's the same with me, John. I'm leaving, but everyone and everything I love is here."

That day, John took her to the cemetery. At first, she couldn't make herself get out of the car and so she sat there for some time as if she were someone else viewing her life. Images of Sammy and Gabe and Julie so overwhelmed her, she could do nothing but grieve them all over again. She finally was able to move from the car and walked slowly to their graves. Her love was so deep, she almost wished God would take her to heaven with them. Then, a profound truth took over her thoughts. The truth was she had never really lost them, because her love for them had never died. She wondered why it had taken so long for her to realize this. It was far easier to love these precious souls than to bury their images in some dark world. She'd been a fool to believe that somehow holding onto her suffering would bring them back to her. As she stood there, she understood the direction her life must take.

She thought of Andy. She never could have imagined that she would ever love someone the way she had loved her family, but somehow her heart opened up to him. Her love for him was as deep as her love for Sammy and her precious children. She knew she would carry him in her heart the way she did them. Still, he was as far removed from her as they were. Just as she knew she had to let her family go, she had to let Andy go, too. She had to let him go so that he could live his life to the fullest. She had to let him go so that she could have a chance to be whole again.

The day that Hannah left Blossom, she said her *goodbyes* to the people she considered her family. Grace, Ann, and John had taken her from the brink of death and nurtured her back to life. She said *goodbye* to Ann and John first. These souls had been in a sense, her surrogate parents since her accident. They had to promise that they would take care of Grace and let her know if her condition started to deteriorate again. She had to promise that she would call them should the situation with her father ever become intolerable. She gave them a framed pastel sketching of Jeff. Initially, she had thought to give it to Andy, but as time passed, she knew this wasn't a good idea. She had done the sketch the weeks he stayed with them, just before he had moved to Austin with his mother She also entrusted them with her most cherished possessions to keep while she was away—mostly items that had belonged to her family, such as clothing, pictures, and trinkets.   She told them not to worry about her finances or legal situations. She gave Elaine and her firm the responsibilities of taking care of her property and investments.

They held her for some time before leaving her alone with Grace. They decided it was best to let them have their time together—alone and without interruptions. After all, they had been each other's sole companions for so many years. She gave Grace a vase she had hand painted with a daisy montage. Daisies were Grace's favorite. She always said they reminded her of bottled sunshine. Leaving Grace was Hannah's most difficult hurdle, mainly because she loved her so much. She also wondered if perhaps this would be the last time she would ever lay eyes on her.

Hannah stayed with her most of the morning. She bathed and dressed her, did her hair and nails, and they looked through endless pictures of the two of them together the many years they had known each other. Grace gave her all the pictures she wanted to take with her, understanding that Hannah was as much a part of her as was John and Ann, and her three grandsons. Hannah couldn't resist tucking one of Andy in with the bunch. It was a recent photo of him with his three boys when he had taken them to his friend's cabin in Arkansas. Grace nodded at her and patted her shaky hands.

"You must promise to write me often and call me. You know how we love to talk. Call me collect if you want. I have to know that you are all right."

"I will call you, Grace. You know I can't go too long without hearing your voice."

"Hannah," she cried. "I can't imagine my life without my sweet little bird living next door to me."

"Grace, don't cry. I won't be able to leave if you cry."

"You tell your father to take good care of you. You tell him he will have to deal with me if he doesn't. And don't be afraid to take the medicine that the doctor prescribed for you. Don't be too proud to take it."

"I'll take it if I need it. I promise. Now, give me a hug. If I don't leave soon, I won't ever leave."

As Grace held Hannah, tears flowed down both of their faces. Grace brushed her aged hands over her precious Hannah's soft face, as if trying to memorize each detail. Her touch was like therapy to Hannah's broken heart. Grace whispered in her ear.

"He loves you, Hannah. I know my boy. He will always love you."

"Take care of him," Hannah barely said.

Grace nodded. Hannah stood up, cleared all the pictures off Grace's bed, and put them in a neat stack on her dresser.

"Let me tuck you in for your nap and when I leave, it will be like any other day. Maybe this will be easiest for both of us."

Missing Hannah already, she complied. Hannah took off Grace's shoes and rolled back her bed. She lay down and Hannah pulled the covers over her. Knowing Grace liked to have her fan running during her sleep to block out the noise, she turned it on. She closed the blinds and moved to kiss her on the forehead.

"Sleep tight, my Darling. I'll see you soon."

Grace reached for her hand and gripped it.

"Don't forget us."

"Never.

"Come back home soon."

"I could never leave you forever."

Grace let go of her hand and watched her until she reached the door. Hannah blew her a kiss before she moved out of sight.

At home, she waited for Elaine. Her bags were packed and she sat watching the clock. She looked about her house, that had been her sanctuary for so long and she was suddenly overcome with the fear that had plagued her for so many years. To aid her, she reached into her purse that held the items she could never part with—the envelopes that had the locks of hair from her family, her wedding ring, her mother's gold heart necklace, and the note Andy had written her when he gave her the toy soldier. Around her neck, the toy soldier hung on a gold chain and she clutched it for support. Her heart was so overwhelmed with sorrow and fear she was immobilized.

God, I can't do this!

Just as she was about to go into a full-fledged panic, the cell phone inside her purse rang. The ID on the phone read *Tony DeJane.* She answered it quickly.

"Hi, Daddy. Yes, I'm ready to leave, just waiting for my ride. I'm fine—really. Why? Don't I sound fine? Yes, I can make it. No, you don't have to come get me. I know you would. I'm facing my fears, Daddy. Just promise me you'll be at the airport to rescue me. Elaine's taking me there. You remember Elaine, don't you? I'm excited, too, Daddy—so excited. Yes, it's been a long time, too long. I can't wait to see you, either. I know...I love you, too."

In her state of complete and utter uncertainty, she failed to realize that she was taking Andy's phone with her.

TWENTY-THREE

"Call me the minute you get to Malibu," Elaine ordered. "You understand?"

"I will," Hannah said nervously.

"I mean it. Oh, hell, why do I feel like I'm throwing a lamb to the wolves?"

"You're not, Elaine. This is my choice. I want to go. I want to see my father."

"You got your bags? Your money? Oh, and did you take the little pill your doctor gave you? Don't try to be brave. You *will* need it. You have your address book and your cell phone? You have all my numbers, right? The lake house? My mom's? Now, you're sure your dad knows that you get in at five-thirty? I don't want you stranded at LAX."

"Elaine! You're falling apart worse than I am. I'll call, I promise. Yes, I have my bags and money and I've already taken the medication. I knew I would need it. I have my phone and everything I need in my purse. Daddy will be there—I think."

Elaine hugged her as if she might never let her go.

"I miss you already and it's not because I'm losing my best employee. You're my best friend—the dearest person I know. Write and call me often, you hear? Don't stay away too long or I might just have to fly to California to get you. Don't worry about the house. Nick will take great care of it. And anytime you decide to come home, he's outta there."

Hannah sat down in a nearby chair, just now allowing herself to let go of the despair of leaving everything she loved behind, her friends, family and security. She clung to Elaine. She broke into tears.

"I don't know how long I'll be gone, Elaine. It could be a while."

"I was wondering how long it would be before you realized what was happening. You've been so brave."

"Oh, Elaine, I'm not brave. I'm not ready for this. I'm not ready to go out on my own. I don't want to say *goodbye* to you. I need you. Daddy is a stranger to me. Elaine, you're right. I can't go. I can't. I was a fool to think I could."

"I was just letting my emotions get the best of me, Hannah. You are ready. Just think about all that you've accomplished in such a short time. I still can't believe it."

"I had you and John and…" She fell short of saying *Andy*.

"But, you're the one who did it."

"Elaine, talk me out of this."

Elaine gripped her firmly.

"Hannah, if you want to turn back now, no one will think any less of you. You can stay with me. You won't have to live in Blossom. I just don't think that's what you want. You told me yourself that you were tired of letting fear control you."

"I know," she cried out. "That was before."

"Before what, Hannah?"

"Before leaving became so real."

"Just concentrate on getting to know your father again. Leave the rest behind."

"My father? Yes, I do want to see my father. I've missed him so much."

"I know you have. In less than four hours, you'll be with him. Now, give me one more hug. This is as far as they'll let me go. You will go through security. There are people all around who can help you find your boarding gate."

Hannah clung to Elaine as if she might never see her again. Their eyes locked together. She brushed back Hannah's matted hair, along with a mass of tears. She kissed her cheek.

"Go, scoot. I'll stay until your plane takes off. If you get nervous, just look out the window. I'll be standing right here until I know your plane is in the air."

"I love you, Elaine."

"I love you, too, Sweetie. Best friends forever?"

Hannah smiled, "Best friends forever."

They stared at each other as if lost in time, and then, Hannah turned and walked down the long walkway that led to security and eventually her plane. Not once did she look back at Elaine, but by the time she boarded her plane, she had pretty much fallen apart—tears, shaky hands, and jumbled stomach. She felt like she was going to be sick. Even before she found her seat, she dashed for the bathroom. Inside, she splashed water on her face until her unsteady body felt somewhat relieved. The pill she had taken was starting to take effect. She wondered what in God's creation ever made her think she could pull this off. Outside, she heard the sounds of passengers boarding and attendants busy readying them for departure. She felt panic setting in at an alarming rate.

God, help me.

She happened to look above the commode and there hung a poster of a cat hanging onto a small tree limb. Below the tree was a fireman with outstretched hands. The caption underneath the picture read, *"You're never alone."* She had to smile. She wasn't going to die in this four-by-four-foot bathroom after all. She thought of Andy for some reason and his image gave her strength.

Oh, Andy, will there ever be a time when I don't think of you?

When she reached her seat, she looked out the window. She couldn't see Elaine, but she pretended she could and waved to her. She adjusted her seat and rested her head back to relax. She closed her eyes and took in several deep breaths. She didn't realize it, but she was gripping the arms of her seat so tightly, her knuckles were white.

"Plane phobia?" a kind voice sitting next to her asked.

She turned to face a woman around fifty, gray-haired, slightly plump, who wore a kind smile. Hannah nodded.

"I used to be the same way. In fact, I used to be afraid of just about everything. Now, I can do just about anything I want to do. I fly, travel, and ski. I've even been bungee jumping. At my age! Can you believe it? My family almost had me committed."

Hannah looked at her as if to ask, *"How did you change?"*

The woman smiled and held her hand out for Hannah to shake.

"Sadie Lodge."

"Hannah, Hannah Martindale."

"One thing about fear," Sadie said. "It's okay to feel it. Everyone does. The thing is not to give into it. It's a fierce tiger, for sure, but once you face it and let it know you're not putting up with it, it somehow becomes more of a pussycat."

She smiled taking Hannah's hand.

"It can be a boulder, or a stone. It's your choice."

Hannah blew out a deep breath. This person had no idea the extent of her fear. She was put out with her presuming.

"When you were a child, Hannah, what place did you always love? I mean, if you could go back, where would you go?"

"That's easy. The ocean."

"Ah, me, too, especially just as the sun is setting over the horizon and most of the tourists have gone home. I like to imagine I'm part of the ocean, like the birds and the sea life. When you close your eyes, Hannah, and think of the ocean, what do you hear?"

Hannah closed her eyes. "The flapping of a sailboat."

"It flaps slowly," Sadie's voice said softly. "It's in no hurry. The sea is its home. It feels safe. What do you smell, Hannah?"

"Mmm, salt and fish and my father's cologne, something spicy, I think."

"Can you feel the sun against your face?"

296

Hannah nodded. Her eyes were closed imagining such a scene.

"What else do you feel?"

"The warm wind, sprinkles of water against my skin, and the feel of sandy wood under my bare feet."

"And as you're sitting in this sailboat letting the sun's rays' ream through you, you're relaxed, because you're like the sailboat. You're in no hurry. The only sounds you hear are those of nature around you, the seagulls, the wind, the slight flapping of waves against the boat. You inhale the salt air and as you do, it flows gently through you, becoming a part of you, part of your soul. You wiggle your toes and fingers and the sand between them feels like a second skin. When the breeze sweeps softly over your face, it's like a gentle kiss of love."

A tear fell down Hannah's face and she was suddenly aware that she no longer felt the rushing anxiety she'd felt just moments ago. Her hands that earlier gripped her chair had fallen limp in her lap. She opened her eyes to look at Sadie, who was smiling at her warmly.

"It's called visualization," Sadie said. "It's a relaxation technique. The principle is to focus in on a serene vision and your body naturally reacts to the peacefulness and relaxes. Anxiety can only remain in a negative home. The technique works, Hannah. Look, we've taken off. We're in the air."

Hannah let out a curt laugh. "I didn't feel or hear us taking off."

"I know. The captain was talking and you were almost asleep," she teased.

Hannah looked at the clouds in the sky and turned to Sadie.

"The clouds look like the waves in the sea."

"You're good at this, Hannah. It took me weeks to accomplish what you did in twenty minutes."

"Twenty minutes, Ha!" she laughed. "It's taken me four years to get on this plane."

Tony DeJane's house was within walking distance of Malibu Beach. Palm trees and California spruce surrounded his stucco house. He fixed up one of the bedrooms for Hannah, making it as homelike as he could, with his limited skills. His selection in curtains and matching bedding wasn't exactly what she would have chosen, but the pink flamingos grew on her considering the love that went into picking them out. The walls were bare except for a small shelf where some seashells and a worn out jewelry box sat. When Hannah opened the small box and the miniature ballerina danced to *The Waltz of the Sugar Plum Fairy*, she turned to her father with tears in her eyes.

"It's mine. The one you bought me when I was a little girl."

"It's comforted me these past years. When I couldn't take the loneliness any longer, I'd open it up and you'd be with me."

She fell into his arms, and at that moment, the years of separation became a faint memory, a testament of lost lives now found. She looked into his dark eyes and wondered how she'd ever believed he didn't love her. She soothed back his once black hair that was now almost completely gray. He still had his trademark mustache that had also grayed in the course of time. He was fuller now, but certainly not heavy, healthy from months of taking care of himself. He had the typical California tan, was as handsome as she'd ever remembered him being, and his smile, always the primary focus of his appeal, still charmed her, melting away her reserve.

When Tony wasn't working at the dock part-time, he and Hannah spent every free moment getting to know each other again. Her favorite times were their daily walks on the beach. Then, she felt free and uninhibited. Fear was far from her mind. Even though the waters were too cold for swimming, she couldn't resist dipping her feet in them. They frequented the strip within walking distance of Tony's house. Hannah's favorite place to browse was a mall area that had quaint specialty shops. Since it was the off-season, they were able to shop without the usual crowds and the shops had daily bargains to entice the local customers. Tony liked a bakery where almost daily he bought some type of sweet roll, usually jelly or pecans, to satisfy the sweet tooth he'd developed since he quit drinking.

Hannah's preferred shop was a unique florist called *Lily's Field*. She loved to look at the different cut flowers and arrangements, some distinct to the area, some more mainstream. Once, Tony suggested she apply for a job there since she knew more about flowers than just about anyone in the world did. She shrugged him off, but in the back of her mind, was a twinge of excitement at such an idea. She hadn't worked in public since before Julie was born.

She monopolized his time completely and he never complained, but listened patiently as she talked about her life in Blossom now. She talked about her past, as well as about Sammy, Gabe, and Julie. She came to realize that her father had suffered greatly too at their passing, losing both his grandchildren, his son-in-law and in reality, his daughter, through his own recourse. She talked about everything and everyone, except Andy. He told her he was proud of how far she had come and she said she was proud of him, as well. He went to AA meetings and she went to Al-Anon. They built their relationship slowly and Tony never promised her things the way he had in the past. This was something he had learned in AA. She learned in Al-Anon that you have little control over the actions of those you love, but only over your reactions.

She called Elaine often and she kept her abreast of Grace's health, via John and Ann. Elaine told her that her house was fine and that her nephew was taking good care of it, as much as a twenty-four year old could take care of a house. He wasn't one for wild parties or anything like that, just working on his doctorate. Hannah never asked Elaine about Andy and Elaine offered her little information. She did say that once when she went to visit her nephew, there were quite a few cars at Grace's and that it looked like some sort of celebration. She knew Andy drove a red '72 Chevy pickup and didn't recall seeing it there that day. Hannah thought it a little strange that Andy wouldn't be at a family celebration, especially knowing he wouldn't be running into her. It never occurred to her that whether she was there or not, the memories were always present.

She missed him terribly and every night, she would write him as if they were together, only separated by distance. She knew this wasn't good for her, but she couldn't help herself. In a sense, it was her way of letting go. She wrote him about her father, Malibu, the beach, the tiny shops, and the idea of her working at a floral shop. She told him of her love for him and how she missed him more each day, rather than his memory fading. After she wrote her letter, she would tuck it neatly in a drawer with all the others she had written, all sealed, addressed, stamped, but never mailed.

Tony came upon the letters quite by accident one day when Hannah and he were heading out on their morning walk by the beach. The wind had taken a turn to the north and there was a chill in the air. She asked him to get one of her sweaters out of her drawer. He opened the wrong drawer and when he did, he saw the letters. He noticed that the they were all written to the same person. He stewed on this information all day. At suppertime, he confronted her.

"Hannah, who's Andy?"

Her jaw dropped. Had Andy tried to contact her? She could feel her heart racing.

"Why do you ask, Daddy?"

"I came across some letters in your drawer when I was getting your sweater this morning. Mind you, I wasn't snooping and I didn't read them. It's just that a father can't help but to be curious when he sees so many letters written to the same man, letters that have never been mailed."

"He's just someone I know."

"He's a Padgett?"

"Yes."

"One of Grace's grandsons?"

She nodded.

"Hannah, you obviously care about this man. Why haven't you mailed your letters?"

"Daddy, please don't press this."

"All right, but there's something I want to tell you."

"What is it?"

"Don't follow your old man's footsteps and run from your problems."

"I'm not running, Daddy. I'm trying to get on with my life."

He kissed her forehead.

"Okay, Honey, I can see this is difficult for you. Just know that I'm here if you ever need to talk. It just might help. And now, there's something I need to tell you."

"What?"

"Well, I didn't tell you this yet, because I didn't want anything to come between our times together. It means too much to me. But, well, I met someone about five months ago. Her name is Janet Perry. She's pretty special to me and I'd like to continue seeing her. She knows about you and me, and our past situation. She's been patient, but I miss her company. She's asked me to go to a movie tonight. I'd like to go, if you'll be all right by yourself for a while."

"Oh, Daddy, all this time. You should have told me. Of course, go."

He drew her in his arms. He kissed her cheek.

"Janet's number is by the phone if you need me. Hannah, think about what I said about this man you've been writing to."

"All right, Daddy. I'll think about it."

When Tony left, Hannah suddenly felt so alone. The reality of losing Andy became so damn real. She cried for what seemed like hours before she finally gave into the fact that she couldn't get through this without help. She reached for her purse. Inside her wallet was a business card. Hannah recalled with admiration the woman she had met on her plane trip to Malibu, the one who had helped her to cope. Later on the flight Hannah learned that she was a therapist, who specialized in behavioral management of chronic anxiety disorders. Her practice was less than thirty miles away in Santa Monica. Hannah traced over the name on the card: *Sadie Lodge, PhD, specializing in Anxiety, Agoraphobia, and Depression.*

Tomorrow she would call her. She didn't know if she believed in fate, but she did believe in a higher power. God had placed Sadie Lodge on that plane for a reason.

Tony drove Hannah to Santa Monica so she could meet with Sadie Lodge. Their first meeting would be a private consultation, but Sadie insisted that her clients very quickly get out into the mainstream and that meant ridding them of their social phobias. At their first meeting, they comprised a set of goals and a timeframe in which to accomplish them.

"We have an expression around here, Hannah. The job won't get done unless you do it and only you can do it. But, don't worry. We'll give you all the tools you need to get the job done."

Hannah was pleased that Sadie thought she was beyond the need of regular medication, but she prescribed anti-anxiety medication for those times when she just couldn't cope. They measured her levels of anxiety to certain conditions and situations. Sadie explained that she would be using cognitive behavioral techniques to desensitize her fears and phobias.

"I have found that for the most part, traditional psychotherapy doesn't rid people of panic and anxiety, even though, as in your case, it may have begun with a trauma. Your thought process has conditioned your body to react a certain way. What we hope to do is to reprocess your present thoughts and in time, your body's responses."

302

"Sadie, do you think I'll ever be normal again?"

"As in normal, do I think you'll ever go bungee jumping? Probably not. However, I do think you'll be able to perform such daily tasks as going out in public without panic, driving, easing away social phobias, and breaking the cycle of believing you're afraid when you are not. I call it losing the fear of fear."

Hannah smiled. "I can't wait to get started."

Sadie studied her goals.

"You wrote down that your first goal is to drive again. I have to tell you, Hannah. That's an ambitious goal for a first goal."

"I know, but it's the one I want most, for more reasons than you know."

"Is it because you associate losing your family to cars and driving?"

"Partly, but also…"

"What, Hannah?"

"Well, not driving keeps me dependent on others."

Sadie smiled. "You're so much further along than you realize. Okay, so goal number one is to drive again. Let's start out with driving to a safe place first, like a home, or a store."

"I know just the place. It's a mall area several blocks from my father's house."

"Good. Now we have to be very specific about things. Can you draw a map for me? You see, you have to practice driving in your mind before you actually get into a car and go into the field. We do this through affirmations and visualizations."

"Sadie, there's a slight problem."

"Just one," she smiled.

"I don't have a license."

"Do you have someone to drive with?"

"Yes, my father."

"Perfect. We'll get you a permit. Later, you can get your license. Now, let's get your tapes and cards ready. They will be your bibles. You must read the affirmation cards daily and listen to your tapes. Also, practice the visualization technique I'm about to show you. Before you know it, you'll be driving and once you start, there won't be any turning back."

TWENTY-FOUR

Andy unloaded the last box from his truck and took it inside the farmhouse. Moving days were hell, but today he was pumped. He and Liz had been busy packing the final items left in the apartment all day. Andy took the last load to the farm while Liz and her mother stayed in Dallas to clean up the apartment. When Liz gave the keys to the complex manager, Andy would be ending a chapter of his life that had brought him unthinkable sorrows, but had ended up with the joy of Patrick's birth, perhaps his greatest accomplishment. He and Liz decided to spend tonight in Dallas at her mom's, but tomorrow they would begin their new life in their new home. This first step was a promise for their future.

Too grubby to stand himself, he jumped into his newly restored shower and felt a sense of pride at what he'd accomplished these past months, even though there was so much more to do. He didn't care. His heart was light and for the first time in months it felt hope. Tomorrow, he was not only moving into his house, but he was bringing his son home. He dressed and walked inside Patrick's room to double check the details.

He sat down in the rocker by Patrick's crib—the surprise from his mother. It was the rocker in which Jean had rocked his sons, the one his mother had rocked him, and the one Nana had rocked his father. Little league curtains hung on the windows and matching sheets and blankets covered the bed. The room was filled with stuffed animals, plants, and flowers that had been sent to him these past weeks. Andy had been certain he wrote thank-you notes to all of those who had been so generous. His eyes caught hold of an arrangement his father had brought over a week ago. It was ivy, adorned with cut baby blue carnations and decorated with baby blue, silk bows. Inside the pot, a ceramic figurine of a father bear holding his infant cub in his arms nestled within its soil. Inscribed on the bottom of the figurine were the words: *For Baby Patrick, God's brave, little soldier.*

Andy had intentionally not written a *thank-you* for this gift. His reason was justified. The ceramic figurine had been cast and lovingly painted, as a symbol of closure by Hannah, a woman Andy still loved, despite all his well-intended efforts to forget her. Andy touched the figurine and he was compelled, for one last time, to let his heart feel the love he felt for Hannah. He closed his eyes and an image of her as she looked the night he'd first approached her on her front porch emerged. The moonlight had cast its light on her beauty, her dark hair flowing recklessly, her eyes, nose, and mouth, so erotic and surreal, her voice, both childlike and completely woman.

She was more spell bounding than perhaps the moon itself. Her white robe clung to her body, so perfectly, he wondered if perhaps it weren't too perfect. His senses were entranced by her smell and touch and sounds. He let his lips fall upon hers one last time and his arms wrap around her in farewell.

Hannah, my heart still belongs to you.

His loneliness for her was intensified by the news from his father that she had left Blossom in an effort to begin a new life. When Andy asked him where she had gone, he told him she was going to see her father and try to begin a new relationship with him. After that, he didn't know. He told Andy that she had rented out her home to her friend Elaine's nephew, so he knew her stay would be extended. Andy feared for her well-being, knowing how her father had rejected her over and over again.

So many times since the news of her leaving, he had thought to pick up the phone and call her. He never did. He didn't have the right. Besides, it would serve no purpose but to

306

reopen a wound that would never completely heal. Tears filled his eyes. He was the one who was supposed to take care of her and reassure her, but he had let her down as much as her father had—maybe more. He knew for her sake as much as his, he had to bury her image. He wiped away his tears as if he were wiping her memory away. When his tears were gone, he vowed never to resurrect his love for her again. He vowed this for his son, who was a hero in the truest sense of the word, more gallant than any he'd ever known.

Andy found Liz sitting in the middle of a barren floor that had once held his living room furniture. Except for a nearby streetlight casting slight streams of light into the room, she was sitting in total darkness.

"Hey," he said sitting down beside her. "What's wrong? Your mom said you'd be here."

"So you went to the hospital. How is Patrick?"

"Patrick's fine, Liz."

He turned her face so that he could look at her. He saw tears and pain and something like fear on it.

"Liz, what is it?"

"Promise me one thing?"

"What can I promise you?"

"That you won't hate me."

He let out a quick laugh and held her near.

"Not likely. Not after what you've given me."

She covered her face in shame.

"Liz, I don't understand."

"I know you don't."

As she began talking, her voice was drawn, almost disconnected from her mouth. His heart was flipping out of control. He watched her with mixed emotions.

"When I was sixteen, I started dating a boy. We were crazy about each other. The problem was that he was from a very wealthy family and I was from a middle class family. His parents disliked me simply for that reason and tried to discourage us any way they could. They couldn't. When I was eighteen, I got pregnant.

"Doug, that's his name, well, he was nineteen and his parents had high expectations for him. They wanted him to go to law school. I wasn't part of these expectations. Eventually, they talked Doug and me into giving up our baby."

"Oh, Liz," he said, trying to understand the fear and sorrow of one so young going through something like this. "I know where this is going."

"You do?"

He took her gently in his embrace. "Patrick has made you realize what you lost. Honey, you're grieving the loss of this child. But don't you see? Patrick is your blessing. You've been given a son."

She smiled bitterly through her tears. "Believe me, Andy. I've grieved plenty for my lost child. That's only part of what's wrong now."

"What, Liz?"

"Even after the baby, Doug and I still saw each other. We were careful this time and managed to escape his parent's scrutiny for a year, but then they discovered we were still seeing each other. They did everything to make my life hell. But, we were so in love. I couldn't imagine my life without him."

"Liz, are you trying to tell me that you're still in love with this man?"

"No. I'm not."

He listened to her relive her past, realizing just how little he knew of his wife.

"When Doug was in law school, we became engaged. Well, his parents flipped, but the more determined they were, the more determined we were. One day, Doug went to his apartment, the utilities were cut off, and he had an eviction notice. His parents gave him an ultimatum—me or his career and inheritance. I knew they meant it. I couldn't let that happen, so I left him. That was two years ago."

"Liz, what does this have to do with us?"

"When I met you, I fell hard. I didn't think I could, not after Doug. But, you were so wonderful, I couldn't help myself. Do you remember Houston and how incredible it was? I fell in love with you that weekend, even though we had been dating for quite a while before then. I guess I started believing then that we'd always be together."

"I'll never forget that weekend, Liz. It produced our living legacy. That's pretty incredible, I agree."

She stood by the window looking out into the blackness. Even in the dark, he could see her silhouette slump forward.

"Do you remember what happened the next week, Andy?"

He remained sitting on the ground.

"Yes," he spoke solemn. "I broke it off with you."

"Yes, and you flaunted your new founded independence in front of me at the restaurant. What was her name?"

He closed his eyes. "Who remembers?"

"I do. It was Candice. I decided the only way to forget you was to play your games. I stayed drunk for weeks after that. I went out to the clubs as often as I could."

A frightening shadow hovered over him. "What's all this leading to, Liz?"

She broke down in sobs. He was too shaken to get up and comfort her, too leery about the undercurrents in her words.

"I ran into Doug one night. We shared some drinks and laughs and ..."

Andy stood in absolute horror. "Don't you dare tell me another word. I don't see what this has to do with us."

She fell to her knees and buried her face in her hands.

"He's not yours, Andy. Patrick's not your son."

He turned from her so enraged he knew if he looked at her, he might strike her. The empathy he felt for her was lost in the threat that she was taking his son from him.

"No!" he shouted. "No!"

"Oh, Andy. I wish to God he was yours. I can't bear the thought of Patrick being near that family."

He looked at her hopefully. "Maybe you're wrong. I mean, he could be mine. You were with me and him around the same time."

She shook her head. "He's not yours."

"How do you know? I mean, you can't be sure."

"I know," she said emphatically.

"Liz," he negotiated desperately. "It doesn't matter. I don't give a damn. I couldn't love Patrick more, if he were my flesh. No one has to know but us. I'll raise him as my own."

"Doug knows about Patrick. He put two and two together. He insists on a paternity test. He'll take us to court if he has to."

"Let him!"

"Don't you see? He'll win. He's the father."

He shook his finger at her in rage.

"Patrick's mine! Mine! I held him in my hands when he was no bigger than my hand. I fed him and gave him treatments and painted his room. Yesterday, I bought him a little tractor that has his name on it. He's my son. You can't take him away from me. I can't lose him."

"Dear God, don't you see? We could both lose him."

Andy went to the hospital to see Patrick. Even though it was after visiting hours, Andy was given special privileges, because everyone knew him. He'd become part of their hearts as they watched him care for little Patrick. He held him against his chest, inhaling the scent that belonged specifically to Patrick. He rocked him and hummed a lullaby. Liz had followed Andy to the hospital and watched as he held Patrick. She sat next to them in an empty rocker.

"Will he ever know how much I love him?"

"Yes. I'll tell him."

"I remember when I was young, a lady name Lula Brown lived down the street. She took in every kid no one wanted, black, brown, green, it didn't matter to her. If a kid needed love, she took them in. I used to wonder how anyone could love someone who wasn't theirs. Now I know."

They sat for some time in the darkness, lost in a void they had no control over. Then, Andy spoke, as if relinquishing his right to Patrick.

"Will Doug be a good father?"

"Yes. He just needs to break away from his parents."

"Does he have the balls to fight them?"

"I'll make sure he does."

"Will you two marry? Patrick needs a father and mother."

"I don't know, Andy."

He looked at her fully devastated.

"I understand why you did what you did, but for as long as I live, I'll never forgive you."

"I know. And that fact breaks my heart."

He took Patrick's tiny hand and kissed it. Then, he pressed it against his cheek.

"Take him, Liz. Take him now, or I'll never be able to let him go."

Liz took him from Andy's arms. A cold impression where Patrick's little body had just been pressed harshly against his chest, so harshly, he felt as though all the air inside of him had concentrated itself in one part of his body—his heart. He didn't look back when he walked away, and only when he was in his truck and driving away, did he let out a breath. Where once his heart felt crushed, it now felt like scorching liquid, burning a hole in the center of his soul. He let out a heinous bellow so foreign to him, he imagined himself to be in the presence of the demons of hell, forever separated from love. Another cry came forth until he found himself on the side of the road vomiting away the poisonous truth that was killing him.

As the cars passed by, he thought it would be so easy to run in front of one and end it all right here and now. An image of Patrick fighting for his life for so many weeks brought a measure of sanity back to him. Patrick had taught him that no obstacle is too large if you're willing to tackle it. For Patrick, he got in his truck. He drove and drove until he found himself on Interstate 35 South, headed for Austin. Only the touch of his sons would get him through this night.

It had been almost a month since Liz had told him the truth about little Patrick. Almost immediately, he sought out a lawyer to take the necessary action needed to dissolve his sham of a marriage as he so put it. In this short time span, he nursed his wounds by working himself to the brink of exhaustion. He began each day before the sun showed its face and didn't stop until well into the evening, long after the sun had set behind the horizon. He would shower and collapse on his bed, unwilling to let himself feel anything. He was driven like a mad man and refused to give into his sorrow. His only goal in life was to farm and finish his house before Christmas, just five blessed weeks away. That's when his boys would be with him. His boys were the only people he willingly allowed in his heart — and Patrick — on the rare occasion when loving him was bearable.

Today, he woke up feeling light headed and nauseas. The clock near his bed read five-thirty. Usually by now, he was up, dressed, and out the door with his thermos of coffee in his hand. He couldn't muster the energy to get out of bed. He had been tired lately and attributed his lack of energy to the calamity of his life. He gave little thought to Liz and what she was going through, nor did he pine over the loss of Jean as he always had in the past. Yet, more times than not, exhaustion wasn't enough to free his mind from thoughts of Hannah, even though he fought it adamantly.

Sometimes, his regret over her was so thick he was certain he would suffocate on it. This merciless monster played havoc with his mind and soul. It would be so easy to drown himself in self-pity by drinking his life away, but he found he couldn't go back to being that man again. He couldn't because it would be like slapping Hannah in the face a second time. He wondered how she was doing so far away from her home and the people she loved. He wondered, too, if she ever thought of him. If she did, did the fond moments outweigh the heartache? He knew he had no right to assume that she might still care or that she should ever think of him affectionately, not after he had cast their love aside. This left him a hollow man.

His whole body ached and he knew he'd overdone the lifting this past week, cleaning out the barn at the main house, purging it of years and years of junk. He reached for his cell to call Dennis and tell him he wouldn't be working today because he was sick—a stomach virus or something. He told him that if he felt better, he might try working later on in the day. Dennis told him to rest up, that he had done enough yesterday for a week's worth of work. Andy closed his eyes and fell back asleep.

Three hours later, he woke up feeling tightness in his chest. His arm was numb and he thought that maybe it was because he had slept on it. He finally managed to get up and slipped on a pair of jeans. The tightness in his chest intensified. He couldn't breath. For one short moment, he wondered if perhaps he was having a heart attack. He dismissed this almost immediately.

Thirty-four year old men don't have heart attacks, Andy. You've just overdone it.

He finished dressing and made some coffee. He looked for some antacids in his bathroom, but all he found was the pink stuff he gave the boys when they had stomachaches. He swallowed a few tablespoons of it. Anything was worth a try. As he moved about the house, the tightness eased somewhat.

He needed to pick up some supplies for the house and because the kitchen was bare, he decided to drive into Greenville and take Dennis' advice. He needed a break from his usual routine. He got in his truck and headed toward Greenville, just thirty minutes or so down the road. Halfway there, his chest began to burn. He began sweating profusely, so he rolled down the window, letting the cold November breeze slap at his face.

Something's not right here.

He picked up his phone and called his brother Charlie. He labored with his breathing.

"Charlie, it's Andy. Listen, I'm not feeling too well. Thought I'd run myself by the hospital in Greenville. Honestly, I think I might be having a heart attack. Do you think you could call Dad and meet me there?"

Andy was kept in the hospital for a few days so the doctors could observe him. He didn't have a heart attack, but the doctor on call reported that his system was on overload—both physically and emotionally. He needed to make some changes or one day he would end up in the hospital with a heart attack. The symptoms that made Andy feel like he was having a heart attack were due to the physically extreme measures to which he was driving himself. His body was worn and he was dehydrated. His inability to release his feelings also contributed to his condition. He was, in fact, a broken man.

Because Andy refused his father's invitation to come to Nana's house and rest there for a few days, the three of them, John, Ann, and Grace, went to Andy's farm. Nana took Andy's room, because she couldn't negotiate the stairs and the others slept upstairs in the boys' rooms that were not quite finished. At first, Andy was belligerent and didn't want their help. He soon realized that he could do little to sway them, so he gave up his arguments. The first day home, he slept the entire day and night. When he woke up the next morning, he felt somewhat

314

rested, but still depleted. The sun was beaming through the window and John was sitting in a chair next to him.

"Hey, Dad, what time is it?"

"Almost ten."

He let out a deep breath. "I guess I was tired."

John's smile was apprehensive. "You gave us quite a scare, Son."

Andy looked at his father and for the first time in weeks, he admitted to his father and himself that he wasn't all right.

"I'm scared, too, Dad."

"You're going to have to find a way to let things go, Andy. You have to find a balance."

"I know," he admitted. "But how? When I'm working, I don't have time to think about what I've lost."

"Count your blessings, Son. That's a start."

He smiled at his father. "You're one of my greatest blessings, Dad—you and Mom and Nana. I know it hasn't been easy putting up with me, especially lately. I'm sorry I've caused you such pain."

John rubbed his son's arm affectionately. "I'm sorry, too, Andy."

He looked at his father confused. "What are you sorry for?"

"I gave you bad advice. I should have trusted your instincts. I was looking from the outside in, instead of seeing things from your point of view."

He knew his dad was referring to his decision to marry Liz and let Hannah go.

"No, Dad, you were right. From where we all were then, it was right to give Patrick a chance for a real family. I knew this and so did…"

"Hannah," John finished.

"Yes," Andy whispered. "Hannah."

"We got a card with a little note from her a week or so ago," John said.

Andy's heart felt something like hope. She would never be completely out of his life, because of her ties to his family.

"How is she, Dad? Really?"

"I can't say for certain, but I would imagine she's a lot like you, Andy. She's trying to be strong, trying to cope. She wrote about her father, mostly, and how they were getting to know each other. She wrote about California and the beach, things like that. It was a short note."

"Did she mention…"

"You, Andy? No, she didn't, but then she wouldn't."

"Does she know that Liz and I are divorced, that our marriage has been annulled?"

"I haven't told her, Andy, and I'm sure Nana hasn't. It's not our place, the way I see it. Maybe it's time you told her."

John handed Andy a piece of paper with an address on it. It was the address of Tony DeJane. Andy stared at it for some time before he handed it back to John.

"My heart can't handle another rejection."

John nodded and put the address in the top drawer of the table next to Mathew's bed.

"I understand, Andy. Just in case you change your mind, you know where it is. Now, do you think you can get up and join the world of the living? Mom and Nana have cooked you a breakfast fit for a king."

Andy laughed for the first time in weeks. "Be there in a moment."

John walked toward the door and then stopped. He turned and spoke to Andy directly.

"Think of the courage it took her to leave, Andy. Think of how much love it took."

When John left, Andy stared at the closed drawer. He closed his eyes and he saw Hannah smiling at him. He finally understood what she must have been going through all of these years—her fears and isolation. Fear is a deadly culprit that cripples the heart and soul. He knew, because it had found its way to his spirit. Would he find the courage to deal with it as Hannah had? He reached for the slightest bit of hope that she might still care for him.

Oh my Love, is there still a place in your heart for me?

TWENTY-FIVE

Andy picked up the phone and called Campton Brothers' Law Firm in Greenville. When the voice on the other side of the line answered with *Campton Brothers Law Office*, he knew it was Elaine Greene. He recalled her brassy voice. He cleared his voice and answered back to her.

"Elaine Greene?" he asked just to be certain.

"Yes," she said, recognizing his voice, as well. She knew who he was and didn't pretend she didn't. "Hi, Andy. How are you?"

He liked the fact that she didn't put on false pretenses. He let out a heavy sigh, wondering where to begin this conversation.

"I'm calling about Hannah."

"I figured as much."

"How is she?"

"Hannah's good, Andy. Better than good."

"I'm glad," he said honestly. "I...I need your opinion on something."

"My opinion? What about?"

"I know you talk to her and you're closer to her than any person I know. I was wondering, I mean I was thinking of contacting Hannah and wondered if you thought she would be open to hearing from me."

"I can't speak for Hannah, Andy, but if you really want my opinion, leave her alone. If you want to talk to someone, talk to your wife. Hasn't Hannah been through enough? I mean, she's moved almost fifteen hundred miles just to get away from you. This is just my opinion, mind you. You see, I'm a little protective when it comes to Hannah. I don't want to see her hurt anymore."

"I deserve that, Elaine. I know I do. I don't want to see her hurt anymore either. It's just that..."

"Just what, Andy?

"It's about Patrick."

Elaine knew that Andy's son had been premature and that he had been in the hospital for a lengthy stay. She knew he had been very sick. No matter what she thought of Andy, she didn't wish any ill will on an innocent child.

"Is your son all right, Andy?"

"From what I've been told, Elaine, he's doing great."

"What do you mean from *what you've been told?*"

"That's what I wanted to talk to Hannah about. You see, Elaine, Liz is no longer my wife. Patrick's not my son."

Hannah began working at *Lily's Field* to help during the Christmas Season, which actually began before Thanksgiving. What started out as a part time job soon developed into a fulltime one. Hannah didn't mind. The work kept her mind and hands busy. The shop flourished with her ideas and knowledge. Lily, the owner, saw very early Hannah's value at the shop. She was one of those rare employees who worked relentlessly and never complained about anything. By now, she was driving to and from work, with Tony always in the passenger's seat. Tony got a kick out of her progress.

"Pretty soon, you'll be taking over the delivery man's job at the florist."

"I think his job is secure, Daddy. At the rate I'm going, I'll be ninety before I get my license."

At the shop, she was in her element and she didn't have much time to think about home and those she loved and missed. Yet late at night, particularly when her father had gone out with Janet, the loneliness set in and she could do nothing but think of Blossom. She missed her morning chats with Grace and her walks with John and Ann. She missed her work with Elaine and the friendship that had bonded them for so many years. Most of all she missed Andy, though she tired so hard to forget him. She soon came to the realization that forgetting Andy would take a long time, maybe years — maybe forever.

Andy walked into the old school house. His heart was beating out of control. His nerves were on edge. Twice he turned back to leave, but something kept him going. A group of a dozen or so men and women sat in the classroom. When he sat down, he felt like he was sixteen again — awkward, insecure. He looked around at the people in the room. They seemed like normal people he'd happen by on any street. Only, they weren't. They were all here for the same reason.

The man in charge brought the meeting to order and Andy thought if anyone said a word to him, he'd leave. Maybe they sensed this, because no one did. For fifty minutes, he listened to people talk about their lives, both good and bad. Tears and laughter filled the classroom and a challenge filled Andy's heart. When the meeting was just about to be adjourned, Andy stood, he thought, to leave.

Then, a gentleman asked if he had anything to share. What the hell would he share? Within a scope of several minutes, his life the past two years came rushing past him — his divorce, Liz, Patrick, his boys moving to Austin, and Hannah. Hope soared in his heart for perhaps the first time in months. Hannah's smile filled his mind and he wanted so badly for her to be with him — now and forever. Once again, the gentleman asked if he had anything to share.

"I think I do, yes."

"Go on," the man encouraged.

Even though Andy hadn't had a drink in months, the desire to drink was always there. He cleared his throat and spoke softly.

"My name is Andy. I'm an alcoholic."

Close to midnight, Andy's cell phone rang. It startled him so much, he almost fell out of the bed to get it. When he looked at the ID from the incoming call, his heart jumped to his throat. The call was from Hannah. Apparently, she had kept the cell phone he had once given her. Throughout their months of separation, he never had the thought to sever this final connection from her. He always kept the line active, just in case she might ever need him. She must have felt the same way, too. *Thank God.* He was so nervous, surprised and excited all rolled up in one. It was all he could do to contain his emotions and he was all thumbs, barely able to hit the button to connect the call. When he did, his shaky voice said *hello,* and then he heard her faintly say *Andy.* His heart bolted with something like joy just hearing her voice.

"A...A...Andy, it's me, Hannah."

"H...Han..."

He never quite got her name out, but at that moment, his heart made peace with himself. He gripped the phone praying he would say everything right to bring her back home. He was shaking so much, he didn't know if he could get the words out, but he knew he had to try.

"Hannah," he said clearly emotional. "You're going to have to give me a moment here. I'm just a little shaken by the fact that I'm actually talking to you."

"I know," she said as equally dazed. "I...I... just called to say that I'm so sorry."

Andy could hear her crying. He knew she was struggling

"Why are you sorry? Oh, Hannah, don't' cry. I'm the one who's sorry."

He heard her blow her nose.

"Oh, Andy, I..."

"What, Baby? What?"

"Elaine called me, Andy. She told me about Patrick. You should have called me a long time ago."

"I was a little crazy for a while. I wasn't talking to anyone. Also, I didn't feel that I had the right after all I had put you through."

"Oh, Andy, what you must be suffering. I…I'm so sorry for your pain."

Never in all his imaginings did he expect her to be so compassionate, so forgiving. He had imagined all sorts of scenarios with her forgiving him, but none fit the reality that was playing out tonight. He closed his eyes and felt tears streaming down his face.

This is Hannah. What did you expect?

Now, he had to make things right with her.

"Hannah, I'm trying to be the person you deserve."

"Oh, Andy, you…"

"Shhh, please let me say this before I lose my nerve."

"All right," she whispered. She closed her eyes and imagined him sitting next to her, pouring his heart out. Her heart ached as he replayed the sad events of his life these past months. He told her about Patrick and his annulment from Liz. He told her about his near brush with fate. He talked about the farm and how he was building a home, he hoped where she would some day want to live. He told her he was attending AA meetings, even though he never drank. He started attending Mass again. Then, he said the words he hoped would send her home to him.

"I love you, Hannah. Please forgive me."

"Andy," she swallowed hard. "There's nothing to forgive. I…I love you, too."

With these words, he released months of bottled up emotions and insecurities. He felt a peace flow within him that he hadn't felt in ages. He let out a heavy sigh of relief.

"Hannah… I thought I'd lost you forever."

"Oh, Andy, I've been so lonely."

"Come home to me, Hannah."

"Andy," she managed to speak through her tears. "I'm changing, too. At least I'm trying to change."

"I know. Come home and we can grow and change together."

"I'm just getting to know my father again and…"

New fear filled his heart.

"And what, Hannah?"

"My job. I've made a commitment at least through Christmas."

"We have jobs in Texas," he said only half-joking.

"Andy, I'm seeing a therapist. She's helping me so much, but I have a long way to go."

Where moments earlier he was feeling peace, now he was churning with self-doubt as she threw him one excuse after another.

"Hannah, you *are* planning on coming home, aren't you?"

"I love you, Andy. Even if I wanted to stay away from you, I couldn't."

"Do you want to, Hannah — stay away from me?"

"No, believe me when I say this, Andy. I don't want to stay away from you any longer than I have to."

Then come back to me now.

"Well, okay then. I guess it doesn't matter when you come home, so long as you come home. Hannah, I know you are building your relationship with your father and that you're making changes in California that are keeping you there. I'm going to honor your wishes and give you the time you need to do this. But, I swear, if you don't promise me right here on this phone tonight that you're coming home to me, I'm going to jump on the next plane to California to come get you myself."

She laughed into the phone. "I just might stay here long enough to see if you do just that."

Andy put the finishing touch on Jeff's room. It was the pastel sketching Hannah had done of him. He looked around the upstairs, feeling proud of his work. The boys would like it. In a week, they would be home for Christmas. He had been working until the late hours of each night trying to have everything ready by their arrival. His brothers and dad had helped him. Andy wanted Christmas at his house this year.

Where he had been distant from his family, he now understood how much they meant to him. His mom and Nana, of course, still had full rein over the menu. They decided, they might let Debbie and Careen help. He invited Jean and Frank, but they would be at her mom's. Andy took each day one at a time, and despite the steps he was taking toward a better life, his loneliness lingered.

Hannah, come home to me soon.

Andy drove home from the Larkin's Ranch around six the day before Christmas Eve. Tomorrow, his boys would be running and screaming and causing havoc around the house. He couldn't wait. Just as he was about to turn into his drive, a small animal ran out in front of his truck and he swerved into a small ditch to keep from hitting it.

"Damn," he cursed as he got out to inspect his truck. He didn't see any damage, so he walked toward the driver's door. Just as he was about to get back inside, he happened to see a small, black puppy about the size of a five-pound potato sack hunched up in a ball. Andy guessed he had hit it after all. He found an old blanket in his truck and decided to take it to the main house and bury it in the back pasture.

When he reached for it, he felt it squirm around within the blanket. He carried it to his truck and placed it on the seat so he could get a better look at it. He couldn't tell for sure, but he didn't think the puppy was hurt, just scared. He scooted it on the passenger's side and managed with little effort to get his truck out of the ditch. By the time he had reached the house, the little puppy had wiggled out of the blanket and was curled up next to him. Andy carried him inside so he could look him over in better lighting.

"Well, I'd say you're just fine, little fellow."

Upon further review, he realized that this little, black ball of energy wasn't a little fellow after all.

"You're a bitch!" he laughed aloud. "I should have known. That's my luck. The puppy licked his face. "Oh, no, you can't sweet talk me. I'll just break up a little bologna and give you some water, and that's all. Tomorrow, we find you a new home."

Andy showered and dressed. Then, he fixed him some dinner and moved into the den, where he could watch the news and eat. That's when he caught sight of the puppy sleeping under the Christmas tree, snuggled up within its skirt.

"I'll be damned. You know I have a soft spot for a girl with dark hair and brown eyes, don't you?"

As Andy ate his dinner, he knew that mutt wasn't going anywhere. That night, for the first time in ages, Andy didn't sleep alone. *Hannah Two*, as he called his new canine friend, slept contented by his side.

"You're not exactly what I had in mind, but I guess you'll do until the real Hannah comes home to me."

On Christmas Eve, Hannah and Tony had a quiet dinner to celebrate the holidays. Tomorrow, Tony would be going to Janet's house to have Christmas with her family.

"Hannah, I wish you'd reconsider and come with me."

"Don't worry about me, Daddy. I'll be fine. As tired as I am, I'll sleep through Christmas. It's been pretty hectic at the shop."

"All right, but I'll be home tomorrow evening. We can go look at the lights down Malibu Beach."

"Sounds good and try not to worry about me."

He sat down beside her and took her hand. His mood was serious.

"Hannah, I know you and Andy Padgett are communicating again. I know you talk to him almost every day. He sends you cards and letters. I'm assuming you're writing him, as well. Want to know what I think?"

She looked at him hesitantly.

"I'm not sure I do, Daddy."

He smiled. She was so much like her mother and too much like him.

"I think it's time you decided just what you want from this relationship."

"What I want?"

"Yes. Is Andy someone you want to spend the rest of your life with?"

"I do love him, Daddy — with all my heart. I feel like I've been given a second chance."

"But you're here and he is there. It doesn't make sense to me."

"There are just some things I have to take care of here." *She pointed to her heart.* "And here." *She pointed to her head.*

"Hannah, am I keeping you from him? I wouldn't trade these past months with you for anything in the world, but I think that maybe I'm holding you back and keeping you from living your life. It's so obvious that you love this man. And just as obvious how miserable you are without him."

"I just don't want to let this go, let us go."

"It's not like before, Hannah. I'm not the same man. Our relationship is solid and it's only going to get stronger — no matter what the distance between us."

"It's not just you, Daddy. It's Sammy."

"You're afraid that if you give your love to him, you're somehow betraying Sammy. Is that it?"

"A little, but I have made peace with this for the most part. Sammy would want me to be happy. It's just that…well, what if Andy just thinks he loves me and later discovers later that my limitations are just too much for him to handle?"

326

"Hannah, from everything you've told me about him, I'd say he's a man who's with you for the duration."

"I'm afraid of losing him, Daddy. He deserves someone who can give him…"

She was babbling, letting her anxiety get the best of her. He knew she was terrified of taking the plunge. She had always needed that extra push when fear held her back, even as a child. She always second guessed her happiness, as if she didn't deserve it. She did this even more now since the death of her family.

"Don't settle, Sweetheart. Don't settle for half a life because of something that may or may not happen. Besides, I have a feeling that the moment you are in his arms, these insecurities will melt away."

"You sound like Sadie, Daddy."

"Your therapist? She's encouraging you to go back to Texas and Andy."

"She's encouraging me to face my fears. She calls facing Andy my bungee jump."

"Bungee jump?"

"It's the terminology she uses for taking a leap of faith—in yourself."

Andy picked up the boys on Christmas Eve from their grandmother's house, Jean's mom. They made a few stops before heading back to the farm. The first stop was to buy a bed, some toys, and puppy food for the newest family member, *Hannah Two*. Then, Andy took them to an exclusive part of Dallas near SMU so they could enjoy the Christmas lights. The boys were surprised when he actually stopped at one of the houses.

"Who lives here, Dad?" Mathew asked.

"Patrick. You remember the little tractor we got him while he was in the hospital,   the one with his name on it? Well, I thought it would be nice to let him have it for Christmas. What do you think? "

"I think that's cool, Dad," Mathew said.

"Yea, "Andy choked. "Well...Patrick's a pretty cool, little dude, himself."

On Christmas day, Andy's house was lit up with lights and cheer. Nana and Ann had prepared turkey with all the trimmings and everyone stuffed themselves until they could barely walk. Bobby had Christmas music blaring through the stereo system Andy had just installed. John played along with Bobby and the two sang Christmas songs all day until Charlie decided to put on his earmuffs to stifle the sound. Soon, everyone in the house was wearing earmuffs looking utterly ridiculous. But they didn't discourage Bobby and John. They just sang even louder. Andy's phone rang and he called out *"Saved by the bell."* He saw Hannah's name on the ID and smiled.

"Merry Christmas, Beautiful."

"Merry Christmas, Andy. Sounds like you have quite a crowd."

"Yea, I do. The whole gang is here."

"Oh, Grace too?"

"Are you kidding? She's the ring leader."

"Tell everyone *Merry Christmas* from me," she sniffed. He knew she was crying.

"What's wrong, sweetheart?"

"I just miss everyone, that's all."

"Everyone misses you, Hannah."

"I love you, Andy."

He moved outside on his porch so he could have more privacy.

"I love you, too. You have to know this. Something is wrong, I can feel it. What is it?"

328

"Nothing. It's just that it's Christmas and I miss you and…"

"And what?"

I'm all alone and I love you so much I don't think I can take another day without you.

"Do you love me, Andy? I mean really love me?"

"Do I love you? Of course, I love you. Hannah, I named my damn dog after you. That's how much I love you. You know what's going on here, don't you? It's Christmas. You're alone, when you should be with me. You're miserable. I'm miserable. Why not put us both out of our misery and come home?"

For the first time tonight, she smiled.

"Did you really name your dog after me?"

He let out an air of exasperation.

"Hannah, everything I do has something to do with you."

"I know, and I love you for this. Be patient with me, Andy. Don't give up on me."

"I'm trying, but sometimes…"

"Next Christmas, I promise," she said tearfully, "we'll be in each other's arms."

"Next Christmas, hell! It had better be more like *this* New Years."

TWENTY-SIX

After church, Andy went by his house to pick up *Hannah Two*. They were going to spend the day in Blossom. Nana was crazy about the silly puppy and so he thought he'd bring her along. Andy knew Nana would keep the puppy permanently if he'd let her, but he found he couldn't part with her. She kept him company on those dark days when the aloneness became almost too much to bear. Today, his mom was fixing her special fried chicken dinner just for him, with mashed potatoes and gravy. She had even made an apple pie. *An apple pie*, he mused. This made him think of Hannah and the pie she had made him so many months ago.

It was Ground Hog's Day and the weathermen forecasted six more weeks of winter. Andy looked at the hazy sky and it almost looked like it might snow. It rarely snowed in East Texas, but when it did, there was nothing more beautiful than the hills covered with a blanket of new fallen snow. *Hannah Two* cuddled next to him. Her snout was resting on his thigh. Andy rubbed his hand over her warm, soft fur. She let out a slight breath of contentment. A loneliness that sometimes caught him off guard struck him. He guessed it was the slow, lazy silence of winter.

As he drove into Nana's driveway, he couldn't help but to look toward Hannah's house. It was a habit of his and he doubted he would ever break it. He parked his truck near the back of the driveway and the first thing that he noticed was there were no cars around. He guessed his dad must have parked Nana's car in the old garage out back. He had to assume that his mom had him running errands at the last minute and that's why their car was gone.

He got out of his truck and the wind whipped at his back. He let *Hannah Two* down to relieve herself after the long drive. When he tired to go inside, the back door was locked, an oddity, since Nana never locked her back door. He tried the front door, calling out to his parents and Nana. No one answered him. He looked in the windows. *Hannah Two* followed him, moving back and forth, as he did.

The house was dark and the curtains drawn. He was beginning to worry that something might be wrong, even though he had just talked to his dad less than an hour ago. He fumbled through his key chain to see if he had a key to Nana's house. He knew he did — somewhere. Maybe there was one in his truck. He opened the passenger's side to look in his glove box. Andy could hear footsteps from behind him and when he heard a soft voice speak out to him, he thought his imagination was getting the best of him. It sounded so much like Hannah.

"They aren't home, Andy."

His head darted up, but he didn't turn around. He couldn't. What if he were wrong? He dared to speak.

"Hann..."

He never quite finished her name. A burning sensation pressed over his chest. He held in a hard breath and then let it out. When he turned around, his heart fell at the very sight of her. She was dressed in a black knit dress that fit slightly tight about her long, lush figure. Only a woman built like Hannah could make a dress of such simple design look the way it did. She was completely sensual, completely bewitching. Her thick hair fell unruly about her shoulders. Her smile was for him, he knew, and his eyes couldn't get enough of her.

He stared so long and so hard, he didn't notice the snow beginning to fall. Neither did she. They just stood there, lost in the moment of seeing each other after such a long time. He leaned against his truck for support. She watched his chest heave in and out, watched his arm and neck muscles try desperately to gain control. His dark hair fell below his collar now, full and smelling fresh.   He was tone from working outside and he'd lost weight.   She took in his essence, earthy and completely masculine.   Months of separation had not diminished one characteristic about him.   She was more drawn to him than she'd ever been.   He finally found his voice.

"When did you get in?"

"Early this morning. Elaine brought me.   I thought about calling, but I wanted to surprise you."

"Well," he laughed.   His heart was in his throat.   "You did that."

Neither one reached to touch the other, somehow knowing if they did, they would have no control over themselves.   He looked at her still reeling in disbelief.

"You came back," his voice cracked.

"Oh, Andy," she almost touched him.

"Hannah, can we take this inside?   I think it's snowing on us."

She looked at the sky and held her hands out as if trying to catch the snow.   Then, she looked back at him.

"What I'd really like, is to see your farm, Andy."

It took a good forty minutes to reach his farm.   *Hannah Two* separated them and kept them sane the distance of the ride. She told Andy that her father was getting married again.   He told her that he'd built a screened in porch that would be an ideal place for an artist to work.   She told him she was driving now.   He said he couldn't believe it, but then after talking with her a while, he could.   She'd grown confident.   She told him about her therapy.   They talked about the boys and Grace and his parents.   Once, she reached to pet *Hannah Two* and their hands touched.   He withdrew his, but she didn't. Then, he decided he liked his hand on hers and put it back.   She let out a soft laugh.

He was nervous as hell.   She wanted to hold him so badly, she almost told him to stop the truck.   When they neared his farm, she knew instantly that it was his. He'd named his small ranch *The Lamplighter* and a black, iron archway at the entrance of his driveway had the name of his ranch inscribed. On either side of the archway stood a lamplight. She held her face, just now letting the emotions she was feeling surface.

"Andy, I...I can't believe...you did this."

"Don't fall apart on me yet, Hannah. I haven't showed you everything."

He led her to the front porch, where there was a swing, much like the one on her front porch. Andy built a bed for flowers over the window that faced the front of the house. They were empty and she knew he'd left them that way for her to fill. She wanted to see more of the outside, but Andy had already put his key in the door. Without speaking, he guided her inside. The flooring was all hardwood, shiny and clean, but also bare. There was little furniture and what was there appeared lonely and displaced, like he must have felt all these months. Oh, but there were so many possibilities. He'd put in new plumbing and shelves in the bathrooms, one upstairs and one downstairs. The three bedrooms upstairs were for the boys. Andy's bedroom was downstairs. That's where they stopped.

There, in his bedroom he stood by a window. One hand rested over his head as he leaned against the frame staring out of it. The other was tucked casually in his pocket. She stood by the antique bed, a bed that had been Grace's before she got sick. She hugged the post and let his voice fill her mind with his plans for the farm. She noticed a patchwork quilt on the bed that looked strangely familiar and then she remembered it had also been Grace's. For some reason, she stroked it.

He turned to her slowly as if he wasn't certain what to do next. He was weary and she knew he was afraid to let go, afraid to let himself believe she was really with him. His heart had been broken so badly. His love had been tested to the limit.

"Do you want to drive around and see my acreage?"

"Do you want to show me?"

"No," he said, but made no attempt to move toward her.

She still hugged the bedpost.

"Andy, your place is beautiful. I knew it would be though."

"Our place," he corrected.

She walked and stood next to him, leaning her head on his arm. His face bore his insecurities like an open book.

"Hannah, I know why you left. Why did it take so long for you to come home?"

"I had to be sure, Andy."

"Sure of us?"

She shook her head *no*.

"Of me. I think I was hiding, Andy, like always. I was, I am so afraid of having everything, and then, having it ripped away."

He contemplated some time just staring out the window before he reached to hold her. They stood facing each other. His hands moved gently through her hair.

"I'm not going anywhere."

She closed her eyes, dropping her hands onto his chest. He kissed her slightly, then took her hands, and kissed them, one at a time. She wondered how he would be when they first touched. Now she knew, cautious, tender. He kissed the top of her head and her breath flowed over his chest. He drew her close.

"I love you," he said into her hair.

"I love you," she said into his chest.

He leaned down to catch the bottom of her dress and slid it upward over her hips, over her head, until he let it drop into a puddle on the shiny hardwood floor. She watched as he continued to undress her, slip, bra, and panties, all scattered around Andy's bedroom floor. She stood before him, completely unclothed, completely vulnerable. Still, she never felt so secure. He moved his hands, rough from working outside every day, over her body that was smooth as silk. Even though he had imagined a million times what she would look like standing before him in raw beauty, his imaginings didn't come close to what he was actually seeing.

"You're so beautiful. My God, so beautiful." And then, out of the clear blue sky he asked her, "Hannah, are you still able to have babies?"

She knew he would bring up this topic, but she hadn't counted on it today. Still, she couldn't be too surprised. It was something she had thought about almost every day since she fell in love with him. Of all the concerns she had about their relationship, this was her deepest concern. To her, having his baby seemed the most natural step considering how much they loved each other. They had both lost so much. A baby would be a benediction of such. But, there were obstacles. She lowered her head, tears formed and she leaned on him for support.

"I knew you would ask me this some day. That's why ..."

He lifted her chin. He saw the answer written on her face.

"Hannah, it doesn't matter. Your love is enough. You are enough."

She took his hand and gripped it tightly.

"You want to know the main reason why I waited so long to come home? This is why. It was for us, Andy. Everything I do is for us. I had to know for sure. In California, I went to see a fertility doctor. You see, I wasn't sure what damage the car wreck had caused and when I was institutionalized, I didn't know what medicines I had been given or what procedures were done on me. I..."

"Stop," he begged. "I don't even know why I brought it up. The only thing that matters is that you're finally here. I love you, Hannah. My cup is filled to the rim with love for you. I'm not sure I could handle any more."

"I know I'm enough, but..."

"But nothing," he hushed her by placing his hand over her mouth. Then he kissed her gently, yet firmly. Through his kiss, she mumbled the word *yes*. He pulled her gently away so that he could look into her eyes. She smiled through her tears.

"Yes, I can have babies."

He closed his eyes in relief. Another wound healed by a future blessing. He lay on the bed moving her on top of him. She was exposed. He was completely clothed. Her pumps made a thud as they fell to the floor—the last of her clothing. He explored every inch of her beauty with his eyes, hands, and mouth. He left no part untouched but her lips. Her lips would be saved for later. For now, touching her was all he wanted. She moved to undress him, but couldn't with the finesse he had shown undressing her. She looked at him with sultry eyes.

"Andy, take your clothes off."

He rolled her on her back and got up in one agile leap. She watched as he undressed before her, slowly. When he had taken off the last of his clothing, she gazed upon him with absolute love. He was so handsome, so tender. She held her arms out to him.

"Love me, Andy."

He lay down slowly on her, pressing himself firmly against her. Her hands moved carelessly over him. She couldn't touch him enough. She kissed him recklessly, wrapping her arms around him, moving his body with hers. When she reached for his lips over and over, he let out a lustful laugh.

"Oh, Hannah, I'm happy to know I'm not the only impatient one."

"I'm sorry," she said withdrawing slightly.

He drew her back. "Don't you dare get shy on me now."

"Oh, Andy, I'm so…"

"Beautiful," he finished.

She smiled shyly. "I was going to say *in love*."

At that moment, passion overtook both of them. Within this passion, their hearts began to heal and the months of loneliness and searching ended. They drew life from each other. She rolled on top to take the initiative. Within minutes, their lovemaking became undirected. His mood that had earlier been cautious was now possessive.

"I thought I had lost you forever," he said.

"I thought we would never be together like this."

"Marry me, Hannah. Be my wife. Have my baby."

"Yes."

In this moment of consummated love, past sorrows were laid to rest. They took and gave love as easily as they took in and let out air. Andy closed his eyes and thanked God for this moment, for Hannah, a gift to a humble man. Hannah lay next to him and understood that the door to happiness was never truly closed forever. Love had found a way.

Their lovemaking took them away from the mid-afternoon hours into the sunset hours of the day. Andy watched as Hannah slept beside him. He brushed her cheek and edged off the bed. He searched the floor for his jeans and slid them on as he moved by the window. He happened to catch the beauty of the snow falling and had an impulse to wake up Hannah to go outside on their swing and watch it fall. *Hannah Two* had made her bed within Hannah's dress. He smiled. His heart was full of love. He walked to the bed and leaned to whisper in her ear.

"Oh, Hannah," he sang softly. "Wake up sweet angel."

She only budged slightly. He lay next to her and nuzzled against her neck, brushing it with slight kisses.

"Come share the snowfall with me. It's the second most beautiful wonder I've seen today."

She smiled, but didn't open her eyes.

"Oh, so you can hear me, huh?"

She smiled again.

"I get it. You like sweet talk."

She giggled out. He whispered again in her ear.

"If you get up and share the snowfall with me, I'll give you a surprise."

"Mmm. What is it?"

"Oh, she can speak, too."

He took her right hand and kissed it. She felt him slide a ring on her finger. Her eyes bolted open and she jumped to a sitting position.

"What?" she asked surprised.

"I bought this for you on your birthday. Well, we both know how that night turned out. I want you to have it now."

"Oh." Her left hand flew up to her mouth, while she held up her right hand and admired the ring, a rose with glittered gold and a diamond. Then, she looked at the man who had given it to her.

"Oh, Andy, it's beautiful. You're beautiful."

The sheet that covered her had slipped down to her waist. He stared at her exposed body.

"No, you're beautiful."

She watched as his eyes filled with desire for her.

"Kiss me," she husked.

"If I do, we'll never make it to see the snowfall."

"Just one."

She pointed to her lips and held out her other arm as a signal for him to hold her. He knew as soon as his mouth touched her lips that this one kiss she requested wouldn't be enough. He couldn't deny her and just as he'd predicted, their kiss had managed to escalate into more kissing and touching. Before he knew it, his jeans had hit the floor again.

"Andy, please don't be upset with me about the snow."

"To hell with the snow, Hannah. Who needs it when I have the whole damn world in my hands?"

Outside, two lamplights shone their light over the snow-covered ground, like hope casting its light on new love.

Made in the USA
Charleston, SC
16 March 2016